"Karon knits Mitford's small-town characters and multiple story lines into a cozy sweater of a book . . . 4/4 stars."

—*USA Today*

"Jan Karon reflects contemporary culture more fully than almost any other living novelist." —*Los Angeles Times*

"Loyal fans of Karon's Mitford novels and Father Tim will be delighted once again to spend time in this quintessential American village with its leading citizen and his colorful coterie of friends, family, and dependent souls." —*Booklist*

"With the homecoming of much-beloved characters and a few new additions, Karon's latest provides a return to a setting readers have been clamoring to revisit. Longtime readers will not be disappointed by the author's latest cozy redemption tale."

—*Library Journal*

"The faster and more impersonal the world becomes, the more we need . . . Mitford." —*The Cleveland Plain Dealer*

MITFORD BOOKS BY JAN KARON

At Home in Mitford

A Light in the Window

These High, Green Hills

Out to Canaan

A New Song

A Common Life

In This Mountain

Shepherds Abiding

Light from Heaven

Home to Holly Springs

In the Company of Others

Somewhere Safe with Somebody Good

~

Esther's Gift:
A Mitford Christmas Story

The Mitford Snowmen

Jan Karon's Mitford Cookbook & Kitchen Reader:
Recipes from Mitford Cooks, Favorite Tales from Mitford Books

The Mitford Bedside Companion:
Essays, Family Photographs, Favorite Mitford Scenes, and Much More

～

Patches of Godlight:
Father Tim's Favorite Quotes

A Continual Feast:
Words of Comfort and Celebration, Collected by Father Tim

CHILDREN'S BOOKS BY JAN KARON

Jeremy: The Tale of an Honest Bunny

Miss Fannie's Hat

The Trellis and the Seed:
A Book of Encouragement for All Ages

Somewhere
Safe
with
Somebody
Good

JAN KARON

BERKLEY BOOKS

NEW YORK

BERKLEY

An imprint of Penguin Random House LLC
375 Hudson Street, New York, New York 10014

Berkley trade paperback ISBN: 978-0-425-27621-1

The Library of Congress has cataloged the G. P. Putnam's Sons hardcover edition as follows:

Karon, Jan, date.
Somewhere safe with somebody good: the new Mitford novel / Jan Karon.
p.   cm.—(Mitford; 10)
ISBN 978-0-399-16744-7
1. Kavanagh, Timothy (Fictitious character)—Fiction.
2. Mitford (N.C.: Imaginary place)—Fiction.   3. Clergy—Fiction.
4. Episcopalians—Fiction.   5. Christian fiction.   I. Title.
PS3561.A678S66   2014   2014012105
813'.54—dc23

PUBLISHING HISTORY
G. P. Putnam's Sons hardcover edition / September 2014
Berkley trade paperback edition / August 2015

PRINTED IN THE UNITED STATES OF AMERICA

10   9   8   7   6   5   4   3   2   1

Cover photograph of town © Panoramic Images/Getty Images.
Cover design by Lynn Buckley.
Interior map by David Cain.

Penguin
Random
House

I know the plans I have for you, says the Lord, plans for good and not for harm, to give you a future and a hope.

—JEREMIAH 29:11

Heartfelt thanks to Candace Freeland, First Reader; Brenda Furman, Scrabble Queen; The Right Reverend Frank S. Cerveny; Chief Eric Brown; Polly Hawkes; Dan Caton; John Grotberg; Mayor J. B. Lawrence; Jenny Dixon; Gerry Newman; Tom Fenstermaker; Brad Van Lear; Terry Pate; Professor Dale Brown; Dr. Neal Kassell; Dr. Mary Laughlin; Bonnie Setzer; Margery Daniel; Father Peter Way; Cathy Kane and the many devoted Mitford readers who cheered this book on; Dr. Lee Kassell; Dr. David Burt; Buck Bland; Becky Dyer; Barbara Bush Foundation for Family Literacy; Dr. Daniel Bara; Steve Pekary; Lieutenant Angel Mahaffey; Dr. Leslie Olsakovsky; Carolyn Wilson; Paul Richardson; Reverend Gale Cooper; Beth Tyree; Julie Arbelaez; Steve ('Mr. Wilson') Wilson; Mike Wilcox; Dr. George Grant; Dr. Elizabeth Hazelgrove; Robert and Lottie May Hazelgrove; Amanda Cempre; Bobby Ball, Dr. Ross, and Carol Rhoads; Donald and Elise Orenstein; Carolyn Schaefer; Jerry and Rosalind Richardson ('Go, Defense!' forever); Father Randall Haycock; Christina Ball; Jerry Torchia; Dr. Diane Snustad.

Boundless thanks to all who reread the entire Mitford series to prepare for the reading of *Somewhere Safe with Somebody Good*; and to Dr. Charles (Bunky) Davant; Dr. Christopher Holstege, Mark Ratzlaff, and Ray Russell.

Remembering our beloved Margaret Ann Lehmann (1944–2013).

Oh, the inexpressible comfort of feeling safe with a person: having neither to weigh thoughts nor measure words, but to pour them out. Just as they are—chaff and grain together, knowing that a faithful hand will take and sift them, keep what is worth keeping, and then with the breath of kindness, blow the rest away.

—DINAH MARIA (MULOCK) CRAIK, 1826–1887

Chapter
One

His wife was determined to march him to the country club this Saturday evening. Worse, he'd have to stuff himself into his old tux like sausage into a casing.

The Irish breakfast—more properly, a resplendent banquet on a plate—was the culprit. He had tried to restrict himself to three such repasts during their stay in County Sligo, but ended up devouring seven, two of them out of view of his wife. He didn't know about Saint Paul, but the grim baggage of diabetes was definitely this cleric's thorn.

'I'm still jet-lagged,' he said.

'Jet-lagged? After ten days? Try again, sweetheart.'

There was a busy silence. They sat in his study, finishing a second cup of coffee. Rain gleamed on the leaves of the maple outside the vast window; fog capped the mountains beyond. 'Our observatory,' he reasoned, when faced with the alarming cost of so much glass.

'It's an important occasion, Timothy. Your doctor is retiring after decades of sleep loss and patients who won't do what the doctor ordered.'

So? Hardly anyone ever did what the priest ordered, either.

'Then he's volunteering to serve in one of the worst areas of famine in the world.'

She pressed her case as he wrestled an unsettling truth—with Hoppy Harper out of the picture, he would fall into the hands of Dr. Wilson, who, in his opinion, was yet the unlicked cub, medically speaking.

'And Father Timothy Kavanagh,' she said, 'highly esteemed friend and longtime priest of the guest of honor, wants to sit home.' The cocked head, the raised eyebrow, the gathering of hoarfrost.

'You're absolutely right,' he said.

'So you're going!'

'Cynthia, Cynthia. I didn't say I'm going, I said you're right that I want to sit home.' He gave forth a sigh.

'You're so southern.'

His Massachusetts-born spouse was keen on the notion that southerners were over-fond of sighing, something apparently beneath the dignity of Yankees. 'You won the war,' his father would have said, 'what's to sigh about?'

Did she have so much time on her hands that she could spend it conducting his business? Since she had started a new book, she should be insensible to life's vagaries for at least ten or eleven months.

'I just read an article,' she said, 'on what can happen to priests when they retire. Some of them end up refusing to leave the house.'

'I have left the house religiously,' he said with feeling.

And there she went, hooting with laughter. It was very hard to have a dispute with a woman who wouldn't stay aggrieved, but was ever looking to put a shine on things.

'I suppose it doesn't count,' he said, 'that I went to see Hoppy on Tuesday and we had a long talk and I prayed for him and wished him well and promised we'd stay in touch with Olivia and Lace whenever he's away.' He watched her eyes; this was clearly not enough.

'I gave him a nice pair of nail clippers,' he said. No need to say it was a pass-along gift from his cousin. 'In a leather case.'

The blank look.

'That was lovely, I'm sure, but it will honor him to have people there, like at a funeral. How would you feel if no one came to your funeral because they'd already said lovely things before you croaked?'

'Okay, okay, I'll do it. Peace be with you, Kav'na. Where are my studs?'

'In the right-hand section of your top bureau drawer. And also with you.'

He thought she looked pretty pleased with herself.

HE HEADED UPSTAIRS to try on the tux, to look Veracity in the face, and assemble the required paraphernalia.

His dog lay sprawled and oblivious on the landing, warming himself in a patch of sunlight.

Barnabas raised his head, blinked.

Soon, he would have to move the Old Gentleman down to the study, as stairs were increasingly nonnegotiable for his twelve-year-old Bouvier/Irish wolfhound. He had put off doing it; it would be unsettling for all, even for his wife's cat, Violet.

When Cynthia moved into his bed on their wedding night, Barnabas, ever sensible of common courtesy, had excused himself to the hall and staked new territory. Later, when they moved from the rectory to her house next door, Barnabas again established his night watch in the hall. Even with the increase of arthritis in his hind legs, he had lately made it home base, declining any comforts offered on the ground floor.

Perhaps he would engineer the shift today—carry down the water bowl, the dog bed and blanket, the raccoon with the stuffing gone. He squatted on his haunches, gave a good scratch beneath the wiry coat.

'What do you think, buddy?'

Barnabas gazed at him, solemn—morning light picked out flecks of amber in the dark pupils.

He couldn't do it today. He could not. They would make the trek again tonight, downstairs for food and a trip to the hedge, and up again, slowly, each step a challenge and then a small triumph. Tomorrow, then.

He stood, trying to focus his attention on the blunt instrument of retirement and how and why the blow still left him reeling. Five years had passed since he'd departed the active priesthood, and as busy as he'd remained, the stunned sense of loss or deficit wouldn't entirely go away. Cynthia was right. If he didn't keep after himself, he could easily disappear into his armchair in the study and not be found again. 'To withdraw someplace,' read a sixteenth-century definition of retirement, 'for the sake of seclusion.'

Retirement, of course, hadn't been his idea—he had been urged by his doctor for health reasons. Cynthia had agreed and in the end, so had he.

As for his retiring doctor, Hoppy was as fit as a forty-year-old with no such health reasons. Weren't doctors, like clergy, called to run the race to the all-consuming end? Only then could the crown of laurels be legitimately received. In his own case, diabetes, overwork, and stress had forced him out to pasture at age sixty-five, though he'd supplied pulpits hither and yon ever since.

He remembered how things had progressed. When his bishop announced to the parish the news of Tim Kavanagh's retirement after sixteen years as the chief laborer in their vineyard, he observed more than a few mouths dropping open like the doors of roadside mailboxes. He heard a sharp intake of communal breath, primarily on the gospel side; a polite handkerchief or two fluttered out. That was expected.

Following the initial shock, however, came something altogether unexpected: their yawning indifference.

At the coffee hour, everyone crowded around, laughing, slapping him on the back and wishing him all the best, and then, like a shot, they fled home to their pot roast, as if no central loss had just occurred.

Where were the emotional breakdowns he'd dreaded, or even, perhaps, guiltily fancied? Where was the long, mournful line at the end of the service, with at least one or two flinging themselves upon him, possibly sobbing, and begging a reversal of this cruel decision?

Dream on. In truth, it was goodbye, Charlie, and have a swell time lounging around the house in your sock feet.

No one had warned him that something quite other would follow. On the heels of indifference came their anger and resentment. The sheer insult of his retirement raced along Main Street like a brush fire—oh, yes, he remembered.

In the how-could-you category, there was everything from the pained look and refusal to wish him a decent good morning, to full-blown righteous indignation. He was theirs, he belonged to them, they had got used to him, and now they were forced to go searching about for a total stranger, never a pleasant task, and God only knows what they'd come up with in this day and time. And it wasn't just his parishioners, but the Baptists, the Presbyterians, the Methodists, and every other Tom, Dick, and Harry who felt wantonly betrayed. A veritable Benedict Arnold, he skulked along in the shadows for weeks before the whole thing blew over and they liked him again. Small wonder that retired clergy refused to leave the house.

This missionary impulse of Hoppy's was, of course, noble; he, Timothy, had had such impulses himself—but wasn't being a small-town doctor in today's world noble enough for anybody?

He fought his way to the rear of their overstuffed closet that was once, they suspected, a nursery, and, in the dim light of the bulb they'd been meaning to convert to a blinding spotlight, found the morose thing in its dusty wrap. He took the wrap off, sneezed, and dragged the tux into their bedroom.

He laid it on the bed and stared at it, unseeing. When was their last black-tie affair?

Miss Sadie's party for the newly wed Harpers, of course. How extraordinary that the frugal Miss Sadie had done such a wondrous and extravagant thing, even having Fernbank's shut-away ballroom restored for the occasion. He recalled tables shining with crystal and silver, the music of the eight-piece orchestra, the coved ceiling swarmed by painted angels with gilded wings— and all of it bathed in the glimmer of candlelight. It had been an evening unlike anything Mitford had ever seen, and would almost certainly never see again.

He took the pants off the hanger, inspired. All would be well—the tux would be a tad form-fitting and in need of pressing, but nothing more; he was overreacting.

He glanced toward the corner of their room at the full-length mirror, which presented Absolute Truth morning, noon, and night, whether you wanted it or not. Indeed, unless the need to know was critical, he seldom looked into it.

The need being critical, he shucked out of his clothes and walked to the mirror in his shorts and socks.

It was an inarticulate sound, like a small animal surprised in the woods.

Heaving a fairly shuddering sigh, he set about doing what had to be done. The pants wouldn't zip all the way, much less button; any promise the jacket might have afforded was nil; and the cummerbund, albeit with Velcro, was toast.

He went to the bedroom door and closed it. This wasn't something he wanted even his dog to witness. As for Saturday night, it was obvious that he wasn't meant to leave the house.

He found Cynthia in the kitchen and confessed only 'a slight gain since Miss Sadie's party nearly a decade ago, but enough to, you know . . .'

'I can let it out,' she said. As far as he knew, she had never used a needle in her life. Having Cynthia Kavanagh do his alterations was as reckless as letting their son, Dooley, cut his hair.

'Puny could help,' she said, earnest. 'She's very good at that sort of thing.'

'We don't have a sewing machine,' he said.

'Right next door! Remember Hélène has a sewing machine. It's in the living room by the piano, with all those sheets of music stacked on it. Maybe Hélène sews.'

'People who sew don't stack things on top of the machine.' He knew that much, for Pete's sake. 'Besides, it's an antique, it doesn't actually work.' His sense of doom was literally breathtaking.

'We would use it over there,' she said, oblivious. 'It would be too heavy to carry through the hedge. It was her grandmother's.'

'Have you ever . . . ?'

'Never. I would only show Puny or Hélène the inseams and tell them how much to let out. They would do the rest.'

For years, Puny Guthrie had kept house for him as a bachelor and thereafter for the two of them, yet he'd never heard her mention any sewing skills she may possess.

'Have you checked the inseams?' he asked.

'I'll go up and do it now. Where is it? And by the way, it's time for your raisins.'

'Hanging on the door.' He was too weary to say which door. She gave him the raisin box and he emptied a few into his hand.

If he were a drinking man, it would be a double single-malt scotch, straight up—he could be that specific. Or, not wanting to betray his Irish bloodline, maybe a Paddy's.

SHE FOUND HIM STARING OUT the window of the study, still cupping the raisins in his hand.

'It doesn't have inseams,' she said, pale.

'Of course it has inseams. What else would hold it together?'

'No, I mean, it has them, of course, but they're so *narrow* . . .' She looked desperate.

'Cheap,' he said.

'What?'

'It was cheap. It must cost extra for inseams that can be let out.'

They sat on the sofa, where so many details of life had been threshed.

'The Internet,' she said. 'Overnight shipping, which gives us time to hem the pants.'

'No way,' he said.

He didn't want to talk about the last time they trusted the caprice of shopping on the Internet, and the thing arriving without screws to assemble it. He would never mention again how he had tracked the screws through a jungle of recorded phone messages, which eventually led to a real person who said he would take care of it immediately. He would never again speak of the many additional phone calls unanswered by the real person, and the weeks that ensued before the screws were delivered—not to his door, oh, no, but to the Local down the street, where the minuscule package had somehow fallen into a basket of California avocados and remained for a further week.

'Why are we doing this at the last minute?' he said.

'Because I thought all along you were going. Why wouldn't you go to the retirement party of a man who was your parishioner for sixteen years, your doctor for as many, a close personal friend, and the adoptive father of Dooley's sort-of-maybe fiancée?'

He held a raisin between his thumb and forefinger, examined it, dubious.

'It's also worth mentioning that he saved your life,' she said. 'Twice.'

There was the real rub, of course. 'Okay, okay, I said I'm going.' He could take to his bed from this ordeal, become an invalid sipping water through a bent straw. 'Why can't I just wear a suit and collar?'

She gave him a look containing its own vocabulary, then stared at the bookshelves, possibly thinking of dust; he studied his loafers, thinking of nothing in particular.

He was thrilled when the doorbell rang. He leaped up and sprinted along the hall like a released felon.

'Puny!' Her good face, freckles and all, had cheered him ever since he first saw it more than a decade ago.

'I know it's my day off, but I brought you somethin'.'

'Where are the twins?' He knew the older set to be in school at this hour.

'In th' car, I don't have but a minute. I jis' come from seein'
Joe Joe at th' station, he might git to be police chief.'

She was radiant, dazzling him.

'Holy smoke. He just got to be captain.'

'Don't tell nobody, just Miss Cynthy.'

'Of course. When will we know?' he asked.

'Maybe in a week or two is what they say.'

'Is Rodney Underwood retiring?'

'Kind of.'

'Kind of?'

'It's still a secret, but yes, he's leavin' to be chief at Wesley.'

'A big step up.'

'So y'all pray, okay? And here's th' little somethin' I brought
you.' She handed him a small envelope. 'Take it with a full glass
of water in th' evenin' an' don't leave th' house.'

He pocketed the thing, feeling the heat in his face.

'You're . . . kind,' he said.

'CHESTER MCGRAW!' she exclaimed as he walked into the
study.

'What about him?'

'He was your size exactly. I remember seeing him from behind
at Logan's in Wesley, and thinking it was you. Timothy! I said.
What are you doing in the pantyhose section? But it was Chester.'

'What was he doing in the pantyhose section?'

'I have no idea, he didn't say. Anyway, he's, you know . . .'

'*Morte,*' he said. 'Last February. A good man, Chester, we were
in Rotary together.'

'Who was at the door?'

'Puny.'

'Really? What about?'

'Just checking in, says Joe Joe might be made police chief.'

'Wonderful. When?'

'We don't know,' he said. 'Don't tell anybody, it's a secret. Have a raisin.'

'No, thanks. He had a tux.'

'Joe Joe?'

'Chester. Chester had a very nice tux.'

'Whoa, now, Kav'na.'

'He wore it to the Children's Hospital benefit last year, remember? When he gave that huge check. So if Irene hasn't thrown it out . . .'

'Wait a minute . . .'

'Why not? He made a barrel of money in the timber business, it would be a very nice tux. I'll call Irene, she's a darling woman.'

He felt a provoking urge to flee to Lord's Chapel and kneel at the railing.

'Irene didn't answer, she's probably in the garden.'

How his wife knew so much about Irene McGraw was beyond him. He knew only that Irene was said to look like a film star whose name he didn't recognize. He scanned his mental file on the McGraws: Baptists. Florida residents for the annual requisite of six months and a day. A lot of grandchildren.

'Shouldn't I . . . that is . . .' If he was going to wear another man's getup, shouldn't it be that of somebody in his own parish? 'Maybe somebody at Lord's Chapel . . .' he said, hating this.

'Nobody at Lord's Chapel is your size, Chester was an absolute duplicate.'

Useful beyond the grave—it was everyone's hope.

'Besides,' she said, 'anyone who has a tux at Lord's Chapel will be wearing it Saturday night.'

His wife knew everything. An honors graduate of Smith, of course—he wondered if all Smithies were like this.

'Ride with me,' she said, taking her keys off the hook at the kitchen door.

'Why?'

She gave him a doting look. 'Because I love your company.'

But there was nothing at all to love about his company. He was a certified crank these days. Not that he wanted to be, but he seemed unable to control the mean streak that had cropped up somewhere over the Pond, possibly around Greenland.

'Besides,' she said, cheerful as all get-out, 'that's what retirement is for.'

'I'm still trying to hammer out what retirement is for.'

'It's for jumping in the car and going somewhere on impulse.'

'I'll stick around here,' he said, loath to beg handouts from a recent widow.

'Irene won't even see you, I'll park in front of the hedge instead of in the driveway. Take your newspaper, I'll just be a minute. Then we can run by the Local.'

She gave him the look that was code for the rare pint of Ben & Jerry's. He was suddenly cheered.

'I'm in,' he said.

SHE BACKED HER MAZDA out of the garage.

'What if she gave it to the Salvation Army?' he asked.

'Too soon, I think.'

'So there's a timeline for cleaning out the spousal closet?'

'Usually six months to a year. Some people do it immediately after.'

He chewed on this arcane information, especially curious about the marital revelations of 'immediately after.'

'By the way,' she said, 'if I croak first, my clothes go to Puny and my jewelry to Lace, except for your mother's ring.'

'Where does that go?'

'If Dooley and Lace marry, to Lace. If not, it could pass to your next wife.'

He refused to comment.

She made a right onto Main. 'Just kidding, of course. Do you think you'd marry again?'

'Absolutely not. I was barely able to marry the first time, much less again.' She had just asked him this ridiculous question in Ireland.

He could sense her staring at him.

'What?' he said.

'I know how you hate hearing this, but . . .'

'But.'

'You need a haircut.'

'I just had a haircut. Two or three weeks ago.'

'That was a trim, not a cut. They left it too long.'

His wife needed a steady, paying job, not one in which she could do as she pleased, with time left over to mind his business.

'Merely a word to the wise,' she said.

He turned his attentions to Main Street, which was literally sparkling after a good wash by morning rain. He realized again how Mitford wasn't unlike an Irish village—colorful storefronts, hanging baskets, benches, a brisk early business in the shops.

'The big news while we were gone,' she said, 'is that Avis painted his bins.'

How had he missed that on his two wimpy morning runs through town? Beneath the green awnings of the Local were the famed outdoor produce bins, now as red as any tomato and filled with pots of yellow chrysanthemums.

'Very Irish, all that color, don't you think?'

'I do.' There was Avis Packard, standing outside his grocery store, smoking a cigarette.

In the end, the real difference between Mitford and the Irish village was pretty profound—Mitford was home, Main Street was his beat. After a year in Whitecap, a year at Meadowgate, the long sojourns in Mississippi and Memphis, and the trek to Ireland, it felt good to ease his foot into the old shoe.

'Irene is a gifted artist,' she said. 'Paintings of children. We've talked about doing a show together, a benefit for the Children's Hospital.'

'You hadn't mentioned it.' Children's Hospital in Wesley was his all-time favorite charity. Never one to relish asking for money, he had nonetheless helped raise $350,000 in the last campaign and thanks be to God for the Florida people who summered in Mitford and environs.

'Sort of waiting 'til we know more about her schedule. Her daughter lost a baby last year, but now there's another on the way. Then there are two little ones in California and four in Texas and one in Germany. She's very busy.'

'Blow the horn,' he said.

He rolled down the window. J. C. Hogan, editor of the *Mitford Muse*, was legging it across the street to Town Hall.

'Tea shop, noon tomorrow!' he shouted.

A thumbs-up from J.C.

He didn't like blaring it all over town that he was headed to the tea shop, tomorrow or any other day. They needed to change the blasted name, make it friendlier to the Mitford demographic.

He left the window down, inhaled rain-washed September air into his lungs. 'Maybe we should try a new flavor this time.'

'It took decades for you to upscale from vanilla to butter pecan.'

'One cannot upscale from vanilla to anything. Vanilla is the crème de la crème, and butter pecan merely passing fancy. However, I have felt the call of a completely different flavor for a couple of years, but never had the guts to buy it. How about Cherry Garcia?' *Carpe diem.*

She patted his knee, laughing. 'You are a wild and crazy guy.'

He didn't know how he felt about being patted. When she did that, and she often did that, he felt four years old, or possibly one up from a small-breed canine.

He moved his knee away, impatient, and opened the *Mitford Muse*. The local weekly had grown considerably thinner of late, but the front page still gave forth a blare of four-color process.

'Timothy?'

'Speak, Kav'na.'

Mule Skinner was running a quarter-page real estate ad below an ad for residential sewage treatment. Not a good placement. And there was the Helpful Household Hint for the week—he'd never admit to anybody but Puny that he looked for it each Thursday.

'Are you listening?' she said.

'I am, I am.' *Shoes can be shined with a banana peel. Clean off mess with a dry cloth.*

She wheeled right on Lilac—a little sharply, he thought.

'Do you think you might try what Puny suggested yesterday?' she asked.

Never one to mince words, Puny Guthrie had told him that what he needed was a good . . .

He buried his face in the newspaper.

. . . purgative.

HERE HE WAS SITTING in a car when he might be running up to the stone wall and looking upon life in the valley—the train hammering through the gorge, with a winding river and blue mountains beyond. It was a mild and perfect day, golden with sunlight after rain—one of his favorite weather conditions.

How would Irene McGraw feel about him bowling around town in her husband's gear? He considered that Irene may even be at the party. In times past, the spouse left behind waited a year before rejoining the social gambol, but the way things were going these days, this had likely been tempered by half.

The tux business was beyond him, he couldn't think about it anymore. He crossed himself and gave kit and caboodle to the creator of all that is seen and unseen.

Good News At A Cut Above

Mrs. Fancy Skinner of A Cut Above Hair Salon, has announced TWO new additions to her shop starting next Monday.

One is Wi-fi service (bring your iPads and laptops!) and last but not least, here's the biggie—a new stylist, Ms. Shirlene Hatfield, formerly of The

Hair Loft in Bristol, Tennessee, and a sister of Ms. Skinner!

Ms. Skinner says Ms. Hatfield will offer a full-complement of beauty services including spray tanning. In a phone interview with the Muse, Ms. Hatfield said: "I will be proud to introduce spraytan to Mitford. With spraytan, everybody in the mountains can look like they just drove up from Florida."

Not a good marketing tactic. Mountain folk wouldn't aspire to looking like the tanned horde arriving from Florida every May to take up all the parking spaces.

A hearty Mitford welcome to Ms. Hatfield! See below for the "Shirlene Hatfield $2.00-off haircut coupon" from the popular Cut Above Hair Salon where walk-ins are always welcome. Another $$$-saving bonus from the Muse—we print GOOD news!!

No expiration date on the coupon; he would clip it for Dooley's long weekend home in October. A coupon in the *Muse* was as rare as hen's teeth; the Wesley weekly was eating J.C.'s lunch by giving readers an entire page of coupons every Friday, not to mention a crossword.

In his shirt pocket, his cell phone did its marching band number, very festive.

'Hello?'

'Hey, Dad . . .'

Static.

'Dooley? Can you hear me?'

' . . . out . . . thinking . . . got to . . .'

'Dooley, you're breaking up. Can you . . . ?'

Gone.

They were pretty high on the mountain, no service up here, he supposed. He hated to miss a call from his boy.

Chelsea TEA shop Adds Children's Plate

He refolded the newspaper, read on.

Clearly, the tea shop was being forced to go with the times and expand their customer base. Only yesterday, he'd heard the new ownership said there would be no more fancy names the average customer couldn't pronounce, including *croissant*. More to the point, the ruffled pink curtains had vanished during their Ireland trip, the flowered wallpaper had disappeared under a coat of green paint, and the radio was tuned to Top 40 instead of Easy Listening. Now here was the children's plate, which he hoped grown-ups would feel free to order when short on cash or not very hungry. But the real work had yet to be done—in his opinion, they needed to dump the name of the place, pronto, give it more of a family flavor. Who took their kids to tea? Nobody that he knew of.

Cynthia appeared at the car window.

'She's not in the garden, and the front door is open. I went in and called, but no answer, and I looked in her studio out back.'

'There's a car in the garage.' He'd seen it as they drew up to the hedge.

'That's not her car, it's Chester's. I wonder if I should go upstairs and look for her.'

'Maybe she's in town, or visiting a neighbor.'

'Remember what happened to Norma Jenkins.'

Norma's front door had stood open for two days as she lay upstairs following a stroke, unable to cry for help and paralyzed throughout her left side.

'I'm sure she's fine,' he said. How many times had he left his own doors wide open as he worked in the backyard or the basement? Of course, those were his early years in Mitford; things were different now, as they were everywhere.

'I don't think she's the sort to leave her door open if she isn't home.'

'You seem to know her pretty well,' he said.

'We've had three art classes together. I taught two of them, she taught the other.'

'What about household help?'

'Her housekeeper goes back to Florida around the first of September,' she said, 'and Irene goes back late October.'

'I have an idea—why don't we head to the Local and forget Chester's tux? I'll rent one from Charlotte, they could put it on the plane to Hickory.'

She wasn't listening. 'I'm going inside and look for her, I feel creepy about this.'

He glanced farther along Bishop's Lane. Only one neighboring house in view, perhaps half a block away.

'Go in with me,' she said. 'Remember what happened to Norma.'

'Okay. I'll wait downstairs and make feeble excuses when she comes home.'

But she didn't come home. While Cynthia called Irene's name upstairs and down, he ambled about the living room off the foyer, peering at a series of five large oil paintings of what appeared to be the same young girl, signed Irene McGraw. He saw in the faces an interesting detail so small that he surprised himself by noticing it at all. The eyes of each subject contained a subtle, but compelling, reflection: the nearly minuscule image of the subject. He adjusted his glasses and leaned close. It was as if the large subject were looking at herself dressed in different clothing—a yellow dress. The painted pupil was a miniature gem—to render such a feat required inordinate skill and, perhaps, the merest hair of a sable.

He looked at his watch, heard Cynthia calling Irene's name.

On the grand piano, family photographs in silver frames. A lot of grandchildren, a perfect flock of them. He had missed having grandchildren, but Puny's two sets of twins had stood in the gap very well.

He thought of his brother, Henry, so recently known to him after all these years, and of what they'd gone through together in Memphis and Holly Springs, and wondered what his Kavanagh family portrait would look like now, with Henry among them.

In a large photograph of the McGraws in this very room, the couple was surrounded by roughly two dozen good-looking progeny dressed to the nines. A life had been lived here—all those grandchildren tumbling and laughing, someone shouting, Don't run in the hall, someone playing the piano, cousins kicking around a football. Like a lot of people who also live in tropical places, they probably spent Christmas and Thanksgiving here, hoping for snow. Now one was missing from this glad company. As for Irene, she would go on and things would be good again—but different, very different.

He'd always thought Irene an unusually attractive woman, but with a subtle air of sorrow or distraction, as if she were actually living elsewhere and had beamed in a likeness for a fund-raiser. He remembered that she played tennis and wore what his mother had called 'good' pearls.

He was turning away from the photograph when he realized that Chester—ha!—was sporting the much-talked-about tuxedo.

He moved into the hall as his wife came downstairs.

'She's not here.'

'I think we should go,' he said. 'You could call later.'

'This doesn't feel right, Timothy. You should see her bedroom. Things thrown all over the place. Not like her. Come and look.'

Clothes tossed on an unmade bed, drawers pulled out, closet doors standing open, clothing on the floor, an exercise mat with an open bottle of water beside it.

'What do you think?' she said.

He shrugged. 'This is the way a lot of people's bedrooms look.' Dooley's room in the early days of living at the rectory, for instance.

'It doesn't feel like Irene, she's fastidious. Always cleans her brushes and palette and puts them away in her carryall.'

'She's plenty gifted,' he said. 'The paintings . . .'

'Yes, and she's never shown or sold anything. I was thrilled when she said she'd consider the Children's Hospital benefit.'

'Who's her best friend?' he asked. 'We could call somebody.'

'Everyone likes her, but I don't know about best friends.'

He looked around again, paying attention. Message light blinking on a phone by the bed, windows raised a few inches, empty hangers on a closet door pull. They walked into the bathroom. Windows open a couple of inches. Drops of moisture on the glass door of the shower. A towel on the floor.

He stooped and felt the towel—damp—then looked out to the

rear lawn. That would be the studio, surrounded by a fairly ambitious garden with an open potting shed. Beyond, a dense thicket of rhododendron and oaks.

'What do you think?' asked his wife.

'I think she's in town or maybe she drove to Wesley; we need to get out of here.'

'I pray she's all right. Should we close the front door?'

'Best to leave things as we found them. I'm sure she's fine.'

How did they manage to everlastingly insinuate themselves into other people's business, Ireland being a prime example?

She sighed; he declined to mention it.

'Maybe we should do our shopping at the Local,' she said, 'and come by again before we go home?'

'Good. Let's do it, let's go.'

'I'd really like to check out her closet to see if Chester's tux is in there.'

'Good Lord, woman, leave off.'

He took her hand and led her to the top of the stairs, and down they went. Cherry Garcia.

Chapter
Two

If not for her, he would eat the entire pint at one sitting. But she would seize it at the halfway point, preach him a homily, and stick it in the freezer behind lamb chops wrapped in butcher's paper. A week might pass until she deemed it timely to let him finish it, straight from the carton.

He hated this monitoring business, for her and for him, but where would he be without surveillance? Lost, he supposed, in some diabetic coma, as twice before. Lord knows, he hoped Wilson would be up to it if anything dire ever happened again. With Hoppy in South Sudan, he could be as *morte* as Chester McGraw with a mere slip of the fork.

She waited for a northbound van to pass, and turned right on Main. 'Remember you have an appointment with Dr. Wilson on Monday.'

'Got it,' he said.

He hiked his pant leg and surveyed his right ankle. No swelling. Same with the left. What a life, when a man had to check his ankles and shoot himself with a needle and leave half a pint moldering behind the chops.

'I meant to tell you,' she said. 'Olivia called. Lace will be home for fall break on October eighteenth.'

'And Dooley comes in on the twenty-sixth and out on the

twenty-ninth.' He mused on the unfortunate juxtaposition of dates. Being in separate schools with different holiday schedules was tough on romantic, not to mention sleep-deprived, relationships. On the occasional long weekend, the round-trip drive time between UVA, where Lace was a sophomore, and UGA, where Dooley was a junior, was fifteen or sixteen hours.

'We'll have him all to ourselves for two days and three nights,' she said. 'And he seems happy about it.'

'No mention of going out to Meadowgate?'

'Not a peep. I think he misses us.'

He couldn't remember when they'd had Dooley's company for two days running—given the boy's fondness for disappearing out to Meadowgate Farm and honing his veterinarian skills.

'What do you think about two dinners?' she said. 'One for Dooley and the young siblings, and Buck and Pauline, of course. I think it would be good for Dooley to spend more time with Jessie and Pooh. We know Sammy and Kenny won't see their mother, so we could have Sammy and Kenny the following night.'

'There's Harley,' he said.

'He could come both nights.'

'And what about Hélène the first night? She's a terrific landlady, he says.'

'Fun. How many is that?'

She nosed the Mazda into a parking spot across from the Local, a pretty good grab.

'Dinner One, nine. Dinner Two, six.'

'Dinner One, burgers, coleslaw, and baked beans, two pots,' she said. 'Dinner Two, your special ham, Puny's potato salad, and we'll have the second pot of beans.'

'I'll get Esther to make the OMC,' he said. 'It'll serve both nights.' He loved doing this stuff. 'I'll just take my low-fat yogurt and enjoy it in the garage.'

He could see the whole thing—the gathering in the study around a long folding table laid with Nanny Howard's tablecloth, the view to Baxter Park, sunlight slanting through the window on Esther Bolick's unbeatable orange marmalade cake . . . and Dooley, there was Dooley wolfing his food and glad to be home but never letting on, and laughing, Dooley laughing, and later they would shoot pool in the dining room, and on the night of Dinner Two, Sammy would hammer the lot of them. Which reminded him . . .

'Which reminds me,' he said. 'I promised Sammy I'd learn to shoot pool.'

'Sammy being your instructor?'

'May as well learn from the best.'

'When Lace comes home, we'll have her over,' she said. 'Lunch, I think. We'll get to see the ring.'

Ah, the ring. Lace's ring from Tiffany was being resized when they traveled up the mountain the other night from the airport. Not exactly a friendship ring, Dooley had said, but not exactly an engagement ring, either.

'Excellent,' he said. 'Yes.' He needed to talk with the bright and beautiful girl whom he first met at Fernbank. She had worn a battered felt hat and carried a mattock and sack; he'd surprised her in the act of stealing Miss Sadie's ferns. Now she was the adopted daughter of the town doctor and his wife, an honor student at the University of Virginia, and Dooley's 'intended,' as they used to say in Mississippi. Things seemed to be coming up roses, albeit with a fair amount of thorns.

Cynthia took the key from the ignition. 'Remind me to get treats for Violet.'

Heaven knows, his wife's white cat was the biggest breadwinner in the family. In addition to being the star of the long-famous *Violet* books for young readers, Violet was a winsome and agreeable creature whom he'd come to like very much.

There had been, so far, a total of four white Violets to pose for and inspire the work of the author/illustrator, all but the current Violet now deceased. In their fictional incarnations, one or the other had gone to Paris, visited the Queen, attended school, vacationed in the country, played the piano, lived in a bookstore, you name it. Out rolled the *Violet* books and in rolled the dough.

'Will do,' he said. 'Let's keep Violet happy.'

IMPRESSED BY THEIR RECENT international travel, the proprietor of the Local checked them out personally.

'Buy one, get one free,' said Avis, bagging the two pink grapefruit.

'Great. Thanks.' He pulled out his wallet. 'You should do coupons in the *Muse*.'

'Too expensive,' said Avis. 'A Magic Marker, a sheet of butcher's paper, and a little tape to stick it on the window—that does it for me. How about today's special?'

'Missed that.'

'Medley of Root Vegetables. Beets, turnips, parsnips, carrots—already washed an' in a reusable bag—four bucks. A little olive oil, a little thyme, rosemary, and sea salt; roast on four twenty-five for twenty minutes.' Avis kissed his fingertips in the Italian fashion.

'We'll take a bag. But four bucks?'

'Fresh and full of flavor, not wilted and half dead like in some stores I could name.'

'Can we get fingerlings instead of parsnips?'

'No substitutions,' said Avis, punching around on the register screen.

'How about a ham?' he asked Avis. 'Bone in. Third week of October.'

'How about a valley ham you can cut with a fork—old-fashioned flavor, low on sodium, and exclusive to the Local? Free-range hogs, meat succulent and sweet. Bottom line, the best ham between here and Smithfield . . .'

Avis leaned into the clincher. '. . . bar none.'

'Book it,' he said. 'Ten to twelve pounds. Do you have a spoon, by any chance?'

'IF WE GO BY IRENE'S, the ice cream will melt,' he said, piteous.

She gunned the engine. 'We spent an eon in there. We hadn't really stocked up since we got home.'

'I have a spoon,' he said, taking it out of his jacket pocket. He held it forth, awaiting her pronouncement. He had made sure that the bag with the pint was within easy reach on the floor of the backseat.

She eyed the spoon, sighed. He would let this one pass, too, but one more and she could never again call herself a Yankee.

She pulled out into early afternoon traffic. 'You want to eat it now, in the car?'

'I do,' he said.

'And let the rest melt?'

'No, I want to eat half in the car and go home and put the rest in the freezer, and call and see if Irene answers, and if she doesn't, I'll ride up with you.'

'That's very sweet,' she said. 'Really it is.'

The cruise along Main Street was the best thing since his first milkshake in the backseat of his Grandpa Yancey's touring car in Holly Springs. He thought he hadn't recently been happier—and then he thought again of his doctor.

Hoppy Harper was heading for South Sudan to do good in this broken world, and here he was with nothing better on his agenda than going after a block of Cherry Garcia with a plastic spoon. He realized he'd been greatly pestered by the idea of Hoppy's bold future, for it made him despair of his own. He had a future, God willing, but bold?

He wished Irene McGraw would get herself home ASAP and shut her blasted dadgum door.

HOPE WINCHESTER MURPHY stood at the window of Happy Endings Bookstore and watched the Mazda go by with Father Tim in the passenger seat. He was eating something, maybe with a spoon, and looked happy.

She had walked past Lord's Chapel the other day on her way home and for the first time in ages, popped into the rose garden.

She wouldn't say a word to Father Tim, for it would disappoint him to know that the rose garden he'd planted behind Lord's Chapel had gone to ruin. Aphids, Japanese beetles, you name it, they had all enjoyed communion and left the leaves in shreds.

The Malmaisons, the thorny Gertrude Jekylls, the Pink Dawn that had shot so joyously up the side of the old Sunday school building—maybe they would make it, and maybe not. She had looked around for a hose and found one buried in weeds and attached it to the spigot and watered the beds, which made her feel somehow victorious over death and destruction.

Soon after his Ireland trip, Father Tim had dropped in to shop her annual S for September Sale, which gave fifteen percent off all titles beginning with S.

She had looked up from Pat Conroy's memoir of his reading life, and there he was, smiling in that boyish way that had caused her to have such a crush on him before she met Scott Murphy and went head over heels for the first time in her life.

'No fair buying by author name, as I recall.'

'No, Father, sorry. Just titles.' She knew he knew that, and was only teasing. 'What author?'

'Strindberg.'

'Strindberg! I can't imagine you reading Strindberg.'

He laughed. 'Just thought I'd see if you were paying attention. I believe it was Strindberg who wrote, "No matter how far we travel, the memories will follow in the baggage car." Not bad, you must admit.'

'And there's what he said,' she countered, 'about people who keep dogs. He called them cowards who don't have the guts to bite people themselves.'

How good it was to laugh with him. He was the only customer she knew who could quote Strindberg, who had read Steinbeck's complete works, and was an expert on Wordsworth, Cowper, and even the poor deranged plowboy poet, John Clare.

With all his fondness for the old and familiar, he was also willing to take a chance on authors he'd never read—not often willing, of course, but she had introduced him to Gabriel García Márquez and he had thanked her, and gone on to Jorge Luis Borges. She remembered him standing by the shelf with the Borges volumes and copying something in a little notebook he carried. He had shown it to her when he checked out.

All that happens to us, including our humiliations, our mis-
fortunes, our embarrassments, all is given to us as raw mate-
rial, as clay, so that we may shape our art. JL Borges

'Biblical,' he had said, smiling.

She couldn't imagine that he'd known misfortune or embar-
rassment or humiliation, but her notion of clerics was at that
time unrealistic at best. She was blinded by the pomp of the
office, and could scarcely comprehend the humanity of those
ordained to it until she came to know Father Tim. It had been
oddly inconvenient to see, if only so far as literary tastes allow,
into the day-to-day life of a religious—more inconvenient than
she had then cared to undertake, for as Mr. Emerson had pointed
out, changing one's mind was nothing if not vexing. Though
she was once content to view the cleric as a blurred figure in the
background of a photo, knowing Father Tim had brought such
imagery into sharp and agreeable focus.

It was he who had hired Scott as chaplain of Hope House, and
he who had performed their wedding ceremony at a lovely old
mountain church with the smell of beeswax and apples, and a
view to Tennessee. He had even baked a ham for their reception.

Above all, he and Cynthia had been two of her biggest sup-
porters when, scared out of her wits and not knowing how she
could possibly make it, she bought the bookstore and moved
upstairs and hung curtains at the windows and came to believe
in God.

Margaret Ann leaped onto the bench at the window and
settled into a patch of sunlight.

She reached to stroke her yellow cat, and there it was—the
warmth of her blood trickling down as if from a tap. It had been
like this for days. She had missed two appointments with Dr. Wil-

son because a fill-in for the store was hard to find and the money for a fill-in harder still. For some reason she couldn't comprehend, she had declined to talk about the baby with anyone except Scott and Louise and Dr. Wilson—it seemed natural to keep such news private and close until it was made obvious. Hoping to please, Scott had agreed. If her sister still lived in Mitford, she would tell her about the bleeding, but Louise was in Charleston, in a stressful job, and she wouldn't wish to alarm her.

And why hadn't she told Scott about the bleeding, or called the doctor's office to make an appointment? She was nearly four months, and surely this was not the time for secrets. What was she waiting for?

She pressed her forehead against the cool pane of the window. She was waiting to grow out of the terrible fear of too much happiness, or too much sorrow.

THEY HAD PUT AWAY four bags of provender, made a hasty lunch, and checked on Barnabas, then lay on the study sofa—his head to the south, hers to the north.

They woke at three, disbelieving.

'You see,' he said, 'jet lag doesn't disappear overnight.'

'Let's call Irene,' she said.

Irene Schmirene, who, he'd bet anything, had come home from her own shopping expedition and was putting away her own provender, or possibly waking up from a nap . . .

No answer at the McGraws'.

'What does her phone message say?' he asked.

'The usual. You've reached the McGraw residence, no one can come to the phone right now, please leave a message.'

'Did you leave a message?'

'I hung up.'

'You could have left a message and when she comes in, she would call back.' His wife didn't know everything, not by a long shot. 'Call her again at five o'clock.'

She sat up, took Violet in her arms, and wandered to the window, staring out. When his wife stared out windows, wheels were turning—walls may get glazed, chandeliers removed and replaced by lamps, draperies changed to a more seasonal color, and now what? Irene McGraw's door was driving her crazy.

For years he had mildly resented her ardent labors at the drawing table, which for months on end took her out of his life into another. He must have developed a kind of mental callus, for now he wished her there at the table in her small studio—the familiar sight of her bowed head as he walked down the hall, the crick in her neck that he would willingly rub out, her struggle to produce a higher work than she had produced before—even the rice bubbling and then burning on the stove would be a consolation compared to this meddling business.

He never thought he'd hear himself say it. 'Go work on your book, Kav'na.'

'Okay,' she said, obliging, and turned and disappeared down the hall with her cat.

He couldn't believe she was actually doing something that wasn't her idea. This woman could take charge of his life like a house afire, but she had the poignant and childlike side, too, that moved his heart every time.

IT WAS QUIET NEXT DOOR.

After he and Cynthia remodeled the yellow house a few years ago and moved through the hedge from the rectory he'd purchased from the diocese, he had rented the place to Hélène Pringle. Hélène was a French-born piano teacher and, to his everlasting surprise, a half sister of the deceased Sadie Baxter—a circumstance which turned out to be more rose than thorn, thanks be to God.

Subleasing the basement apartment from Hélène was Harley Welch, a sixtysomething reformed moonshine runner and gem of a mountain fellow, who once acted as self-appointed guardian to Lace Turner before her adoption by Hoppy and Olivia Harper— all that being an opera of considerable magnitude with many arias yet to be sung. Indeed, the basement had become home, also, to Dooley's two younger brothers, Sammy, seventeen, and the nineteen-year-old Kenny, recently returned from the four winds to which they'd been flung as children.

Suffice it to say, the trio made the occasional racket. In addition to the keyboard melodies pouring from Miss Pringle's studio windows, ten until four, there was the racing of the engine of a derelict pickup on which the tenants labored into the night. No less clamorous was the hammering at the back stair treads which were slowly but surely being replaced. Through it all ran the threnody of country music from a boom box, turned full blast while reclaiming a rectory toolshed formerly lost to briars.

It was the stuff of life over there, though something of a blow to the neighborhood.

How the seemingly prim Hélène Pringle could bear all this, he didn't know. She said a few weeks ago, when he found her weeding along her side of the hedge, that 'they' kept things 'cheerful, more like a home.'

'*Pardon moi*, Father, but before they congregated down there, I found the old place a bit . . .' She looked up at him, apologetic. '. . . *morose*,' she said in the French way.

Now you could hear a pin drop. Before they arrived home from Ireland, Harley had taken the boys to visit a branch of the Kentucky Welches, and Hélène had flown to Boston to settle her mother's estate.

He found himself pacing the floor, as if waiting for something unknown.

HE PORED OVER HIS CALENDAR and a stash of notes scribbled to himself.

A Rotary meeting. A Kiwanis Club dinner. Cleanup day on the lawns at Children's Hospital.

Return the call from the mayor—he was pretty sure Andrew Gregory wanted him to run for town council, an idea he'd dodged for years.

A request to speak to a clergy group in Holding.

The cure in Hendersonville looking to fill their pulpit for a month.

And there, of course, was the unopened letter from the new bishop. The new bishop. He had liked the old bishop.

He wasn't busy enough, pure and simple. And yet such a list didn't engage him at all. Dashing uphill and down, his tongue hung forth like a terrier's, had lost its luster.

In the years he was heaped with responsibility and a flock that buzzed about him like bees, he'd been fine—except, of course, for the two diabetic comas. He had never lacked for something to do, some problem to solve, someone to try and make happy. Then came the course in clergy counseling, and the contemporary notion that he couldn't possibly make someone else happy, such business was entirely up to the other person.

He wished, albeit briefly, that Emma Newland was still his

erstwhile secretary. She would call around and cancel or decline as he directed, and leave most of them afraid to try again.

In sum, he wanted more out of life than meetings and dinners and confabulations of every sort and kind. He had thought Holly Springs and Ireland might give him some answers, but both seemed only to emphasize the questions, What now? What next?

He supposed he would do as he had always done—he would perform whatever duty his calendar dictated, and he would try to like it.

SHE MADE YET ANOTHER CALL AT SIX-THIRTY.

'Still no answer,' she said. 'I left a message.'

'The towel was damp when we were there this morning around nine,' he said, musing.

'So let's say she left soon after. It's six-thirty now; that would be—at least nine hours. Would you leave our front door open for nine hours?'

'Only if I forgot it was open when I went out through the kitchen to the garage and drove somewhere.'

'Maybe she drove to the airport and is gone for two weeks to . . .' She threw up her hands, unable to think of a destination.

'Ibiza,' he said.

'Do you think we should call the police?'

'I do not. You know Rodney Underwood. He would rope off the house with yellow tape, and such a crowd of squad cars and theatrics you'd never see again. The poor woman couldn't get in her own driveway when she comes home.'

'It's a good thing there's a glass storm door, at least the bugs and squirrels can't get in.'

He opened the *Muse* to finish what he had started hours ago.

'But since it will be dark soon,' she said, 'don't you think we should go up and close her door? Wouldn't that be the neighborly thing to do?'

Here was his all-time favorite *Muse* column, Mayhew's Mitford. Worth the cost of the paper right there, as Hessie Mayhew knew everybody's business and wasn't afraid to tell it.

'Timothy?'

He glanced up.

'This *is* Mitford, after all. Remember what we say about ourselves.'

'"Mitford takes care of its own!"' He quoted their longtime, albeit former, mayor's classic slogan.

She made a beeline for the key rack. 'I'm going up there.'

'I'll just get my shoes on,' he said.

THEY HAD HOPED for the welcome surprise of seeing Irene's car garaged next to Chester's, but it wasn't there. They pulled into the driveway. In the approaching dusk, a nearly full moon had risen; the house had a vaguely lost look.

'We should have called the post office and asked if she put a stop on her mail.'

'I wonder,' he said, 'about the message light that was blinking. Maybe there's a phone message that would give us a clue.'

'We could try it. Should we?'

'Maybe,' he said, getting out of the car.

They stood on the front stoop, indecisive. There was a definite drop in temperature, as often happened when the sun dipped behind the mountains.

They stepped into the dark entrance hall. He wasn't feeling

so good; something in the pit of his stomach. What was it about an empty house, any empty house where the human or even canine spirit was absent? He looked up to the stair landing, nearly vanished in the shadows.

'I just remembered,' he said. 'We don't have a password to pick up her messages. Besides, I don't really want to go up those stairs.' They were not his stairs to go up.

'How about her windows being open? What if it rains? Did you hear a weather forecast? It's hurricane season.'

'They were up maybe two inches, for Pete's sake.' He was curt without meaning to be.

She looked at him, wounded. 'Sometimes rain blows sideways.'

She appeared twelve years old in the diminished light. Though she'd recently had her sixty-fourth birthday, she was occasionally mistaken for his daughter.

'I'm leaving,' he said. 'This is it for me.' He took her arm, felt her stiffen.

'Did you see that?' she said.

'What?'

'Something moved out there.'

'Like what?'

'A person, maybe. To the right, in the driveway.'

They were fresh from a burglary in Ireland, and a lawless freak jumping from the armoire in their room . . .

He saw movement, too, then; a blur through the glass door. The sudden impulse to run with his wife out the back door came forth as paralysis. He couldn't move.

'Deer,' he whispered, hoarse.

'Yes?'

'As in doe and buck. They're after what's left of the hosta.'

They came in families most nights to the Kavanagh hosta, but only after they finished off the azaleas.

She was trembling, an ash leaf; his heart hammered. Dear God, for the comfort of home, the innocence of his dog's snore . . .

Maybe She Who Always Had an Idea would come up with something; he didn't know what to do.

'We can't stand here all night,' he said. It was fish or cut bait. 'Stay there, don't move, it'll be fine, I'm going out.' But only if he could walk with knees turned to water.

The movement of the door latch was nearly inaudible.

His wife's shriek; an inferno of white light emptied into his face.

'Put your hands where I can see 'em.'

He said something unintelligible, his vital forces blinked off.

'Father Tim?'

Another blaze of light, a young face, a gun.

'Joe Joe?' he said, aghast.

Joe Joe grabbed him as he fell and stood him against the doorjamb like a cooked noodle.

'I can explain everything,' he said. But why bother? Let his wife do the talking.

Chapter
Three

I'm off,' she said, giving him a kiss on the cheek.

'To?'

'Concrete World, for a birdbath and two frogs under an umbrella.'

'Don't do the frogs,' he said. 'Go and be as the butterfly.'

Out she went to the garage, in breezed Puny from the stoop.

'It's your short day,' he said. 'You don't have time to torment me.'

'I've always got time for that, Father.'

She was mischief itself, he could see it coming.

She removed her sweater, rolled it into a ball, stuffed it in her bag, put the whole business under the counter, and stood up, grinning.

'Joe Joe says you fell out when he shined that light on you.'

'And shoved a Glock .45 in my face. Wouldn't you fall out?'

'I'd drop dead on th' spot.'

'The truth is, I did not fall out, as you say; my knees went weak, that's all. I trust he won't be spreading such foolish news around town.'

She took the cushion off a kitchen stool, pummeled it. 'He would never say a word, but I don't know about Officer Greene, th' ol' so-an'-so. He might tell Ruby, an' then, you know, party time.'

'Party time?'

'Everybody will know you fainted. But that's okay, men faint a lot, it's not just women that faint. A woman tells her husband she's havin' twins, an' what does he do? He falls out. A man goes to th' doctor an' when he hears th' bad news, he pitches headfirst off th' table.'

'How do you know this?'

'I have a friend who's a nurse in Wesley. She says men fall out all th' time.' She gave what-for to another stool cushion.

'Did Joe Joe do that when you announced you were having the girls?'

'He actually did, I forgot about that. Hit his head on the bedstead.' She was having a pretty good laugh about it. 'It didn't hurt him none, though.'

'What about the second time around?'

'Cool as a cucumber. Lord knows, twins don't run in that family, they gallop. It's nothin' that ever come out of my family, I can tell you that.'

'So tell Joe Joe I'll keep quiet if he'll keep quiet.'

'More coffee?'

'Half,' he said, holding forth the mug.

'All that uproar over nothin',' she said. 'Who wouldn't git in their car an' shoot down to Georgia with their door wide open? Especially if her daughter was havin' a baby a whole month early an' lost th' last one. If one of my girls was in that fix, I'd be leavin' my door blared open, too.' She rattled a handful of flatware out of the dishwasher and into a drawer. 'It's a good thing her neighbor spotted your car over there and called th' police. It's nice to know people still keep an eye out for each other.'

'All's well that ends well.' He snipped the coupon from the *Muse*.

'Seven pounds four ounces and a great pair of lungs, she said when Joe Joe an' her neighbor called down to Georgia. An' think about it—if you and Miss Cynthy hadn't gone over to check, who knows what criminal element might've backed a truck in there an' emptied th' place?'

She lifted the lid on the Dutch oven, peered in. 'Are you movin' Barnabas down today?'

His heart sank.

'I'll help you. It's got to git done.'

'No, no. I mean yes. Monday. I think Monday. He likes it up there, you know. That's home.'

'But he'll like it down here, too, once he gits used to it. Y'all are down here so much, it'll be company for 'im. Where's Miss Cynthy at?'

'Buying a birdbath and two frogs under an umbrella.' Actually, that was his wife's code for buying art materials in Wesley.

'She don't need to buy those frogs, ever'body has frogs under a umbrella. You could not *give* me frogs under a umbrella. Does she want these beans cooked?'

'She does.'

'Did she soak 'em overnight?'

'She did.'

'Did she add ginger?'

'I believe so.'

'What are you doin' today?'

'Lunch with J.C. and Mule.'

'Fancy Skinner's sister is movin' here from Tennessee, she'll have 'er own chair at A Cut Above.'

'So I hear.'

'You need a trim really bad.'

Here it comes, he thought. For a full decade, Puny Guthrie

had monitored his barbering regimen—in truth, had a particular zeal for it.

'I had a trim a couple of weeks ago.'

'That was in Ireland,' she said.

'How much could it grow in two weeks?'

'I been wantin' to say it, but I hated to—they left it too long. It's throwin' money down th' drain when they leave it too long, I can tell you that.' Out with the mop bucket.

'*Miserere nobis.*'

'What'd you say?'

'Talking to myself.'

How many times had he wanted to tell her to back off, he had a wife to mind his business? But he couldn't say that to this spunky mountain girl whom he loved like a daughter. Puny had ministered to him as tenderly as any angel before Cynthia came on the scene—trouble was, she never stopped doing it, and he didn't have the heart to rebuke her.

'You said you'd never go back to Fancy again in this life, an' Lord knows, I don't blame you, but maybe her sister would work out. It'd save you th' trip to Wesley. You know th' price of gas these days an' Joe Joe says it's not goin' down anytime soon.'

Talk about meddling; he was a novice.

She ran hot water in the mop bucket and turned, green eyes wide, to pin him to the wall of the study.

'So?' she said.

'So, what?'

'You know. What I brought you.'

'Thanks,' he said, stiff as a board. 'A very helpful household hint.' End of discussion.

'It sure made you nicer this mornin'.'

He fled upstairs to don his running gear.

. . .

'I'M HAVIN' TWO CHILDREN'S PLATES,' said Mule, looking pleased with himself.

'Why a children's plate?' said J.C.

'I want to see if it's any good; it's their new promo.'

'And why two, for God's sake?'

He didn't have much to contribute to the conversation, but he'd give it a go. 'He likes children,' he told J.C.

'So order one children's plate,' said J.C., 'and if you don't like it, you won't be stuck with two.'

'But I really like macaroni and cheese,' said Mule.

'Which comes with a grilled cheese sandwich, for crap's sake. You want to detonate your arteries?'

'You only get half a grilled cheese with it.'

'But if you get two plates, one each with half a grilled cheese, that's a whole grilled cheese plus a double macaroni and cheese. Why not just order a grilled cheese and a side of macaroni and save a buck fifty? I thought you liked to pinch a penny.'

'I want two children's plates, one at a time.'

'If you ain't th' cuckoo clock,' said J.C.

'Leave him alone,' he said. 'Let the man order what he wants.'

'But he's not goin' to like havin' two children's plates. You don't even get a pickle with that deal.'

'Children don't generally enjoy pickles,' he said, conciliatory.

'And look around. Do you see any children in here? I don't see any children in here, which tells you where this promo is headed.'

He examined the menu card.

'I guess you read about Fancy's sister coming in?' asked Mule.

'I did,' he said. 'Clipped the coupon this morning.'

'She's single.'

'Aha.'

'I heard she's movin' here to look for a husband.'

'She might want to rethink that,' he said.

Lunch and dinner only

No breakfast served, you are on your own

Soup of the day: Cream of chicken

Pie of the day: Cherry

*Special salad of the day with our
homemade poppyseed dressing*

*Try our house specialty: Banana pudding—
sorry about leaving out the bananas last week*

For restroom key, ask Mindy

'I think I'll have the special salad,' he said.

'Maybe I'll have that, too.' Mule looked hopeful.

J.C. did an eye roll. 'Every wife's dream—for hubby to have a salad.'

'What's in the special salad?' asked Mule.

'I don't know,' he said. 'It just says special salad.'

'You'd order a salad and not know what's in it?'

'Why not? Whatever it is, you get fiber.'

'You order salad just for fiber?'

Why did he continue to have lunch with these clowns? Had he been a bona fide psychiatric case all these years and people were too kind to confront him with the truth? Lunch at home, that was the ticket. Or better still, in Wesley once a week, to get out of the house. Mule was too cheap to drive to Wesley for lunch, and J.C. went to Wesley only on Thursdays, so if he avoided going to Wesley on Thursday, he would have complete freedom the other four days to do what he wanted, and with no dithering conversation thrown in. It came to him that under such circumstances, he'd be at liberty to eat a whole pepperoni pizza with nobody the wiser. He wondered why he hadn't thought of this before.

He rechecked the menu. 'Or maybe I'll have the vegetable plate.'

'What are th' choices?'

'Green beans, mashed potatoes and gravy, cooked apples . . .'

'I don't like green beans.'

'. . . black-eyed peas, coleslaw, glazed carrots . . .'

'Nothin' glazed for me,' said Mule.

'. . . sweet potatoes, or cabbage. Choose three.'

'How would mashed potatoes and gravy go with cooked apples?' Mule eyed J.C., who refused to comment. 'But maybe not, maybe th' gravy would run into th' apples.'

Pizza, his wife would say to the coroner.

How do you know that, ma'am?

I smelled pepperoni. He could never fool me.

Their favorite server, a young mountain girl with consummate charm, was nowhere to be seen. Someone tall, big-boned, and tricked out in an apron and cowboy boots was taking orders.

'That's th' new owner,' said Mule. 'She sold her other place down th' mountain. Cracker Barrel came in and she went out. Heard this place was up for sale an' jumped on it.'

'News you can use,' said J.C.

'We pumped regular together at Lew's this morning.'

'Hello, boys.'

A hand shot his way. He stood and shook it.

'Father Kavanagh?' she said. 'Wanda Basinger.'

'Ms. Basinger, this is J. C. Hogan, editor of the *Mitford Muse*, and I believe you've met Mule Skinner, our erstwhile realtor, at the gas pump. Welcome to Mitford.'

'So this is th' Turkey Club I've heard so much about.'

'Where's that young woman used to wait tables here?' asked Mule.

'I had to let 'er go.'

'Let her go? What for?'

Wanda Basinger raised an eyebrow. 'She was nice to th' customers.'

Mule adjusted the knot in his tie, stricken. J.C. mopped his forehead with his napkin. As for himself, he sat down.

'We'll start with you, Mr. Skinner, what are you havin'? I can recommend the special salad with Gruyère, sliced figs, and onion.'

'Sliced figs,' said Mule, dazed. 'Onion. No, thanks.'

'The cows'll come home before you get an order out of him,' said J.C. 'I'll have th' chopped barbecue plate, double hot sauce, double fries, double pickles, and a large root beer.'

'A man who knows what he wants. Father?'

'The vegetable plate. Coleslaw, black-eyed peas, sweet potatoes, hold the corn muffin.'

They all looked at Mule; J.C. drummed the table with his fingers. 'Sink or swim, buddyroe.'

Mule faced the wall, avoiding eye contact with Wanda Basinger. 'I don't know,' he snapped. 'Ask th' father.'

'Bring him two children's plates,' he said. 'One at a time.'

. . .

'I'M NEVER COMIN' BACK HERE.' Mule stared at children's plate number two, disconsolate. 'Who would fire a girl like that? She was th' best thing they had goin'. She always gave me an extra roll and butter, and extra whipped cream on th' chocolate pie. Since when is it a crime to be nice to customers? Right there is what's wrong with th' world today.'

'How was the barbecue?' he asked J.C.

'Good. Real good. Amazing barbecue.'

Wanda was patrolling the room with a water pitcher. 'Everything all right over here?'

Mule shoved his untouched second order to the side.

'Would you like this in a take-out, Mr. Skinner?'

'For my dog.'

'Whose barbecue was that?' asked J.C.

'It was yours, honey, you're payin' for it.'

'What I mean is, who made it?'

'Somebody in east Tennessee.'

'The menu says it's North Carolina barbecue.'

'You do not have to live in North Carolina to make North Carolina barbecue. Just open th' vinegar bottle and pour it in there, you can do that in Tennessee, Mississippi, or Detroit, Michigan.'

'May be a little misleading,' said J.C.

'North Carolina is a *style* of barbecue,' said Wanda, 'just like Memphis is a *style* of barbecue. My husband makes Texas barbecue without steppin' foot out of our backyard on Little Mitford Creek.'

She filled their water glasses.

'If you know what you're doin'—an' my husband, Lloyd, knows what he's doin'—it tastes like the real thing, you can't tell it from th' real thing. You take Kansas City barbecue, they make it over in Alabama and Arkansas and all around down there . . .

'. . . which,' she said, taking her leave, 'would make that a *style* of Kansas City barbecue.'

'Nowhere to run, nowhere to hide in this town,' said J.C., slapping a couple of quarters on the table.

THEY STOOD ON THE SIDEWALK and watched Mule head out with his foam box.

'I didn't know Mule had a dog.'

'He hasn't had a dog since fifth grade,' said J.C. 'He'll eat the second go-round when his stomach settles down. That woman needs to be rustlin' cattle, not hustlin' food.'

'She does make Velma look cordial.' J.C. had engaged in a verbal brawl with Velma Mosely, co-owner of the old Main Street Grill, thereafter taking his lunch trade to the tea shop.

They stared at a black limo moving north on Main, the driver in uniform.

J.C. gawked. 'Who do you think that is?'

'A tourist with money to burn,' he said, walking.

'Didn't look like Ed Coffey at th' wheel.'

Ed Coffey, liveried to the max, had driven Edith Mallory for years in a black Lincoln town car with tinted windows. 'Ed Coffey's in Florida with Edith,' he said. 'I hear she's having a tough recovery.'

He remembered the inferno boiling into the night sky, and the looping shriek of fire engines. He'd run out to the street and looked at the ridge above Fernbank where Edith Mallory's Clear

Day was ablaze. By the time their local engine and a backup from Wesley hacked through the overhanging rhododendron, the house was destroyed and Edith had suffered a severe head injury.

'Is she talking yet?' asked J.C.

'We had a card from her when we got home. Said she's doing better.' *Doing better*, she had written, *pray for me.*

'I guess you heard what's going on at Lord's Chapel?'

'What's going on?'

'Actually, nobody really knows, but rumors are flyin'. The story I get is—'

'I don't want to hear it,' he said. 'I keep my nose out of parish rumors.' Not only was that expected of the former priest, but he really didn't want to hear it. It would do him no good to know whatever it was nobody really knew.

J.C. wiped his face with his lunch napkin. 'You'd never make it in my business.'

'True.'

'That was some good barbecue, you should try it. But the fries came with aioli.'

'So?'

'I thought they weren't servin' anything people can't pronounce.'

'You just pronounced it. Maybe you and Mule can overlook the owner's personality and we can settle in and be regulars.'

'Or maybe we'll go back to Lew Boyd's an' eat bad sandwiches . . .'

'Your sandwiches were bad, not mine.'

'. . . an' sit on those dinette chairs by th' vending machine, suckin' up exhaust fumes from th' garage . . .'

'Snow blowing in . . .'

'Freezin' our ass to th' chair,' said J.C.

'Those were the good old days.'

'It was just a few months ago.'

'*Tempus fugit.*' He was going to coax his Latin back if it killed him.

'Find a hole and fill it, that's my motto. If I was a rich man, I'd put a real restaurant in this town.'

They were legging it up Main Street—a grand, soft day, as the Irish would say. He was glad he'd run this morning, if only a couple of miles; he'd get back to a regimen, he would straighten up and fly right.

'We have a real restaurant,' he said. 'Lucera. Miss Sadie's old place. Great food. Terrific atmosphere. Romantic.'

'That's the problem—you pay for romantic. I don't need romantic.'

'Adele might enjoy romantic, ever thought of that?'

'Oh, boy, Dr. Phil comes to Mitford.'

'Remember who helped you land Adele.'

'Right. Mitford's leading citizen.'

'Who would that be?'

'Wait'll you see next week's *Muse.* I paid big money for this piece.'

'What piece?'

'Wait an' see. Inspired by the McGraw incident. You'll like it.'

'Come on. What are you talking about?'

'Number one, we're posing an important philosophical question to this community. Number two, a couple of people called you Mitford's leading citizen and we're taking a survey—you could end up th' winner.'

'Wait a minute. I am not a leading citizen. No, no, that's embarrassing. Are you serious?'

They stopped outside the men's store.

'For one thing, I don't lead anybody.'

'You led a hundred and twenty people, give or take, for sixteen years.'

'That's a completely different matter, and that was five years ago, it's history.' He didn't like the feel of this. 'You need to cancel that story,' he said. The McGraw *incident*?

'Freedom of the press, buddyroe.' J.C. opened the door to the Collar Button, the bell jingled. 'I'm droppin' in here to pick up a half-page ad, looks like th' local economy's on the upswing.'

HE GUNNED HIS VINTAGE RAGTOP up the hill to Hope House, dismissing J.C.'s blather. He would give J.C. a call tomorrow, nip this thing in the bud—he didn't like what he was feeling.

There. The kick in the engine, like a tic, then the feel of something disconnecting and firing again.

For a year or more, they had thrashed through whether to sell his Mustang, trade it, put it on blocks in the backyard ('Too rural,' said his wife), save it for Dooley, or auction it off at the fiftieth anniversary benefit for Children's Hospital. Cynthia was keen on the benefit, Dooley didn't appear to want it, and storing it on blocks, anywhere, seemed uselessly sentimental.

If he knew the ropes of Internet commerce, he would put it on eBay or one of those lists he'd heard about. Or maybe park it at Lew's with a sign on the windshield.

The benefit was probably the answer. A completely trouble-free way to let it go and get a deduction into the bargain. But he'd miss it, of course. Cynthia had given it to him a few years ago as a birthday present; it had marked a memorable chapter of his life.

He pulled into the parking lot at Hope House, liking the ease of the steering, the worn leather seat—an old shoe on wheels. He got out and locked it, then stood back and looked at what the boys in Holly Springs had called 'a sharp little ride.' A collar in a red Mustang convertible had raised a few eyebrows along the way, which, if nothing else, had been fun.

He heard the familiar buzz just beyond the treetops to the north, and looked up and, yes, oh, boy, there it was—Omer Cunningham's yellow ragwing, making a pass over Hope House.

He threw up his arm and waved to beat the band. Omer dipped a wing and roared south.

Omer's personalized wing dip was a tribute cherished by more than a few. Uncle Billy, a recipient of one of these dips, had marked the occasion by saying, 'That'd bring tears to a glass eye.'

It gave him a thrill to see Omer gunning around in his slap-dash contraption. Not that he, Timothy, had been the perfect passenger the time or two that Omer had taken him up. He remembered trying to hold on to his minimal breakfast; remembered looking down at the floorboard, where a ruined bath mat failed to cover a gaping hole—a hole through which he gained an uneasy view of treetops and power lines.

Where Omer got the wherewithal for such entertainment, he had no idea. 'He's a decorated 'Nam vet,' J.C. said. 'Let 'im do what he dern well pleases.'

The door to Room Number One was open, as he usually found it, and the real Number One was sleeping in her blue recliner.

The chair faced out to the nurses' station where the action was, and had been called the best seat in the house or the worst, depending. All the world was right there, just through the door, still living and using a walker, still dying and being rolled to the elevator on a gurney, still uttering the occasional epithet, still bringing flowers and removing the perished ones, still bearing trays of food, some you could eat and some you couldn't, and once in a blue moon there came the brightness of children passing, going in to their great-grandma—or great-grandpa, though there were currently only three of these good souls, one still with an eye for the nurses.

The children were especially worth waiting for, hoping for, they seemed to come most often around Easter, bringing baskets, conducting something into the world of the hallway that reminded Louella of her own youth, those long days ago when she was raised by Miss Sadie, seven years her elder, and pulled around town in a red wagon like a sack of seed corn.

For Miss Sadie to raise a little dark girl as her own and to give her the family name if she wanted it, and then to take her in again years later, when her beautiful husband had died and her step-grandson was transferred to Los Angeles—to do all that and then put in her will that Louella Baxter Marshall was to have the many satisfactions of Room Number One until the day, according to the handwritten will, that 'Louella, my sister in the Lord and dearest friend,' was herself rolled to the elevator on a gurney.

'Miss Louella, you see too much goin' on,' a nurse once said. 'It's too stimulatin'. You need rest.'

'I'll rest in th' grave,' was the reply.

Louella had asked him which cost the least, a casket funeral or cremation. Cremation, he said. She didn't want the price of a fancy casket to bear on the funds Miss Sadie had set aside to take care of Louella Baxter Marshall's needs. She wanted to choose cremation, then, as Miss Sadie had done. She had never heard of a Baptist being cremated, though Episcopalians did it all the time.

'I was 'piscopal all my young days,' she once told him. 'Then Baptist with my husband all my middle days, then 'piscopal all my old days. I guess I'll go out th' way I came in.'

'Cynthia and I will keep your urn,' he said, 'or we can sprinkle your ashes.'

'I'd hate bein' closed up in that little thingamajig. Where would you sprinkle me?'

'How about into the valley where the train runs every day blowing its horn, and the river turns its face to the sun and catches the reflection of clouds passing over?'

'That sound good,' she said, thoughtful. 'I'm not afraid to go. You might get Dooley to sing.'

'He'd be honored.'

'No organ back of 'im, just 'is voice. An' you could put a little pinch or two on that place where you buried Miss Sadie's urn in th' churchyard.'

Beloved. He had written the word on a slip of paper and, unable to speak, handed it to the fellow who would engrave Sadie Baxter's small headstone.

'An' a little pinch in th' ol' part of th' buryin' ground where some of my people are at.'

He took her hand and held it.

'An' you might maybe put a teaspoonful in th' bushes up at Fernbank.'

He laughed. 'I'll be burning some fat on this run.'

'In th' lilacs. Th' ones on th' south side by th' porch steps. Miss Sadie an' me used to drag a little bench out there an' peel apples in th' sunshine.'

'Consider it done,' he had said. 'But I believe we've got a while yet.'

He slipped into the room and sat by her chair on the low stool he always occupied during these visits. On the stool, he was twelve years old. Indeed, he felt some primordial consolation when he was with Louella, something that reached back beyond his earthly beginning. Perhaps because it was Peggy's dark-skinned arms in which he slept as an infant as his mother and father drove the Buick from Grandpa and Nanny Howard's town house out to a new life in the Mississippi countryside. It had been Peggy he ran to when his heart was broken or his knee gashed when he fell on a rusty plowshare. It had been Peggy he always ran to, except when he turned ten, and suddenly there was no Peggy to run to.

He had a moment of yearning for those days. The 'old fled days,' the Irish called their years of tribulation. In tribulation, there had been a certain sweetness, too, as marrow in a remorse-less bone.

Louella opened one eye, then the other. 'I see you,' she said, chuckling a little. 'I see you on yo' stool. Where you been so long?' She pressed the remote on the chair arm and raised the recliner to an upright position.

He stood and kissed her on the cheek. 'Been to Ireland,' he said, happy.

Louella reached for her dentures on the TV table, installed them. 'Where th' fairies are!'

'That's it. Where have you been?' He sat again on the stool.

'Dreamin' I was in that little wagon, bumpin' all over town. I dream a lot 'bout that wagon, 'bout Miss Sadie pullin' me around, darin' somebody to call me that bad word we don' use no more.'

I have a brother, he wanted to say, but couldn't.

Then again, maybe he could. Maybe he should. As a kid, a dime had burned a hole in his pocket before he learned the secret promises of saving. This far greater secret, kept from all but Cynthia and Dooley and Lace, had burned a hole somewhere in him, and it was still smoking.

'Can I tell you something . . . that no one else needs to know just now?'

''Tween us an' th' Lord.'

Louella would be ninety years old any day. What if she forgot her declaration and told a nurse, or . . . He felt the shame of his selfishly endless noodling.

'I have a brother.' There it went, like a string winding off a ball.

'I declare.'

'My father,' he said.

'Oh, yes.'

'With the woman who helped raise me.'

'Black like me,' said Louella.

'Yes.'

'Happen all th' time. When you find out?'

'July, when I went down to Mississippi.'

'They some bad jokes 'bout Miss'ippi.'

'Don't I know it.'

She looked at him with the inexplicable fondness that came from that other dimension.

'I met him,' he said.

'He's a good man?'

'A very good man. Tall, handsome—like my father.'

'He dark?'

'Not very, but yes. He writes poetry.'

She nodded, affirming this in some way.

'His mama livin'?'

'She's about your age. I saw her for the first time since I was a boy. Peggy is her name—she left when I was ten, it was a hard thing. No one knew why she left, though she thinks my mother knew.'

'How old a man?'

'Sixty. Retired from the railroad. He was a porter, and later a conductor on a train that ran from New Orleans to Chicago. The *City of New Orleans*, it's called. He once got a hundred-dollar tip from Elvis Presley.' He was oddly pleased with the Elvis scrap of Henry's history.

'A porter was a fine thing to be back then. A society of gentlemen, is what my gran'ma said.'

'He didn't have enough red blood cells, he would have died without a transfusion of cells, so I gave him some of mine.' Tears sprang to his eyes; Holly Springs and all that came with it had been a time of tearing apart and putting back together, and then Ireland with its own riving and mending, and now home to try and find his center again.

'He gon' make it?'

'We believe so, we pray so.'

She patted the arm of the recliner. 'This th' prayer chair, you know.'

'His name's Henry. Henry Winchester.'

'A fine name,' she said. 'I'll pray for Henry an' Peggy and you th' same. I'm glad you got a brother, honey, real glad.'

'Thank you.' He had hung on to Miss Sadie; he was hanging on to Louella. All that they were he would never have again. He remembered what Peggy told him her mother had said after the cruel loss of her young son. *All us got is us.*

'This is the prayer stool,' he said, taking her hand. 'We need to talk about you now.'

HE MADE A RIGHT off the elevator, hoping to connect with Dooley's mother, Pauline. She was dining room coordinator at Hope House, and a darned good one.

Pauline's years of alcohol addiction had been damaging in the extreme. Sammy was probably six or seven when she deserted four of her five children, taking only her son Pooh with her. Her husband, Clyde, in many ways more dysfunctional than Pauline, had taken Sammy. Kenny had been traded by his mother to a complete stranger for a gallon of whisky, a move which, in the end, was a very good thing. Jessie, the youngest, had been abducted by a psycho cousin of Pauline's, and Dooley ended up on the rectory doorstep at age eleven. He had driven to Lakeland with Cynthia and Pauline a few years back to recover Jessie, and thus most of the worst scenarios, he hoped, had played out for the Barlowes. And thank God, there had been healing in Pauline's new life as a believer—she had married Buck Leeper, also a recovering alcoholic, and they seemed to be coming along better than expected, with Jessie and Pooh doing well in Mitford School. Dooley would see his mother on occasion, but was reserved; Kenny and Sammy refused to see her at all.

'Father!' she said, standing from her desk in the small office. The tears began. There were nearly always tears when they met. He gave her a hug and handed over his handkerchief.

'How are you?' he said.

She smiled a little, nodded. 'God is good.'

'I've noticed that myself. And Buck?'

'The best. He's doing well.'

'Any work?'

'Comes and goes.'

'Feast or famine,' he said of the construction business in general.

'How is Sammy?'

'Hurting.' He never veiled the truth with her if he could help it.

She nodded, wiped her eyes with the handkerchief.

'And Kenny is a wonderful young man. The couple he ended up with—it was a blessing, as you know.'

'So thankful.'

'Dooley will be home toward the end of October, I'm hoping we can arrange something, break bread together.'

'Thank you, Father.'

'And Sammy—back to Sammy. When it comes to shooting pool, he's a genius. All we have to do is figure out how to channel genius.'

She looked away from him. 'One day . . .'

'Yes, oh, yes, definitely. One day.' One day there would be an end to the hurting. There had to be an end to it.

THEY WALKED OUT with Barnabas to the flower borders, carrying mugs of Earl Grey.

His wife looked west over the trees; a breeze stirred her hair, the sleeves of her blouse. ''T will be a lovely sunset,' she said.

Hydrangeas blooming, digitalis thriving, black mulch from the pile where the garage once stood. Harley had done a fine job of keeping things in order.

'I told Louella about Henry.'

'Wonderful.'

He cleared his throat and made the announcement in what she called his Old Testament voice. 'I'm wearing a suit tomorrow night.'

She laughed, put her arm around him. If he never wore a tux again, it would be too soon.

'Forgive me for pushing you to the brink?' she said.

'Always.'

'Bookends?'

'Always.'

'Puny left you a wonderful salmon and pasta dish, but I'm hungry for liver and onions tonight, will you have some? It might be fun just to *try* it, darling.'

'Never,' he said.

Chapter
Four

At first light, he got up and sat on the floor by his dog and buried his hand in the bristly coat and prayed, silent.

Almighty God, whose Son our Savior Jesus Christ was lifted high upon the cross that he might draw the whole world unto himself: Mercifully grant that we, who glory in the mystery of our redemption, may have grace to take up our cross and follow him; who liveth and reigneth with thee and the Holy Spirit, one God, in glory everlasting.

His dog rolled on his side and looked up—it was that slow, lingering look that spoke volumes could he but read them. He thought the look might be saying, It's okay, it's fine down here; I don't mind, you can stop feeling guilty now.

'Hey, Dad.'

'Hey, yourself.' Always the unabashed joy of hearing, *Hey, Dad.* 'What's up?'

'Off to the doctor. Hoppy's retired, as you know, so it's Wilson these days. How about you?'

'Killed,' said Dooley.

Midterms. 'Hang in.'

Dooley laughed. 'Is that the best you can do? Hang in?'

'It works, buddy, it works. I'm praying. Don't worry about anything.'

Dooley was doing well in school. Long haul that it would be, the boy was keeping his eye on the ball of having a successful country vet practice, maybe raising a few cattle.

He remembered bearing down hard on the books, going for the high marks and professorial praise, believing he would no longer be a shadow in his father's eyes, but a viable being pumping real blood and real sweat and hitting the mark.

'How was Hoppy's retirement party?' asked Dooley.

'A little tearful here and there. Hoppy's been good medicine for us, we'll miss him keenly.'

'Lace said you told the Uncle Billy joke.'

'They asked me to say a few words. Uncle Billy's still bringing the house down. Lace was a great surprise, by the way, didn't know she could make it. A lot of people noticed the ring.'

A long pause. No information forthcoming.

'She denied that it was an engagement ring,' he said, assuring Dooley of her discretion. 'I guess friendship rings can look a lot like engagement rings.'

'Maybe,' said Dooley.

'Big doin's down here for your October weekends. We look forward to seeing her midmonth, and you on the twenty-sixth.'

'Can't wait. When do the guys come home? I can't get through to Kenny or Harley's cell; I guess they're pretty much in the boonies.'

'Miss Pringle arrived this morning from Boston, she says Harley and your brothers will be here tomorrow evening. We're loading up on ground sirloin and buns.'

'We can talk about Kenny when I get home?'

'Absolutely.'

'About the college business.'

'And maybe figure out something for Sammy.' Sammy the willful, Sammy the shark, Sammy who would not be tethered or tamed. He loved Dooley's younger brother but couldn't manage him, and maybe that was a good thing—or maybe not.

'THERE WE WERE, two of three misfits who didn't show up as penguins. Deep breath.'

'Any man can be roped, Doctor, but not every man tied.'

'I was just out of the shower when the call came—had to get to the hospital and yank an appendix, or else. Long story short, too late to go home and don the tux—deep breath—wife already at the club and couldn't bring it by the hospital. So—into a clean set of scrubs and off to the revelry.'

'You were the envy of every man there.'

'Who was the other fellow out of uniform? I've seen him around, but can't remember his name.'

'Omer Cunningham, our former mayor's brother-in-law. He's flown Hoppy in and out of a few tight spots in these mountains, though his aircraft is hardly suited to the job. The poor man's helicopter, he calls it.'

'A character,' said Wilson.

'Great guy. 'Nam vet. I've been up with him a couple of times. Flies a ragwing taildragger.'

His doctor sat on a rolling stool, palpated his feet and legs.

'Greek to me. Was that a pair of overalls he was wearing? I'm a city boy, Father, we don't know these things.'

'Overalls with a hammer-hanger, as I recall. Which city?'

'Born in Boston, moved to New Haven young enough to lose the broad *a*. Exercise?'

'Just starting to run again after a trip with my wife. Two miles now and then, I'll do better.'

'Ireland, wasn't it?'

'County Sligo.'

'The Wilsons populated a good bit of the Eire. My set came over from Tyrone.' His doctor looked up. 'You had a rough time a couple of years back. Any depression these days?'

'Nobody will let me be depressed,' he said. 'I have two women watching me like hawks. Of course, there was that moment in front of the mirror a few days back. That was pretty depressing.'

'Why?'

'Obviously over the line by ten pounds, maybe twelve.'

'Let's check it.'

He stepped out of his loafers and pulled off his watch, vain soul that he was; Wilson popped him on the scales. *Miserere nobis.* One seventy-nine.

He was nearly always 165 on Hoppy's scale, but this was obviously not Hoppy's scale. This thing had big red numbers and was digital.

'Who changed this scale?' he said.

'This is my scale.'

'What was the matter with Hoppy's scale? It could have stayed right here.'

'Dr. Harper took his scale with him, carried it home on my golf cart. He's fond of it, it weighs him four pounds lighter.'

There was professionalism for you. So if he had weighed 165 on Hoppy's scale, plus the four Hoppy had cheated him out of, that was 169, and so he had, indeed, gained ten pounds since his last visit—if Wilson's scale was accurate.

'Is this scale accurate?'

'On the money.'

He stepped off the thing. 'There you have it, then, Doctor— the depression you were asking about.'

Nurse Kennedy handed him a prescription on the way out. He eyed it, nonplussed, and handed it back. 'What does it say?'

'It says, "Run three times a week. Three miles a day first week, four miles a day ensuing weeks. Drink plenty water. See you Nov."'

'Four miles one way or round-trip?'

'Round-trip. He's too easy on his patients. Dr. Harper made grown men cry.'

See there, Hoppy had been out of here only a few days, and was already spoken of in past tense. That was retirement for you.

'Dr. Wilson is a runner,' she said.

'Really? Does he follow his own prescription?'

'He's hard on himself, but soft on others. He does fifteen miles three times a week, sometimes twenty.'

He couldn't take any more.

'Are you going to retire, too?' he asked Kennedy. She had been at the hospital clinic a hundred years; she was the one who welcomed him back when he awoke from the last coma; he was accustomed to her.

'Heavens, no, Father, I'll be here 'til the cows come home.'

'Good,' he said. 'Thank you.'

THEY LAY ON THE STUDY SOFA under a couple of blankets, her feet to the south, his to the north, the fire on the hearth turning to embers.

Though he couldn't see it rising over Little Mitford Creek, a waning moon silvered the branches of the maple, the Japanese cherry, the pickets of their fence. He raised his head for a better view of the celestial vault, wishing he could see Cassiopeia and Perseus and Camelopardalis—constellations whose names he loved pronouncing as a boy—but moonshine obscured such aloof regions.

'I brought you flowers last Tuesday for our anniversary,' he said, 'but I'm due for another round.'

'I should bring you flowers. I've been bossy.'

'I've been . . .' He thought about what he'd been. '. . . caustic.'

'I wonder if my being bossy makes you caustic. Or did your being caustic make me bossy?'

'All I know,' he said, 'is that Barnabas is downstairs and seems to like it, the checks are still rolling in to Violet, and I love you better than life.'

'I love you back,' she said.

'To carry forth the full confession, I'm also sorry I fell asleep after your great dinner on Tuesday.'

'I consider it a compliment.'

'Falling asleep on our anniversary and not even helping with the dishes. That's a compliment?'

'You feel comfortable with me. I don't think I'm a particularly comfortable person. Besides, we celebrated early in Dublin, remember?'

He grasped her foot, held it tight—so much was loose in this world. 'Thanks for helping keep watch.'

'If you're sleeping down here, I'm sleeping down here. How many nights?'

'One more, I think.' He closed his eyes, spoke aloud their favored prayer from the Compline.

'Before the ending of the day / Creator of the world we pray . . .'

She joined her voice with his. 'That thou with wonted love shouldst keep . . .

'Thy watch around us while we sleep . . .'

The prayer ended, the fire crackled and sighed.

'Are you drifting off?'

'Not immediately.'

'Let's write love letters again,' she said. 'Like we did when I was stuck in Manhattan all those months and we were trying to figure out what we meant to each other.'

'Love letters are hard.'

'But that's what makes them good.'

On his bed by the hearth, Barnabas whimpered in his sleep, his squirrel whimper; Violet slept in the armchair.

'How often?' he said.

'Twice a week?'

'That's way too much, Kav'na.'

'Once a week, then. That's absolutely the best deal I can make.'

The small rattle against the window of maple branches in a September wind. He was completely content, apt to say anything.

'Let's do it.'

PERHAPS SOME BY-PRODUCT of nocturnal energy poured off celestial bodies, rained on the hapless, jangled human nerves. In any case, he couldn't sleep.

He breathed a mantra known to pacify his nervous system— *Thank you, thank you, thank you,* again and again, and finally, on to his nightly petitions for Cynthia, Dooley, Lace, Sammy, Kenny . . . off he went, naming the legions, lingering on some blurred or precise image of each, all this followed by supplications for the Church, this country, her leaders, her enemies.

He could usually manage that much in a lateral fashion before his petitions drifted like clouds before a leeward wind. He found drifting to be the provoking nature of prayer—and there was the water tower in Holly Springs and Henry and Peggy in the house with the swept yard, and his breathing coming easier now, and he was no longer lifting up the living, but poking around in the dim chambers of those gone before.

If wakefulness persisted, as it was doing tonight, he often applied himself to the useful soporific of 'praying the town,' which meant going in his imagination from door to door, interceding for Mitford families, with special intentions for the sick. If he lasted long enough, which was rare, he included the merchants, who needed all the help they could get.

It had been thoughtless to buy into Cynthia's letter-writing scheme, as if he had nothing else to do. Though, come to think of it, he had nothing else to do, except three miles three times . . .

So if he was going to write her, where would he go for inspiration? He had used the Song of Solomon more than once, which was also more than enough, being the sticky business most people knew it to be.

Better still, if he was going to get serious about it, he needed first to answer the letter from Henry, which had arrived days ago. He considered getting up and doing it now, but if he moved, the whole sleeping arrangement would come to pieces.

O Lord, I call to you, come quickly to me, Hear my voice when

*I call to you. May my prayer be set before you like incense; may
the lifting up of my hands be like the evening sacrifice . . .*

Somewhere in the fifth verse, his mind drifted.

Camelopardalis, he was thinking as he fell asleep.

DAWN. THE LIGHT SHY, the sun hidden; low-hanging fog.

Still in his robe and pajamas, he took his coffee mug out to
the maple beyond the study window and looked toward the
dark stain of mountains along the horizon.

What he needed was a new route. In the past, he'd run up
Wisteria and across Church Hill Road, cut up Old Church Lane
and hung a left at Fernbank, then a left on Lilac Road and a
right toward Farmer. He wasn't crazy about the Farmer leg of
that run, some drivers insisted they paid taxes on both sides of
the road and were determined to get their money's worth. The
road to Wesley was busier still, with more carbon monoxide to
suck into his lungs, so what to do? A parochial route; that was
the ticket, though he hated having ten extra pounds flapping in
the face of every Tom, Dick, and Harry on Main Street—fat was
a private matter.

He'd give the parochial plan a try. If he didn't like it, he
could change it. He would cross Main and hook a right toward
Farmer, then a couple of rights to the tower monument, then
up Lilac, hit Church Hill, and home. Easy.

Okay. And if he had any wind left when he hit Lilac, he
could keep going and run around the monument, then twice
around the parking lot at town hall, then over to Church Hill
and home to Wisteria.

Forgetful of the morning dew, he sat on the bench under
the maple tree, exhausted just thinking about it.

. . .

Dear Henry . . .

The morning was close, humid; he was sweating as he hooked a right toward Farmer. Any advantage of the running he'd done in the past was long used up; he was strung tight as a mountain banjo.

Out of the Irish skillet and into the fire, it appears that C and I cannot avoid all manner of boondoggleries.

But no, he wouldn't go into the McGraw affair, too much work composing all that drivel, and to what end?

We're plenty glad to be back at 107 Wisteria. As I said when we talked, we arrived home in the middle of the night, Dooley and Lace driving us up the mountain. What I forgot to say is that I wish you could have seen our little town sleeping at two in the morning—I was especially moved by the sight of the streetlamps glimmering as if under the spell of sober thought, and the silent mountains beyond. It is cause to believe that one day, all will be well with the world.

He would like to say, *You must come and have a look for yourself.*

But he couldn't say it; it would commit him to something he couldn't fully undertake.

Thank God for your steady improvement. This six- to twelve-month stretch of your immunodeficiency is a tough pull—but I should think everything depends on it. On the upside, your hundred days of staying out of the fray will soon be over—maybe a matinee (usually only a few people in the theater) and a box of popcorn?—I'll Google your low-bacteria diet to see what is approved. No Milk Duds would be my guess.

Thanks for your letter received on the seventh. We still have tomatoes in plenty, and will indeed save our seeds for your patch. You are a better man than I if you get anything useful from them.

If Henry should ever come to Mitford, he wondered whether he could introduce him as his brother. The thought had presented itself in Ireland, but hadn't concerned him. Now he was home, and the anxiety had come back. It wouldn't be so easy with others as it had been with Louella.

He had stopped to adjust the bandanna around his head when he looked up and saw the limo headed north toward Farmer.

Identifying the plate was a lost cause; the car was in the opposite lane and moving fast. He didn't care for tinted windows, though they had their virtues; he wasn't even the man for sunglasses. He regretted that he'd gaped like a moron.

The point was, Henry's bloodline made itself clear even to the casual observer. What would his former parish have to say? And why in God's name would it matter what was said?

It mattered because the fact of Henry's existence revealed their father's duplicity, which was a slap in the face of his mother. Or worse, in his view, was that some may think his mother had been the one for duplicity. Either way, his mother's memory would bear the brunt, and the fault would rest on his shoulders. He had not let sleeping dogs lie, he had roused them up and they had gone baying.

The Methodist chapel was coming up on his left—he imagined himself resting on the bench in the memorial garden, shaded by a hedge of privet; he saw himself making excuses to Wilson, but no, he couldn't worm out of this, not with Wilson doing twenty to his three.

The vastly more important thing was that his half brother now freighted a population of Tim Kavanagh's stem cells. That his cells would have been a match for Henry's was given less than a five percent chance, but they matched—an indisputable miracle, according to members of the Memphis medical team. The miracle had kindly extended itself to a successful transfer of his cell soup, which vanquished—for how long, no one knew—the acute myelogenous leukemia.

Clearly, God had given him this particular brother, and his cowardice to fully accept that was shaming.

ESTHER CUNNINGHAM was driving home from the Local with a sack of fingerling potatoes when she saw Father Tim running east on Lilac Road. Now, there was a sight for sore eyes. She threw up her hand, but he didn't see her. While everything else was changing, there was their retired priest running his legs off, just like he'd done for years. It was a consolation to see somebody doing the same thing over and over again.

Take this bag of potatoes—used to be, as far as she knew, there had been Idahos, Irish, and russet—period. Now there were four thousand types of potatoes, including fingerlings that looked like a bag of noses with warts. You couldn't just have a *potato* potato anymore. Avis Packard was over the moon for fingerlings, and here she was, falling for it and paying double. Why hadn't she resisted such extravagance? She hadn't resisted because she was too exhausted to resist.

She didn't know when she'd been stripped so bare, all the way to the bone and down to the marrow. Ruined, as her mother used to say.

Had she seen the doctor about it? Of course not. Why go to a doctor for being exhausted? For having cancer, yes, for ulcerated stomach, yes, go to the bloomin' doctor, but for worn-out, it was simple—rest, lose forty pounds, walk to the mailbox every day, think positive, breathe deep, eat right, and be regular—just the thought made her want to lie down.

She had confessed this to Ray a few weeks ago. And what wisdom of the ages had he rattled off? 'It's the economy, Sugar Babe.'

Yesterday, he rolled out another brilliant observation. 'It's our age, Doll Face.'

And now he was going to fix everything, which was what he always did—she knew better than to complain to Ray Cunningham. He would be taking them out West for three months in their Coachman Freelander. 'This'll put pep in your step,' he said. To Ray, a few weeks in that old RV could cure every ailment from ingrown toenails to congestive heart failure.

They would experience the Oregon Trail from Independence, Missouri, all the way to the Willamette Valley. They would ride in a Conestoga wagon, meet Indians, and sit around smoking a peace pipe, though she would not inhale, no way. How anybody had the gall to smoke a peace pipe with people they had decimated was beyond her. It was a Wild West bonanza Ray had signed up for, and while he was out of his mind with excitement, she was dreading it like a double root canal. How she would endure being cooped up in an RV with his unending torrent of 'Cupcake' and 'Sweet Lips,' she had no clue. She'd been cooped up with it many times in the past, but that was then and this was now.

Mayoring Mitford for going on two decades had nearly put her under, and even though she served her last term three years ago, she still hadn't completely recovered. She had been diced, sliced, barbecued, and fried trying to run this town. She'd rather have mayored Chicago, Illinois.

Everybody thought Mitford was just this quaint little village with people runnin' around prayin' for each other. So let *them* try to placate the boobs on the town council, the nitwits in Raleigh, and the sleazy developers from parts unknown. Let them try to keep taxes from escalating, and the merchants from doing exactly as they pleased and thinking they owned the place. Let them keep the Independence Day parade from wandering down side streets everywhichaway, leaving llama poop scattered from one end of town to the other.

And that was just the small stuff. As for the big stuff, how about the moment that deserved to be recorded forever in the history of Mitford, USA?

Just as she'd known it would, the nasty business of the box stores had landed on the council table in '95.

Whop! The council and the whole bloomin' town split down the middle like a ripe melon dropped on concrete. Right there was where the cheese got binding, and stayed that way for a full year before it finally came to a vote.

Ray had driven her to the council meeting. She was a basket case. If this thing went through, Mitford was chopped liver; it was every other desperate small town in America, with their acres of asphalt and windowless buildings looming over the struggling enterprises of Main Street.

The votes came in. It was a tie. Ray's grin lit up the entire back row.

When they called for her vote, she stood and gave it the Big Jack Benny. She looked to her right and she looked to her left. One side of the council was grinning; the Other side was shaking in their boots. They all knew where she stood, they all knew how much she loved this town, and they all knew that a tie and only a tie gave the mayor a vote.

Horace Greene, a Catholic on the Other side, crossed himself in plain view of God and everybody. And she had reared back, squared her shoulders, and lowered the boom on box stores. Nada. No way. Not in this town.

People always said Esther Cunningham was a tough cookie, but no, on too many issues she had been as soft as the inside of a cathead biscuit. If she had it to do over, she would take no prisoners.

And then Vanita Bentley askin' her, Is Mitford still takin' care of its own, Miz Cunningham?

No! she wanted to shout. Absolutely *not!* Why ask such a foolish question? You have two eyes in your head, figure it out. See the trash blowin' around on Main Street, and th' plastic bag that's been snagged on th' awning of the Woolen Shop since the storm in August? August! And what about th' candy wrappers an' chewin' gum an' cigarette butts litterin' the sidewalk an' the dirty display windows in half the shops? What was the matter with retailers who couldn't get out there with a broom once in a while, and keep their windows washed so shoppers could see the bloomin' merchandise? Not to mention Avis Packard and his pile of cigarette butts along the curb at the Local, shame on him. You had to go in and talk to merchants like this was their last day on earth if they didn't get their act together.

And last year's Christmas parade—if that wasn't pathetic, nothing was. There was Santy Claus ridin' in on his float, the star of the show, the big kahuna, and the spectacle of him throwing out that little dab of candy was mortifying. A handful! A pittance! She was shocked and the children were crushed. 'Not a budget item,' was what a council member said. If she was mayor again, she would show them *budget item*. What kind of town had a Santy that didn't give out enough candy to stick in the toe of a stockin'?

And what did Andrew Gregory know about filling the oil drum of an old woman and her halfwit son in a hard winter, or pulling a few strings to see that a fatherless family got fed or had clothes on their backs? Oh, no, he was busy tryin' to make an inn out of Evie Adams's old house and run a rubber-tire trolley up Main Street, everything but stand on the sidewalk in a clown suit to bring in the tourist trade. She hoped her successor was having a happy life, thank God he didn't marry Cynthia before the Father got to her.

As for th' mess at Lord's Chapel, which nobody seemed able to figure out, she'd been around the block a few times and could absolutely guarantee that whatever was going on down there would sooner or later blow up—in more faces than one.

As she pulled into the driveway, she noticed the blotches on her right arm. Ha. On her left arm, too.

She looked in the mirror on the back of the sun visor, to see if her face had broken out. Was the Pope Cath'lic? Just like the old days when she was mayor, her entire mug was one big splotch. Stress, Hoppy Harper had said. Sausage biscuits, said her grandson, Joe Joe, who would soon be the best police chief the MPD ever had.

She killed the engine and stared at the garage door. Ray was playing golf today with his crazy pilot brother, Omer. She would have an early lunch, fix herself a salad, and no way would she dig out the leftover rum cake hidden behind the organic peas Avis Packard had conned her into buying.

She sighed, close to bawling. She didn't want any of that lonesome grub.

What *did* she want?

She turned the key in the ignition, cranked into reverse, and backed out to Church Hill Road. She was going to Wesley, where she would swing in the drive-through at the Highlander, park in the shade, eat her chili dog and fries in the car, and listen to Rush Limbaugh.

'LOOK THERE,' said Hessie Mayhew, who sat by the window of the Woolen Shop, having coffee with Lois Burton. 'It's Father Tim, I thought he was still in Ireland.'

'I can't believe you didn't know he came home days ago.'

'I can't know everything,' snapped Hessie.

'But you're *paid* to know,' said Lois, 'bein' a reporter on th' *Muse* an' all.'

'Fifteen dollars an hour,' said Hessie, 'does not buy universal knowledge.'

Only yesterday, she had pictured Father Tim salmon fishing in waders and a tweed cap. And there he went, blowing up Main Street in shorts and a T-shirt, letting it all hang out. She didn't think clergy should run or even jog. It was too up-close-and-personal a thing to do in front of people trying to mind their own business and get a little shopping done. Besides, without his collar, he looked positively naked. She took out her notebook, jotted something in green ink.

'What did you just write?' Lois craned her neck to see for herself.

'A Helpful Household Hint,' said Hessie, slamming the notebook shut.

'I didn't know you wrote th' Household Hints, I love th' Household Hints. I used a banana peel on my pumps just yesterday. It was a mess to get off, but it worked.'

She had no intention of saying that Vanita Bentley, whose official job was Classifieds, was now writing fifty percent of the Hints, including that ridiculous banana peel business. This was a job Miss Heloise Bentley had taken on without asking a by-your-leave of yours truly, who had done all the important writing at the *Muse* for twelve long years, including the Lady Spring pieces which everybody was crazy about, and Mayhew's Mitford which had made her famous in two counties, if not three.

Out of the blue, Vanita had scribbled a snowstorm of Hints, and, unable to fit another scrap onto the hog pen J. C. Hogan called a desk, piled a shovelful in his swivel chair.

So did Mr. High and Mighty say, I'm sorry, but Hints is Hessie's job? No way. Traitor to the end, he grinned over that jumble like every jot was a Shakespearean sonnet. You'd think he'd won the lottery when he came to "Restoring Color to Your Carpet," a Hint he said his wife, Adele, would put to immediate use in their den.

Don't think that little episode didn't bring forth the bitter memory of Mitford's first celebrity wedding, when, following graduation from Appalachian State, the daughter of a former governor's ex-girlfriend's first husband's niece who'd had a bit part in *As the World Turns* got married at the Methodist chapel.

Had Vanita ever written anything but Sofa-for-sale and Used-baby-carriage-dirt-cheap? Could she write, punctuate, or even *spell*? Nada. Yet she took it in her head to cover the wedding in case it had somebody famous in it. Quick as a fox, Vanita Schmita slapped a story on J.C.'s desk before the bride could stuff herself into a going-away pantsuit that was the wrong shade of green for sallow coloring.

She, Hessie, had slapped a few impromptu stories on the so-called editorial desk herself, and many had never been seen again.

But let Vanita toss her scribbles in that Dumpster with drawers, and he would sniff them out like a hound. In a heartbeat, there was the wedding story splattered over the front page, and a color photo mostly showing the backs of people's heads.

She would long remember the intense rush of pleasure it gave her to read:

Spring Brake Leads to Fall Wedding

No indeed, she would not be writing the tacky Hints so dear to the hearts of Vanita Bentley and J. C. Hogan, like how to shave fuzz off a sweater or make your own underarm deodorant. She would stick with such time-honored Hints as how to remove red wine stains from white napery, or how to make old knives as sharp as new. She would never stoop to serve the lowest common denominator—those who didn't wish to remove stains or sharpen their knives. This week, her Hint was "How to Clean Leather Book Bindings," though hardly anyone cared about books anymore, much less leather-bound.

The only person she knew who owned such treasures was Father Tim—he had a bookcase full. Years ago, when she was still in floral arrangements, she went to the rectory to meet with him and Cynthia about their wedding flowers. She recalled that Cynthia wanted roses and lilacs and had to be told very firmly that there was no such thing as roses and lilacs in *September*, Mitford weddings were done with what people had in their *yards*. And hadn't everybody raved over what Hessie Mayhew had fashioned out of twigs, berries, and pods with a few hydrangeas thrown in?

The point was, if the Hint for this week appealed to just one person, that was enough. Such disagreeable crumbs as "The Homemade Smell Remover" were not her bailiwick, though it was certainly one way to attract the huddled masses—didn't they have dogs and cats and even pet pigs that slept anywhere they liked, on furniture of mixed description and in people's beds?

'I wonder if he saw any fairies,' said Lois.

THERE WAS NO WAY TO miss the sandwich board at the foot of the steps leading to A Cut Above:

Welcome to Mitford

Shirlene Hatfield!!!

All hair services

The famous Spraytan

Acrylic Nails

Wi-fi

Free Wine and cheese this week only

Trims $10 this week only, MEN ONLY

Special on color through Sept. only

The Collar Button man, whose name, for some inexplicable reason, he could never retain—Eddie? Freddie?—emerged from the men's shop next door and lit his meerschaum pipe.

'Glad to see you, Father. Going up for a haircut?'

'Not if I can help it. Going up yourself?' The subtle force of pipe smoke on the morning air . . . The Collar Button man raised an eyebrow. 'Wi-Fi? Barry White? Cheap wine? Not I.'

'I've seen a black limo cruise through a couple of times,' he said, 'but didn't see where it's from.'

'North Carolina. I've also heard California. Definitely a car service plate.'

'Any idea what it's all about?'

'Winnie Kendall has had two sightings and is hoping for Elvis. Fancy Skinner has had one sighting and is rooting for George Clooney on a search for mountain real estate.'

The Collar Button man released a veritable plume of smoke.

He sprinted by the shoe store, formerly the Main Street Grill, where for four decades Percy Mosely had curmudgeoned his customers, local and otherwise; and where, for all Percy's love of menu experiment, the Livers and Gizzards Special had been the great hosannah, the magnum opus of the Grill's long history.

Before he retired from Lord's Chapel, the rear booth had been generally known as 'the Father's pew.' He always sat with his back to the front door, symbolic, perhaps, of shutting out the maelstrom for an hour.

He'd been fond of those days.

SITTING ON A BENCH beneath the awning of Happy Endings Bookstore, Coot Hendrick looked up to see Preacher Kavanagh balling the jack up Main Street. Out of respect, he stood and held out his hand, which the preacher stopped and shook.

'Coot, how are you?'

'I never growed up with people runnin',' said Coot. 'Some of 'em, they run right out in traffic.'

'How's your mother?'

'Mean as a rattlesnake.' Coot grinned, baring a set of gums appointed with stubs for teeth. 'I heered you fainted like a woman when th' cops come on y'.'

'Good to see you,' the preacher said, and there he went like a shot, didn't think that was funny a'tall.

THEY WOULD BE SLEEPING AGAIN tonight on the sofa— there was an odd comfort in seeing the blankets folded at one end, the pillows stacked at the other. She was squeezed in between the bedding gear, reading; he had commandeered the wing chair with Violet on his lap.

He looked at his wife over Thomas Traherne's *Poems of Felicity*—her glasses had skied to the end of her nose. As always when reading, she had left these parts for an obscure outer planet.

He had a go at his own book, but his mind dipped and reeled like a swallow in summer air. He had no idea what he had just read, possibly because he had occupied himself with scratching a rash on his neck which appeared today for no good reason. Just there, under his left jaw, suddenly populating the privacy of his flesh.

'A rash,' he told his wife, jabbing a forefinger in its general direction.

She looked up, unmoved.

'Can you see it?'

'I can,' she said. 'These things happen.'

She was so cool, so distant from suffering, always a better

man than himself. Why should he be pitiable and complaining, and she ever stalwart? He was the priest, she the mere deacon, appointed by himself without official credentials of any kind, yet ready, of course, in all situations to stand for what was right and good. Even with the ankle business throughout their Ireland trip, she was undaunted save for a single weeping spell which helped alleviate the tribulation of sitting for days with her foot elevated.

He hated this about himself, his whimpering. Churchill's mandate to never explain and never complain was baloney. He had read the man's letters to Clementine and was hardly surprised to learn that the old so-and-so had grumbled as bitterly as the rest of the common horde.

Here he was, seventysomething, and still whining, though God had woven like a gold thread through every chapter of every book of Holy Writ: Rejoice! Know that I am with you and for you and will never leave you; take courage that I will fight for you and be your shield and buckler and provide for you when you are old; I will supply your every need, I will give you victory over death, I have prepared a place for you in heaven . . .

Every imaginable love and consolation had been and was currently being delivered to him, and yet he had no wit or gumption to receive it. Abject, a worm, he lifted a silent petition for grace.

She turned a page.

'Besides the rash . . .' he said, eager to divulge the entire calamity, 'my right eyeball is scratchy.'

The blank look.

'Like sandpaper.'

'What's really the matter?'

'What do you mean?'

'It isn't the rash or the sandpaper. What's really wrong?'

He opened his mouth to protest, but knew he couldn't cover himself. What was really wrong was . . . He felt tears in there somewhere. 'I've lost something,' he said, swallowing down the knot.

'Like?'

'Like . . . passion.' It was hard to use that word, which was so often overused, but there it was. 'Like . . .' He closed his eyes. 'I feel useless,' he said, humiliated to confess this, even to her.

'Feeling useless is a good thing.'

He had no comment on such ridiculous thinking.

'There have to be rest stops in music. There must be winter for the roots of a plant to dig down and grow strong for spring. There—'

'Please,' he said.

'You do this at least once a year, ever since you retired. In fact, you just did it in Ireland! And I drag out all my homilies and metaphors and somehow we manage to push on.

'Listen to me, sweetheart. What happened in Sligo? The woes of an entire household fell on you; souls were spared because of a meddling priest. You had just come from saving the life of a total stranger who happily turned out to be your brother. Before that, there was our year at Holy Trinity, where you restored a parish gone to ruin for forty years.'

'You always say these things.'

'Somebody has to say these things. You have an insatiable craving to always do more, nothing is ever enough. You want God's job.'

'Cynthia.'

'It's true. It was this very refusal to slow down and be useless once in a while that forced you to retire. You were killing your-self.'

He had no words; words were impotent, tiresome.

'Remember the cave and how you'd been plagued with always wanting to get it right, whatever that means? Remember realizing that God and God alone is the only one who always gets it right?'

'I know this,' he said, angry. 'I'm not a child.'

'Think how you rounded up a scattered family, lost from each other for years—all Dooley's siblings together now, and Dooley—you took a thrown-away boy into your heart and helped him become a young man of character—look at him and what he's making of himself. Look carefully at him when you're feeling useless, and remember Morris Love while you're at it, and Buck Leeper and Dooley's mother and legions of others too numerous to mention.'

It was that numbskull write-up in the *Mitford Muse*, it was Hoppy Harper going out there to make a difference, it was time racing by, it was his complaining in the face of God's benevolence, it was his dog growing old, it was—it was *jet lag*, he didn't care what anybody said.

He put his head in his hand. *And as yet my love is weak*, he prayed as did Thomas à Kempis, *and my virtue imperfect and I have great need of your strength and comfort . . .*

She stood and came to him and sat on the arm of the chair. 'Honey . . .' she said.

He liked it when she called him honey, which she almost never did. Yankees were accustomed to using the word exclusively for the produce of bees.

'I could get started on your new studio,' he said. He had promised it to her when they were in Sligo; he saw the light-filled space as clearly as if it were real. 'I could call Buck and we could get estimates.'

'No,' she said. 'Thank you, darling. It's too much right now. Sawing, drilling, hammering, people in the house. I like my little room, it's been good to me. Maybe one day. I was thinking you might raise some money for the Children's Hospital. That always puts you in a bright mood.'

'No, no, raising money puts me in a dark mood.'

'Yes, but once it's raised, you're in a bright mood. The capital campaign will be announced soon. As the auction chair, I'll know more next month. We're desperate for beds, Timothy, they're starting to turn children away. I think we'll be going for five million.'

Five million! He was literally stunned.

She got up and went along the hall. Talk about sweeping from a room.

Violet jumped from his lap and followed. He got up and did the same as Cynthia vanished into the guest bath and closed the door.

In his years as a donor, they had never gone out for such a sum. Historically, it had been a roof repair here, a few new beds there, a van, a 'gently used' ambulance, a geothermal system. But five million? Where on earth would they find it in these mountains? Maybe a half million if they burned up the road, knocked on every door, and with begging cup in hand cornered the stray tourist. He felt he'd done all he could in recent years, having worked each potential donor he knew, save, of course, the fabled North Star of Donorship which was Edith Mallory. Others had tried Edith and failed, and since the fire, hardly anyone tried anymore.

There went the flush; out she came. He tagged along to her studio and sat on the minuscule love seat.

'What?' she said, giving him the eye.

'You're right. I just did this in Ireland, the whining. I had forgotten that. I'm sorry.'

'Just because we've been away for three weeks doesn't mean 't was a grand holiday we were havin'.'

'No picnic, I grant you.'

'I love everything that happened in Sligo, even the ankle business for what it gave me in return—but it was exhausting.'

She came and squeezed in next to him. 'Do us both a favor and give yourself a break. Let's have a rest stop before the next fanfare.'

Maybe he'd thought there wouldn't be a next fanfare, that the fanfares were over. He took her hand in his. What he'd ever done to deserve her was a complete mystery.

She rested her head on his shoulder, sighed.

'You're so southern,' he said.

Chapter
Five

He read the Hint, and realized it made no impression whatever on his psyche.

Why prolong the agony? He turned to the *Muse's* midsection.

As was his wont on the occasional Thursday, he read aloud to his wife, who was filing her nails at the other end of the sofa:

Does Mitford Still Take Care of Its Own?

by VANITA BENTLEY, Special Correspondent to *The Muse*

Mitford police recently surprised a local couple in the front hall of the McGraw Residence on Bishops Lane.

'Wait a minute,' he said. 'What does this have to do with Mitford taking care of its own?'

'Read on,' she said, 'I'm sure there's a connection in there somewhere.'

"At seven forty-five in the evening," said Mitford police Captain Joe Joe Guthrie "we got a call from a neighbor on Bishops Lane who said a strange car had been parked at the McGraw residence twice that day. I made the decision to go up with Officer Lonnie Greene.

"We approached the darkened house on foot as we did not want to go rolling in there without knowing more of the situation. The moon was about full which can be very useful in Police work. We could see two people moving around in the front hall. Office Greene and I took up a position on either side of the front door."

"Intruders usually come out the door they go in," said Officer Greene "and we figured this was the door they went in."

Well guess what people it was not intruders, it was . . .

'Get this,' he said.

    . . . it was Father Time Kavanaugh and his wife Cynthia . . .

'Father Time,' she said. 'I love typos.'

'And Kavanagh with a *u*.' He looked at her, disbelieving. How many years did a person have to live in a town for the local paper to get their name right?

    . . . who were checking on Ms McGraw to see if she was OK!!

The Kavanaughs said they had called the McGraw Residence twice that day and gone by earlier to check on Ms McGraw when she didn't answer her phone. They found the front door open and decided to go in and look around to see if maybe Ms McGraw had fallen down the stairs but she was not there. They left the door open, but&^ returned at sundown with the intention of closing the door if it was still open.

Unfortunately Father Time fainted when he saw Captain Guthrie's Glock 45, but he did not hurt himself in any way thank the Lord.

He dropped the paper in his lap.

'A miserable affair, this newspaper. A disgrace. Besides, I didn't actually faint.'

'Don't stop now,' she said. 'This is our fifteen minutes of fame.'

He poked the miserable affair with his forefinger. 'Right here is the trouble with living in a small town. I don't like everybody knowing our business.'

'But we've known their business for years.'

He soldiered on.

It turns out that Ms McGraw was actually in Georgia watching her grandson being born!! Michael Jason Holbrook!! Seven pounds eight ounces!!

"As for why Ms McGraw would leave her front door wide open while she went off to a whole other state, she said in a phone interview "My brain was rattled." Well now isn't that true of all of us at some time or other??

The point is, the Kavanaughs were taking care of their own.

This made us think about our former mayor, Esther Cunningham, who invented the famous slogan, Mitford Takes Care of Its Own, and used it as her campaign platform for many years!

Generally speaking do you believe Mitford still takes care of its own??

Here is what several townspeople said in a sidewalk survey:

"As for myself I try to take care of my friends and neighbors by offering fresh local meat and produce at a fair price. As for running around town doing good, no." Avis Packard, The Local

"I do not see the same eagerness to address the needs of those less fortunate. That is all I have to say and don't quote me." Former Mayor Esther Cunningham

'Ask the press not to quote you,' he said, 'and what do they do?'

'When Esther was mayor, heads rolled for less than that.'

Oh, his wife was amused; she was over the moon about every jot and tittle of this farce.

"We are taking care of our own when we work to share our beautiful village with others, when we seek to expand our economy and quality of life by bringing in businesses that enhance the lives—and the livelihood—of all. We are taking care of our own when we raise taxes only when critical to the

welfare of our community, and when we elect to
have the finest fire and police departments in this
county or any other." Mayor Andrew Gregory

'Well put,' he said.

"Come to think of it the Girl Scouts have not
tried to sell us cookies for three years, so it is hard to
take care of our own if the opportunity is removed."
Lois Burton, The Woollen Shop
"I always thought Father Time was the real
mayor of Mitford if you don't mind me saying so. It
seems like he takes care of everybody."

'That's it,' he said. 'I'm done.' He would cancel their subscription immediately, buy an iPad, read the *New York Times* online,
and never look back. He tossed the newspaper on the coffee
table. She snatched it up, found the editorial, read on.

"Remember how he was so good to Uncle Billy
and Miss Rose and how he goes to the hospital every
day and visits Hope House and keeps his yard looking so nice? In my opinion, he should be officially
named Mitford's Leading Citizen and the embody-
ment of what we should all be doing if we weren't so
busy." Jena Ivey, Mitford Blossoms

He felt the heat in his face. He no longer went to the hospital every day, nor did he make regular calls at Hope House.
Plus it had been a while since he'd done anything at all in his

yard, now that Harley had the job. Blast J. C. Hogan to the moon and heaven help Vanita Bentley.

'Listen up,' she said.

> "Father Time brings us a plate from the All-Church nearly every year and Mrs Bolick brings us a cake with orange slices on it every Christmas which is the best my mama and me has ever tasted." Coot Hendrik

'Where does this bloody Father Time business come from?' he said.

'When you type Tim it's easy to hit the *e* key, I've done it a lot, actually. You'll love this one.'

> "Look for example at Father Time Kavanuagh who makes us all feel like his own! He retired but he didn't quit. Maybe he's no longer talking the talk in the pulpit, but he's still walking the walk on the street.
>
> "The point is, any of us can take care of our own. I am going today to deliver a hot meal to somebody old and downtrodden and so what if it's KFC. If I can do it, anybody can do it. Get off your butts, people!!"

'Who authored that literary gem?'

'Anonymous,' she said. 'Vanita closes the piece thus.'

> Are we still taking care of our own/ Who do you think is our leading citizen??? If you would like to way in on these crucial topics, please write to Vanita

---

Vanita Bentley at the Muse or look for me on Main
Street and thank you.

His wife patted him on the knee. 'Father Time,' she said.
He could see it coming, and oh, yes, there it came, in spades.
His wife could hurt herself laughing like this.

HE TOOK HIS COFFEE to the desk in the study, glanced at the calendar.

A good time to call and cancel their subscription. But no—the self-styled feature writer of all mankind would herself answer the phone, which wouldn't be a good thing.

He chose instead to pore over the agenda he'd pored over on Tuesday. The Rotary meeting, the Kiwanis Club dinner, the cleanup day at Children's Hospital; the call from Andrew Gregory, the subject of which he was certain; the talk to the clergy group in Holding, which meant a full day and evening down the mountain. As for the church in Hendersonville that wanted him to supply for a month next January, and the letter from the bishop which he hadn't yet opened . . .

It was fish or cut bait.

She answered on the first ring; Snickers barked in the background.

'Hello, Emma?'

DEAREST CYNTHIA was to the point—nothing wrong with that.

Darling Girl had a nice tone, she liked such terms of affection.

Ha.

He uncapped the pen and wrote.

Dear Bookend.

Good. That was it.

He had rather take a whipping than do this. Didn't she know he loved her? What was she looking for in this exercise? It seemed a waste of time—he could be sanding the basement steps, which needed two coats and a sealer.

Nothing more came forth. He laid the pen down and sat as if turned to stone. His mind was Arctic tundra—hither a scrap of stunted moss, yon a dwarf tree.

His ankles had begun to swell when a beguiling thought pushed through, something like blood forcing passage in a heavily blocked artery, but he resisted such thinking.

Then again, why resist? And so what if it had been done before? She would love nothing better than being told the answer in scrupulous detail.

He took up the pen, ritually shook down the ink, and wrote.

How do I love thee? Let me count . . .

There was more than one way to skin a cat.

'I CAME RIGHT OVER.' Emma had let herself in through the garage, and stood at his desk looking flushed.

He glanced at his watch.

'I know, I know.' She thumped her purse into his out-box; he hated it when she did that. 'It's nine o'clock, and you said ten, I'm runnin' early. Better an hour early than a minute late, you always said.'

'Have a seat.' He shuffled papers to conceal the letter. 'How are you?'

'I thought I'd never hear from you, I had to find out at the post office that you'd actually gotten home.' The arched eyebrow.

'Takes a while to get back in the swing,' he said, dry as crust.

She removed something from her purse, took it over to Barnabas. Down the hatch it went. 'Peanut-butter dog cookie with glucosamine,' she said, giving his dog a perfunctory scratch behind the ear. 'Tried one myself. Not bad.'

She sat down in front of his desk. 'So you fainted. Dead away or just partially?'

'Partially.' He drummed the desktop with his fingers.

She had herself a good laugh. His relationship with Emma Newland personified what he'd heard about childbirth—one forgot the agony 'til the next time around.

'How's Harold?'

'Depressed. Retirement coming up next year.'

'Oh, that.' That can of worms, that hoisting by one's own petard. 'I'd like you to make some calls for me, write a letter or two, if you'd be so kind.'

'Excellent. I have Tuesdays free.'

'I was thinking a couple of hours today.'

'I could use something more permanent,' she said. She slid her glasses down her nose, gave him a look. 'Like we used to have.'

He opened his mouth to speak, but produced only the odd gasp.

'Remember who rescheduled you with the airline and bailed

you out of Ireland for a measly five-hundred-dollar penalty. And remember who got you into that fancy Dublin hotel at the last minute, in the middle of high season.' She crossed her arms, satisfied, complete.

If he lost this round, he was toast. 'And perhaps you remember,' he said, 'who sent you a *large . . . Waterford . . . vase.*' He let the words suspend in the air.

She grinned. 'Thanks.'

'You're welcome.'

'Okay,' she said, 'I'm good for a couple of hours.'

'So make my apologies to the Rotary president for what he calls an important meeting.' He handed her the jumble of notes he'd made; she scanned them.

'Why do you want to skip the Rotary meeting? Rotarians do great things for people. Harold is a Rotarian.'

'True. Great things. I need a break.'

'Ireland wasn't a break?'

'I need another break.'

'How long have you been a Rotarian?'

'Thirty-five years and twice a club president.'

'Okay,' she said, 'you can have a break. I'll call.'

'What will you say?'

'That you're taking a break.'

'Okay, but say nothing more.' Emma relished the elaborate excuse. 'That will do.'

'Same for the Kiwanis?' she said, ticking off the list. 'You're taking a break?'

'Just decline. No need to say why.'

'Cleanup day?'

'I'll do it, I always do it. Ask for Jane Moreland, tell her I'll prune and mulch the hedge.'

'Do they have more than one hedge? They might get confused if there are several hedges. Take the old Fernbank place, for instance, there are three different hedges up there— hemlock, boxwood—'

'The privet hedge.' He'd worked on the Children's Hospital hedge for eight years, but privet was privet and it still looked bedraggled.

'So about this call from Andrew Gregory,' she said. 'Do you think he wants you to run for mayor next time?'

'He seems perfectly happy doing the mayoring himself. He'll ask me to run for council, I'm certain, but don't say I said it.'

'You should run for mayor.'

'Why on earth do you think that?'

'You'd be perfect.'

'I would be no such thing. I have no patience for budgets and five-year plans and whatever else goes on in that office.'

'Then you should definitely run for council. It's your town.'

'So? It's your town, as well. I don't see you serving on the council.'

'They haven't asked me.'

'Call the mayor's office, please, and say I'll get back to him next week.'

'Got it. What do clergy down th' mountain want with you?'

'They want me to tell them everything's going to be all right.'

'Is it?'

'All I know is that the gates of hell shall not prevail against the church. I can't be more specific, thus I'm not the man for the job.'

'So I'll tell them you're taking a break,' she said.

She was hitting her stride; her chest heaved with the joys of power and purpose. Not one among the many would know what hit them.

'Hendersonville,' she said.

'Father Buster Baldwin, Priest in Charge,' he dictated, handing over the address. 'Dear Father Buster, I must decline your invitation to supply St. John for the month of January upcoming, while you and Mary are in the Keys. Thank you for your prayerful consideration and for the very generous offer of your home during that time. I will pray for the right soul to provide the needs of your growing parish. In his grace.'

'Hendersonville in January,' she said. 'You dodged a bullet. So what's with this letter from the bishop?'

'Open it and tell me what it says.'

She slid her glasses down her nose. 'You can't open it and read it yourself?'

'Read it and give me the gist of it.' He had avoided the thing like the plague. Maybe he was still holding on to Stuart Cullen, his former bishop and oldest friend. In any case, Bishop Martin wanted something, he was sure of it. In his early days as a priest, he developed a nose, an instinct about people who wanted something. He could see it in the way they looked when approaching him, even sense it by glancing at the envelope containing a request. As for this missive, they would be after him to raise funds, he could smell it.

'It's dated September third. How long have you had it?'

'Eons,' he said.

'"Dear Father Cavanaugh."' She was silent for a moment, glanced up. 'He misspelled your name big-time.'

'With a *u*, I suppose.'

'With a *c* and a *u*.'

Call him prideful, call him contrary, he disliked it very much—very much—when someone misspelled, and in this case totally botched, his surname. What was the matter with people?

'So much for your new bishop,' she said.

'Read it and tell me what he says.'

She adjusted her glasses, bent to the task, read silently, shook her head, squinted, looked up, and met his gaze.

'He's leaving for the airport in thirty minutes and has just been advised of a grave issue in the diocese. He tried to call but your mailbox was full. Um, he wants you to come to Asheville.'

'And do what?'

'Meet with him about something private.'

He felt his brow furrowing, quite of its own accord. 'What else does it say?'

'It says you were beloved by your former parish.'

'That's nice. What else?' He did not want to go to Asheville, however appealing the land of the sky may be.

'He says he's going to the Bahamas . . .'

'Bishops always go to the Bahamas.'

'. . . to a remote property with no cell phone service, and he'd like to see you when he returns in two weeks, he'll call as soon as he gets back—which, if it was written on the third and this is what, the seventeenth? He should be calling any minute.'

'What else?'

'He asks you to pray.'

'For what, exactly?'

'He doesn't say.'

'He doesn't say?'

'Right.'

'Let me see the letter,' he said.

'It's about time—you acted like a snake would bite you if you touched th' thing.'

I will covet your prayers in this desperate matter which
must remain unspoken until we meet.

'You haven't drunk a drop of water since I've been here,' she said. 'You're supposed to drink a lot of water. You may forget, but I remember these things.'

'How's Snickers?' he said.

'THREE HOURS EVERY TUESDAY MORNING, at the old rate, for somebody who knows how to dot every *t* and cross every *i*.' She collected her handbag from his out-box. 'You won't get an offer like that every day. Think about it.'

He had already thought about it.

SHE HAD GONE THROUGH the garage and out to the sidewalk when he remembered and ran after her. 'And call Vanita Bentley at the *Muse*,' he shouted, 'and give her the correct spelling of my name. Both names, for future reference.'

'*Both?*' she yelled back. 'She can't spell either one?'

He walked out to her at the curb. 'Didn't you read today's *Muse*?'

'Are you kidding me? I don't read that rag.'

'Who told you what you said when you came in?'

'Ruby Greene. She called me the day after it happened.'

'Isn't it against the law to tell things known only to police officers?'

'It was on the board down at th' police station, they post reports of all their calls, don't you remember? Anybody can go in an' read th' police reports.'

He walked back to the house, wondering where he and Cynthia might move. Possibly to Linville, where they had no newspaper, a loss more than generously repaid by the Thursday night seafood buffet at the lodge.

COOT HENDRICK WAS LATE getting home, as three people had stopped him on the street and talked his head off about the question going around town.

He heard the *Wheel* as soon as he walked in the house, and went to his mama's room, hollering. 'I got m' name in th' paper! I got m' name in th' paper!'

He had folded the *Muse* to show off the article just right, and held it close to her face so she could see it good.

'What'd ye git it in there f'r?'

'F'r answerin' a question.'

'What was th' question?' She was deaf as a doorknob, and talked loud enough to bust a man's eardrums.

He sat in the chair with the broke seat and one arm missing, and leaned in to her good ear. He said what people on the street said the question was, and said it slow so he wouldn't have to say it again.

'Does . . . Mitford . . . still . . . take . . . care . . . of . . . its . . . own?'

'What kind of question is that?'

He honestly didn't know.

'What did ye answer, then?'

He wasn't sure what he answered, he'd been so rattled by

the woman on the street poking a thingamajig in his face. 'Talk right in this,' she said.

He would give most anything to find out what he'd answered, but he couldn't read nothing but his name. 'Look there,' he said, pointing to his name, which he had tirelessly searched for after picking up the paper from the street rack. 'Can you see that?'

She lifted her head off the pillow and squinted at the two long columns of printed words. 'What's it sayin'? Read it out.'

She knew he couldn't read, it was hateful to ask him to do such a thing. His daddy had run off when he was four years old and never come back, and if he'd knowed how hard it was to live with this old woman, he'd of run off with him.

'I cain't read over th' dadblame TV!' He hated her TV, it went 'til way up in the night, he had to get in bed and cover his head to keep from seein' the light flickering on his walls from her room next to his. He would set it on the road one day, and let the town crew get out of it whatever torment they could.

'Shut it off, then, f'r th' Lord's sake.'

The room seemed to tremble in the silence. He sat down again by the bed.

'It *says* . . .' He was going to make this up out of his head. 'It says Coot Hendrick of Rural Route Four says Mitford has been good to me and my mama.'

'That's right,' she said. 'Keep goin'.'

'We have many friends and family here and th' weather is good except in winter when water freezes in th' sink and we have to bust it with a hammer.'

'That's dead right,' she said. 'A good answer.'

He felt warm all over. She hardly ever spoke kindly of anything he said or did.

She turned her head on the pillow to give him a look. 'Who's th' family we got here? We don't have no family here, why'd ye say a thing like that?'

He made out like he didn't hear, and plowed on and went to conjuring again. 'At Christmas, Miz Bolick brings us a orange marmalade cake. It is the best cake me and my mama ever et.'

'It is that, all right.' Her hair was gray as fog against the pillow.

He remembered the first time Miz Bolick ever showed up at their door. It was snowing, and she was about covered up with it, as she wasn't wearing a hat, but she was wearing red gloves and she was holding out that cake with the orange slice on top. He had busted out crying and been mighty embarrassed because her husband was standing right behind her. He hadn't known what to do, if he should take the cake and leave them out in the snow or invite them to come in the house. He had never invited anybody to come in the house, the neighbor woman just came in whenever she took a notion, and the nurse sent by the county done the same. But Mr. and Miz Bolick had gone on home, saying Merry Christmas and waving bye-bye, and he remembered Miz Bolick's red glove shooting up in the dark night.

It was hard to keep his eyes glued to the paper and make something up at the same time. 'At Thanksgiving, th' church people bring us a plate from down at th' All-Church Feast, one f'r me and one f'r Beulah Mae Hendrick.'

She sat up and glared at him. 'You mean to say I got *my* name in th' paper?'

He hadn't meant to say her name because she didn't deserve to get her name in the paper. But the mule was out of the barn.

She was wagging her bony old finger like a hickory switch. 'How come you didn't say nothin' 'bout my name bein' in there?'

'It's a . . .' He almost said a bad word. '. . . *surprise!*' He'd be runnin' for the county line if he'd of said that word.

She snatched the paper. 'I'll be et f'r a tater,' she said. 'Let me see my name. Where's it at?'

Lord help. She could read a little bit. His finger trembled as he poked at a jumble of words in the middle of the page.

'Well, I'll be,' she said, sinking back on the pillow. 'You tear that out where my name is and put it in th' Bible. An' go on and keep readin', this is mighty good.'

He felt a terrible need to pass water, but wanted to stick with this and see where it was headed; he never knowed before that he could make out like he was reading.

'Sometimes it is a Baptist that brings our plates from th' All-Church, and sometimes it is th' Methodists, an' one time it was th' Presbyterians, but most of th' time it's Father Tim who used to preach down at Lord's Chapel.'

'That's right,' said Beulah Mae. 'Most of th' time, that's who it is. What else did ye say?'

His mind was empty as a gourd. 'Let me think a minute.'

He didn't know when they dropped off to sleep, but they woke up at the same time as a clap of thunder broke directly over the house.

She sat up, hollering. 'Let me die, I'm too old to live!'

'Stop that now, dadgummit!' He was sick of hearing it. His mama was going on a hundred, maybe already was a hundred, since she won't too sure when she was born.

'Let me die!' she hollered again.

'Stop eatin, then!' he hollered as he went into the kitchen.

'Go to meetin' men? Are ye crazy as a bedbug?'

You're a mama's boy, they said in school—whenever he

went to school. But he didn't even like his mama, whose people come over from Ireland—she was mean as a wet cat.

'What d'ye want for supper?' he shouted.

'Warm milk and buttered toast and you could boil me a egg if we got any.'

'We ain't got any eggs n'r any milk. Our checks don't come 'til day after next.'

'Why'd you ask, then?'

'To hear m' head roar!' he hollered.

He would bake her an onion, right in the skin, then take the skin off when he put it out in the bowl and salt it a little but not much, given she had high blood pressure and fluid around her heart and he didn't know what all. And he'd put a piece of buttered toast with that and a cup of hot tea with a spoon of sugar. Don't say that wouldn't be good, and he'd fix the same for hisself.

He heard the rain on the roof, coming down hard; he liked rain and snow and weather of all kinds except high wind. He fairly hummed as he took two yellow onions out of the basket and set about doing what had to be done in this life.

'I LOVE THEE WITH the breath, smiles, tears, of all my life,' he read aloud from the Browning model. Hard to beat. Impossible, actually. He would give cash money to be released from this torment.

He picked up the pen, wrote.

> I love thee for the way you look in the morning, like
> the girl next door which you once were and ever shall
> be to me . . . for the way you forgive me even before

I commit the unforgivable . . . for believing that I am
all the things I thought myself never to be—

How she occasionally raved on, his heedless, imaginative
wife, and how he loved her with everything in him.

. . . for being brave when I am not, for being cheerful
when I am sour, for putting up with me.

Somehow, it wasn't coming together as he hoped. Though
each sentiment was supremely true, the words lacked something
visceral—bells needed to chime, bands needed to march.

The rain had stopped; he had enjoyed the sound of it peck-
ing at the window. He looked to the kitchen, to the wall clock.
Nine p.m. Cynthia had gone up to bed with a book; his crowd
snored by the last embers of the fire.

He removed his glasses, rubbed his eyes. A *desperate matter*,
the bishop had said.

He stood and stretched, feeling newfound muscles in his
back, in his legs, as headlights flashed into the rectory drive
next door. Sammy, Kenny, and Harley were home from the hills
of Kentucky, safe and sound as he'd prayed them to be.

He pulled on his cardigan and walked out to the stoop. He'd
get a breath of air, maybe go over and welcome them home.

Truck doors slamming, the crunching of pea gravel beyond
the hedge, voices.

'Tote my grip in, somebody.' Harley, his old buddy. 'I got t'
find th' door key. Leave th' truck lights on, hit's dark as a dun-
geon out here.'

'I ain't g-goin' back to school, I don't c-care what you say.'
Ah, Sammy.

'I just said Dooley wants to talk about it when he comes home.' Kenny's deep baritone. 'Talk about it, that's all.'

'D-Dooley th' king, dude of th' earth, Mr. m-money f-freak!'

'Chill, Sam. Dooley loves you, he's good to you.'

'You been mouthin' off th' last twenty miles,' said Harley. 'I'm gon' yank a knot in y'r tail if ye don't hush.'

'I'd like to s-s-see that. You ain't th' b-boss of me.' This followed by a stream of language.

'Miz Pringle don't want t' hear such talk,' said Harley. 'She'll give ye y'r walkin' papers.'

'She won't g-give me n-nothin'. But she might g-g-give you somethin', parley voo f-francay.'

'Whoa, now, dadgummit.'

The back porch light switched on.

'Pour l'amour de Dieu, cessez ces vilains cris tout de suite! N'avez-vous donc aucune consideration pour nos bons voisins?'

Hélène Pringle spoke French when vexed, and though he hardly understood a word she'd just said, he definitely got her meaning.

'Yes, ma'am,' said Kenny. 'We apologize. We're sorry.'

Harley chimed in. 'We sure are, Miss Pringle. Real sorry.'

'You have roast *poulet* waiting downstairs in your oven, though I can't think why I did such a thing for shameless hooligans.'

'Yes, ma'am,' said Kenny. 'We thank you.'

'It won't happen ag'in,' said Harley.

We'll see about that, he thought, stepping inside.

Chapter
Six

So he was a laughingstock, he thought as he gave himself the morning insulin shot. Big deal. Clergy were known to do worse than go weak in the knees. He would get out there and face the music, let the chips fall where they may. Not for him the blighted syndrome of retired-priest-who-won't-leave-the-house.

He did his stretching in the study, tied on the bandanna Puny had laundered, made a swing through the kitchen to stuff the bakery list in his shorts pocket, and paid his respects in the studio.

'Pray for me,' he said, kissing his wife.

'Go and be as the butterfly, sweetheart.'

He went out through the garage and hit the sidewalk running.

In this desperate matter . . . can't be spoken. He learned long ago that it was useless to second-guess a bishop. Cynthia would go with him on the drive to Asheville; they would have a nice lunch, maybe put the top down and live a little.

Truth be told, he was more concerned about tonight's pool lesson and how much a fool he'd make of himself. He'd shot a few games, of course, though he hardly had a clue what he was doing; he just tried to get a ball in a pocket—any ball, any pocket.

The morning was unseasonably warm and humid, not unlike the flatlands in late spring. He crossed Wisteria and stood for a moment on the corner, observing Main Street in motion at seven-thirty—two workmen on ladders, replacing the awning at Village Shoes, a pickup truck off-loading bushels of valley apples into the Local.

And there was the cloud of aromas sent forth by the Sweet Stuff Bakery ovens, fired six days a week at five a.m. sharp. For his money, the yeasty fragrance diffused by clean mountain air was the best thing about Mitford—where could you find another town that smelled this good every morning?

He dodged Shirlene's sandwich board and buzzed three times at the bakery's side entrance—he being one of the few customers allowed entry before the front doors opened at eight. The kitchen curtain parted, Winnie Kendall peered through the window. The monitor buzzed, the door swung open.

'Good morning, good morning!' he called out to the kitchen.

Winnie stepped into the hall, wiping her hands on her apron. 'Father! We're just glazin' the Danish an' slicin' th' cakes. What can we do for you?'

He loved her good face, it was all smiles, all the time—the sort of face you wouldn't mind wearing every day.

'Just dropping off an order and I'll get out of your way.'

He dug in his shorts pocket for the list. 'I can swing by for it later this morning.'

Odd. It was in a small envelope. He hadn't noticed that when he grabbed it off the kitchen counter.

'Let's see.' He opened the envelope, and knew at once this wasn't the list. Something like joy leaped in him. What to do? Put it back in his pocket and wait to read it later? But then, why wait?

'This is not the list,' he said. 'I'll just . . . sit a minute in the coffee nook.'

'Good! Away from the window where nobody can see you, or they'll be comin' in through th' air vents.'

He glanced at his watch; Winnie and her husband, Thomas, had forty-five minutes to fill the display cases. Her accelerator was definitely floored.

'Can you remember your list, Father?'

'Yes, yes. Let's see.' The mix-up had rattled him. Maybe if he recalled who would be there tonight . . . 'There's Sammy, he's sixteen, no, wait, he's seventeen. And Kenny, he's nineteen, a strapping fellow. And Harley, he's just driven from Kentucky, so he'll have an appetite. And there's Miss Pringle.'

A timer going off in the kitchen.

'That'll be th' bran muffins,' said Winnie. 'Sounds like you need a cake. The triple-chocolate would be my recommendation.'

'A cake! That reminds me. I need to stop by Esther Bolick's and order a two-layer orange marmalade for Dooley's visit home.'

Now Winnie seemed rattled.

'What is it, Winnie?'

'Oh, my. Well. Nothing, just . . . nothing!'

'It wasn't a cake we're after,' he said. 'Let's see . . .' His mind was a complete blank.

'Two teenagers, you said. That's brownies for sure.'

'Of course! That's it. Your famous brownies. A panful, please. And two sugar-free lemon squares. And a chocolate pie. No, wait, we talked about the pie for Lace, for the weekend of the seventeenth.'

'Of September?'

'No, no. October.' He was a basket case; he could handle only one social event at a time. 'Let's see. Yes! And a crème brûlée!' For Harley, who had no teeth at all. 'And a napoleon for Miss Pringle, she's French, you know. And a pan of yeast rolls and two bags of hamburger buns.' He was drained.

'A pan of brownies,' she said. 'Two sugar-free lemon squares, a crème brûlée, a napoleon, a pan of yeast rolls, and two bags of buns. I can have it ready at nine-thirty, but that's a long time for you to wait.'

'No, no, I'll be back at nine-thirty. I'll just sit here a minute, if you don't mind.'

'I can't turn th' lights on in here 'til eight or they'll be bangin' on th' door.'

'Of course, that's fine.'

'How about a cup of coffee?'

'Please, don't trouble yourself, you have your hands full.'

'Never too full for you, Father, you helped me hang on to this old place, remember?'

'Well, then, black as coal, Winnie, and thank you.'

He felt eighteen years old as he withdrew the triple-folded sheet from the envelope. Her scent of wisteria . . .

She had gotten ahead of him by a mile, and with things going the way they were, he wouldn't be able to turn his in 'til tomorrow. *Sic vita est.*

'You look happy as a chigger,' said Winnie, delivering his coffee in a real mug instead of foam.

He laid the folded letter by the coffee mug and waited. He would not be tempted to read it in haste, as her words would be wonderful and one must prepare, as best one ever can, for what is wonderful.

And maybe reading it here wasn't such a good idea, after all. Maybe he should take it to the bench at the Methodist chapel, where there was a large bird feeder and a good bit of birdsong. He blew on the coffee to cool it down. For that matter, he would be running right by Lord's Chapel, where he could sit on the bench in the rose garden he'd planted himself.

He saw her as she might have looked when writing it, the way she held her mouth when she worked—and yes, she would have worked on this, for his wife, like Flaubert, minded every word. She was earnest in all she undertook, and now this tangible gift, this endearing artifact of her affections . . .

He felt a slow flood of happiness, like a tide coming in, and made the sign of the cross and lifted the fold.

My dearest husband,

As a child with parents who scarcely knew me, I remember distinctly what I yearned for—to be somewhere safe with somebody good.

When I was recovering from the clumsy attempt to end my life and just awakening to His life in me, I remember asking, Please, God, let me be somewhere safe with somebody good.

Your goodness to me has been overwhelming. How tender you are, though I am often as tough as gristle. How patiently you have loved me since you made up your mind to love me always.

By His grace, I am safe at last. But to be safe with you is grace beyond measure.

Thomas Traherne said "We are as prone to love as the sun is to shine."

*I was always prone—as prone as one could
possibly be, I feel. But could I actually love? Not
until I met you, Timothy, who is Love's truest
yeoman.*

*For everything that you are to me and to many, for
your kindness of spirit and unbounded generosity, I
love and cherish you with all my being, and if God
choose—please forgive me for borrowing this—I shall
but love thee better after death.*

Bookends forever,

C

Thomas blew into the room bearing an enormous tray. Jelly donuts, cookies, Danish, crème horns, lemon squares. The still-unlighted room hummed with energy.

'Winnie's comin' with th' muffins, but we're runnin' behind on th' cakes,' said Thomas, mildly desperate.

'I'll pray!' he said, and did. Retail these days needed all the help it could get.

'Anything you'd like before you go, Father? We have sugar-free Danish, you know.'

'No, thanks, Thomas, and much obliged for the coffee. I have everything I need.'

He checked his pocket, making sure the letter was there. 'Absolutely everything.'

HE WAS BREATHING HARD AS he came around the bend at the Methodist chapel, looking neither right nor left, and ignoring the thought of the bench—there would be no more sitting, he was done with sitting. He was flying now, zooming, really, in some rare transport he'd seldom known. And while there was no real need to stop by Esther's—he could call, Cynthia could call—he liked the idea of seeing his old parishioner and personally delivering his OMC order. Besides, three miles was three miles, nobody said he couldn't make stops along the way.

How could he top such a letter? He could not, and anyway, topping it was not the point. That she could say such things to him, as woolly as he'd been of late, was yet another testament to her own boundless generosity. As for the pitiable effort sitting unfinished in his desk drawer, surely he would get his wind—be able to go deeper, step up higher, somehow hit the mark.

He would be wringing wet by the time he reached Esther Bolick's; maybe he should call her, after all. And maybe he should order a three-layer, not a two. While the two-layer was heaven's gate, the three-layer was heaven itself.

There went the mailman tooling along in his mail cart; he threw up his hand in salute, reminded that he was feeling letter-challenged. He couldn't seem to finish the one to Henry, either. He would give a shout to Holly Springs on Sunday—voice-to-voice was always good—and say hello to Peggy while he was at it.

As a boy, he had prayed with desperation for a brother—roughly sixty years later, he had one. For that reason alone, the business of Henry was beyond blood or color or Matthew Kavanagh's duplicity. The smart, sensitive, considerate Henry Winchester was a tailor-made brother with whom he shared major understanding from the get-go.

He remembered their talk while sitting on Henry's garden bench in the frying heat of a Holly Springs morning. They had connected on a level too profound to plumb straight off, but which, with time, might be plumbed for the rest of their lives.

In the end, his mother's memory could not be shamed by a

gift from God. Don't worry about me, she would say, and never
worry what others may think. I worried too much about what
others thought—I can tell you it's a tragic waste of time and
energy and pokes God in the eye.

Yes, yes, and yes. If allowed, the dead still spoke.

On his left, Lord's Chapel, built of stone laid by local workmen in the early twentieth century. He glanced toward the
rose garden, but the trees had grown up considerably in just a
few years, and he couldn't see much that lay beyond.

This had once been the center of the universe for him; sixteen years of memories stored in a vault to which he alone held
the key. Dooley's confirmation, his own wedding day with the
church packed and the bride late and the groom on search-and-
rescue and the organist hammering away to fill the gap and the
two of them running, no, racing down Main Street, and how
she ever did it in high heels was beyond him. Uncle Billy's
funeral, which turned into a laugh-in he'd never forget; the long
procession of cars with people paying their last respects to Sadie
Baxter, his favorite parishioner of this life or any other; the
annual Advent Walk and everyone's freezing fingers warmed by
the heat of apple cider in a paper cup; the annual All-Church
Thanksgiving that made ecumenism so lively and quick in
these mountains . . .

He noted a bit of trash caught in the overgrown hemlock
hedge, and stopped, blowing like a horse. He removed the bandanna and wiped his head and face and neck. What salve was
the common bandanna.

But if he picked the stuff out of the hedge, where would he
put it?

A fast-food wrapper, a plastic fork, a grocery receipt, a baby
diaper, of all things, and the inevitable plastic bag, which he

stuffed with the other detritus. He hadn't noticed the trash before, perhaps because he'd been running on the opposite side of the street. Trash had never lingered in the hedge when he was priest. Dooley's now-deceased grandfather and church sexton, Russell Jacks, had seen to that.

He moved along, stooping, filling the bag. Where did this stuff come from? Tourists, some might accuse, but that dog wouldn't necessarily hunt.

He straightened up, looked at the church building in the September light. There was a spirit about it that he didn't quite recognize—something—he searched for the word—doleful, perhaps. As they were members now of the Wesley cure, he hadn't kept up with his old parish—it was, in fact, against church tradition for him to meddle in the business of a former congregation. Some hierarchy hadn't been thrilled that he'd chosen to remain in Mitford—most retiring priests moved to other pastures to make the severance complete.

He started his run again, jogging to the curb, where he paused before crossing Main.

The limo was moving south, flying. Headed down the mountain, apparently, and too fast for a good look at the license plate. Either George Clooney had closed the deal with the realtor and was in a hurry to get home, or Elvis was after barbecue on the bypass in Holding.

He continued up Old Church Lane toward the minuscule office he had shared, for what seemed eternity, with Emma Newland. How had he done that? Emma, Emma, Preacher's Dilemma, someone had said. But she was loyal. Oh, yes, and to a fault. She would flog any man, woman, or child who stepped out of line with her erstwhile boss.

And there was the time he'd been minding his sermon and

Russell Jacks brought his grandson to that very door. He could see as plain as day the barefoot Dooley Barlowe in filthy overalls, looking up at him. 'You got anyplace where I can take a dump?'

Right there, their lives had changed forever. X marks the spot.

He was wiping out too quickly this morning, but avoided looking at the memorial bench under the tree on the office lawn. That's pretty much where he'd been standing when half the parish showed up for his Big Six-Oh. They had wheeled in a red motor scooter for their priest, who had given up driving a car eight years prior, and set him on the thing and turned the key. Drunk with astonishment and adrenaline, he had gunned it up the hill and out of view with everybody whooping and hollering like pagans.

Ah, but his bit of carless Lenten devotion had been exactly what was needed to put him on the street. Wearing out shoe leather was how he got to know his parish up close and personal—he wouldn't take anything for those years. Was he looking for something like that again, and if so, wasn't he bound to be disappointed?

He surprised himself by hooking a right straight to the bench, where he sat clutching the trash bag, grateful for shade. He felt the letter in his pocket, and considered taking it out and reading it again.

'Timothy?'

Father Talbot stood in the doorway of the office, athletic, tall, and good-looking. It was as if the Search Committee had been mandated to pick the polar opposite of Tim Kavanagh. A head full of chestnut-colored hair streaked with silver and a poster boy for the dazzling smile, Henry Talbot was said to wear a 'piece' and bleach his teeth, and what was wrong with that, after all?

The man had aged considerably since he had seen him

before the Holly Springs trip. Talbot had come over to him at Rotary and wished him a happy birthday.

'How did you know such a thing?' he asked, flattered.

'A very busy grapevine,' Talbot had said.

He stood and shook the hand of his successor at Lord's Chapel. 'Just using your bench for a little R&R. How are you, Henry?'

'You're looking fit.'

'Not so fit as yourself,' he said. Talbot was what he would call a serious runner, replete with Nikes, who kept himself trim through all weathers. 'Still running?'

'When I can,' Talbot said.

'What's your route?'

'Up the hill and through the woods. There's a path, you know, behind the hospital. No exhaust fumes.'

What was he sensing in Talbot's demeanor? Exhaustion, perhaps, maybe depression, a kind of shocked daze, in any case. Perhaps it was something like his own daze during the early stages of diabetes. Burned out, strung out, a condition endemic to clergy, diabetic or not—that would be enough right there to cause rumors.

He felt he needed to keep moving, but was oddly stuck, uneasy.

'Your laundry?' asked Talbot in an attempt at humor.

'Picked up a bit of trash.'

'Ever helpful,' Talbot said.

'Well, then, off I go, and great to see you.'

'Perhaps we could . . .'

In the north light, Talbot's blue eyes were the color of water.

'. . . get together . . .'

'The tea shop,' he said. 'Lunch?' He would have suggested a time, but Henry turned to go inside.

'Best wishes to Mary.'

He sensed that Henry had purposely turned away at the offer of a meeting.

Depression—he could smell it. But surely this wasn't the 'grave matter' the bishop wished to discuss. Depression was merely the heavy bear that went with a rising majority of the priesthood.

He huffed his way up Old Church Lane, carrying the plastic bag and remembering why it isn't good to stop along the way—one lost momentum, and an extra push was needed to regain it.

There was Esther's house at the end of the pebble drive, with its baskets of geraniums gasping their last since the first nipping frost, and how could he not knock on the door and say hello and tell her he was remembering Gene, and that he wouldn't forget? The trouble with dying is that the living so quickly forgot.

He jogged up the drive.

Suffering. That's what he'd tried to put his finger on. Henry Talbot was suffering.

EVEN ESTHER BOLICK SEEMED OLDER since he'd seen her last, and smaller. How could she be stout last June and fragile in September? What was going on with people?

'Come in, Father, come in, I'm tickled to see you.'

She was wearing what his grandmother had called a 'housecoat' and old slippers resembling rabbits with whiskers.

'No, no, I won't come in, Esther. Too sweaty. Just stopping to order an OMC and say I miss seeing Gene, I think of him often.'

'He was my taster,' she said, taking a tissue from her pocket.

'I know.'

She wiped her eyes. 'If you won't come in, I'll get you a glass of water and come out. You sit over there in the swing, you're just what the doctor ordered.'

No way would he argue with the legendary baker of his wedding cake. He watched a female cardinal at the feeder until Esther came out.

'I'm done, Father. That's that.' She handed him the glass of water and sat in a wicker chair. 'You'll be takin' your cake orders up th' street. From this day on, Sweet Stuff is bakin' th' OMC.'

'Good Lord, Esther. Surely not. Only you can bake the OMC.' He was an ardent fan of her celebrated orange marmalade cake, even if it had nearly taken him out—one slice at the wrong time and he'd plunged into a nonketotic coma in which he enjoyed a lengthy dinner with Charles Spurgeon.

'People have bootlegged my recipe for a hundred years without so much as a thank-you-ma'am. And what do they do with it? They *change* it—to make it their *own*, they say. Oh, no, they say, this is not *Esther's* recipe, this is *my* recipe, new an' *improved*.

'*Mangled* is what it is, when they get through dumpin' nuts in th' batter—nuts! Not to mention th' screwy bunch that pours in a bucket of Cointreau. Can you believe it? No, you can't believe it, because *that* is *un*believable.'

'Absolutely!' He was riled, himself.

'Fame,' she said, 'is a wicked thing.'

'Indeed it is.' Not that he'd ever had any. 'But why?'

'My legs an' my back. It's either this or knee replacements.' She gave him a fierce look. 'Bakin' is hard work, Father.'

'It is, it is.' He had baked a cake once, it half killed him. 'But with you, it's also an art form.'

'I don't want to quit,' she said. 'I'd bake th' OMC 'til th' cows come home, but my bakin' days are over. Winnie and I signed th' letter of agreement yesterday afternoon. It says she'll never, under any circumstances, add, delete, or falsify any part of th' recipe. Where it says one tablespoon grated zest, that's what I mean. *One tablespoon grated zest.* Where it says five *large* eggs . . .'

'You do not mean small or medium.'

'That's correct,' she said, 'I do not.'

'I don't know, Esther, this is kind of like losing the town monument.'

'It'll be advertised as Esther's OMC, made from th' recipe I've used for forty years. And you'll never guess what she's askin' for every two-layer ten-inch she sells.'

He drained the glass, afraid to guess.

'Thirty-five dollars! In this town! How 'bout *them* apples?'

'People will come from all over,' he said. 'Wesley, Holding . . . shoot, maybe even Charlotte!'

'And every one that flies out of her case, I get ten percent— for sittin' on my behind readin' Danielle Steel.'

'Gene would be proud.'

'Every cake I baked, he tasted th' batter before it went in th' pan. Hon, he'd say, this'll be your best yet.' She looked away, wistful. 'Did you see th' sign over town for Fancy's sister? I ought to go up and get my hair dyed, I've never had my hair dyed. They're runnin' a special.'

'Well, got to get these dry bones moving. It's wonderful to see you.'

He went to her and stooped and kissed her forehead. Esther without Gene was a lost Esther.

She squinted up at him. 'Do you think Mitford still takes care of its own? I've been thinkin' about it. I don't know.'

He didn't know, either. Indeed, he had nearly left her house without offering what was needed most. 'May I pray for you?'

'I thought you'd never ask,' she said. 'It's certainly nothin' Father Talbot ever troubled himself to do. Set your bag down right there and go for it.'

'I DIDN'T WANT TO SAY anything 'til th' sign went up and it was official.'

He hadn't seen Winnie look so solemn since Edith Mallory tried to sabotage the lease on Sweet Stuff.

'I mean, while I'm truly honored to bake th' OMC, I'm against th' whole idea.'

'You are?'

'Totally,' she said. 'Esther shouldn't quit bakin' th' OMC, it's her joy.'

He agreed.

'But it's official, Father, and I'm ready to put th' sign in th' window. Or do you think it should go on th' door?'

'On the door.'

They stood on the sidewalk and stared at the computer-generated sign, not speaking for a time.

'The end of an era, Winnie.'

She looked at him. 'Eras have a way of endin' all over th' place.'

PUNY MET HIM at the side door and took the bake shop bags.

'They was a man here to see you,' she said. 'In a black car with tinted windows.'

He was floored. 'What did he want?'

'He wanted to see you an' I said you were out runnin' and then 'is cell started beepin' an' he answered an' said yes, ma'am,

a whole lot of times an' then he said they had to git down th'
mountain an' off he went in a hurry.'

'It wasn't Ed Coffey?'

'Definitely not Ed Coffey. Had on these really dark wrapa-
round glasses an' a uniform like I never seen on anybody. But
not armed services or anything.'

'He said *they* had to go?'

'That's what he said.'

'Did he say anything else?'

'Nothin.' Miss Cynthy told me to answer th' phone an' th'
door, she's workin'.'

'How did he ask for me?'

'He said, Is Father Timothy Kavanagh available? That's when
I said you were out runnin'.'

'He didn't ask where?'

'No, that's when 'is cell phone beeped.'

'He said they had to go down the mountain? Those were his
words?'

'Exactly.'

Yes, ma'am. The driver was southern. *They.* There would
have been another person with him, or two. *Down the mountain.* Usually only people who lived *on* the mountain said *down*
the mountain.

He sat on a kitchen stool, fairly whipped from the run and
the heat. 'Aren't you here late?'

'I'm leavin' in ten minutes. I tol' Miss Cynthy I have to bring
th' babies to work on Monday. Can you stand it?'

'I'll eat my Wheaties,' he said. 'Any calls?'

'Mr. Skinner left a message, I couldn't git to th' phone right
then. He said, Tea shop today, high noon. Th' only other call
was th' man who said bring your car in tomorrow mornin'—first

thing, he said, or it'll be late next week 'til he can take a look at it. Here's your raisins.'

He ate the raisins, dutiful, walked Barnabas to their side of the hedge, went to the studio and looked at what his wife had done today, which was bloody amazing, thanked her for the letter, and said, More later, and went upstairs and showered and put on a knit shirt and a pair of khakis. He had time to clean the outdoor grill for tonight before he went to lunch. Run, clean the grill, go to lunch. Life was short, how long could he afford to do nothing? In the afternoon, he would work on his own letter. God help him.

So Mule was over his huff about the tea shop, and J.C. would probably show up, too.

What next? What now?

And how long could he avoid J.C.? The answer was, not long. Nobody had mentioned the *Muse* piece today, so he wasn't the only one dismissing local reportage as rubbish and twaddle. He crossed himself, lifted a prayer, forgave the old so-and-so, and went downstairs to report the real news, which was Esther's.

'You DIDN'T LIKE IT,' said J.C. 'I can tell.'

'I didn't, you're right.'

'I think you'll change your mind.'

'Good. I hope so.' His wife had the winning strategy; she laughed at nonsense. He wanted to learn how to do that.

'So let's be productive today,' said Mule, joining them at the table, 'an' name this place.'

'In the interest of time,' said J.C., 'we ordered for you.'

'What did you order?'

'Surprise,' said J.C.

'A children's plate,' he said, 'with chocolate pie.'

'Fancy told me last night I have to quit chocolate.'

'Oh, boy,' said J.C.

'Okay, okay, but just this once,' said Mule. 'Here's th' deal—I thought about it a lot last night. The Lunch Box!'

'How about this place is also open for dinner and that won't get it?' said J.C.

'Okay, here's one that comes off of th' fact we're at thirty-six hundred feet above sea level. High country, mountains, like that. So how about . . .' Mule leaned in, confidential. '. . . Pie in the Sky?'

'Too much of a dessert theme. People are tryin' to lose weight.'

'Man,' said Mule. 'This is hard. Those were my best shots. How about Foggy Mountain Dew?'

'*What?*'

'Kind of senseless, but kind of intriguin'.'

'Way off message,' he said. He knew that much about marketing.

'What's th' message?'

'Good food, reasonable prices, come and get it.'

'I don't know,' said Mule. 'Maybe we should leave it alone, it's none of our business what th' name is. Chelsea Tea Shop—fine with me. But what's a Chelsea? I've been meanin' to ask for a couple of years.'

'A district in London,' he said.

'There you go,' said J.C. 'Definitely not th' local feeling we're lookin' for. Th' family thing might be good to weave in. My mother called us to th' table saying, Soup's on. How about Soup's On?'

'Then they think the menu's all soup,' said Mule.

He took a long draught of his iced tea; J.C. ogled the ceiling fan.

'How about the Daily Blessing?' He definitely wasn't good at this.

'Not bad,' said Mule. 'If you're hungry, any food's a blessin'.'

'Too religious,' said J.C.

'We ought to put th' owner's name in,' said Mule. 'You know, like Pete's Barbecue in Wesley, or Cindy's Lunch Spot on th' highway. Owners go nuts over havin' their name in th' name.'

J.C. sat for a time, eyes closed.

'He's in a trance,' said Mule.

J.C. looked up. 'How about Wanda's Feel Good Café?'

'Whoa!' said Mule. 'Where'd that come from?'

J.C. shrugged.

'Does that mean you feel good when you're in here?'

'Not particularly,' said J.C. 'How about you, Tim?'

'I've felt better in other places,' he said. 'But since this is the only place . . .'

'So there you have it.' J.C. ended the presentation to Wanda Basinger, who had joined them at the table. 'New ownership, new name.'

Wanda displayed a decidedly crooked grin. One side of her mouth appeared to smile, the other side read, Back off.

'I love it,' she said from the smile side.

'Free lunch for five days,' said Mule.

'For which turkey?'

'Th' whole flock,' said Mule.

'Five times three is fifteen,' she said, 'which at roughly ten dollars a pop is a hundred and fifty bucks. Way out of line.'

'Free lunch, five days,' said Mule.

There was a staring competition between the realtor and

the proprietor. Pretty heady stuff, he thought. He took a turn looking at the ceiling fan, J.C. wiped his face with his lunch napkin.

'All right, all right,' said Wanda, speaking from the back-off side. 'But no tips included, you can forget that.'

'Deal,' said Mule.

He'd just witnessed how Mule Skinner was able to make it in today's real estate market.

HE'D GONE OUT to the recycling bin and saw Harley in the driveway next door. He dodged through the hedge.

'Harley! Welcome home, buddy!'

'Yo, Rev'ren'!'

Hugging the slightly built, highly metabolized Harley Welch was like grabbing on to a field hare that smelled, curiously, of cologne.

'Ye're a sight f'r sore eyes. Boys howdy, I'm glad to be back, we was out in th' boonies, I can tell y' that.'

He stared, dumbfounded.

'Harley?'

'It's m' teeth, ain't it?'

'But you said . . .'

'I know. I said teeth never give me nothin' but trouble—what didn't rot out was knocked out; I didn't want nothin' more t' do with 'em.'

He was feeling oddly betrayed, accusing. 'You said you'd gotten used to the way things were in there.'

'I thought teeth'd jis' take up too much room, but I was dead wrong. I tried to git Sammy to git a set, but he won't be havin' none of that.'

This was a whole other Harley, and he didn't much like it. Harley with teeth? It was . . . he couldn't find the word.

'HARLEY'S BRINGING HIS FAMOUS BROWNIES,' he said. 'We can freeze Winnie's for the October crowd.'

His wife sniffed the air. 'What's that smell?'

Hugging Harley had left its mark. 'Harley's cologne.'

'Harley's *cologne?*'

He would have to change shirts.

'Just a warning,' he said. 'Harley has teeth.'

'*Teeth? Harley?* What for?'

'For Miss Pringle, he says, out of respect.'

'Miss Pringle! Good heavens. Do you think . . . ?'

'I can't imagine it, no. Just being thoughtful of others, surely. I have to tell you, the teeth scared me to death.'

'When did this happen?'

'In Kentucky. A cousin cut him a deal.'

He loved the look on her face.

'Just a warning,' he said.

HE'D SEEN SAMMY toward the end of July, before the Ireland trip. Now he marveled again how people can change so noticeably, so quickly. Striding across the yard to the porch, Sammy seemed taller, more muscular; the old scar on his cheek more noticeable. Really noticeable was the boy's mane of red hair caught back in a ponytail. Though younger than Dooley, Sammy could easily pass for Dooley's twin.

Sammy pounded up the porch steps carrying the cue stick he'd given the boy for Christmas last year.

'Hey,' said Sammy.

'Hey, yourself.' He gave Sammy a hug, slapped him on the back. They'd been down the road together, so to speak. 'Great to see you. Welcome home.'

Sammy peered at the dozen quarter-pound burgers on the fire. 'Smells good, I could smell 'em c-cookin' from over yonder.'

'Where's the rest of your crowd?' It was hard to picture Hélène Pringle as part of this particular mélange.

'They're comin'. Where's ol' B-Barn at?'

'Under the deck chair. How was Kentucky?'

'They cain't sh-shoot pool, I can tell you that, I whipped ever'body plus somebody's granmaw, she was eighty-two. She was a wild ol' woman, sank five balls in one turn. I hope you g-got coleslaw.'

'We've got it all.'

Sammy drew a cigarette from his shirt pocket.

'No smoking, remember?'

'I was hopin' you'd g-got over that notion.' A word, then, that wasn't allowed.

'Watch your language, buddy. You know the rules.'

Sammy looked at him with distaste, spit over the porch railing. 'You ain't changed any.'

'Just a little older,' he said. No wiser.

As a French-born only child of a Parisian mother, Hélène might rightly be fascinated by sibling relationships and the less cosmopolitan ways of her tenants.

During dinner on the porch, he watched her watching them. He was amused by her generous laughter, a side of Hélène Pringle he hadn't previously seen.

. . .

'You ready?'

'As I'll ever be. Remember this is a tutorial.'

'A what?'

'You're just teaching me the basics this time. It's not about winning, right?'

Sammy was incredulous. 'It's always about w-winnin'.'

When Dooley wanted to buy Sammy a pool table a few months ago, the only problem was where to put it. Not many women would move the dining room furniture to the basement and replace it with a pool table.

He gave his wife a pat on the back. 'You're the best,' he said as they gathered in what Dooley called the Kavanagh Ball Hall.

'I already racked 'em f'r eight ball,' said Harley, glad to be of service.

Though he'd shot a few games with Sammy, he was as nervous as a cat. In truth, he hadn't really learned anything; the instructions had passed through his head like a drift of smoke.

He could grow roses, he could make a decent soufflé, he could quote long passages from the old poets and Holy Writ, he could run five miles—what was his problem? He took a cue stick from the rack. Why was everyone staring? So intently did Hélène gaze at the preacher chalking his cue, she might have been front row center at the opera.

'I'll b-break,' said Sammy. 'Don't want you to strain yourself.'

Sammy hunkered down, scattered the balls, made a stripe, kept shooting, pocketed four stripes in a row.

Cynthia stood by the window with Hélène, another opera buff hoping for the best, yet he'd somehow known from the get-go: there would be no aria from him tonight. He was too old to eat fries and a burger-all-the-way before shooting pool with a seventeen-year-old shark.

Sammy missed a shot, said something under his breath, looked up. 'I could of hammered that 'un, just wanted to make you l-l-look good.' Sammy pointed at the six ball. 'Okay, there's your six. Shoot it in th' side pocket.'

He stepped to the table.

'It's a easy shot,' said Sammy, 'unless you're like a t-total beginner.'

He leaned over the table, sighted the ball.

'Remember your bridge hand,' said Sammy. 'Grip on c-cue. Hit th' cue ball in th' center. Now, sight through th' cue ball to th' s-six ball. Got that?'

'Got it.' Not really, but God knows, he was trying.

'Put th' six in th' side pocket—it's pretty much a straight-in s-shot.'

The silence in the room was unnerving.

'T-two words of advice,' said Sammy. 'Don't miss.'

He stroked the shot, smacked the cue ball, and sent it into the six ball, but at the wrong angle. The six ricocheted off the cue ball and rolled to the left of the side pocket; the cue ball careened to the right of the pocket, bounced off the side rail, rolled to the end rail, and wedged behind the four ball.

Harley and Kenny erupted in laughter.

'He's sandbaggin' ye, Sam!'

'You've met your match, dude.'

The scar flamed on Sammy's cheek. 'Where's your head, man? I told you to hit th' freakin' six ball into th' s-side pocket.'

More laughter.

Sammy's violent strike of the cue stick against the table rim snapped the stick in two. Harley and Kenny ducked as the cue end flipped into the air, fell to the floor, and skittered into the hall. Sammy stood as if paralyzed, then slammed the butt-end onto the table.

He heard Hélène catch her breath, the sound of Sammy's feet pounding along the hall, the screen to the side door slapping shut . . .

He turned to Kenny, stricken. 'What happened?'

'Your shot left 'im with a really bad leave,' said Kenny. 'He had nowhere to go.'

'Y'r shot was real good,' said Harley, hoarse with feeling. 'But he sure handled it bad. Lord help, I'm sorry.' Harley looked at the floor, shaking his head. 'Lord help.'

'We shouldn't have laughed,' said Kenny. 'But it was pretty amazing, that shot.'

'Yeah,' said Harley, fighting to put a shine on things. 'It was . . . real good.'

But it hadn't been real good. Not at all.

HARLEY FOLLOWED HIM TO THE KITCHEN.

'That was a fine spread, Rev'ren', we thank ye.'

He poured a cup of coffee for Hélène. 'Enjoyed it myself. Glad you're home safely. We missed you.' He and Harley were avoiding eye contact.

'Me an' Kenny'll stay an' give y'uns a hand.'

'Not tonight, thanks.' He set the sugar bowl on the small tray. 'How did the boys do out in Kentucky?'

'Kenny done fine, he's a upstandin' young 'un if I ever seen one, but Sammy, he was always tryin' t' fight m' cousin's boys. It's a wonder he didn't git 'isself shot.'

He put a napkin on the tray, a spoon.

'He'll be feelin' bad about 'is cue stick you give 'im. I don't think he meant t' do that, he was real attached t' that stick.'

He turned and looked at his old friend. 'What's it going to take for him, Harley?'

'A strong hand, a real strong hand—which I ain't exactly got. He's a pain in th' butt, Rev'ren', but he's m' boy an' he's gon' be all right.'

'You really think so?'

'Yes, sir, I do. He's gon' be all right, don't you worry.'

Harley's earnest face.

He wanted to bust out crying, but no. 'Thanks,' he said. 'I needed that.'

HÉLÈNE LINGERED AT THE FOOT OF THE PORCH STEPS.

'What shall I do, Father?'

'How do you mean?'

'About the boy. I'm so sorry for . . .'

She was choosing her words.

'. . . the heartache he caused this evening.'

What solution could he possibly come up with right here, right now? What could he say to her about what she should do?

'He needs help, he needs love, he needs prayer. Let's continue to trust in a brighter outcome.' How ineffectual this sounded.

'Merci, Father. I would hate to turn him away. I do pray . . .' She cast her eyes down. '. . . ever since the time he—God, you know—made himself present behind the curtain.'

'I remember you telling me,' he said.

'He's not behind the curtain any longer, there's nothing between us now. Do you . . . understand?'

'Yes,' he said. 'Yes.'

Not knowing what else to do, he took her hand for a moment, then watched as she went along the path to the dusky hedge where Harley waited to see her through.

HE SAT ON THE FLOOR next to Barnabas, who had made light work of his own burger and fallen asleep immediately after their walk. He ran his fingers into the bristly coat, searching out the steady rhythm of his good dog's heartbeat and feeling his own separation anxiety.

'Visit this place, O Lord,' he prayed into the darkened room, 'and drive far from it all snares of the enemy; let your holy angels dwell with us to preserve us in peace; and let your blessing be upon us always; through Jesus Christ our Lord, amen.'

THEY HAD MADE IT to the bedroom and changed out of their clothes through a feat of singular endurance. He hung up his gear; his barefoot wife sought the consolation of her wing chair.

'He has two older brothers,' she said. 'One with money, which Sammy sees as raw power, the other with a special kind of patient wisdom. Sammy has pool. I think that losing the game to you, a total beginner, proved how easily he could lose that identity. Then the brothers would have everything and he would have nothing.'

'Maybe a garden,' he said. 'He's as adept at gardening as he is at pool. Helping Harley with his lawn work around town is good, but . . .'

They were trying, God knows they were trying.

'His whole world has been unpredictable and unsafe,' she said. 'And he's fallen for what was preached to him by his father's abuse and his mother's neglect—that he's unlovable and incompetent—disposable, really.

'Wanting to teach you how to shoot pool was a gift, I think— a way of proving he isn't disposable, that he has something to offer.'

'Look at Dooley,' he said. 'I don't know if that could happen again, it was a miracle, really. We didn't know what we were doing.'

'We were loving him, that's what we were doing. But . . .'

He looked at her in the lamplight, in her white gown. 'But?'

'I don't think we can do it again, raise a broken boy.'

Lon Birdie had said, 'Sammy has his daddy's temper, you don't want to cross him.' But Sammy would be crossed in this life again and again, and how would he learn to handle being crossed if the people who cared never crossed him?

The thought was too weighty; he let it go. It had been a long day.

'No matter what,' he said, 'I need to get rid of any notion that Sammy could be another Dooley. We mustn't hold him to his brother's standard, it wouldn't be fair.'

He went to the chair and took her by the hand and led her to bed, and they crawled beneath the duvet and felt the ease of this familiar place and the way nine years can have with love.

'Now,' he said, 'about that letter.'

Chapter
Seven

His wife lolled around their bedroom in bare feet and nightgown, a working girl commanding the favors of Saturday morning.

'I've been thinking about your visit with Esther,' she said. 'She'll never get her hair colored if left to her own devices.'

'True.'

'So why don't we buy her a gift certificate while the special is on? We can deliver it after church tomorrow.'

'Great idea,' he said. Maybe that would put the spark back in Esther's eyes. 'You'll pick it up today?'

'No, no, when I bring you back from the mechanic in Wesley, you can take my car and pick up the gift card on your way to the apple stand.'

He had forsaken the services of A Cut Above years ago, but not before Fancy Skinner turned his face seasick-green with a concoction guaranteed to make him look 'fresh.' It was humiliating that he'd fallen for such a dumb trick, and he hadn't set foot in the place since.

On the other hand, the gift for Esther would be a mission with true significance, unlike taking the Mustang in for evaluation—a couple thousand plus change, he could feel it coming.

'Okay,' he said, 'and I'll drop in to see if there's anything new in Hope's S for September Sale.'

'Bring home a Maurice Sendak if she has one—any Maurice Sendak.'

'No author names with S on sale, just titles,' he said, privy to such knowledge.

A whole morning of missions—and apple pie, albeit sugar-free, at the end. He felt the small excitement of it.

HE CIRCLED THE BLOCK in the Mazda, didn't find a parking spot, and drove to Lew Boyd's. He would walk up to A Cut Above and swing by Happy Endings on his way back. He liked the old bookstore, with its board-and-batten walls, the creaking floor, the yellow cat that minded its own business and never jumped on his lap when he sat reading in an armchair.

'Park in front of that RV yonder,' said Lew. 'He ain't goin' nowhere.'

'What's the trouble?'

'Crankcase. Th' PCV system is disruptin' th' normal air/fuel ratio balance.'

'That'll do it,' he said.

'Where's your ragtop at?'

'Wesley. It may be ready for last rites.'

'Wish I could take care of it for you, but I don't do Mustangs. Too finicky.'

'How's Earlene?'

He liked to inquire after the Tennessee wife Lew Boyd had kept secret for months, then sprung on Mitford like a jack-in-the-box.

'She got the Christmas decorations down.' Lew wiped his hands on a rag looped around his belt.

'The Christmas decorations,' he said.

'Th' ones left up since Juanita passed twelve years ago.'

'Have you seen a limo come through lately—driver in a cap?'

'Oh, yeah, he came in for a fill-up, decked out in a uniform. Used th' coffee machine.'

'When was that?'

'Maybe two, three days ago.'

'Anybody you ever saw before?'

'Nope.'

'Anybody in the car with him?'

'Too dark to see in th' back. I asked him if he had Mick Jagger in there; he said, Not this time.'

'What else did he say?'

'Nothin' comes to mind. Looked like he was in a hurry.'

'Where was the tag from?'

'North Carolina. A car service. He pumped premium, I checked th' oil, he bought two packs of peanuts, a Coke, and a water. Paid cash, Bud took th' money. End of report.'

'So. Anything else new?'

'I got a great sandwich vendor; you boys need to come back here an' eat. What you doin' for lunch these days?'

'We're down at the Feel Good.'

'Th' Feel Good? Where's that at?'

'The old tea shop. The new name's not official yet, the sign goes up next week.'

'Weird name. Plus I put in a microwave at th' Red Man rack—state-of-th'-art—an' a coffee machine you won't believe.'

'I hear folks in Virginia sell fried chicken at their gas stations.'

'I'm not doin' fried chicken. Don't hold your breath on fried chicken, I got all th' grease I can handle.'

. . .

To atone for a paltry two days on the asphalt, he ran up the stairs.

Shouldn't have done that. He stopped on the landing, heart racing, to catch his breath.

Fancy Skinner would not be allowed to talk his ear off, nor would he be lured into her chair for any reason whatsoever. He would conduct his business and get out of there.

The marching band. He needed to figure out how to change his ringtone.

'Hey, buddy.'

'Hey, Dad. I hear Sammy acted out.'

'He did.'

'Wish I could be there. Kenny says he busted his cue.'

'Yep.'

'He loved that cue.'

We often break what we love, he thought, but didn't say it.

'What can we do?' said Dooley.

Counseling, a special school . . . These were easy answers, but they didn't seem right and he didn't know why.

'He was getting a grip on things,' he said, 'when he was with us at Meadowgate.' Or so it seemed.

He felt responsible for whatever had gone awry, for the momentum lost in his relationship with Sammy. He had no choice but to take the game seriously and become a pool-shooting family member able to fill in for Harley or Kenny or Dooley as needed.

The rules Dooley had laid down for his brother were tough but good: The table was for practice, and sharpening his game with an eye toward competition. As for who was allowed to play, it was family and family friends only. Dooley had helped hammer out the house rule of no language, no smoking, and Sammy would arrange table times with Cynthia.

He gave Dooley the only answer he had. 'We must keep praying.'

He wanted life to feel simple, for college and vet school to be over and Dooley established in his practice at Meadowgate. He and Cynthia would go out on weekends and give a hand around the place—he would bake a ham, help with the weed-eating. And maybe there would be grandchildren. He hadn't known he wanted all that until just now, this moment.

'We miss you, buddy.'

'Miss y'all back. Gotta go, Dad.'

He knew what it had taken for Dooley to call him Dad, to give the word life in their relationship. He remembered the first time he addressed his father, Matthew, as Dad. It was a naked, intimate designation compared to the formality of Father. He'd been embarrassed to say it and his father had been astonished. But he kept saying it because he believed the word itself would somehow soften things, change things.

He stood on the landing for a time before opening the door.

'I hope th' roof won't be fallin' in.'

Dressed in pink tights, pink V-neck sweater, and spike heels, and pushing a broom, Fancy Skinner stopped dead in her tracks. He gawked. Mitford's premier hairstylist was an entirely different skin color.

'Fancy? How are you?'

'We haven't seen you up here since Clinton left office. How was your trip to Italy?'

'Ireland,' he said.

'Meet my baby sister, Shirlene Hatfield from Bristol; she's new in town. She'll be introducin' Mitford to spray tan.'

He shook hands with Shirlene, who, unlike her blond and
fairly shapely sister, was a big girl with a bushel of coal-black
hair, wearing an orthodontic smile, and a caftan printed with
tropical birdlife.

'Tim Kavanagh. Welcome to Mitford.'

Shirlene pumped his hand, bracelets jangling. 'I just pushed
your population count up to eleven hundred an' thirty-two.'

'Terrific. Congratulations. We're glad to have you.'

'Would you like to see our spray tan booth?'

'Your . . . ?'

'Spray tan booth, right there in the corner.'

Something like a round phone booth loomed in the corner.

'It's th' first in the high country. It was a huge investment; I
personally brought that into the business. You just walk in, take
your clothes off, an' a recording tells you what to do.

'It is so easy, you won't believe it. You just do like this . . .'
The clamor of bracelets as she flung forth her arms.

'Then you turn like this . . .' She gave a balletic whirl. Tou-
cans flew from banana trees.

'Wow,' he said.

'Plus it's very private, I mean, we don't *look in* at you or anything. As for your choices, I'm personally wearin' th' Boca, and
Fance got th' very popular Palm Beach.'

'A gift certificate,' he said, hoarse. 'While the special's on.'

'Or,' said Shirlene, 'if you're watchin' your budget, which we all
have to do, we can give you th' Miami or th' West Palm Beach.'

'You won't believe this,' said Fancy, 'but we were talkin' about
you just five minutes ago.'

'Oh, my gosh, is this him? Father Tim?'

'Shirlene has a question for you. I told her you know everything
and everybody.' If looks could kill, he'd be *morte*.

'I wouldn't say that. Just dropped in to get a gift certificate for color. While the special's on.'

'For your wife?' said Fancy.

'A friend.'

The cocked eyebrow. 'Cynthia still colorin' her own hair?'

'She is.'

'Speakin' of color,' said Shirlene, 'what do you think about our new look? I told Fancy we can*not* make it on perms and acrylic nails, we need to get more men in here. We didn't want ya'll runnin' over to Wesley 'cause our walls are pink.'

'So now they're green.' Fancy gave him the fish eye. Clearly, this woman would never forgive his infidelity.

'A great improvement!' he said.

'Do you run over to Wesley?' asked Shirlene.

'He does,' said Fancy.

'I need a gift certificate.' He spoke as if to the deaf.

Fancy shoved the broom in a corner. 'Let me go in back an' find th' dern things. Do you want it in an envelope?'

'Thank you. That would be good.'

'Shirlene, he needs a trim. I've got highlights in ten minutes, you'll have to do 'is trim.'

'No, no,' he said, 'I'm not here for a trim.'

'See those little puffs over 'is ears? They look like chrysanthemums. An back there on his neck, see his collar? We like to keep his hair off his collar at all times.'

'You really ought to do it while th' special's on,' said Shirlene. 'This is th' very last day you can get a trim for ten dollars.'

'A deal you will never see again in this lifetime,' said Fancy. 'Why anybody would blow good gas on a trip to Wesley is beyond me. Give 'im a glass of wine, Shirlene, I'll go find th' bloomin' gift cards.'

'Wine?' he said. 'It's ten forty-five.'

'Well, it's there if you want it,' said Shirlene. 'It's been a very successful promotion.'

'Hello, baby . . .'

'Oh, shoot, that's my cell.' Shirlene snatched the thing from the folds of her caftan and checked the ID. 'No way am I takin' this—it's Charlie Jackson, th' big creep.'

'Hello, baby . . .'

'If he ever said what's on his mind, he'd be speechless.'

She hit the Off button and held the phone aloft. 'Ta-da, my new Barry White ringtone. You gotta love it. So here's my question, Father. Where are the single men in this town?'

'That's a hard one. Very slim pickings.'

On impulse, he walked to the window and looked through the slats of the blind. 'There's one right there.' He could count on Avis.

Shirlene peered across the street at Avis Packard, who, innocent of visual interrogation, stood under his green awning smoking a fag, as the Irish liked to say.

'Oh, boy, I've seen him a time or two. He'd have to quit smokin'. Yes, sir, he'd have to quit that foolishness. An' that haircut looks like his mama did it. Lord help, get a load of those high-water britches. He'd be a handful.'

Shirlene turned from the window; bracelets chattered. 'Anybody else you can think of?'

'That's my best shot.'

He wouldn't mention Tony Nocelli, Lucera's chef and co-owner, who was a good-looking Italian and brother-in-law to the mayor. Local lore credited Tony with making more than one heart go arrhythmic.

'There are actually two or maybe three single men in Bristol, but they just aren't, like, *qualified*.'

He checked his watch.

'You know what I'm lookin' for?' Shirlene sat in her swivel chair. 'Somebody to play Scrabble with—you know what I mean, Father? Somebody to cook for, I love to cook—somebody who has a garden and is kind to others. Oh, and I'm crazy about yard sales, it would be nice to have somebody fun to do that with.

'So, it's not like I'm askin' for th' *moon*—I know better than to ask for th' *moon*. I had th' moon one time an' I'm totally over that, it stayed in full eclipse for fourteen years.'

Shirlene heaved a sigh. 'I sold my house in Bristol an' most of th' proceeds are standin' right over there in th' corner.'

They looked toward the corner, respectful.

'Spray tan is a lifetime investment. But I'm bankin' on it bein' a big hit in Mitford.' She blinked, close to tears.

'That's the spirit!'

He noticed a tic in his left eyelid. Where were the barber-shops of yore, where a man could go for peace and understanding, a doze in the chair? Nowhere, that's where. It was over, the good life was gone with the wind; a man was forced to seek the comfort of his own home.

'I cannot find th' gift cards,' said Fancy. 'I'll have to hand-write th' dern thing, or we can just call *whoever it is* and tell 'er to *come in.*'

Fancy was fishing for a name. 'Hand-write it, then,' he said, 'and thank you.'

Shirlene circled their lone customer. 'You would look *gorgeous* with a light application of spray tan, wouldn't he, Fance?'

'Don't even think about it,' he said.

'I would definitely recommend th' Miami for you. It's not a real heavy beach look as much as a sun-kissed look, you know what I mean? It's more like, Hello, I've been down at my sum-merhouse fishin' for a couple of days.'

He pulled out his wallet. 'How much?'

'Depends if it's full color, highlights, or both.' Fancy drummed her fingers on the counter.

'Both!' he said, reckless. Definitely the last time he'd climb the stairs to this Gehenna.

Fancy popped in a stick of Dentyne; the chewing commenced. 'You ought to get th' conditionin' treatment with that. Only fif-teen dollars extra—it puts th' shine back in. I personally use th' conditionin' treatment every time, otherwise you don't get your money's worth out of th' highlights.'

'Fine. Okay. The works.' Though he cared very much about Esther Bolick, this was ridiculous. He gouged a couple of fifties from his wallet.

'Keep goin',' said Fancy.

'What's that?'

'Another fifty, an' I'll give you change.'

He was grinding his left molars. Keep calm and carry on, the Brits liked to say.

'How'd you find your wife?' asked Shirlene. 'I hear you were pretty old when you got married.'

'She moved next door and asked 'im to go steady,' said Fancy.

Shirlene threw back her head and hooted with laughter. 'That is so *funny*, I am *crazy* about that. Moved next door an' asked you to *go steady*?'

'It worked,' he said.

HE HUNG A RIGHT toward Happy Endings. It was getting cooler. Breezy. Fall was in the air.

For the first time since coming home, he had the content-
ment of feeling rooted into Mitford like a turnip.

On impulse, he sat on the bench in front of the shoe store and
dialed the unpainted house in the Mississippi countryside, the
house with the swept yard and the gregarious garden patch and
Sister's pink Cadillac parked out front. God had opened a window for him in Holly Springs, with a view into lives he wouldn't
have known save for the note that read, *Come home.*

'All right?'

'Peggy!' he said. 'It's Timothy.'

'Oh, Timothy, we been talkin' 'bout you, Henry was gon'
call if we didn' hear.'

'How is he?'

'Not too good jus' now, not too good. Bad rashes all over his
skin—he has to stay greased up like a chicken, an' his eyes so
dry they sometimes stick shut.'

He felt the desperation of it in his bones.

'An' he's droppin' weight,' said Peggy. 'That's what worry me.'

Keeping Henry in the clear was like keeping a feather in the air
by the force of one's own breath. 'What do the doctors say?'

'Say stay out of th' sun, rest good, an' keep th' faith. It's somethin' like GVD, I don' know . . .'

'GVHD. Graft versus host disease. His cells recognize my
cells as foreign and go on the attack.'

'Somethin' like that, yes.'

'The good news is, the immune cells can also attack any leukemia cells that may be left.' He was putting a shine on things for
her sake, but felt a nauseous anxiety in his gut. 'His medication
seems to be doing the job?'

'Oh, yes, he has it all, he's gon' be all right. God didn't send
you to save his life, then drop 'im like a hot potato.'

'Does he feel like talking?'

'Th' nurse is with him. He'll be awful sad to miss talkin' to you, can he call you back?'

A car drove by, honked, he threw up his hand.

'I'll give him a shout this evening. How are you, Peggy? Are you all right?'

'Holdin' on,' she said. 'I'll be ninety 'fore we know it. Sister took my broom away las' week.'

'Uh-oh.' Peggy loved her yard-sweeping broom.

'Said, Give me th' keys to that broom, Mama, you flyin' it over th' speed limit.'

They had a small laugh, as they often had more than sixty years ago. 'You and Henry and Sister are faithfully in our prayers. It's wonderful to hear your voice.'

'I thank you for the rest of my days, Timothy. We sho' love you an' your wonderful wife.'

'We love you back,' he said.

HOPE TURNED AWAY TO HIDE HER TEARS.

'I'm sorry, Father. It's just so hard right now. Dr. Wilson says I must go to bed at once. He sent me to the hospital in Wesley for an ultrasound and . . . it isn't good. This is my last day at work, I don't know for how long.'

'Who will run the store?'

'I really can't afford . . . I mean, I don't know. I thought of closing it, but . . . it's . . . we just want the baby to be . . .'

She was sobbing. He had forgotten his handkerchief; it would have helped to have it.

The bookstore was operating on a shoestring, he knew that. Though the bottom line didn't always show it, a lot of people would be seriously disappointed if it closed. He loved seeing schoolkids sprawled on the floor, drinking in a story, exercising their imaginations. Jefferson had famously said, I cannot live without books. How could they live without their bookstore? Happy Endings was an institution; right up there with church and school, it was a bridge from the uncivil to the civil. Where else could he take his dog and read Sunday's *Times* on Monday morning?

And now, a baby, and something gone wrong.

'My body is making a terrible trap for the baby. Please don't tell anyone.'

'You have my word,' he said. 'Please. Sit.'

He led her to a chair, brought her the box of tissues and a glass of water from the coffee station.

'I can't talk about it anymore right now.' She gave in completely to her suffering; he sat close by, let her be. Her body making a trap . . .

'I'll give you a day a week,' he said. He could hardly bear seeing her like this.

'Oh, but Father, no, I couldn't . . .'

'Thursday!' he said, suddenly wild with this dangerous notion.

On his way to Lew's, he fingered the bookstore key in the pocket of his sweater, and noted a definite spring in his step.

Lew was waiting for him at the pumps. 'Bud told me some stuff. Th' driver said he had to get to the airport.'

'What else?'

'Bud said while I was checkin' th' oil, th' guy opened th' door behind th' driver's seat an' a bag of some kind fell out. A big leather kind of bag, an' he handed it back in an' closed th' door an' stooped down and picked up whatever fell out of th' bag an' opened th' door an' handed that back in. Bud found somethin' after they left, prob'ly rolled up under th' chassis an' th' driver missed it.'

He walked inside with Lew, who reached under the counter and handed him a glasses case.

Two initials on the cover—KD—in what he reckoned could be actual gold. A light fragrance suggested itself when he opened the case. Empty. Soft leather; maybe kidskin.

'Nice case,' he said, handing it back.

'Guess we'll hold on to it if they come this way again.'

'What else?'

'That's it.'

He walked to the Mazda, frowning. An old parishioner passing through, most likely. K.D. He ran a few names from the past. Kitty Duncan—not likely, she was in her eighties a decade ago. Katherine Daily. Married again, if he knew Katherine, and still serving artichoke dip too runny for the cracker, bless her heart. He being a slow learner and a hungry bachelor, her artichoke dip had landed on his shirtfront more than a few times.

On the way home, he had a moment of remorse. God knows, he'd never done retail and didn't have a clue. But how hard could it be? Ring a sale, take a little money, make change—if that's all there was to it, no problem. And definitely no gift wrap.

But that was the small stuff. What could be so very wrong with Hope's pregnancy?

HE DUMPED THE MOUNTAIN WINESAPS into a bowl in the kitchen, stacked their new books on the table in the study, and went looking for his wife.

She was at her drawing board—pale, oblivious to his presence in the doorway, squinting. Her eyesight had been diminishing over the last couple of years. She didn't need to be baking pies tonight; he needed to take this woman to dinner. But first things first.

'I have a job,' he said.

She looked up, mildly startled. 'You also have a message from the bishop.'

'You go first.'

'He's very apologetic for leaving you hanging.'

They probably wanted him to approach Edith Mallory and ask her to remember the diocese in her will—but what was so grave about that?

'He's a very nice man and eager to meet you.'

'Good, good.'

'He would have canceled his trip to the Bahamas, but the family was coming—they have three children and nine grandchildren. The airfare was nonrefundable and he hadn't gone on vacation with his wife in two years. His wife's name is Eleanor.

'He'd like you to be at the cathedral Monday morning at nine. A cold front is moving in tonight for two days, and unlike the Mustang, the heater in my car actually works.'

His deacon had it covered. 'No clues as to . . .'

'None. We'll take coffee in a thermos.'

He went to her and massaged her neck. 'You need a break.'

'We just had a break.'

'Ireland was no break. How about a week at Whitecap?'

'I'd love a week at Whitecap. But not right now, sweetheart.'

'How about dinner tonight at Lucera?'

'I'd love dinner tonight at Lucera.'

'What don't you love, Kav'na?'

She turned and looked up at him. She Who Never Hesitates

looked hesitant. 'I'll tell you over dinner,' she said, smiling now. 'What kind of job?'

'Selling books. Thursdays ten to five. I'll pack a lunch and take Barnabas with me.' He was excited; he was twelve years old.

THANK HEAVEN it was Saturday and she would have tomorrow to try and find someone to come in for a day, any day, she could not be choosy now. Together with Father Tim's day, perhaps they could cobble things together and she could keep the business.

She had tidied the reading area, thrown out old newspapers, dusted the bookshelves. It was all she could do; the pain was there again. Now she must lock the door and turn the sign around to say CLOSED, and Scott would park at the curb and open the car door for her and she would see the love in his eyes and the alarm, and beyond that, they would know nothing more until she saw the specialist in Charlotte next week.

She was afraid of being afraid. And yet she could not, even with prayer, hold it in check.

She looked at her yellow cat lying contented on the sales counter. Margaret Ann had always lived at the bookstore, but things were different now. 'Let's go home,' she said. She coaxed the bewildered feline into the book bag, the book bag that read HAPPY ENDINGS.

Dr. Wilson had not been able to make that promise.

'I DREAMED OF OUR FATHER LAST NIGHT.'

He heard a kind of elation in Henry's voice.

'He was real, Timothy. So real. How can this happen when I never met or knew him? Surely it's the picture you gave me, I've studied it many hours these last months.'

He, too, had studied photographs of his father, searching for clues.

'His presence was real, it had bone and marrow,' said Henry. 'Have you ever experienced this?'

'There was a parishioner at Lord's Chapel, whom I knew for many years. She was a type of mother to me—or aunt or grandmother—and a tender friend. Sadie Baxter. I've dreamed of her several times. It's always very real, even one in which she was sitting in a tree and calling down to me.'

'The one who remembered Dooley in her will.'

'Yes, because she saw something exceptional in him. She also gave the town a state-of-the-art nursing facility and other gifts we seem to take for granted these days. In any case, I count such dreams a benediction.'

'We didn't talk,' said Henry. 'It seemed he'd come just to let me look at him. He was sitting on the bench in my little patch where you and I sat, and was gazing at me in a steady sort of way. I was afraid I wouldn't measure up, and then I felt joy that he would come at all.'

He completely got the power of Henry's encounter, felt his own tears rise.

'He was solemn.' Henry's voice broke.

'Solemn,' he said. 'That would be our father.'

'And then he nodded. Just . . . nodded. And I sensed he was giving me his approval. There was beauty in his face, and I had the feeling it was my turn to study him, that he was offering that privilege to me. And then I woke up, dumb as a stone. I had no desire to make a sound or to be real to myself—I wanted the dream of our father to be the reality.'

This was his very first taste of what sibling rivalry might feel like. He was honestly happy for Henry, for this fragile mite of contact, but he wished his father would also appear to him, Timothy, and give a nod of approval. Would he never rid himself of this damnable neurosis? Perhaps diabetes wasn't his Pauline thorn.

For some reason, they didn't talk about the rashes or the weight loss or the alarming battle raging in Henry's blood.

OPERA, great smells from the kitchen, and a bottle of Madame Cliquot's midrange brut in an ice bucket by their table.

Tonight, they would dine on Tony's Pollo alla Griglia in the room where they'd savored Louella's fried chicken and biscuits. Then they would visit the ballroom with the painted ceiling where he and Cynthia had danced beneath a heaven brimming with angels.

By Mitford standards, not a bad night out.

'Just under the wire,' he said, handing over his letter.

'Bedtime reading.' She smiled, happy, and slipped the envelope into her purse.

'How about a toast?' he said. 'To Miss Sadie, who helped make us all better than we might have been.'

'To Miss Sadie.'

They clinked, they drank.

'I love toasts,' she said.

'You were going to tell me what you don't love.'

'Retirement in all its forms, wrinkle cream that makes nothing disappear but misguided hope, and, of course, age spots.'

This had been his cue for years; he took her hand, examined the back of it with absorption. 'These aren't age spots, Kav'na. They're freckles.'

She laughed, one of her real letting-go laughs. While he was at it, he kissed her hand.

'Great to see y'all havin' such a good time,' said their server.

Chapter
Eight

Out there, the gray stain of first light and the stinging cold. In here, the toasting heater, his favorite sweater, his favorite wife.

In the coffee-scented car on the open parkway, they were children on a field trip, owning the light that grew and changed and made luminous a nascent gold on early autumn hills. The mist steaming along the ridges was theirs, and granite cliffs, and stark silhouettes of wind-shaven trees, and then the sun rising full-bore, to have its way with all that crept and crawled and walked upright.

He had to wonder—why travel across oceans when this vast and sublime world lived at their very door?

JACK MARTIN WAS GOOD-LOOKING, or perhaps striking would be the word.

Medium build, blue eyes, silvering hair. Even the magenta of the clerical shirt, which flattered very few, suited the bishop's coloring.

'You had a good trip, Father?'

'Very good, thanks.' Broad windows with a mountain view, a fire on the hearth. 'We took the parkway to Linville Falls, 221 to Marion, then I-40 here. The Alleluia Highway, we decided to call it.'

'We, you say?'

'My wife, Cynthia, is with me.'

'Not waiting in reception, I trust.'

'No, no. She's in town at a bookstore.'

The bishop gestured toward one of two wing chairs before the fire.

'They opened early for her visit; she's signing a few editions of her work. She's a writer and illustrator of children's books.'

'As I know very well.' The bishop leaned to the table beside his chair, removed a book from a pile, displayed the cover of *Violet Comes to Stay*.

'I sent out for her books when we returned from our trip. I now have them all, save one, which is shipping right away. They'll end up with the grandchildren.'

'She'll be pleased. Many thanks.' Two walls of books had already accumulated here.

It was fair to say he hadn't been greatly alarmed by the bishop's invitation and its cloak of mystery—curious and perplexed would be closer to the truth, though he was surprised now by a certain tension, even dread, that he hadn't expected.

'We'll have coffee in a moment, then move straight along. As I'm sure you know, Father, I gave Mrs. Kavanagh my deepest regrets for the muddle of this whole business. Let me offer my apologies firsthand.'

'None needed,' he said. 'Not at all.'

'A comedy of errors. I couldn't phone you from the island because we were quite remote, with no cell phone service. I had to give the matter into God's hands entirely, where it belongs in any case.'

The modest rap on the door, and the bishop's assistant with a coffee tray, and the standing and the introductions. While the bishop agreeably chose all that was offered, he declined cream, he eschewed sugar, and passed on the offer of a chocolate. The retreating assistant closed the door, soundless.

'In a fairly short time, I've learned a great deal about you, Father. Good stuff. Good stuff. You married late.'

'Never too late,' he said. 'But yes. Sixty-two.'

Jack Martin stirred his coffee. 'I understand marriage suits you.'

'I think I never knew much about who I really am until she told me. I like her version and I'm sticking with it.'

The bishop's laughter was contained, but genuine.

Romantic, Cynthia had insisted from the beginning; deeply sensitive, a brilliant diviner of character—but that was his little secret. He smiled at the bishop, sipped his coffee. Definitely not church coffee. More secular.

'You chose to settle in Mitford after you retired. Permanently?'

'We have no aspiration to live elsewhere. It's an easy town, quite beautiful in its hanging valley, and still with a certain innocence that appeals to us.'

'You had sixteen years at the Chapel of Our Lord and Savior. Growth was steady, and I'm told you made a sizable addition to the building.'

'A second-floor Sunday school, yes.'

'It's quite the reverse in many parishes, as you know.'

'The parish is fortunate to have summer people who help pay the bills. A good mix—I was very fond of it all.'

'Your retirement was for medical reasons. Complications of diabetes, I believe. How is your health currently?'

'Stable. My wife doesn't allow otherwise.'

'Was there something about a suicidal Pepsi?'

'Coke,' he said. 'I drank a Coke on an empty stomach, and my system went haywire. I drove my car into a stop sign and injured a dear friend who was out walking his dog. The dog was killed instantly.'

This was hard, painful; he despised it. 'And cake,' he said. 'There was also a cake incident. So, there were two diabetic comas. I was rolling the dice—something I'm not known to do and something I'll never do again.'

Jack Martin drew in his breath. 'You've had a bout or two with depression.'

'More than one or two.'

'Chronic?'

'No. But with some frequency in my forties—I was a priest without a heart for God. Then an especially tough time after what we call the Coke incident.'

'You're a straight shooter, Father. Nor am I one to roll the dice, to use your term. I've read your file very prayerfully and talked to several of your close associates.'

The bishop fingered the chain of his pectoral cross. 'Together with a few people whose opinions I regard highly, I feel that you and your wife make a good model for marriage, a good model for living. Especially in the wake of a tragic model. Henry Talbot is divorcing his wife and leaving the church.'

Something went on with his heart, a beat or two skipped.

'Talbot came to me just hours before we left the country. He confessed he'd let his parish down, and cheated on his wife for some years—I won't go now into the details of who, what, and why. As desperate as that is, there's more.'

Jack Martin sat back in the chair as if suddenly fatigued.

'Other issues have surfaced. Less troubling by comparison, but there nonetheless.' The bishop gazed toward the windows and the mountains beyond. 'It's a man breaking down in many ways at once. I've seen some disasters in my time, but this is a train wreck.'

Not just leaving the church, not just cheating on his wife, not just a divorce, but other issues as well. He was struck by the calamity of it.

'I spoke with the senior warden at Lord's Chapel.'

'Bill Swanson,' he said. 'A good man.'

'Bill says the vestry has been able to hold things together, but barely. Bill was ready to come to me, but Talbot beat him to it. Apparently, everyone knows something is terribly wrong, but very few know what or how much. When the truth breaks, the floodwaters will come in over our heads.'

He saw himself going to Talbot's office, trying to find words to counsel or console, but it was a shallow offering. For the first time, he noted the sound of the hearth fire—the sharp spit and crackle of hardwood.

'Any one of these issues begs immediate dismissal. It was imperative for Talbot to leave Lord's Chapel at once, but he implored me to allow him a final voice. Your Methodist pastor, I believe you know her, will supply September thirtieth, and I agreed to give Talbot October seventh. He wants to make a type of confession to the congregation, an apology for letting them down, for not . . . caring for them as he'd hoped to do.'

The bishop took a folded handkerchief from the breast pocket of his jacket, pressed it to his eyes. 'He gets good marks for that.

'He begged for this concession, and I granted it. I've made arrangements to be there, of course. I said earlier that I don't gamble, but this is an exception. His apology to the parish could be healing for all concerned—or it could be a further disaster.'

He agreed, but said nothing.

'Parishes seldom get closure when a priest leaves under strained circumstances. It could help them, and the interim, considerably.'

'I saw him at the church office a day or two ago.'

'He may have been there removing a few personal items—discreetly, I hope. We won't say anything to the parish until the seventh. There's no need to extend the agony over roughly two weeks. They'll simply know the bishop is coming—which I hope will give us a stronger turnout and more people to hear Talbot's remarks firsthand.'

'Bill knows what's going on?'

'He does. And he knows I'm talking with you, but I trust him not to spread any of it. The parish was told that Talbot is taking a little time off with family, which I presume to be true.'

Jack Martin got up and used the poker to rearrange a log, then stood with his back to the fire. His eyes weren't blue, they were green. Startling.

'I need the right person to step in at once. On the eighth, actually, if such a miracle could be wrought.

'There's a priest from Colorado who would do well in this circumstance—he's been through it all before. He would supply until the Search Committee finds the right candidate, then perhaps he'd be a candidate for the long haul.'

'What sort of man?'

'Ex-Marine. Sixty-three. Hikes, stays fit, likes the mountains. Lost his wife to ovarian cancer two years ago. Very good at this kind of thing, though probably not available 'til January first. On the other hand, Father . . .'

The bishop returned to his chair, thoughtful.

'On the other hand, you know your way around the cure, you're a familiar figure and a trusted friend. That counts for a great deal.

'We wouldn't ask you to be the one for the short stint, to fill in 'til Father Brad comes in January. We'd be asking you to step in at once and stick with it 'til the Search Committee secures another priest.'

Good Lord.

'I'm asking you to supply as vicar until we find the right candidate.'

He was fairly stunned. To be asked at all, and then to be asked for such a quick turnaround . . . the eighth of October was two weeks away.

'This is scary,' he said.

'For both of us. Talbot's movers arrive Monday morning, following the service on the seventh. The field would be clear for the interim to make a fresh start.'

He took a glass of water from the coffee tray, drank; collected himself. 'What about his wife, Mary?'

The bishop gave a faint smile. 'She's said to refer to Mitford as a hick town. That happens often, you know—the spouse feeling disaffected. As it turns out, Talbot says she loves him unconditionally and doesn't want to lose him—even in view of his misdeeds. He admits that he cares for her deeply, but sees divorce as punishment to himself. A selfish view, of course, that often masquerades as noble.'

'She knows about the infidelity?'

'He says he confessed it to her.'

'His repentance . . .'

'Is genuine, I feel. But it's regretful that he didn't confess the whole story to me, I would have liked that for his sake. What do you know about him?'

'We got on well enough, but the parish was a bit standoffish and it was hard for him. He's a man who likes to please and be accepted. But don't we all?'

'God help the fellow who follows a well-loved priest of sixteen years—a tricky business.'

'I must discuss this with my wife, of course, and commit it to prayer. I can't give you an answer today.'

He would say, What do you think? And she would say, What do you want? And he would say, I don't know. And she would say, You'll make the right choice. During this conversation, her eyes would do the real talking. Because she had watched his health go south when he was full-time, her eyes would say, No.

He had worked hard at being retired, at battling with the psychological upheaval of losing an entire identity—there were times when he even missed the stress of it—but he was running the course pretty well now; had actually gained a bit of momentum. Going full-time at this point would create another upheaval, one guaranteed to be deeper still.

But hadn't he wanted something greater than the middling life, hadn't he battered the door of heaven with his endless, What next, what now?

'Though my retirement was pretty much doctor's orders,' he said, 'some of the parish were upset by it. I don't know how they'd take to a revolving door.'

'You're a healer, Father. Your former bishop, Stuart Cullen, says so, and I'm a Cullen fan.'

He'd never thought he was a healer; he'd always felt the need of healing, himself.

'The way you brought the mountain parish back last year was

most extraordinary—mite nigh impossible, as my Kentucky grandfather would say. The diocese is proud of what you did there with God's help.' Jack Martin rubbed his forehead, thoughtful. 'What would you say you're about as a priest?'

'To see the useless made useful, the scattered made whole.'

'The Coke and cake business. I trust there will be no more of that, whatever you decide.'

'Absolutely.'

'This invitation is somewhat unsettling, I should think. After several years of retirement, you may have found your sweet spot. But there's what Bonhoeffer said: "We must be ready to allow ourselves to be interrupted by God."'

'You understand that it would help to know right away. If you decline, we can find someone to supply for a few weeks and then the candidate from Colorado would step in, but that's a lot to put a parish through. It would be lovely if . . .'

The bishop's words hung in the air like mist in the hollows.

'What can be done for Henry Talbot?' he said.

'We have three clinicians. He could see one or all, and all of it would be completely private. I told him this, but he doesn't believe he deserves help. Perhaps that can change.'

They sat for a time, silent, looking at the fire. The bishop turned to him as if startled by a thought.

'Let me pray for you, Father.'

'Thank you,' he said. He bowed his head, sentient to the rigors of the bishop's distress and his own.

'Lord of healing, Lord of grace, thank you for your servant, Timothy, whom you raised up to share with others your unconditional love. Thank you for his steadfast faith in you, and for his gentle ways among your flock. If Lord's Chapel again be his charge, Father, equip his every need and send him out with strength and vigor to do your perfect will. May his shepherd's heart be a healing balm to the parish, and a witness of your infinite love for each of us. Thank you, Lord, for your Holy Presence in our lives as we struggle to love one another as you love us. May your name be glorified now and forever, through Christ our Lord, Amen.'

'Amen. Thank you.'

'Whatever you decide, Father, I'd like you to be there on the seventh.'

'Consider it done.'

'To return to your wife for a moment—she's well liked, as you know, a woman of considerable character and, it's said, strong opinion.'

'*Alis volat propriis*,' he said.

'Flies with her own wings.' Jack Martin smiled. 'I have such a one, myself, thank God. In any case, I'm sure Mrs. Kavanagh would be a great help to you, and we'll help her however we can. If she'd like someone to talk with about this, have her call me.'

They stood and walked to the office door together and shook hands, each holding the gaze of the other.

'Say nothing to anyone but close family. If you decide to step in, you'd begin October eighth. It will be a kind of holocaust for a time—I'll look after you and send help when needed. You realize that the length of your stay at Lord's Chapel could be six months, a year, possibly longer.'

'Indefinite,' he said. 'Like everything else in life.'

'The Lord be with you,' said Jack Martin.

'And also with you.'

They embraced, and he turned and walked down the hall and went into the nave, where he knelt at the silent rail.

His mind was clamor itself, a hectic marketplace with hawking on every side. They were coming up on the Feast Day of Saint

Matthew, who quoted Christ's injunction to forgive 'seventy times seven.' For some of the parish, that would not be enough. He envisioned himself standing once more in the Lord's Chapel pulpit and felt a terrible thirst, not so much for water as for—what?

'Jesus,' he said, unable to form a further petition. He pressed his forehead against the railing. He would take any wisdom right now—not the big decision, that would be asking too much too soon; the smallest scrap would do. He remained at the railing for a time, then stood and bowed to the cross, and walked out a side door into the sublime mountain air.

THE SIGHT OF HER CAR coming up the hill was a benediction. 'Good timing,' he said, climbing in.

She handed him the box of raisins. 'Did your six o'clock oatmeal see you through?'

'Barely,' he said, buckling up.

'We're off to the most divine spot for a real breakfast. I'll take the scenic route.'

Along streets mottled by the shade of pin oaks, he told her everything.

'What do you think?' he said, swigging from a bottle of water.

'What do you want?'

'I don't know.'

'You'll know,' she said.

He couldn't see her eyes. 'What about you? What do you want?'

'I would hate sharing you again with so many people.'

She had never gotten used to that, but she had been generous and patient, and he had been grateful.

'Your exhaustion would be hard to watch,' she said.

'But I've been doing better.'

Except for Ireland. He had exhausted himself in Sligo with what she called his 'household parish,' but it had been a wonderful time, really; he would never forget the joy that came forth in the end.

'You will lose families in this fallout, you will try to mend broken hearts; you will try to fix everything.'

Of course he would try to fix everything. What was a priest for, if not to get into people's business and, with God's help, do a little fixing? To operate otherwise cut the parson out of a very big piece of the pie.

She drove into the parking lot of a small restaurant, turned off the ignition, and gave him a steady look. 'But if you decide to do it, Timothy, I'll do it with you. All the way.'

Her eyes were blue, with nothing more said there.

He patted her knee.

Two weeks. He felt the rock in his stomach and doubted that breakfast could fix that.

ON THE WAY HOME, they avoided further discussion of the matter, and spent themselves on foolishness.

'When was the War of 1812 fought?' he said, and she laughed, though it wasn't funny.

They were giddy, a little haywire.

'So, on a cruise ship,' he said, 'what time is the midnight buffet?'

Chapter
Nine

There was something to be said for the invitation being dropped into their lives like a grenade.

One, it demanded that he concentrate every power on making the right decision. If he could focus so obsessively, so completely as this on his relationship with God . . .

Two, there was no room to agonize over what to do about Sammy.

Restless beside his wife, who had fallen asleep at once, he sought peace in the familiar. *Lord Jesus, stay with us, for evening is at hand and the day is past; be our companion in the way, kindle our hearts, and awaken hope, that we may know thee as thou art revealed in Scripture and the breaking of bread. Grant this for the sake of thy love, amen.*

For the sake of thy love, he thought. For the sake of thy love.

Ardent for sleep of any kind or duration, he decided he needed a cutoff date, a personal deadline for calling in his answer. He wished for an easy way out—the parting of waters, the audible voice.

IT WAS FREEZING OUT THERE, with a stern wind to boot. Barnabas had done his morning business and made for the door in under sixty seconds.

On his knees, he brushed back the ashes of last evening's fire and kindled a small one for Morning Prayer—two splits of oak and one of maple, atop kindling that would bring the fire quickly. Flames licked up; he was an acolyte at the tapers.

In any decision making, he'd learned to wait for the peace; it was heedless to make a move without it. There was no time for waiting, and yet waiting was imperative.

He remained on his knees, prayed aloud. 'Heavenly Father, in whom we live and move and have our being: We humbly pray thee so to guide and govern us by thy Holy Spirit, that in all the cares and occupations of our life we may not forget thee, but may remember that we are ever walking in thy sight . . .'

He moved directly then to the abridged version. 'Help me, Jesus.'

In the wilds of New Jersey, Walter was usually stirring by five a.m.

As he dialed, he could see his first cousin, semi-retired from the law firm and a little stooped, in a bathrobe of considerable antiquity. He would be fetching the *WSJ* from the hallway, taking Katherine a cup of tea in bed, then rooting in beside her to read and argue aloud with the editorials.

'Are you out of your mind, Timothy?'

'I feel I should do it,' he said. 'For the parish. It will be a hard time.'

'Should do it? Why should? I'm not party to all God has to say about such matters, but I do know this—the business of killing yourself for other people is a lot of hogwash. Take this on and you'll be up to all the tricks you pulled in Ireland, saving souls right and left with hardly a minute to draw your breath.'

'It isn't the parson who saves souls—you know that.'

'I know, I know, but somebody has to be hands and feet, and you've done that nobly for forty-plus years. Give yourself a break, cousin, refresh yourself, learn how to live before you die. And face it—you haven't even begun to retire. Two years in two different parishes, plus a good year's worth of supply up hill and down dale, not to mention being the very backbone of the Children's Hospital. A question—how many vacations have you had in your adult life? By my count, four, and they were all working vacations. Right? Am I right?'

A sermon from a lawyer. There were few things worse.

HE CALLED HIS FORMER DOCTOR at home and told him of the bishop's offer, then, and walked north toward Hoppy's house.

He would talk with Sammy, posing no threats, avoiding blame, speaking the truth in love.

Sammy was not hopeless. Look at Dooley, how he'd been born into neglect and violence only to become a young man set on bettering himself, sharing his wealth but also conserving it in the right places. It seemed too good to be true.

HOPPY WAS A WEEK AWAY from his first trip to the Upper Nile and a leap into the unknown. Here a leap, there a leap—it was a frog pond.

They sat at the table in the Harpers' kitchen, where for years Hoppy had worked an early morning crossword. His old friend and parishioner was looking terrific, better than ever. Retirement in the early stages.

'What do you know about Hope Murphy?' he said. He felt

reluctant, somehow, to go directly to the issue at hand. 'Are you at liberty to talk about it?'

'Wilson mentioned that she trusts you, says you already know something of what's going on. I feel comfortable telling you more—but in strict confidence. She's a private person, as you're aware. The medical term is placenta previa.

'The placenta, or afterbirth, is a temporary organ that transfers oxygen and nutrients from the mother to the fetus. In Hope's case, the placenta has attached itself to the lower segment of the uterus and is covering the cervical canal. Two problems: the baby has no way to exit, and as the cervix dilates, bleeding can be excessive.'

'The bleeding . . .'

'Increases the risk for preterm rupture of the membranes, which can lead to premature labor. This can be life-threatening—for mother and infant.'

'The outcome as you see it?'

'Wilson says the bleeding has been fairly minor so far, but he's taking no chances. Bed rest will control it to some extent. She'll be under the care of a specialist in Charlotte, with Wilson doing the day-to-day stuff here. They'll want her in Charlotte at thirty-two weeks.'

'A month early?'

'Taking no chances. If anything goes off track up here, there's no safety net, she could bleed to death.

'We're looking at a Cesarean, of course, and with God's help, a healthy baby. Depending on circumstances, there could be a hysterectomy at the time of delivery.'

Hoppy removed his glasses. 'If the delivery isn't successful, needless to say it will be devastating to the Murphys. A hysterectomy would add another kind of death sentence. When you're back at Lord's Chapel, I know you'll encourage prayer for this.'

When he was back at Lord's Chapel . . . everyone would assume he'd go back.

'As to your own predicament . . .' Hoppy gave him an ironic smile. '. . . if you stick to your exercise regimen and keep your weight down, I believe you could manage it physically. So the issue is how you would manage it . . .' Hoppy tapped his forehead with a pencil. '. . . up here.'

'Did you know about Talbot?'

'Nothing specific, just that clergy have their struggles; I thought his disconnect might eventually turn around. Olivia has had real concerns about him, but frankly, I've been too caught up in the Sudan business to pay much attention. How are you feeling?'

He had no words for how he was feeling. 'What if I take it on and can't go the distance? That would be twice for the parish. You know they resented my retirement.'

'Yes, but not everyone. Most people understood. What they resented was you swigging down that Coke and eating the bloody cake. My guess is, they'll kiss your ring.'

'Come on.'

'Trust me. As for your medical aptitude, Wilson says your cholesterol is good and the diabetes is under control. But you know how fast that can go off the cliff.

'If you move forward with picking up Talbot's pieces, you'll need help. You're prone to try doing it all, which took you out of full-time in the first place. To do it all and deprive others of doing is . . .' Hoppy studied the puzzle. '. . . a misguided notion.'

'And how many years were you burning the candle at both ends and calling for more wax?'

Hoppy laughed. 'Touché, Father. In any case, whatever happens, Wilson is up to handling it. Your job is to avoid giving him anything to handle.'

Hoppy turned to a bank of drawers beneath the window seat, pulled one out, removed an open bag of jelly beans, and offered a sampling. 'Have a green, they're the best.'

He did as prescribed. 'I thought you were on the wagon.'

His former doctor laughed, popped a jelly bean. 'I was, and will be again. No jelly beans in Yida.'

Hoppy adjusted his reading glasses, bent over the puzzle. 'Ecclesiastical setback. Blank, *p*, blank, blank.'

'Apse,' he said.

He checked his commitments for today.

> *Lunch @ Feel Good.*
> *Mustang diagnostic*

Another big day on the calendar.

How would he like going from zero to a hundred and sixty mph? Why couldn't there be some reasonable in-between? He loathed zero and despised a hundred and sixty. Why couldn't he ever find a cruising speed?

The pressure of the open-ended timetable was too much; he had to have a cutoff date. 'Jesus,' he said under his breath.

Barnabas looked up from his bed at the hearth. Good! His dog had not lost his hearing. It was he, Timothy, who had lost his, for he was getting no feedback. Zero.

What about Thursday? Maybe he could take a week to make the decision, but he couldn't bear the pressure of it for a week. He wanted, needed it to happen quickly, as quickly as God would permit. Thursday would be extremely fair to all. 'But *late* Thursday,' he declared to his dog.

He consulted his calendar.

Written with a kind of slapdash joy in the slot for Thursday:

Happy Endings 9 a.m.

The Happy Endings stint had completely slipped his mind. He had planned to go in early, take his own beans, and learn to operate a coffeemaker that also did the grinding. But how could he think about stuffing a full day's commitment at the bookstore into Thursday's need for an urgent decision?

Friday was open, a total blank; he could call the bishop on Friday. For that matter, he could do the bookstore on Friday— Friday was payday in these parts, a good day for buying books; he would notify Hope, who, he felt certain, would be just as grateful for help on Friday.

Barnabas came over, lay at his feet, looked up.

No. Thursday was the day he would call the bishop. And Thursday was the day he would work at the bookstore—no way would he disappoint Hope, and no way would he disappoint his dog, who, he believed, was definitely up for sooner rather than later.

'IT'S YOUR CARBURETOR,' said Jeb Adderholt.

Jeb paused to allow for shocked silence or possibly an enjoyable stream of strong language, but he could not bestow this small pleasure upon Jeb Adderholt.

The phone line between Mitford and Wesley enjoyed its

characteristic crackle and hum. Something about a throttle shaft . . .

'Plus your radiator's rotted out pretty bad.'

'Ah.'

'An' your heater, you know that heater's never worked right. Th' old folks say this'll be th' worst winter in a decade.'

'They say that every year.' He was now old folks, himself, and as far as he was concerned, the winter could do whatever it pleased.

Jeb cleared his throat, moving in for the kill. 'Have you noticed your clutch is slippin'?'

'How would I notice that?'

'When you're goin' *uphill*,' said Jeb as if speaking to someone from a foreign country.

'Right. Yes, I've noticed that. Anything else?'

'It's gon' cost more to fix than it's worth.' Jeb named a price, but given the hum, it was muffled and indistinct.

He would pick it up tomorrow and pay Jeb for the diagnostic. So much for his sharp little ride.

Having driven previously used vehicles all his life, he had no idea how to buy a new car. Before the vintage Mustang, there was the motor scooter, and before that, eight years of foot travel, and before that, the antiquated Buick, and prior to the Buick, he could scarcely remember. He would subscribe to *Consumer Reports* or Lew would probably know, or Dooley. Dooley! Of course. Dooley would go nuts over helping him buy a new vehicle.

He left Dooley a voice message, feeling better already.

'ARE YOU HAVING LUNCH with the turkeys?' His wife was whipped from yesterday, and so was he. But would they give in and lie down or whatever people do when they're whipped?

'I don't feel I should have lunch. Things are too . . .' He shrugged.

'But it's the day the sign goes up, sweetheart.' She dumped coffee grounds into the kitchen compost bin. 'I think you should have lunch.'

'All that boondoggling . . .' he said, vague.

'Boondoggling beats sitting around trying to figure out what God is up to. He's given you a target date, which I think you should let Bishop Martin know.'

'Why let the bishop know that I don't know?'

'You'd be letting him know that you'll know by Thursday. He could relax a little. But what do I know about bishops? Maybe they don't need to relax. We, however, need to keep praying and trusting God, and moving ahead to things like lunch and dry-cleaning and a dozen eggs at the Local.'

She was right, of course, but still . . .

'Puny's coming in today instead of tomorrow,' she said, 'and bringing the boys.' She rubbed her eyes, something she did more often these days. 'As for me, I'm having lunch in Wesley with Irene McGraw, she's just back from Georgia.'

'Tell her I enjoyed breaking into her house. Nice artwork.'

'The capital campaign meeting is after lunch. I'll have a report. In the meantime, you and I need to plan something fun—like dinner and a movie. All we ever do is dinner. What was the last movie we saw?'

'*Babe*, I think. Do we have a VCR player?'

'VCRs went out of style ages ago. It's DVDs now. Just a disc. Like a CD.'

'Do we have any?' he said.

'No. We would have to order a movie that comes in through our TV.'

'Do you know how to do that?'

'I've never done it,' she said. 'All I know how to do is watch *60 Minutes* and PBS.'

'Puny knows technology. Get her to show you,' he said.

'Get her to show *you*, and I'll make dinner.'

He was supposed to know this stuff, but he had never, not once, known this stuff. He was pretty good at softball and handy with a hammer and paintbrush, which should be enough for anybody.

'What do other people do in the evenings?'

'Shirlene Hatfield plays Scrabble online. J. C. Hogan once confessed he cleans Adele's Glock .45. Let's see—Mule and Fancy watch reality TV.'

'How do you know these things?'

'People talk,' he said. 'Then there's Esther Bolick. She sleeps in her recliner for a couple of hours after dinner, then goes to bed and watches Johnny Carson reruns.'

'Maybe we just need to get out more.'

'We got out all day yesterday.' She wasn't listening. '*From dawn to dusk.*'

She peered at her reflection in the chrome of the toaster, and did something with her hair. 'That was yesterday. Let's go and be as—'

'Don't even say it,' he said.

'I HAVE GOOD NEWS!' Puny announced as he came downstairs.

She was 'lit up like a Christmas tree,' as Nanny Howard used to say. His mind flew to the good news Puny had handed him twice before in recent years—twins. He couldn't take another set of twins, he just couldn't.

'Joe Joe's our new police chief, he'll be officially installed th' first week of November.'

'Congratulations!' One more frog off the bank. 'Tell Joe Joe I'm proud as the dickens.' He gave her a hug.

'It's goin' to be in th' paper real soon,' she said. 'There'll be a reception at Town Hall, we want y'all to come.'

'Consider it done!' he said.

She looked abashed. 'I guess I should have told you about Joe Joe last, an' told you th' bad news first.'

'What bad news?'

'Your cue stick's missin'.'

'My cue stick?'

'I dust in there ever' week, cue rack an' all, an' th' one in your slot's not there this mornin'.'

He walked up the hall to see for himself, fighting the anger rising like bile. Among other things, that was a pretty nice cue stick.

The empty slot was a slap in the face. He took a deep breath. If he ran this to ground, there would be consequences. He could not do that now, he could not fly off in any direction other than the one he was currently navigating. Unless something forced his hand, he would pretend not to notice.

Puny was peeling apples at the sink. 'Don't mention this to Cynthia,' he said.

IT WAS YES AND THEN IT WAS NO, it was up and then it was down.

He thought of calling Stuart, his former bishop, oldest friend, and fellow seminarian, but a kind of torpor prevailed. Why?

To relieve the constriction in his chest, he prayed for Henry

Talbot and Henry Winchester, two Henrys needy in matters more desperate than his own.

And why couldn't he firmly grasp the idea of returning to Lord's Chapel and logically examine it? The notion seemed a wisp, a snowflake disappearing on the upturned palm.

He needed the solemn confines of a monk's cell; he needed air and open space.

'. . . AND UNDER THE SHADOW of your wings I will rejoice,' he prayed from the psalm. 'My soul clings to you, / Your right hand holds me fast . . .'

Perhaps more than the decision itself, he wanted light in his darkened mind, something luminous to see by.

While shaving, he had an impulse toward the ridiculous. He scarcely ever did anything ridiculous.

Puny's ten-month-old twin boys were in the kitchen in their bouncing chairs, each with a pacifier. He was not a fan of the pacifier but it would be politically incorrect to express that opinion in his own household.

'Tommy,' he said, standing near the door while Puny swept the side porch. 'What do you think?'

Tommy burst into tears, the pacifier fell to the floor; Violet pounced and skittered it to the corner of the room.

Puny opened the door a crack. 'What's goin' on in there?'

'I asked Tommy a question and he started crying. Sorry.'

'Could you please pick 'im up? I got to get these steps cleaned off, you wouldn' believe th' raccoon poop out here.' She closed the door.

He picked up Tommy, all eighteen pounds, jiggled him as he had jiggled Puny's first set of twins, Sissy and Sassy. Jiggling was good—Tommy stopped crying.

Puny opened the door again. 'What did you ask 'im?'

'Oh, nothing much. He's fine now.'

She closed the door; he put Tommy in the chair, went after the pacifier, washed it under the hot water tap, and stuck it back where it belonged.

Timmy, his very own namesake, looked up at him with Carolina-blue eyes.

'What do you think, Timmy?'

Timmy took the pacifier from his mouth, laughed, and handed it over.

'Thanks for sharing,' he said. 'Maybe later.'

Out of the mouths of babes, so to speak. He kissed both boys on the tops of their heads.

THE WIND WAS UP, and bitter; the twelve o'clock news had called this the coldest September since 1972.

He was the Michelin man in long-sleeve knit shirt, clerical collar, crew-neck sweater, vest, wool scarf, flannel-lined jacket, long socks, corduroys, and gloves.

On his way to lunch, he peered through the window at Happy Endings. The dark interior gave him a sinking feeling. He noticed the wind hammering a sign on the door.

Open Wednesday and Thursday

Ten to six

Until further notice

Thank you for your patience

Beneath the text, someone had written in red ink: *Pray for Hope!*

'WANDA'S FEEL GOOD CAFÉ' was rendered in dark green paint on a white background; the whatchamacallit over the E in CAFÉ was a bold slash of red.

He recognized the men on the scaffolding, one without a jacket. 'Hey, Luke, you'll be a popsicle. What are you doing up there in this cold?'

'Need th' money, Father. Pizza, beer, and a month's rent.'

'No beer, no pizza,' hollered Jeff, 'but a whole bunch of baby diapers and a tank of oil. We're just gettin' it screwed into th' brick and we're out of here.'

'You turned it around mighty fast,' he called up.

'Gotta do what it takes. My baby's sick. Pray for us.'

'Consider it done.'

Luke spit off the side of the scaffolding. 'Don't leave me out, Preacher.'

'Don't worry, you're in. God be with you.'

And there was Hessie Mayhew with a point-and-shoot, a notebook protruding from her coat pocket.

'Hessie! How are you?'

She leaned back, shooting skyward at the sign. 'Whoever came up with this wacko name . . .'

'Your boss came up with it.'

'How was Ireland?'

'Green,' he said.

'Well, stand over there under th' sign and let me get a shot. Th' sign's so high up, I have to either shoot from across the street to get you both in, or stand here and get th' sign and just your head.'

'Get Wanda to stand out here, it's her sign.'

'She already stood out here for about two seconds. She was nothing but a blur, the lunch crowd was coming in.'

'So get J.C. to stand under the sign, he likes to get his picture in the paper.'

'He already stood under the sign. But the painters got in front of the F an' th' G, so I told 'em to move and they ended up in front of the W an' th' L.'

'I'd keep it simple and just shoot the sign,' he said, making for the door. 'Tell the guys to squat down.'

WANDA'S FEEL GOOD felt plenty good. Smelled good, too. Glad to be here, he peeled off gloves, scarf, jacket.

The place was packed. He stashed his gear on top of other gear on the coat rack and headed for their table.

'Mule?'

Mule grinned. 'Th' Miami look.'

'Why?'

'I'm tryin' to help Shirlene and Fancy get a little action goin'.'

He pulled out his chair, dumbfounded. Though Mule looked ridiculous in a short-sleeve Hawaiian shirt, he also looked ten years younger, albeit a funny color.

J.C. took a swig of coffee. 'Real estate's so slow he's gone to freezin' his ass as a sandwich board for a beauty shop.'

'Y'all are pasty,' said Mule, giving them the eye. 'Why be pasty when you could look like you've been somewhere and seen a little sunshine?'

'I have been somewhere,' he said, though he hadn't seen much sunshine.

J.C. ripped a paper napkin from the metal holder. 'Wait'll you hear what it costs to get yourself sprayed.'

'It's not about money,' said Mule, 'it's about lookin' good. When you look good, you feel good, and when you feel good, you, ah, look good.'

'Where's he getting this stuff?' he asked J.C.

'From literature that comes with th' spray tan deal.'

Wanda whipped around with the coffeepot.

'Is that you, Mr. Skinner?'

'It's me, all right.'

'Just back from the Sunshine State?'

'Just back from A Cut Above,' said Mule, 'where they have the amazing, not to mention revolutionary, spray tan technology. Why be pasty when you can be tan?'

'It is *not* the season yet for people to be tan,' said Wanda. 'We get tan in summer when we garden and play golf. If this weather keeps up, we will have snow in here before the leaves turn.'

'So you garden?' said Mule. 'And play golf?'

'I kill plants and can't hit a ball. I was usin' a general example.'

'So,' said Mule, 'are you goin' to do a little something to, you know, live up to your new name? To, like, make people feel good?'

'How people feel is their business, not mine. If they like to feel good, fine. If they don't, fine. I'm here to give you a decent cup of joe and a great hamburger.'

He raised his hand. 'I'll have the hamburger.'

'Same here,' said J.C.

'Okay, that's what I'm havin',' said Mule. 'All th' way, but hold th' onions.'

'All the way *comes* with onions,' said Wanda.

'Right, but hold 'em.'

Wanda rolled her eyes. 'I was warned.'

'Who warned you?' asked J.C.

'The poor woman who owned th' place before I bought it. She said th' turkeys will make you crazy.'

'Double fries on th' side,' said J.C. 'And double aioli.'

'And you, Father?'

'Pickle. No fries.'

'Lovely,' said Wanda. 'One more thing, Mr. Skinner. We're *supposed* to be pasty in autumn, that's what autumn is *for*, to rest our faces from the harmful rays of the sun.'

Wanda moved on.

'She has not rested her face in a coon's age, I can tell you that,' said Mule.

J.C. stared into his empty coffee mug. 'What ever happened to the waitress with a heart of gold?'

'Lunch is on me,' said Mule, waving the chit.

'Go home and get some clothes on, buddyroe.' He slapped Mule on the back as they left the café.

'And wash that stuff off!' said J.C.

'Won't wash off, that's how you get your money's worth. It has to wear off.' Mule zipped his fleece-lined jacket, grinned, headed to his vehicle. 'I don't care what you turkeys say,' he hollered from the curb. 'I'm tan, you're pasty.'

'You're goin' to like Thursday's main feature,' said J.C.

Wind rattled the scaffolding, hammered them as they walked across Main.

'Don't count on it.'

'You're goin' to like it big time. It was Vanita's idea. She's a sharp little writer. Adele's making news next week. Front page, four-color. Don't miss it.'

'Great. Can you talk about it?'

'I could, but then it wouldn't be news.'

He was impressed that the *Muse* editor never scooped himself.

'So,' said J.C., stopping off at the bank, 'you still don't want to hear what's goin' on at Lord's Chapel?'

'Out of my precinct.'

'Talbot has a habit, you know. Women. Paid.'

'Enough,' he said, meaning it.

Since he'd sat in a car most of yesterday and running today was not going to happen, he would compromise with a power walk up Lilac, and around the block to home.

Abe Edelman, owner of Village Shoes, peered out the window and threw up his hand.

The marching band . . .

'Hey, buddy.' He kept going, breathing hard.

'What's with the Mustang?' said Dooley.

'Carburetor, heater, radiator, clutch.'

'Don't get another old car.'

'Right,' he said. 'Let's get a new one. What do you think?'

'BMW X1.'

'You're lookin' for something hot to drive when you come home.'

Dooley's cackling laugh.

'What else do you have in mind?'

'You'd like a Jeep.'

'I don't need to go off-road or splash through mud puddles.'

'What are you doing? Running?'

'Walking.'

'So you want a boring vehicle?'

No, he didn't want boring; life was short and getting shorter.

'What's the least boring vehicle to get me to Wesley, and down the mountain on the rare occasion, and over town in bad weather?'

'A Mini Cooper, Dad. Clubman hatchback. Plenty of room for Barnabas. Twenty-seven miles per gallon around town, thirty-five on the highway when you come to see me in Athens. Cynthia would love it.'

'Very small,' he said, thinking of eighteen-wheelers, propane tankers . . .

'You don't need big to run to Wesley.'

'What about emissions? Maybe a Prius . . .' He wouldn't mention the meeting with the bishop, not now.

'Mini Cooper, Dad. I'll go online and shoot you some info.'

'I don't know.' His head was spinning, he was freezing.

'Trust me,' said Dooley.

Someone had stopped by Happy Endings since he'd passed earlier. Strips of paper were taped to the window. Where no tape secured the paper, the wind passed beneath; hand-printed words shuddered and danced.

We read to know we are not alone. CS Lewis

Children are made readers on the laps of their parents. Emilie Buchwald

Everywhere I have sought peace and not found it, except in a corner with a book. Thos à Kempis

Pray for Hope!

. . .

HE WANTED TO BE A SHEPHERD; he wanted to serve others. He was hardwired for that—that would never change—and here was his opportunity. Why was he wrestling with it?

Timmy had laughed and handed over the pacifier—a sacrifice, the gift of himself to the stressed-out bald guy with the worried look on his face.

He needed to do that—hand it all over. Right away. Now.

How long had it been since he'd sat on the stone wall above the valley and prayed through a sunset? It seemed years.

'AN AMAZING THING HAPPENED,' said his wife, putting eggs in the fridge.

'Tell me.'

'Irene McGraw wants to give us those wonderful portraits, all five, for the hospital auction in June. She says they make her sad, she needs to let them go.'

'This is hardly an art-buying community,' he said.

'We'll have to depend on the Florida crowd, bless their hearts.'

The Florida crowd had bailed them out more than once—a new furnace for Lord's Chapel being one example. As for donating the Mustang, he didn't know how that would fly in view of the diagnostic. 'Are those self-portraits of her as a child?'

'She says the self-portraits are in the eyes of the subject.'

'Who's the subject?'

'She didn't say, she didn't seem eager to talk about it. If I were a dealer, I'd put quite a price on them, but of course she doesn't have a name in the art world.'

She poured two glasses of juice, passed one to him. 'She really shouldn't donate them, they seem so personal to her.'

'A great start for the auction,' he said. 'Well done. What's the plan for the campaign?'

'A new wing.'

'Wow.'

'We're going for a new wing with twenty more beds, which will make forty-five.'

His wife was beaming. 'I'm believing we can auction Irene's paintings for big money, plus raise enough to meet the goal.'

Should he pitch in and give a hand? He'd been a donor for twenty years, had even been asked to serve as the director at one time. It was his favorite charity, hands down, but his mother's money was running out and his gifts in the future would be comparatively modest. After years of giving, he was, in effect, spent. He couldn't think about it now.

She was talking hospital business while searching his face for some clue to his thinking about yesterday. But he had no thinking to speak of.

'I'll certainly bid on one,' she said.

DRIVING HOME from the hair salon in Wesley, Esther Cunningham could see that the sunset would be a whopper. She didn't usually notice such things—that was the kind of stuff Ray got a kick out of. Excited as a kid, he'd say, Look at that sunset, Honey Bun! Or, Hey, Doll Face, get a load of that apple tree in bloom! Or, How about that rock over yonder, see th' nose an' all, it looks just like Muhammad Ali.

If she stared herself blind, she could not see Muhammad

Ali, but maybe Teddy Roosevelt if she strained herself. And clouds—Ray loved to study clouds. He could see such as Ben Hur driving the chariot behind a gazillion horses, and pigs, and angels, and somebody on a unicycle, and a woman looking at herself in a mirror.

Speaking of which, she pulled down the sun visor and looked in the mirror. She had requested a style like the Queen always wore—a curl on either side of her forehead, with no part. Twice she had said, *No part.* But plain as day, in a straight shot down the middle, there was a part.

She made a left at Lilac and was putting on the turn signal for Church Hill when she spotted Father Tim walking up Lilac, quick as a field hare. What was he doing out this time of day at his age, and in this raw cold, plus walking uphill so fast? She didn't believe in walking uphill if it could be avoided.

She remembered how he once swore off driving a car. He had hoofed it for seven or eight years, just gave up driving altogether, for Lent or Advent or some such. Baptists weren't required to keep up with the church calendar, which was dandy with her. Easter was Easter and Christmas was Christmas, why confuse people with all those other holidays deeply unknown to the ordinary person, like sitting around in a dark sanctuary with no flowers on the altar, not even any candles burning, the way the crowd at Lord's Chapel did at Advent, or was it Lent?

At least she'd gotten her hair done before the meeting with Andrew Gregory tomorrow. If the matter of age came up, she had a bulletproof vest, namely a list from the Internet that said, in part, 'At one hundred, Grandma Moses was still painting. At eighty-five, Coco Chanel headed up a design firm in Paris, France. At eighty-nine, Albert Schweitzer was running a hospital in Africa.' She was going into that meeting like Sherman took Atlanta, while Ray sat in the car and prayed.

AS HE CRESTED THE HILL, there were the blue-dark mountains and the hanging orb above. Jupiter was out, or maybe Saturn, he wasn't so good with planets.

He was infernally pestered by the image of the empty slot in the rack. How had Sammy come in? They locked their doors now, it was a fact of life since three robberies in a neighborhood behind the hospital.

Sammy needed a lot of help, probably beyond anything he and Cynthia could give. Not least, he needed hard and satisfying work that wore deeply on the muscles and released the sleep-inducing cytokines currently making news. Hard work and hard rest may not solve everything, but maybe they could help. Harley's lawn jobs around town were already drying up, leaving Sammy way too much time and energy.

He would immediately put Sammy on the Lord's Chapel rose garden, which he heard was sorely neglected—out of sight, out of mind was the problem, it was too hidden. Maybe the nearly three dozen bushes should be moved to the lawn facing Main Street where more people could enjoy them. Right there was a task for a small army, with maybe a little something for Coot Hendrick to get at with rake and hoe.

He sat on the stone wall, barely cognizant of the panorama of the evening sky.

The hedge would be another project—the cleanup, pruning, and mulching would take a minimum of two days for Sammy, probably three—and the birdbaths would need scrubbing out. Sammy would take pride in all that. If they could make it happen before late October when Dooley came home . . .

As for the old Sunday school, circa 1916 or thereabouts, it was crammed to the rafters with decrepit pews, battered hymnals, moth-eaten banners—the detritus that comes from being an ecclesial storage unit. The youth group—that was the ticket—they could spend a few days cleaning it out and top things off with a yard sale. Of course, he'd heard the youth group was dwindling, but he would cross that bridge when he came to it.

Then there was the issue of someone to assist him in the church office. Who, he had no clue; five-plus years is a long time to be off any turf, but Bill Swanson would know. Emma would be after him like a beagle after a fox, but he couldn't do that again. Absolutely not. Someone young, upbeat, *cheerful* . . .

He felt the cold of the stone seeping into his very marrow—his body had been present on the wall for twenty minutes according to the illuminated face of his watch, but his mind had been down there—ripping out briars, fertilizing roses, working with the youth group as he'd done so happily in years past. And yet, when he tried to see himself in the pulpit at Lord's Chapel, he could not.

The many petitions of his heart and Cynthia's would serve, but in the end, one supplication alone was equipped with all that pleases God.

He prayed the prayer that never fails, then made his way home at a trot, eager to see the light in their window and feel the consolation of a fire.

'I NEED TO TALK, SON. Is this a good time?'

'Sure. What's up?'

He walked around the room in robe and pajamas, the cell phone pressed to his ear. 'This is confidential.'

'Got it.'

'I've been asked to come back to Lord's Chapel. For an indefinite period. Until they find a new priest.'

'Are you thinking about it?'

'Constantly. I just don't know what to think.'

'I hear something in your voice. What's th' deal?'

'Strictly for your ears and none other. Father Talbot is leaving the priesthood and divorcing his wife. There'll be a good bit of outrage and instability in his wake.' Dooley knew about rage and instability.

He was pleased that Dooley took his time with this.

'That would be a really hard thing to take on,' said Dooley. 'Why would you want to do it?'

'I need to make a decision, fast. Will you pray?'

'I will. For sure.'

When he hung up, he realized he hadn't answered Dooley's question—a question he hadn't honestly asked himself.

He slipped the cell phone into his robe pocket. Why would he want to do it?

The thought that followed literally took his breath away.

He didn't want to do it.

Not at all.

Chapter
Ten

That is a good book which is opened with expectation and closed with profit.—Amos Bronson Alcott

A good book has no ending.—RD Cumming

He read the quotes that had gone up, and with some satisfaction taped his own contribution to the glass:

wear the old coat and buy the new book {Austin Phelps

There. A community billboard of sorts.

'Lord,' he prayed, 'make me a blessing to someone today.' That had been his mantra in years past when unlocking the door to the church office. He jiggled the key the way Hope had instructed. Not working. 'It's a very old lock,' she'd said. 'I've grown to like it.' Hope was a romantic, bless her heart.

More jiggling.

'Father, up to your old tricks?' The owner of Village Shoes was unlocking his shop next door.

'Abe! Which old tricks would that be?'

'Breaking and entering!'

'Ha. Right. I'm working here today, giving Hope a hand. Drop over for a cup of coffee if you get a chance.'

'Will do. We'll be proud to have you on the street. That lock is a coronary.'

The key found the sweet spot, the lock gave forth a soft click, the door opened.

Books! He could smell them. After being cooped up all night, they were crazy to give out their pulpy aromas.

As his dog sniffed about for the cat, he hurried to the finicky thermostat and cranked the heat up according to instructions.

Out of Dooley's old yellow backpack he unloaded water bowl, food bowl, kibbles, coffee beans, a wrapped sandwich, an apple, an orange, a roll of toilet paper which Hope confessed was currently in short supply at Happy Endings, and a coffee mug printed with, *I don't have a short attention span, I just . . . oh, look! A squirrel!*

He stooped to the coffeemaker and studied it, frowning. With some misgiving, he dumped the specified quantity of beans into the grinder bin and hit On. Nothing happened. He flipped the switch to Off, then again to On. Zero.

Nothing worked these days. You could not gain entry into packaging of any kind, nor could you depend on *On* or even *Off* to mean what they promised. It was a black mark against society in general.

He was considering a dash to the Feel Good when he spied a note pinned to the corkboard.

> *Fr T, coffee machine unplugged. Plenty of change*
> *in drawer. Yesterday's sales great. U R very sweet to*
> *do this. Call if U need me. # on door at wall phone.*
> *Thnx for making deposit by five.*
> *Marcie*

He watched the beans grinding with industrial vigor as he filled the water bowl for Barnabas. The antique furnace was heaving around down there; a giant throbbing could be felt in the floorboards. He flipped a couple of wall switches—Beethoven's Ninth, third movement, was succeeded by a constellation of reading lamps lighting the room.

And there went the *Muse* truck up the street and the sound of this week's edition smacking the front door. No way would he fetch it in and trouble his head—he would depend on the greater diversion of the *Times*, albeit last Sunday's edition.

He'd spent Wednesday doing almost nothing, trying not to feel guilty about his decision. He'd taken it as a day to reflect and pray, to know whether the peace he felt about declining was real. And yes, thus far it was real.

Unfortunately, he couldn't put a shine on the consequences. When the bishop's offer came to be public knowledge, as it assuredly would, some might see his refusal as a shirking of duty. A few would be scornful, some would feel betrayed, a handful would understand, and the rest wouldn't care.

He was frankly surprised by his decision—but profoundly relieved. Relieved, for one thing, because it hadn't actually been his decision. El Shaddai had spoken in that way which is not speaking, to a confused cleric vested in robe and pajamas by his home fire.

In truth, he should ring Asheville now, before the shop opened and while his head was still relatively unfrayed. He crossed himself, a schoolboy sent up the hall to the headmaster.

The pleasant but brief conversation was over before he quite realized it. He stood in the middle of the room, dazed.

Bishop Martin had been disappointed though not completely surprised, and would ring up at once the Colorado mountain-climbing priest known to be 'fond of the guitar in the early service.' They confirmed their meeting in the vestry at Lord's Chapel a half hour before the eleven o'clock on the seventh.

'And Timothy,' the bishop said at the end, 'I have every confidence in your decision.'

It was as if he were coming back from a kind of death, and hearing the familiar Ninth for the first time.

Under the watchful gaze of his dog, he picked up a coffee spoon and with something like astonished joy, conducted the remainder of the sublime third movement.

THE BELL JANGLING ON THE DOOR. Ten after ten. He was ready.

'*Esther?*' Good Lord!

'It's me,' said Esther Bolick, thumping a Sweet Stuff bag onto the sales counter. 'The *new* me.'

'I liked the old you.'

'Old? I'm runnin' from that word doin' eighty miles an hour.'

'But a tan? I've never seen you with a tan.'

'I have never been tan, and will never be tan again. I thought, what the heck, you and Cynthia paid to get my hair dyed, why not give that poor child a break and get sprayed?'

'How was it?'

'Hosed down like a squash plant, arms an' legs everywhicha-way. What do you think about my hair?'

She twirled around, a bit unsteady.

'I like it. That's the ticket. You look younger by ten years.'

'I thought I'd never get out of there, Fancy Skinner drives

me crazy. I brought you something to say thanks for your nice gift. It was wonderful of y'all to do that.'

She patted his hand, pushed the bag to him. For some reason he couldn't understand, Esther Bolick didn't get it that sweets were verboten where he was concerned. When news of his diabetes swept through the parish like a brush fire, she delivered him a full-blown two-layer OMC as a consolation. He'd put it in the fridge and slammed the door and leaned against it as if the thing might break out of there and have its way with him. Which of course it did. He had been in the hospital a mere nine days.

'You wouldn't believe what they charge for a single slice,' she said. 'Go ahead, I brought you a fork.'

She thrust her hand into her coat pocket and handed over a sterling dessert fork loosely wrapped in a paper napkin.

'Do you think I should?'

'Why shouldn't you?'

'Well, I mean, you know—*diabetes.*'

'Oh, pshaw,' she said, bored by this confession. 'Just take one bite, and I'll finish it.'

'Deal,' he said, digging in.

'So?' she said, giving him a fierce look.

'It's good. It's really good.'

'But?' She arched an eyebrow.

'But not as good as yours, Esther, and you can take that to the bank.'

'Ha!' she said. 'You have not lost your silver tongue, Father. And look at this.'

She whipped a piece of paper from her handbag, showed it to him up close. 'My first check.'

'Wow.'

'Wow is right, they did a big wedding last Saturday at Linville. Th' OMC was forty-two inches high and seven layers, I took a picture.'

'Forty-two inches.' He marveled. 'Seven layers!'

'How 'bout them apples?'

'Gene would be thrilled. So you think you're going to like being retired from the OMC?'

'I didn't say that,' she snapped. She grabbed the fork, wiped it with the napkin, dug in. 'Uh-huh. I was afraid of somethin' like this. A little too sweet. She deviated from th' recipe.'

'Are you sure?' He felt the need to protect Winnie.

'She's not supposed to deviate from th' recipe, Father. It's in th' letter of agreement.' She waggled the fork at him. 'A letter of agreement is just that—two people *agreeing.* I don't suppose you have a cup of coffee—a cup of coffee would certainly improve th' taste.'

'Right this way,' he said.

First Things First!!!!
A Belated Tribute to
Miss Sadie Baxter

---

by VANITA BENTLEY

My husband says I have never before publicly (much less privately) admitted to being wrong, but I am doing it here and proud to say What was I thinking?

I jumped the gun on trying to find a living lead-ing citizen when we ha=ve a dead deceased leading citizen who needs to be recognized FIRST!!!! Miss Sadie Baxter bless her heart, who left us eight years ago in June (Mr. Hogan pls check me on this) was as generous a benefactor as any lttle town could ever hope to have.

From her house on the ridge above Main Street Miss Baxter is said to have rocked in her rocker and prayed for this town and the little cars and people she could see from up there moving around on the streets below. Have you ever heard anything so sweet as that? I personally have not.

So what I am proposing is that we name Miss Sadie Baxter who never married but gave her ALL to friends and neighbors, is that we name her Mitford's LEADING CITIZEN even though she is crossed over and put a plaque in the town museum so we can always remember where these great gifts came from:

1. Hope House, our state of the art nursing facility for people of all races, colors, religions, walks of life and you name it

2. Baxter Park between Main and Churchill— Little Mitford Creek runs through it!! Have you ever been to Baxter Park? You should GO!! It is so pretty and shady. Remember to pick up your trash and do not park in there at night as the MPD often checks it out.

3. The orchards of Baxter apples that you and I pick from every fall and make apple butter or have somebody make for us is now owned by Mayor Gregory who is carrying on the tradition of

letting townspeople pick there for free. But once again: PICK UP YOUR TRASH!!!! And thank you Mayor Gregory!!

4. Thirteen rooms at Childrens Hospital in Wesley were given by Miss Sadie who said it was one for each apostle plus One room in honor of her dear lifelong friend Louella Baxter Marshall a resident at our own beautiful Hope House. Have you ever been to Hope House? You should go and take the children and sing hymns and kiss the elderly (though not in flu season)—they would LOVE it and so would YOU!!!!

5. The slate roof on the historic Lord's Chapel (her father gave the whole church in nineteen hundred and something—Mr. Hogan w eigh in on the exact date pls)

The plaque will be written by Fr Timothy Kavanagh her dear friend and priest who will say all the wonderful things on the plaque that you and I don't know how to say.

So I hope you will get behind this and go see the plaque at our Town Museum any time after November 1, admission to students and senior citizens $2. $4 to everybody else opposite the monument. Be sure and play the jukebox, all proceeds go to the new Guttering Project.

P. S. We did receive 14 votes for Father Tim as Leading Citizen—7 for Winnie Ivey who gives bakery goods to the needy—4 for Wanda Basinger who has given us such a great place to have a nice lunch (a big YUM on the fries)—2 for Coot Hendrik who is a town fixture and 1 for me, I am so HONORED to be included—thank you!!

AT ELEVEN-THIRTY, he had $32.67 in the till.

J.C. swung in with his briefcase, deposited it on the sales counter. 'So what do you think of today's lead?'

'Very good, excellent. It's about time we recognized all she did for us. I agree one hundred percent. Why didn't somebody tell me I'm writing the plaque?'

'You didn't ask,' said J.C.

'Buy a book.'

'I don't have time to read.'

'Buy a book anyway. We need the money.'

'What should I buy?'

'Something by Churchill. Or David McCullough. Or a book of poetry—that would give you a good worming.'

Or, he wanted to say, how about a book on whacking the exclamation mark, getting to know the comma, giving the quote mark a try?

'I'll pop your briefcase under the counter and you can have at it. Free coffee to your left.'

'I'm in,' said J.C.

'DON'T TRY TO SELL ME A BOOK, Father, I'm not here to buy a book, I'm here to read my needlepoint magazine in peace and drink somebody else's coffee and try to get my nerves settled. Think "freeload" when you see me comin'.'

Winnie Kendall had a frazzled look.

'We have never had such a run on fig newtons, I don't understand it, hardly anybody eats Fig Newtons anymore, but sixteen dozen down th' hatch since Monday, we think it's somethin' goin' on at th' college in Wesley. An' th' OMC, oh, my Lord, it is sailin' out of there by th' slice *an'* whole, 'cause everybody wants to see if I got it right, an' some don't mind tellin' me I didn't even though I go exactly by the recipe. So Thomas said, "For th' Lord's sake, Winnie, go up to th' bookstore for a while and I'll handle things down here."'

'God love 'er, Hope has let me do this little trick for three years—it is a lifesaver.'

'Make yourself at home,' he said. 'Take a chair, any chair.'

'I like th' one in th' Poetry section. Hardly anybody ever wanders back there.'

'Ah, but there's a poetry renaissance coming, I hear. A slender volume recently hit the *Times*' bestseller list. A first!'

'Oh, boy,' said Winnie, giving him a wink. 'That'll run me over to Ancient Greek History for sure.'

HE WAS READING the *Muse* when the best-looking woman in town stopped by.

'Listen to this,' he said. '"Make your magnolia leaves shine! Just rub on any cooking oil and voila! Dry, dusty leaves in indoor arrangements look brand-new." Did you know this?'

His wife handed over a box of raisins. 'We don't have any magnolia leaves in indoor arrangements.'

'Well,' he said, 'in case we ever do.'

. . .

He rang Jeb Adderholt.

'Better let me get it back to you, Father. Wouldn't want you on th' road in it.'

'But you shouldn't be driving it, either.'

'Nossir, we'll tow it over.'

'Put it in the garage next to my wife's car,' he said. 'Back it in for me, if you would.'

Red Mustang turns into white elephant.

No customers were around when the mayor came in, just Winnie reading the bedraggled Sunday *Times* in her hideout.

Andrew sat on the stool in front of the sales counter. 'This is confidential, Father. Anyone about?'

'Someone's in the Poetry section,' he said. 'You might keep your voice down.'

He had never admitted to anyone, including Cynthia, that there had been talk of Tim Kavanagh running for mayor. Esther and Andrew had both suggested it in years past and J.C. and Mule had supported the notion.

But all that time and tribulation and weighing of issues— and no vote? The mayor was but a ceremonial head. As for the pay—last time he heard, it was $200 a month, which was probably commensurate with the weight of the issues involved.

The toughest call the council had faced in the last couple of years was whether to allow dogs in Baxter Park. Why, dogs had visited Baxter Park for as long as he could remember— and now they could enjoy it legally, always a good thing.

Even if he could get elected, it wasn't as if it were a lifetime commitment. Two years and you were done, unless, of course, you ran and were elected again. He could do two years. Maybe he

could make a difference, though things around town seemed
perfectly fine to him. As for the notion of increasing tourism, it
was unquestionably a nonpolluting way of improving the economy, and most tourists were harmless, anyway. All they wanted
was to get out of the heat, have a nice lunch, take up the parking
spaces, and go home until the following summer.

'Esther Cunningham was in to see me,' said the mayor.

'Wanting her old job back!' he said.

'How did you know?'

'I was kidding. But you're serious?'

'Not entirely. It's more like she wants to give me input on
how to handle the job in general and hammer the merchants
in particular. A kind of Mafia arrangement in which she's the
godfather, and I'm the capo who dunks 'em in concrete and
drops 'em in the river.'

'Esther, Esther,' he said.

'She's legendary, of course, and frankly, I wouldn't be surprised if she runs again. How old is she, anyway?'

'Seventysomething is my guess. Maybe more.'

'If she tosses in her hat,' said Andrew, 'she'll have no opposition from me. I will not run against Hannibal and his elephants.'

'Good thinking.'

'But that's not why I stepped over to see you. I'd like to ask
you to do something important.'

So much for the mayor business; this would probably be the
town council pitch. Which meant spending money out of
pocket, giving talks, shaking hands, kissing babies, and trying
to wither the opponents, if there were any. He was glad he'd
worn his best jacket; this was serious stuff.

'This is a big one,' said Andrew. 'We like to work well in advance on this one.'

The mayor was beaming. 'I'm asking you to be grand marshal of the Independence Day parade next July. You'd be driving Miss Sadie's '58 Plymouth Belvedere. It looks like it just rolled off the showroom floor.'

There was something outright consoling about the especially vigorous handshake.

'M' NAME'S IN TODAY'S PAPER.'

At one-thirty, the ravenous bookstore clerk was eating his sandwich and Coot Hendrik was wearing a grin that Uncle Billy would have said 'like to busted his face open.'

'You were one of only four people who got a vote.'

'Five,' said Coot. 'Down at th' café, they said it was five people.'

'Correct, yes. Five.'

'I got m' name in th' paper last week, too.'

'You did, I remember.'

Coot was visibly moved by two such public attentions, and didn't say anything for a time.

'You could read this 'un to me, if you wouldn't object. They read it out too fast at th' café, I could listen to it ag'in.'

He turned to the front page, scanned the piece, and did as directed. 'Four votes for Wanda Basinger who has given us such a great place to have lunch, and two . . . for Coot Hendrik . . . who is a town fixture.'

Coot looked deeply into his coffee cup. 'I was wonderin'— what exactly is a town *fixture*?'

'Let's step over there,' he said, heading for the store diction-ary. He thumbed through to *F*, to *Fi*.

'You are a town fixture because you . . .' He ran his forefin-ger slowly beneath the definition as Coot looked on. '. . . are invariably present *in* and long associated *with* this town.'

Coot nodded, grew thoughtful. ''At means you're a town fixture, too.'

'I certainly hope so,' he said. 'Come to think of it, your name is in this book.'

'They ain't no way.'

He thumbed back to C and ahead to *Co*.

'Right here. *Coot*. Plain as day.'

Coot stooped, had a close look. 'How'd it git in here?'

'It's the name of . . . "an aquatic, slow-flying, slate-colored bird of the rail family, resembling a duck."'

Coot blinked. 'Are they any way I could borry this book?'

'Not this book. But I might have a dictionary in paperback.'

The chances were better than good that Coot couldn't read. How would you go about teaching a full-grown adult to read? Maybe there was a book about that around here . . .

ESTHER CUNNINGHAM WAS PEERING in the display win-dow; he could see her but she didn't see him. Actually, her attention was riveted on the quotes taped to the glass; he saw her mouth moving as she read them one by one.

The bell jangled.

'Esther!'

She was the *Queen Mary* sailing into Boston Harbor, flags flying. 'I hear you're gainfully employed again,' she said.

'No rest for the wicked, an' th' righteous don't need none.' Uncle Billy had authored that particular quote.

'Was it your idea to tape that stuff on th' window?'

'I can't really take credit for that.'

'Credit? There'd be no credit to take for postin' litter that's goin' to fall in the street and blow around 'til th' cows come home.'

'It makes good reading,' he said.

'That may well be, but such clutter on a public display window is not a good model for other merchants. As I recall, I passed a regulation on that very thing. Do you, Father, of all people, want to set a bad example for Main Street? To have every Tom, Dick, and Harry litterin' their windows with fingerprints and gummy tape?'

This was a runaway horse. 'How about buying a book today?' His sales techniques, so far, were pretty limited.

'A book.' Esther looked at him as if from the depths of a coma.

'Pick any title beginning with S and get fifteen percent off. Maybe a picture book for your grandchildren. The last I heard there were twenty-one of them, but that was a while back. What's the latest count?'

'Twenty-four!' she said. 'And more on th' way. You know th' Cunninghams carry out th' biblical injunction to go forth and multiply.'

'I know that, yes.'

'You want to see pictures?' She gouged in her handbag and pulled forth a four-by-six-inch album in the accordion format.

'Do I want to see pictures? Esther, Esther, is the Pope Catholic?'

. . .

BEFORE HE TALKED TO SAMMY, he would talk to Harley. If Sammy kept going like this, he would end up in jail—that simple.

At two-fifteen, voices on the sidewalk. The door swung open, the bell jangled, and in swarmed Unbounded Clamor and Delight, with a couple of teachers in tow. It was story time for Mitford's third grade.

'My name is Hastings. I would like to buy a book, please.' A boy peered at him from just below the top of the sales counter.

'How do you do, Hastings?'

'Very well, sir.'

'What book will you be buying?'

'I don't know. But I have money. I saved it just for a book.'

'Come with me,' he said. He was playing this by ear. He had no idea what the bestsellers were, or what this demographic or that might be reading. It was the blind leading the blind.

The Call of the Wild—he had loved that as a boy. But it was a tearing, violent thing.

He found Miss Mooney squinting into the pages of a slender volume. 'What do you think for young Hastings?' he said. The boy walked ahead and joined a couple of classmates.

'He's gaining on Dickens. But for now, maybe *Around the World in Eighty Days*?'

'How old is he?'

'Nine,' she said, 'but small for his age. Very bright.' She smiled. 'Most of his body weight is constituted by his brain.'

'Have you ever taught anyone to read, Miss Mooney?'

'All the time,' she said, and proud of it.

'An adult?'

'Never.'

'Do you know anyone who might teach an adult to read? For pay, of course.'

'I would be interested,' she said, 'considering I have two girls to put through school.'

Hastings came and tugged at his sleeve. 'Excuse me, are we looking for my book?'

'Absolutely. But help me out here. Is there something you might especially enjoy?'

'Um. Maybe Mr. Wordsworth,' said Hastings. 'I've heard he can be a very good read.'

He turned away for a moment, smacked by the beauty of complete surprise.

'WE CAN'T THANK YOU ENOUGH,' said Scott Murphy. His therapy dogs, Luke and Lizzie, panted at the chaplain's feet. 'What can we ever do for you, Father?'

If there was a trait he especially admired, it was that of being earnest. Hope's good-looking husband was earnest in spades.

'I needed Happy Endings for my own benefit. God made a way for all of us in this—three birds with one stone. I'm the grateful party. How is she?'

'Depressed.'

'Is she ready for a visitor?'

'You,' he said. 'But not yet.' Scott took out his billfold. 'I'd like to buy a book.'

There was the Murphy smile he always enjoyed. 'And what book might that be?'

'A book for you to give someone who needs it. I don't know.'

'Intriguing. Paper or hardcover?'

'Hardcover.'

'Deal,' he said, taking thirty bucks from the good chaplain. 'Will you let me know when to visit? I'll take the Eucharist to her.'

'Yes, please, that would be the best medicine.' Scott's face betrayed a certain pleading.

HE TOTTED UP THE DAY'S SALES, recalling that Esther Bolick had bought an almanac at forty percent off, just for the recipes, and a calendar at fifty percent off, just for the pictures.

Esther Cunningham had bought three children's books and three birthday cards.

J.C. had bought a book on petit point for his wife, Adele, who, while lamenting her poor skills with the needle, was known to be handy with her Glock .45. J.C. had also sprung for a book of jokes which could likely be run in the *Muse* with proper credit to the person who collected them.

Seemingly without concern for the S for September discount, the mayor had stepped up to the plate and bought Ina Garten's latest and a big-ticket coffee table book by Bunny Williams, which, he said, would please his Italian wife, who was doing over their bedroom.

As for Hastings, the boy had forked out $13.95 plus tax for a paper edition of *Eighty Days*, as there was no Wordsworth to be found save in a pricey anthology.

All of which, when added to Scott's hardcover and the teachers' rather brisk business, amounted to . . .

'Two hundred and eighty-four dollars and twenty-six cents,' he reported in a call to Hope. 'Is that good?'

'That's wonderfully good!' she said.

'And my wife gave us an order for a hundred and twenty dollars for items we don't have in stock. Should I pass that list to Marcie?'

'Yes, please. This is such good news, Father; I don't know what to say. How can I ever thank you?'

'Taking care of yourself is all the thanks I need. I'll be over to see you soon, and I'll be here tomorrow, same time. Tomorrow's payday around town, we need to be open.'

Tears.

'My dog enjoys coming in. Must get down to the bank now.'

'You're a saint.'

'If you only knew,' he said.

AFTER LOCKING UP, he gave the new postings a once-over.

> *There is no frigate like a book*
> *To take us Lands away*
> *Nor any Coursers like a Page*
> *Of prancing Poetry*

—EMILY DICKINSON

Pray for Hope!

Push lawnmower for sale, good condition
$45 or make offer
-2895 ask for Lloyd

Esther was right, of course. Their community billboard would have to go. He set the backpack down and peeled the many contributions off the window and put them in his back-pack.

A little white vinegar and the *Times*' Style section and all would be well. He wondered if the *Muse* had ever run that as a helpful hint for glass-cleaning.

HIS MAMA WAS SETTIN' on the side of the bed; he could tell she had dipped a little snuff.

'Looky here,' he said. He didn't even stop to take off his jacket. 'It's my name in a book.'

'What're ye doin', gittin' y'r name ever'where all of a sudden?'

'I ain't doin' nothin', it's jis' in here. Th' preacher says always *was* in here, always gon' *be* in here.'

'Is my name in there?'

'It ain't. What my name's in here f'r is a duck. A coot is a kind of a duck I reckon you named me after.'

'I never heard of such,' she said. 'Your gran'daddy on my side, they called 'im Coot, you was named after your gran'daddy. It wadn't no duck you was named after, I can tell ye that.'

He liked being named after a duck, but he wouldn't say a word about it, nossir, that would be his secret. He took the book and set it on the mantelpiece where he could see it from nearabout anywhere in the room.

AFTER RAW COLD, the air was mild and forgiving. He walked with Harley to the west side of the house and the bench beneath the maple.

'My cue is missing. Do you know anything about it?'

'Your cue?' Then it dawned. 'Lord help!' Harley said.

'He's headed for trouble.'

'I know it, I know it, Rev'ren', I lay awake knowin' it. They was a competition over at Bud's ball hall in Wesley a few nights back, he prob'ly hated to go in there without a cue. I let 'im ride with Jupe from down at Lew Boyd's. Jupe's a good boy, he got Sammy back by eleven-thirty. He done real good in th' competition.'

'I'm going to try talking with him,' he said. 'No accusations, no guilt trip, no conflict of any kind. Just want to draw him out if I can, see if there's something we can grab on to. Just talk.'

'You'll be blue in th' face.'

Life with Sammy had been hairy at Meadowgate, but they'd worked at it and Sammy had settled down. And then came the trip to Holly Springs and Ireland, and what was gained now appeared lost.

Also lost was the chance to commandeer the Lord's Chapel landscaping project and involve Sammy. That was his only regret in saying no to Jack Martin.

RESTLESS, he went to his bookshelves in the study and searched among the Wordsworth volumes. There were many, both by and about the good poet whom he'd loved since boyhood. The paperback bought while in seminary was worn but not wasted. He stuffed it into the backpack.

He wandered up the hall, Barnabas following, to the living room they'd never lived in. Then he peered into the Ball Hall, aka dining room, where they had seldom dined.

He switched on the lights, lonesome for the clattering of balls, the cries of triumph or lamentation. It was as dead in here as a funeral parlor.

The cue rack—it was full. All cue sticks were in place.

Had he and Puny been mistaken? But he'd seen the empty slot with his own eyes and now he was seeing this. He walked to the rack and removed his cue and examined it with some absorption. No marks or damage of any kind.

He replaced the cue and hurried to the study and called next door, expecting Harley to answer.

'Yeah?'

'Sammy?'

'Yeah.'

He couldn't summon whatever it took to ask for Harley.

'Just wanted to say . . . we miss seeing you.' That had flown out, unexpected and true.

Silence.

He didn't know where to go with this.

'Well. See you soon.'

'Yeah,' said Sammy.

ABSALOM GREER HAD BEEN a mighty encouragement. The eightysomething country evangelist had never pulled punches with the town priest. They had been two respectful equals serving from the common ground of one-God-made-known-through-Jesus-Christ, and having a pretty good time of it.

The old man often spoke of the God of the Second Chance. To roughly reassemble Kafka's metaphor, God had sure used his axe to break the frozen sea inside Tim Kavanagh, who, as a priest in his forties, had not yet come to a living faith.

He'd been given the grace of the Second Chance over and over again. More than anything, he wanted Sammy to break the bread of grace.

He sat at his computer and brought up the search engine and

typed in his search. A lot of sites. He clicked on a link, it opened on exactly what he was looking for. Yes, yes, and *yes*.

Holy smoke.

In roughly ten minutes, he hit Add to Cart.

WHEN HE RETURNED Friday morning from walking Barnabas to the monument, Puny was jubilant.

'I have good news!'

'Last time you had good news, you also had bad news.'

'Same this time. But th' good news is, your cue stick's back! Jis' like it never left!'

'I know,' he said.

'You mean you found it and put it back?'

'I just walked in the room and there it was.'

'Oh,' she said, knowing. 'You want to hear th' bad news?'

'Not really.'

'I really don't want to tell you, either.'

'Maybe you shouldn't.'

'You'll be mad.'

'Puny. You've known me for ten years. How often have you seen me mad?'

'Well.'

'See there? So what's the bad news?'

'I had to run up to your room to get your laundry, and because Timmy was cryin', I jis' slung 'im on my hip an' took 'im with me, you know how I do. An' I laid him down a minute on your pillow, I didn't think you'd mind.'

'You would be right.'

'And so . . .' Puny looked at her feet.

He waited.

'And so he threw up all over your favorite pillow-w-w!' A small wail and then tears—a Puny trademark. 'I know you have trouble sleepin' and how you looked for years for that one pillow, and now . . .'

'Now?'

'Now it's really stinky.'

He flashed back to his days as a bachelor. So routine, so undisturbed by dissonance, one might have heard a pin drop in his life. Then a dog as big as a Buick started following him home, and then Dooley showed up, and then Puny came to work, and then Cynthia moved in next door, and then Puny started having twins, and that's how he ended up with a real life. And even though he loved it and wouldn't trade it for anything, he had no idea how he'd find another pillow as beloved as the one just gone south with upchuck on it.

'You're absolutely right,' he said. 'This is very bad news. On the other hand, if we consider the really bad news in the world, this news is actually pretty good.' He was suddenly laughing and didn't want to stop.

'I thought you'd be mad,' she said, looking startled.

'I'm furious,' he said, wiping his eyes.

HE STUCK THE VINEGAR in the yellow backpack. Nine-thirty. He had to get out of here. But while he was thinking of it, he went to the basement and checked the windows. They were small, but not too small. And one was unlatched.

LIGHTS, MUSIC, COFFEE.

The high-ceilinged room was originally a drugstore built and operated by the object of Miss Sadie's unrequited love, Willard Porter. For some reason, the space had a calming effect on him. Add the smell of old wood, the companionable creak of heart pine floorboards, the light through the display windows . . .

He flipped the sign around: OPEN.

He would run tomorrow and again on Monday and Wednesday. As for the Thursday/Friday bookstore schedule, he would see how things progressed.

Chapter
Eleven

While his first letter had sprouted on a dry stalk, now came the bush, ablaze with truth and ardor.

If he'd gone back to Lord's Chapel, Cynthia would have let him off the letter-writing hook. As things stood, two days at the bookstore bought no acquittal. As it happened, the idea for the second letter had struck him quite forcibly; it was the lightbulb above the head of the cartoon character.

Zealous to capture every drop from this underground aquifer, he had written like the wind and now lacked only the ending.

How convenient it would be to trust the inspiration of Duff Cooper, a crackerjack writer of the love letter, but Cooper had stolen unashamedly from Jefferson. All's fair in love, he knew that much, he could not speak for war.

He laid the pen aside and took a break, considering the many sermons he'd composed at this very hour during years of Saturdays. There had been more than a few, of course, that refused to compose—he'd gone into the pulpit on a wing and a prayer, as surprised as the congregation with what the Holy Spirit gave forth.

He was cooking tonight, and needed a few items from town, but first he would finish the letter—and seal it, so he couldn't meddle with it later.

He picked up the pen. It wasn't exactly Beethoven's address to his Immortal Beloved, but with just the right touch at the end, this would be his finest hour. He couldn't possibly top this.

FIRST HE SMELLED IT, then he saw it.

Next to the fireplace, the Old Gentleman had thrown up a fairly unrecognizable portion of . . . maybe a chipmunk.

Whatever he said caused his dog to crawl beneath the coffee table.

The miserable deed had been done, of course, when he walked Barnabas to a tried-and-true spot beyond the tulip bed. While his dog nosed around at the end of the leash, the parson had been oblivious—his mind on the afternoon light, on the chiaroscuro of the mountains, on Henry Talbot . . .

SAMMY WAS AVOIDING HIM, of course. But avoiding Sammy would lead nowhere.

Before he ran out to the Local, he popped through the hedge, crunched across the gravel, and knocked on the rectory's basement door.

'Hey, Father Tim! Come in, an' 'scuse th' mess.'

Kenny was tall and muscular, a bigger fellow than Dooley and Sammy, with a wide smile and the blue-green Barlowe eyes. Hearty, this one, without Sammy's angst or Dooley's steel resolve.

He embraced the boy. 'How's my timing?'

'Good! It's just me an' Miss Pringle's cat. Harley an' Sam's gone to Wesley for pizza.'

Kenny muted the sports channel. The place felt good, like home.

'You can sit right there,' said Kenny. 'It's th' only chair in th' house not upholstered with cat hair.'

Barbizon gave him a cool eye. Maybe a few too many pizza crusts for Miss Pringle's cat, who was one hefty feline.

'Thought I might catch Sammy,' he said.

Kenny sat on the sofa, a relic from the glory days of the rectory. 'He stole your cue, Harley said.'

'But he put it back. I wanted Harley to know.'

'Sammy had it th' worst of any of us. Some people think our mother swappin' me for a gallon of whisky was a tragic thing. Well, it was, but God worked it out to be a good thing.' Barbizon climbed into Kenny's lap.

'Ed Sikes did me a favor droppin' me off on his grandparents. Mom and Pop saved my life. Sammy didn't have anybody to save his life. Our old man's a goon, it's a wonder Sammy made it out of there as good as he did.'

'I agree.'

'You can't knock Dooley down, he's th' iron man, but you can knock Sammy down with a feather. It killed him when he busted that stick you gave him. He never said it, but he grieved that stick. He feels a lot of shame over what he did.'

'Your brother and I need to talk. When do you think would be a good time?'

'In the evenings, right after supper. Harley gets him up pretty early an' they're out of here by seven-thirty. Sam goes nuts in th' morning, he don't like to get up. I have to work on 'im, too, before I leave for th' restaurant in Wesley. He's stubborn. Man, is he stubborn.

'An' their work's dryin' up; Harley's tryin' to get him an' Sammy a few handyman jobs for winter—like shovelin' snow.' Kenny grinned. 'We're prayin' for snow around here.'

'Never too early to pray for snow.'

'Course, Sammy's not prayin' for anything. He don't know th' truth. I wouldn't know it, either, if it wasn't for my grandparents. I told you I think of them as my grandparents.'

'Yes.'

'I'll go back to Oregon,' said Kenny. 'I'll go back. Mom and Pop are old, they need me.'

In October, there would be Dinner One at a table across the driveway, with Dooley and Pooh and Jessie and their mother, Pauline—with Buck, of course. A painful piece of business, but he should mention it, at least. 'You know Dooley's coming home soon. There'll be a couple of get-togethers at our place. All are welcome.'

'Our mother's comin'?'

'To the first one, yes.'

'Nossir, I'm not ready for that an' Sammy's definitely not ready for that. I know what Jesus says about forgiveness, but . . . no way. You did us a favor when you took Dooley in. What you did for Dooley has touched us all, an' will keep on touchin' us. You've done a lot for Sammy, too. I thank you.'

He had no words, only the certainty that he hadn't done enough.

'So you and Sammy and Harley are invited for the second night, okay?'

'Yessir. Thanks.'

I believe we'll see the day, he wanted to say, when we'll all move back and forth through the hedge . . . like family. But he said nothing.

On the screen, figures racing toward the goal line.

'You like the restaurant business?'

'I try to give it my best an' I'm savin' everything I can. I guess if somebody asked me what I'd like to do, I'd have to say build bridges. That's it for sure. But mostly, I just want to go to school. I want to learn, I want to know.' Kenny's voice was thick with feeling. 'I want to *fly*.'

AVIS HAD BEEN PLEASED with the parson's dinner menu.

Pan-seared scallops with roast potatoes and carrots. Endive in a light dressing of avocado oil and lemon juice with sea salt. A crusty bread from Sweet Stuff, and the Local's most highly recommended chardonnay, listing to the oaky side. As always, Avis expected as full a report as the customer was willing to render.

But the letter. When he went to fetch it, he couldn't find it. He sat at the desk and tried to remember any unusual movement he'd made or action he'd deployed.

It had simply vanished.

Where was his mind? What had happened? He remembered sealing the envelope, and yes, he'd been distracted by the chipmunk business—what a cleanup!—but how distracted could he have been? He searched all drawers and pawed through the wastebasket, experiencing a feeling akin to slipping off an ocean shelf into the fullness of the sea.

The letter had been his magnum opus. And while certain parts of it had come easily, other parts had been dredged from the deep, requiring the might of prayer and patience. He had been Michelangelo at the marble of David, if he did say so himself.

As for her letter, he read it by the flame of three candles burning on the kitchen island. He was scarcely able to see his dinner, much less her small, eccentric scribbling. But she loved him, he knew that; he had known it all along and would always know it, and wasn't that the point?

'Can we quit?' he said later, drying the skillet she had washed. 'Writing letters, I mean.'

'Sure. Okay.'

'That was easy.'

She laughed. 'I just wanted to see if we were paying attention.'

He put the skillet in the drawer. 'And are we?'

'We are. I loved learning that you'll always think of me as the girl next door.'

'In this letter, I was able to say other ways I think of you.'

She looked at him, happy. 'But don't tell me the ways,' she said, scrubbing the roast pan. 'I'll wait for the letter.'

'If we find it,' he said. 'A fresh pair of eyes. Sometimes that works.'

She dried her hands and made a beeline for the study.

'I love this,' she said, tearing into his bookshelves.

'I wouldn't have put it there.'

'But if we look only where you would have put it, which you've already done, how will we ever find it?'

'Go for it,' he said.

ON SUNDAY AFTERNOON, he walked with Barnabas along the drowsing street, headed for the monument.

This time next Sunday, things would be different in Mitford. Henry Talbot would have spoken his piece, and perhaps, one hoped, made his peace. One chapter would end, another would begin—Father Brad would bring something of the young Colorado mountains to these ancient hills and life would flow on. He was dreading next Sunday, though he had no real responsibility. All he had to do was show up.

He buttoned his old flannel jacket. A few days ago it had felt like winter, then a bit like spring. Today, a genuine autumn was in the air and he savored it. The leaves would be turning soon, the maples doing their chorus line of scarlet and gold along Lilac Road . . .

He wanted to see Sammy this evening, but Harley had called to say the boy was down with a case of flu. 'You don't reckon ol' Barbizon could carry th' germs upstairs to Miss Pringle, do ye?'

'No, no, I don't reckon so at all,' he said, putting a shine on things.

As he crossed Lilac at Town Hall, the air was stirred by a sweet drone. He braked his dog and looked up to a cloudless blue sky and felt a smile have its way with his face.

Omer Cunningham was out and about in his yellow ragwing.

Chapter
Twelve

Make me a blessing . . .

He jiggled the key in the lock. Nothing.

More jiggling. More nothing.

'I hear you don't cuss,' said Abe, obviously enjoying himself.

'Not if I can help it.'

'When I messed with that lock last summer, I personally could not help it. The air turned blue all the way to the bypass.'

Jiggle to the left, jiggle to the right, as per instructions.

'Easy does it. You're trying too hard. You have to be gentle with it.'

He felt blood thrumming between his ears.

'Hey,' said Coot, coming up at a trot.

'Hey, yourself,' he said. 'Pull up a chair.'

Coot thumped onto the Happy Endings bench, glad to find a little action on the street.

'Good morning, Father!' J.C.'s wife, Adele, was in full MPD gear and looking taller, somehow. 'I see you're keepin' your hand in where criminal activity's concerned.'

Abe and Coot had a laugh.

'Ha, ha,' he said, dry as a husk. Barnabas stuffed himself beneath the bench.

'Want some help?' asked Adele. 'I've worked with that lock a couple of times.'

'It takes a village,' he said, jiggling.

'Is that the right key?'

Of course it's the right key. Why couldn't a man have a little bloody privacy trying to enter his bloody workplace? Thank heaven for the Irish, who saved the day when it came to cussing.

'How does Hope put up with this?' he said to no one in particular.

'It works fine for her. Most of the time, anyway.' Abe crossed his arms, lounged against the display window. 'Lieutenant Hogan here could use her piece on it. One shot and you're open for business.'

Adele tapped the silver badge on her jacket. 'Make that Captain Hogan, if you don't mind.'

He wiped his sweaty palms on his khakis, shook her hand. 'Congratulations, Captain. Well deserved.'

'I've got to open up here pretty soon,' said Abe. 'So can th' captain shoot th' lock or not?'

More laughter. More additions to the crowd of onlookers. Coot passed around an open bag of Cheetos.

'Why, hey, Father! Marie Sanders, remember me? I gave that armoire to th' Bane and Blessin' a few years back.'

'Oh, yes, I remember your armoire.' He had helped move it off the Sanderses' truck. It weighed a ton. He had intensely disliked armoires, including his own, ever since.

'It made a dandy entertainment center for the Bolicks,' she said.

'Yes, ma'am, I remember.'

'We didn't have a place for it anymore.'

It seemed the key wanted to veer right, into an inner sanctum unknown, perhaps, even to the lock-maker of yore.

'Sometimes I miss it, it was very roomy. We kept th' cat litter in there an' th' dog food, then th' mice started comin' in through a hole in the back.'

One more time and he was done, the whole town could have a go. He removed the key, waited a moment, and inserted it again, as if rebooting a computer.

'It wasn't a real big hole or anything,' said Marie Sanders. 'We patched it before we put it in th' sale.'

'Hold it right there! Just keep doin' what you're doin', Father, okay? Great! Super! Yay-y-y! What's goin' on?'

Vanita Bentley had arrived with her iPhone.

Click. The key found the sweet spot. A little short on breath, he escaped with his dog into the silent realm of ink and paper, and closed the door behind him.

Books! Man's best friend.

Next to the dog, of course.

Sandwich. Apple. Raisins. Almonds. Bottled water. Toilet tissue. Kibble. Winnie's peanut-butter dog biscuits. Journal. Fountain pen. Pushpins. Flyer for the front door.

He stashed the empty backpack under the sales counter and moved on to the fun part.

Lights. Beethoven. Coffee.

Since retiring, he hadn't been able to find the groove worn by all those years of priesting. Getting up at five had remained routine, as had Morning Prayer, but from there, routine staggered off the cliff around seven-thirty a.m. and perished on the rocks below. He had missed being in a groove, a fact he discovered by realizing he'd found one at Happy Endings.

Two days of routine and five of the wildly random. Most people would give anything for a plan like that.

He read Marcie's note.

> *Fr Tim, Here's our O for Oct. sale!!!! feels like we*
> *just had it yesterday—I could not do window on Wed.*
> *with O banner which we keep under stairway. Pls put*
> *banner on display window floor with stack of books on*
> *chair with O titles. U r an angel. Call if u need me. Use*
> *stuffed cat that looks like M Ann, also under stair.*
>
> *PS Big box books arriving today U unpack I*
> *shelve OK?*

He pinned his quote to the corkboard.

Tolle, lege: take up and read. —*Augustine of Hippo*

He carried the flyer to the front door and taped it to the glass. If Esther Cunningham came after him for this, he would go to the mat for the right to use the front door as a declamatory venue. He would bend but he would not break.

Open Wednesday,

Thursday & Friday

10 until 4:45

Come in &

Add A Literary Quote

To Our Billboard

He made the sign of the cross and turned the CLOSED sign around.

OPEN.

Yes.

'My delivery truck's runnin' late,' said J.C. 'Here you go, hand-delivered.' J.C. spread today's edition of the *Muse* on the sales counter, tapped a story on the front page. 'You can read that out loud in your preaching voice.'

He skipped the headline beneath a two-column-wide color photo, and read:

> **Adele Hogan has been named Captain of the Mitford Police Department, filling the former position of our new Chief, Joe Joe Guthrie.**

'Wait a minute,' he said. 'Shouldn't you feature our new chief on the front page? I mean . . .'

'He's inside front page,' said J.C. 'Not official 'til November. Read on.'

> **"I will be honored," Hogan said when the news was announced internally, "to serve the citizens of Mitford as ably and justly as I possibly can."**

'Nice, huh?' said J.C.

> **"She's the one for the job," said former Chief Rodney Underwood, who moves to Wesley as Chief of the WPD. "I was impressed when she interviewed several years ago. Some people when they interview, you can tell they just want to carry a gun and drive fast."**

'Adele is truly different,' said J.C. 'She wants to carry a gun, drive fast, *and* be of real service to the community.'

'Noble,' he said.

'DARLING! ANY BUSINESS UP THERE?'

'A couple of tourists from Alabama, one from Statesville. Pretty steady.'

'Have you read the *Muse?*'

'About Adele, yes, but haven't read about Joe Joe.'

'You have sixty-five votes.'

'Sixty-five!' He felt the heat in his face.

'It's looking very promising. And Coot got another vote, he has three now. Here's what the article says:

> **"Every little town needs a town fixture. I cast my vote for Coot Hendrik who once helped my elderly mother cross the street plus he ran after somebody's grocery cart last week when it rolled down the hill behind the Local. Little things mean a lot, people! It doesn't have to be all sparkle and shine. Sincerely, Anonymous."**

'Him again. Did you find the letter?'

'No, but Puny can have a go tomorrow. I thought you'd like what Anonymous said.'

'That it can't all be glitter and gleam? Amen to that.'

'Sparkle and shine, I think he said. You can't get this sort of thing in the *Times*, sweetheart.'

He wanted a five-hundred-dollar day today, he really did, plus he had to find a bunch of O titles and get the window done.

'Any news from next door?' he asked his wife.

'I called this morning,' she said. 'Sammy's some better, but now Harley's down with it. So far, Kenny is unscathed.'

'Okay, gotta go, Kav'na. See you around five-fifteen.'

'By the way, did you order something? UPS dropped off a long box this morning. It's in the garage.'

His scalp prickled. 'I'll tell you everything when I get home.'

The God of the Second Cue had delivered.

'YOU DIDN'T TELL ME you were workin' at th' bookstore.'

He was astounded to see Emma Newland with a tan. They were clearly giving free samples at A Cut Above.

'I didn't know I was expected to report such matters.'

'Which days are you workin'?'

'Thursday and Friday.'

'I still have Tuesday open,' she said.

And he still had Tuesday closed. 'I'll remember that.'

'I voted for you; I emailed it to Vanita last week. But I think this should be a democratic election, so next week, I'm voting for Winnie.'

'Good,' he said, 'she deserves it.'

'I guess a person can have more than one vote.'

'Probably so. I don't recall seeing any rules. How about buying a book?'

'I don't have time to read.'

'For your granddaughter,' he said. 'Grandchildren have time to read.'

Emma adjusted her half-glasses, peered around the store. 'What do they read?'

He didn't actually know, he needed to discuss the whole

issue of children's books with Hope. 'Eric Carle.' He'd heard Cynthia mention Eric Carle. 'Or—let's see, starts with an S—Sendak! Maurice. Yes, he was quite the revolutionary.'

'Nothing political,' said Emma.

He was still conflicted about whether to promote Cynthia's books, which were perennially displayed throughout the store. He headed for the Children's section, tailed by Emma.

'So what did th' bishop want?'

'He wanted to talk something over.'

'What was so *grave* that he couldn't mention it in his letter?'

'It was so grave that I can't mention it in conversation.'

That was sticking the knife in and turning it. He pulled *The Very Hungry Caterpillar* off a shelf.

'It was somethin' to do with Lord's Chapel, I can tell you that.' Smug's truest meaning, personified.

He studied the S authors, found a Sendak, paged through. What if *Where the Wild Things Are* scared the granddaughter? How could he possibly know what to recommend if all he'd read of the children's inventory was *Violet* books?

'Just give me one of Cynthia's,' she said, impatient. 'Or two—Hope needs th' money. So, are you goin' to say somethin' about my tan or not?'

'It's becoming.'

'It's th' Boca. You should try it yourself while th' special's on. And by th' way, I will not vote for Wanda Basinger next time around, I am not that democratic.'

He took two *Violet* books off the shelf and headed for the register, Emma nipping at his heels.

'Nothing she does is out of the goodness of her heart. A restaurant is a *commercial* enterprise; she is *paid* to make great fries, she is *supposed* to stack her garbage in a neat pile for pickup.' She stood at the sales counter, slid her glasses down her nose, gave him a look. 'So where's any leadership involved in that?'

He swiped her card.

'How's Snickers?' he said.

HE WAS ROAMING THE STORE looking for O titles when he heard the bell. Irene McGraw. Irene was in her usual garb of pants and cotton sweater, making the casual appear elegant. He wished he could remember the name of the famous film star people said she looked like, but since he never saw a movie . . .

She didn't see him, so he let her browse. Book browsing had its own set of rules, of course. It was a contemplative pursuit, and he was trying to learn when to reel in a paying customer and when to reel out.

'Irene,' he said. 'I'm glad to see you. I apologize for the uproar we caused.'

She smiled. 'It was very funny. So few things are in today's news. Thank you for your concern, it was lovely to feel looked after.'

'How's the new grandson?'

'A fine, big boy, thank you. He has his Grandfather Chester's eyes.'

'I miss seeing Chester,' he said, meaning it. 'How may I help you?'

She waved her hand, a kind of flutter. 'Lots of grandchildren who love to read.'

'Fifteen percent off titles beginning with O,' he said.

'I'll just wander through, if you don't mind. I may be a while. I like to read the books I give.'

He was impressed, to say the least.

'I'll leave you to it, then. And many thanks for your kind generosity to the hospital. When we went looking for you that day, I waited for Cynthia in your living room. I confess that I studied your paintings. They're breathtaking, really.'

There was the look he always associated with her, the distant, sorrowing, distracted look. A look which was actually rather beautiful, like the face of a Madonna.

She smiled, but didn't acknowledge his praise. 'I believe the children's books are that way?'

'Come with me,' he said.

Two hours later, Irene McGraw was still sitting on the floor in the Children's section, books strewn about in a bright sea of color. For the first time since he'd known her, she appeared . . . what? Relaxed. Comfortable.

'I'm just going to have a bite of lunch,' he said. 'Cynthia made a sandwich with grilled chicken, it's already cut in half. Will you join me?'

He hardly expected her to accept, but she did. She looked up and smiled and said, 'I'm hungry as a bear. Thank you.'

He brought over his sandwich with the apple cut in slices, and the almonds and raisins, and laid it all out on the children's book table with two cups of water, then helped himself to a chair several sizes too small, and passed her the half sandwich on a napkin.

'Since we're in the Children's section,' he said, 'I'll ask a child's blessing.

'God our Father, Lord and Savior, thank you for your love

and favor, bless this food and drink we pray, and Irene who shares with me today. Amen.'

'Amen.'

'I learned that from my first-grade teacher, Miss Sanders—I don't recall if she was married, we thought all teachers were Miss, devoted to us exclusively. We prayed in school back then, saluted the flag, all sorts of wonderful stuff we can't do anymore.'

'My mother was a schoolteacher,' she said. 'She wasn't my birth mother, she was an aunt by marriage. My mother died when I was born.'

'I'm sorry.'

'Though I never knew her, I miss her very much.' She gazed beyond him, grave, then looked at him and said, 'How is that possible?'

He considered this. 'I suppose there's a sense in which you did know your birth mother—she carried you close to her heart for many months, you inhaled and exhaled her amniotic fluid, which provided everything you needed for life and good health. Most important, she's how you got here in the first place and began making a valuable difference in the world. All of that, it seems, forges a pretty close relationship, much to be missed.'

She looked at the sea of books, unable to speak.

'Perhaps you could give me a tutorial,' he said. 'I'm old at book loving, but new at bookselling. Would you be willing to explain why you choose one book and not another?'

'These,' she said, 'are the ones I like so far. All the open ones are under consideration. And that stack is definitely not making the cut. Where shall we begin?'

'Let's begin with the books you like,' he said, interested.

. . .

By THREE-THIRTY, gone from the window were *The Secret Garden, Sense and Sensibility*, and all twelve volumes of the obscure classic *Swallows and Amazons*.

He called his wife to come give him a hand with the O window. Got the answering service. Huffed a wing chair to the window. Thumped the stuffed cat onto a rug by the chair. Installed a floor lamp. Screwed in a bulb.

With Irene McGraw's help, he unrolled the October banner. Placed a book on either end to flatten the thing for the next thirty days. Looked up and waved to whoever pecked on the glass.

One by one, he distributed O titles. Stacked *Of Mice and Men* and *Oliver Twist* on the table by the chair.

Went looking for a title to place on the cushion of the chair.

'*One Hundred Years of Solitude*,' suggested Irene.

Did that.

Displayed *O Pioneers!* by the cash register, with a 15% OFF sign.

Washed his hands at the coffee station.

Done.

At FOUR O'CLOCK, Irene left with twenty-one books, ranging from picture to young adult. She had, in every sense of the term, made his day.

'Guess!'

'I don't know,' said Hope. 'After all you did last week, I'm afraid to think it. Four hundred and . . . maybe ten dollars?'

'Four hundred and ninety-nine dollars and twenty-seven

cents. Plus I found some loose change under the wing chair cushion in Poetry, and put that in to make an even five hundred.'

Tears. Not hers. His.

HE TORE OPEN THE BOX in the garage and dug through the foam peanuts.

Beautiful. He was thrilled.

He grasped the butt with his right hand, and laid the shaft across his left palm. Giving the cue a slow turn, he examined the workmanship of the inlaid forearm and its striking design. He looked at the collar, the ferrule, the tip. Definitely a pro stick as far as he was concerned.

AFTER THEIR EARLY DINNER on Friday, he sat with Cynthia in the kitchen.

'I'm just going to love him.'

'That's the hard way,' she said.

'With God's help, I want to be something like grace to him. I don't know how the shrink stuff works and I don't want to pretend to know or try a bunch of fashionable strategies. So, if it works, it works, and if it doesn't, maybe he and I will both learn something in spite of ourselves.'

'You know he's frightened of attachment, of any real closeness. It's what he wants most from you, but he'll keep trying to push you away.'

'I'm not going away.'

'Let me pray for you.' She took his hand, rested her shoulder against his.

'Lord, you know how crucial this time with Sammy will be. Open his heart, we pray, to your love and to Timothy's. I ask you to give Timothy your words, and to anoint all that he says and does to draw Sammy into the circle of your astonishing grace. May it be a tender time, somehow transforming in ways we can't know. We ask all this, believing, but ask this far more—that your perfect will be done in Sammy's life and in the lives of his siblings. Thank you, God, for second chances, for without them, I wouldn't be here tonight to lift this petition. In the marvelous name of Jesus, we are thine own forever.'

He kissed her hand. 'You're my best deacon.'

'Flu season this year is terrible. I know we had our shots, but a lot of people who had a shot are sick as cats. I do not have time to be sick.'

'If I get sick,' he said, 'I'll quarantine myself.'

'Where?'

'I'll sleep downstairs with Barnabas.'

'In that case,' she said, 'maybe I'll just get sick with you and we'll finish off the soup.'

She took the ladle from the drawer and bent to her task at the stove. 'This may be Puny's best chicken soup ever. I'll put it in three containers. Give them my love, and please use a sanitizer before you go over, and be sure and wash your hands when you come back. Also, it might be good to hang your clothes on the peg by the side door and have a really hot shower first thing.'

The fire crackled and spit.

'One more thought,' she said. 'I'll put wipes by the door. Could you please wipe the doorknobs when you come home—outside *and* inside?'

Florence Nightingale was alive and well and living in Mitford.

. . .

'LORD HELP, REV'REN', I'M HALF KILLED.'

'You look it,' he said to Harley. He stood in the doorway of the tidy basement bedroom next to the oil burner. 'Cynthia sends her love, and to prove it, she sends hot chicken soup. Interested?' Starve a cold and feed a fever? Or was it the other way around? He could never remember.

He lifted the lid from the container; Harley sniffed the air.

'Are they any noodles in it?'

'Sure thing.'

'Yessir, I'll have a shot right out of th' jug, thank ye.'

Harley drank soup and lay back on the pillow. 'Boys howdy, that ought t' do it.'

'Where are your teeth?'

'Law, I don't know, I ain't even thought about 'em in two or three days. Maybe on th' kitchen table.'

'Let me pray for you.'

'Yessir, an' pray for our boy in there, he's been sick as a houn' dog. An' pray Kenny don't git it, some of us has t' work f'r a livin'.'

'Will do.'

'An' pray f'r th' furnace man t' git th' rattle out on Monday mornin'. Ever' time it starts up, it rattles an' bangs 'til a man could jump out th' winder buck-naked.'

'Here we go,' he said, bowing his head.

SAMMY SAT FACING THE WALL on the far side of the bed, his back to the open door.

Not knowing what to say, he knocked.

'What?' said Sammy, not turning around.

'Cynthia sent hot chicken soup.'

'I don' want n-nothin'.'

He made the sign of the cross. *Your words, Lord.*

'I have something for you.'

'I don' need n-nothin'.'

Sammy's shoulder blades as sharp as wings, the vertebrae delineated. So young, so old. He stood transfixed by the sight of Sammy's bare back and its articulation of despair.

He wanted to tell Sammy that he was loved, that he was forgiven, that there could be a new start, a real beginning. He wanted to say, You're safe with us, you're surrounded by people who care for you and we won't let you go. He wanted to pray aloud for whatever succor the words might conceivably offer. But he was mute.

He took the cue to the bed, carrying it horizontally in both hands.

At the altar of defeat, he laid the stick of grace.

Then he turned and went home to the yellow house where he had been given everything and more, none of it especially deserved.

According to caller ID, it was Henry Talbot.

'Father, thank God you're there. Please pray for . . .' The voice broke. '. . . my husband.'

'I'm praying for him faithfully. And for you, Mary.'

Mary Talbot tried to speak, but could not. He was going to say that he would do anything he could, but there was the click, and he stood for a moment holding the receiver.

. . .

THEY HARDLY EVER GOT TO HEAR the innocuous buzz of their doorbell, installed in the seventies by a former priest. Most people came to the side door, and UPS and FedEx historically dropped off in the garage.

Eight-fifteen was late for a visitor; he was already in his robe and pajamas following the prescribed hot shower.

He switched on the front porch light and opened the door. Dooley was grinning. 'Hey, Dad! Let's go car-shoppin'.'

Chapter
Thirteen

Dooley was in the lead and there was Father Tim bringing up the rear.

Hessie peered through the window of the Woolen Shop. They were running along the street close to the parked cars, and laughing.

What had happened to his freckles? Had they been surgically removed? Or do freckles at some point just vanish on their own? His cowlick had also disappeared—that had been her favorite Dooley feature when he was a boy.

Whoa, look at that—muscles, even. The grubby little kid in overalls had turned into one good-looking hunk, pardon the expression.

And what was it about Father Tim that seemed different? Loose, that was the word, as if he were as light as air, just springing along.

She opened her notebook and entered a reminder:

Google fade frkles

AFTER THEIR FOUR-MILER and a shower, he wrangled Dooley into lunch at the Feel Good.

'Hand-cut,' he said, pushing the fries to Dooley's side of the table.

'That's a really nice cue you gave Sam. But nobody gets why you did it. I mean, he thinks it's some kind of joke or a trick. I think it scared him; it didn't make sense.'

In his experience, grace hardly ever made sense. 'If he's going to shoot pool, he needs a decent stick.'

'He probably thinks he should be punished for bustin' the old stick, and he knows you know he took yours off the rack, so it hacks him for you to make a move he can't understand. It's like you're trying to pull something over on him.

'Clyde would have half killed him for what he did; Clyde half killed him for breathing.' Dooley called his biological father by his given name. 'Anyway, I brought him a new one, too, so now he has a backup.'

'Good shooters need a backup,' he said.

'But think about it, Dad. I gave him a really great pool table. You and Cynthia let us put it in your dining room. You took out all your furniture so he could do what he loves. How many people would do that? How can he get his head around that kind of thing? When I was a kid, I could never understand why you were so good to me, I thought you'd end up knockin' me down or kickin' me out, it didn't make sense for you to be good to me. Sometimes I hated you for it, because I didn't know what was in your head.'

He listened; ate a couple of fries.

'So here he is,' said Dooley, 'actin' like a creep. And here we are, givin' him all this great stuff. Is that th' message we want to send?'

'For now, anyway.'

'When I'm home on the twenty-sixth, I'm going to seriously

work on 'im about his teeth. They're a mess. I'll take care of the money; he needs to get that behind him.'

'You'll have to catch him first.'

'And the stuttering. It holds him back; other pool shooters give him a hard time. Maybe I'll work on that when I'm home for Thanksgiving.'

Dooley pushed away the ketchup.

'I thought you liked ketchup on your fries.'

'I do, but Lace is tryin' to get me off sugar. There's a lot of sugar in ketchup.'

'Lace . . .' he said, wanting to talk about that.

'I asked Harley if Sammy's cool with his rent,' said Dooley. 'Sammy's paying on time. It was a good decision for me to quit paying his share. He doesn't want to be out in the cold like he was when he ditched Clyde. He's proud to be livin' down there—it's warm, it's clean, it's cheap. Sammy's no derp just because he acts like one.'

Dooley reached into his pants pocket, pulled out a phone, looked at it, took the phone in both hands, and used his thumbs to . . . whatever.

'A new kind of game?' he said.

'Talkin' to Lace.'

'Talking?'

'Texting, Dad.'

'So how's she getting along?'

Dooley put the phone in his pocket. 'She didn't say.'

That gate was locked, he may as well get used to it. 'You know she'll be home on the eighteenth. Any chance we can get you back our way?'

'I'm slammed.'

'What's on for tonight?'

'Sammy and Kenny—we're goin' out for pizza. Dutch. Then Bud's ball hall.'

'Sammy's better, I take it.'

'He's not contagious at this point, but Harley probably is. I can't get the flu. I've got something goin' on at school Monday and Wednesday.'

'Let's talk about what we can do for Kenny.'

'He wants to go home to Oregon; he'll be here a year this December. He said he'd like to leave early January.'

Kenny had knocked on the door at Meadowgate Farm last Christmas Eve. Though hoped for and prayed for, his arrival was nonetheless unexpected. He had appeared out of the blue as the siblings he hadn't seen since he was seven or eight years old were getting in costume for a Nativity pageant in the kitchen. It had been the Christmas miracle people wish for but seldom get.

'I don't want him to go back,' said Dooley, 'but I understand. He misses his mom and pop.'

'Did you talk about college?'

'He'll work hard to make it on his own, but I know he'll need help. He doesn't think he should take money from us to go to school in Oregon.'

'That's not the point.'

'I told him that. He had great grades in high school, and a year in community college. He thinks he can get into the university in Eugene. It's about thirty miles from his grandparents, he could probably live at home—maybe take a bus, buy a used truck, I don't know.' Dooley was the older brother, for sure; he had the worried look of a parent. 'He's got a girl in Eugene.'

'Well, there you go.' He would also regret losing the wise

and amiable Kenny, who, among other virtues, had a good way with Sammy. 'I'll split some of his expenses with you. You're going to need a good chunk of cash when you finish buying out Hal's practice.'

Dooley laughed and Dooley grinned, but Dooley seldom smiled. Here was a smile to remember.

'Thanks, Dad. Thanks.'

'What about you?' he said. 'Tell me about you.'

'I joined the University Chorus. That's the Monday and Wednesday night stuff. Rehearsals. Brahms. You love Brahms.'

'That's great! Proud of you.'

'A hundred and twenty singers. Big concert in April, full orchestra.'

'Wow. We'll come hear you in April.'

'I thought I could forget about singing, but I really want to do it, I need to do it. Music is in my head all the time. The singing helps me figure things out.'

He realized Dooley had been staring at him intently.

'What?' he said.

'You're lookin' like a wild man.'

'Me? A wild man?'

'Your hair is really long; you're headed into a ponytail. You should let me cut it.'

He laughed and Dooley laughed with him. Dooley had cut his hair once. Not a good idea.

Wanda Basinger was on the move with her coffeepot. 'I hear your boy's in town,' she said. 'This him?'

'Mrs. Basinger, Dooley Kavanagh.'

Dooley stood. 'Pleased to meet you. Congratulations on your new place. Serious fries.'

'Well, thanks,' said Wanda. 'Nice manners you've got there.'

'Prep school.' Dooley grinned. 'They made me do it.'

LAST YEAR, he met the improbably named Bud Wyzer at the ball hall in Wesley, and watched Sammy shoot a few games with a trio of hustlers from the college. Sammy had whipped them badly, which had not gone down well with the college president's son.

Bud was a good man, he would be helpful.

While Dooley was catching the deep sleep of the clinically exhausted and university-educated, he sat at the kitchen counter and consulted the phone book.

'Bud, Tim Kavanagh. Hope to see you soon. Would you keep an eye out for our boy, Sammy Barlowe? You were kind to do that once before. If you see anything going on that shouldn't be going on, I'd like to know about it. Grateful for your help, Bud, here's my number.'

Little drops of water, little grains . . .

He rang Harley and made his proposal. Good. Okay. Done.

He made another quick call, put on his best jacket, and went to the kitchen. His wife was making egg salad, a Dooley favorite which wouldn't be turned down next door, either.

'I'm going to apply for a job,' he announced.

'About time,' she said, giving him a smooch like he hadn't enjoyed in some time.

'Hooray!' said Puny. Bright-eyed and bushy-tailed, that was Puny Guthrie on emergency call to catch up Dooley's laundry.

'Applying is one thing,' he said, snapping on his clergy collar. 'Getting the job is another.'

. . .

THEY SAT ON A MEMORIAL BENCH in the rear churchyard.

'Something must be done about the hedge out front.'

'Th' hedge. Right.'

'Pruning, feeding—and a new dressing of mulch wouldn't hurt.'

Bill Swanson blinked.

'The roses also need to be pruned back, hard. And right away. I recommend a light feeding of bone meal, fish meal, sulfur, magnesium sulfate, Epsom salts. But first, the beds will want refurbishing.'

'Refurbishing,' said the senior warden, blank as printer paper.

'New soil, new mulch. New all around. And of course the old Sunday school has to be dealt with—get the vines off, dig out the roots, replace the gutters—or the building will come down in a heap one of these days.'

'Right, right,' said Bill, not knowing what else to say.

'You may even want to go forward with liming and fertilizing the lawn.'

'A lot of mowing comes with that. Who has time?'

'So, if a parishioner volunteers to get the work done—fine! Great! If not, we'd like to have the job starting next week. When Father Brad comes, he may, of course, want to go another way—also fine.'

Bill looked at him, overwhelmed.

'Free,' he said. 'We'll do it for free, myself and a couple of helpers.'

'Free? Since when have I turned down free?' Swanson's relieved smile, followed by a dark look. 'Is that free labor and free materials or just free labor?'

'Both,' he said.

'Wow,' said Bill.

. . .

As he was walking home from Lord's Chapel, a gust of wind plastered a vagrant piece of paper against his pant leg.

ATTENTION MERCHANTS
OF MITFORD'S MAIN STREET:

Wash your windows—make 'em shine, people!!

Set an example—use the litter bins on Main!!

Sweep your sidewalks daily!!

**And remember—no postings on display windows!
It's a town regulation!**

Be living proof that—

Mitford Takes Care of Its Own!!!

Office **of the Mayor**

He stopped at the next trash bin, tossed in the broadside. No, no, he would never move to Linville. The laughs were better in Mitford.

After Dooley's nap and the job interview and the communal Great Folding of Laundry, they dug out Dooley's laptop.

'Look up the top ten best-gas-mileage sedans,' he said.

Toyota Prius. Volkswagen Jetta. Ford Fusion Hybrid. Toyota Camry Hybrid. Volkswagen Passat . . . too many websites, way too much information.

'I surrender,' he said. He had more fun walking, all those years ago. 'Is the Minivan still your best shot?'

'Mini Cooper. Yeah. Yes. Hatchback.'

'What do we have to do?' He was exhausted just thinking about buying a car.

'We can run down the mountain tomorrow after church, the dealership opens at one o'clock, and I'll leave from there for Athens.'

In his mind's eye, there was the Mustang, backed in and headed out to pasture. For something like four thousand dollars, he could have it fixed and enjoy the manifold comforts of the old shoe.

'It would still be an old car,' said Dooley, reading his mind. 'Four thousand today, a couple thousand tomorrow. YOLO, Dad.'

'YOLO?'

'You only live once.'

'Okay,' he said. 'Okay.'

'I already called. They have exactly what you need, you can drive it home. You'll love it, Cynthia will love, it, Barnabas will love it. And it can kick a little asphalt if you're in the mood.'

'What color?' he said.

'Blue. Your favorite.'

High five. Dooley's laughter.

'Stick with me, Dad.'

'I'm stickin',' he said.

SHE SAT IN HER CHAIR in the bedroom, eyes closed, barefoot. He pulled up the footstool, took one of her feet in his lap, massaged the instep. 'It seems it's always about me around here. What about you? What's going on? How's the book coming?'

'My eyes . . .' she said, giving them a rub.

'Cornflower blue! The color of a volcanic lake!'

'All those years of painting tiny feet and minuscule claws and infinitesimal whiskers.'

'Voles,' he said. 'And cats, of course.'

'Voles and cats and moles and mice and owls and baby birds— so many *feathers* with birds. The strain . . .' She closed her eyes. 'Poor Miss Potter, her eyes were her undoing. That's one reason I liked painting portraits in Ireland. People's heads seemed so . . . huge; the strokes could be so bold. It took more than a single marten hair to get the job done.'

'New glasses, maybe. I'll drive you to the eye doc.' He hated his need for her to be ever strong, fearless, and wise.

'I think I'm beyond new glasses.'

'Meaning?'

'Surgery.'

The word frightened him, always had. 'It could be the light in your workroom, there's so little of it. The new room we talked about in Ireland—that would be the very thing. All those windows facing north! It would help, I promise.' He felt a deep urgency to fix this for her.

'Besides, your workroom shelves are groaning under the weight of your art—and no place to store anything else. Stacked around the walls, overflowing the hall closets . . .'

She smiled. 'It's okay. I'll put some things in the auction.'

'You need the new room, Kav'na. Let me do it.'

'It would be a pain, all that banging and hammering.'

'But the final result would give you pleasure.'

'Yes,' she said. 'It would. Let me finish this book and we'll talk about it.'

'When will you finish?'

'May, I think. Or maybe June, July.'

He needed to remember that he went through something like this with every new book, worrying about her eyes, her right arm, her neck, her shoulders, her lower back. Who said art isn't manual labor, right up there with digging ditches?

'How about a long weekend in Whitecap?'

'Not now, sweetheart. Let me finish the book.' She plopped the other foot in his lap. 'And maybe one day . . .'

'One day what?'

'. . . we can go across the country in an RV.'

He laughed. 'Where did that come from?'

'I think about it a lot. All that lovely freedom—parking in churchyards overnight, stopping at flea markets, sketching in meadows. I'll let my hair go gray and knit while you drive.'

What a wild notion. He never knew what to expect from his wife.

'Speaking of hair,' she said, 'when are you going to get a cut?'

The bloody nuisance of it.

HE LAY AWAKE, listening for Dooley to come home. Barnabas would bark a couple of times, out of courtesy to the household.

Eleven-thirty.

Ten 'til twelve.

Midnight.

Dooley was twenty-two years old. Kenny was nineteen,

soon to be twenty. Yes, but Sammy was seventeen, and there was the memory of the college president's son and his surly minions.

Twelve-twenty.

There went the barking. A light glowing on the stair. Dooley coming up and going to his room across the hall and the stair light switching off and the door closing.

Thanks be to God.

THE PHONE RINGING . . . ONE O'CLOCK.

Addled, he remembered that Dooley was across the hall, so this wasn't the call every parent feared.

'It's Mary Talbot, forgive me, Father. It's Henry . . .'

'Henry.'

'He left the house at six this evening. In his running clothes.' Mary Talbot was breathless, as if she had been running. 'He hasn't come home. I should have called sooner, but I hated to involve . . . You're the only one . . .'

'His car?'

'It's here. His billfold, his watch, everything is here. What shall I do, Father? I mustn't call the police, it would attract attention . . .'

'Let me think. No, let me dress. Don't worry, I'll be in touch.' He hung up, grabbed his khakis from the back of the chair.

Cynthia stirring.

'I'm going out for a time. Henry Talbot.' He pulled on a shirt, a sweater, cords, socks, a jacket; it was cold out there. His wife turned over, sighed, slept on.

He needed a flashlight, he needed Dooley.

'Wake up, buddy. Wake up.'

'What?'

'I need you to come with me. Sorry. Get up.'

Dooley got up, sat on the side of the bed, stared at him. 'What?'

'It's important. Please get dressed.' He handed over the clothes Dooley had just taken off.

DOOLEY DROVE THE PICKUP to the hospital and around to the rear of the building and parked near the entrance of the trail into the woods. In the beam of their headlights, cans, bottles, fast-food bags, detritus.

'What do you think?' said Dooley.

'I'm not thinking, just going on instinct. This is where he runs, I don't know, it could be a dead end.'

They got out of the truck; he switched on the flashlight.

'Spooky,' said Dooley.

'Why anyone would run back here is beyond me.'

They entered the trail, which he had checked out years ago as a possibility for his own route—a round-trip three-mile stretch of rough ground, tailor-made for spraining an ankle or sprawling over the gnarly roots of old trees.

If Talbot left his house at six, he would have had less than thirty minutes of diminishing daylight. An odd time to go running over this terrain.

'Man,' said Dooley.

'Thanks for coming with me.' He didn't like the feel of this. 'How did it go at Bud's?'

'Some guy from Winston merked Sammy, they were shootin' straight pool.'

'That's good.'

'What's good?'

'Losing once in a while will help keep his feet on the ground.'

'Yeah, well, I don't like losing.'

'Who does?'

What had Talbot lost, that he would run only where he could hide?

They concentrated on negotiating the path and ignoring the trash. He was so wired, his teeth chattered. Maybe they were wasting precious time in here, and yet the hunch was too strong to ignore. The night was damp, claustrophobic; a nearly full moon had vanished behind sullen clouds.

Midway into the path, they heard a movement to their right. An animal scurrying through leaf mold. And the smell . . .

'Puke,' said Dooley.

They stopped, panned the trees with the beam of the flashlight. Maybe someone had come in here with a bottle of whisky, but the smell was different—he knew the stink of alcohol-related vomitus.

The small movement again; the sour reek. The hair stood on the back of his neck.

'Careful, Dad.'

He lowered the beam, illumined the form sprawled in the leaves by a tree. 'Who's there?' he said.

A voice—hoarse, unintelligible. Somebody drunk or in another kind of trouble.

He was aware of a slippery feel beneath the soles of his shoes as he walked toward the tree; he stumbled, righted himself, the fumbled beam of light picking out a couple of empty water bottles, a discarded jacket, Henry Talbot's agonized face.

Dear God.

He fell to his knees. Henry lay on his back, eyes open, pupils

dilated. Henry's hairpiece was missing. The sight of him without it was jarring.

'"Living darkly,"' Henry whispered, '"with no ray of light . . ."'

He handed the flashlight to Dooley, pressed his fingers to
the carotid artery, felt the faint, rapid pulse.

'Henry! It's Tim and Dooley Kavanagh.'

The suffocating smell.

'Can you get up? Can we help you up?'

'I was coaching back then . . .'

'Let's get him into a sitting position,' he said. 'Go easy, we
don't know . . .'

Henry Talbot might have been a rag doll, his limbs and torso
dead weight, his upper body and running shirt slick with vomit.
He could not be set upright or brought to his feet; they laid him
again on the ground, on his back. Apparently nothing was broken, or pain would be evident. They needed a plan.

Talbot was easily six-two, one-eighty or one-ninety. No way
to get an ambulance or Dooley's truck into these woods.

'We'll have to carry him out, what do you think?'

'We can do it.' He heard the alarm in Dooley's voice, and
the resolve.

But he'd been too quick. Wilson lived roughly a block from
the hospital, and had a golf cart—Wilson's wife was often seen
wheeling her husband's lunch to the side entrance.

'Better plan. Go to Wilson's house and ask for the golf cart.
Tell him we'll see him in ER, and bring a medic with you if
one's available.'

Dooley hesitated briefly, then set off running.

The light bobbed along the trail and vanished—he was
alone in the night with a man who could be dying.

'Jesus,' he whispered into the darkness.

This was a dream, nothing about it smacked of reality. He shivered in the damp air and felt about for the jacket to put around Henry, but it was saturated with a cold slime, and useless.

He had spent a few nights camping with youth groups, but was hardly an outdoorsman. The silence unsettled him; he needed the sound of the human voice, he needed something to put under the head of a broken man lying in the woods, surrendered to fear and remorse. There was nothing to do but wait. He hunkered on the ground by Henry's side.

"'Living darkly, with no ray of light . . .'" He repeated Henry's quote, drawn from the half-delirious poem by John of the Cross.

"'And darker still, for I deserved no ray.'" Henry's voice might have emanated from an octave never before heard.

'God loves you, Henry.'

"'Love can perform a wondrous labor . . . and all the good or bad in me takes on a penetrating savor . . .'"

His hand gripped Henry's shoulder, to give some mite of warmth.

'It is very hard to die. Or if I have died, I confess I expected more.' A deep tremor in Henry's body, his whole frame agitated, the breath ragged. 'Perhaps this is purgatory, or I have passed directly to Sheol. But the people . . . the people . . .'

'Tell me.'

'They had grown fat on honey and I gave them bitter root. Tell them I learned to love them. Lying here, it came to me that I love them and deeply repent of my cold disfavor toward them and our Lord. I was unable, I was coaching then. Ask them to forgive my manifold sins against God and this parish. It was winter, you see, and I was but ten years old; my sled had come apart against a tree . . .'

He placed his hand on Henry's head and prayed aloud. 'Nothing can separate us from your love, O Lord. Thank you for releasing us from the bondage of believing we are worthless and rejected . . .'

'Up there . . .' Henry's voice coarse from the heaving.

The moon had escaped cloud cover and silvered the canopy of branches. 'Up there, the heavenly realm, and here, O Lord, am I, a worm awaiting your claim. Will you have me?'

'He will have you, Henry.'

'"Living darkly, with no ray . . ."'

Their voices mingled on the night air.

'For you, Lord,' he prayed, 'have not given us the spirit of fear, but of power and of love and of a sound mind . . .'

'". . . and quickly killing every trace of light,"' Henry whispered, '"I burn myself away."'

'HARD TO ASSESS,' said Wilson. 'No way to know how much or when he took it, he's too confused to tell us anything.'

'What was it?' said Dooley.

'Acetaminophen and diphenhydramine. The empty bottles were in the pocket of the jacket you brought in. It's a common mix for the suicide demographic who prefer ingestion.'

'He left the house at six,' he said. 'There were empty water bottles with him on the trail. Let's say he got the stuff down right away. We found him at one-thirty, one-forty . . .'

'It's three forty-five now,' said Dooley, 'so around ten hours.'

'The tests show thickened blood,' said Wilson, 'some liver damage, and the kidney function is off. We hung a couple liters of saline on him, gave him an antidote, and the chopper will have him to Winston in forty-five minutes—before five, say, or about eleven hours from the overdose. Twelve hours out and he's in big trouble. So by a hair, by a hair.'

The doctor he'd recently thought a cub looked pretty old right now.

'What about ID?' asked Dooley.

'On his wrist. A band.'

'Dad notified his wife.'

'She'll have to get here fast.'

'She won't be coming,' he said.

'Not even the children know what's happening,' she'd told him on the phone. 'I've lived the last thirty-four years putting a good face on things for Henry. It's useless for me to come, for there's no longer a good face to be put. I love Henry more than life, Father, but I will go through with the divorce. I declare the agony ended forever on this terrible night. I'm sorry—for everything. Thank you for all you've done.'

'I hope we can keep this quiet,' he told Wilson.

'Nobody will hear it from me, but I can't make promises for anyone else. You know the Mitford grapevine.'

They waited in the hall for Talbot's gurney. 'My son's going to be a doctor,' he said, proud.

Wilson eyed Dooley with approval. 'You'll make a good one, I'm sure. Your speciality?'

'Animals,' said Dooley. 'Not people.'

The doctor volunteered a grin. 'Animals are people, too.'

THE CHOPPER USED TO LAND in Baxter Park; now there was a helipad on the roof of the hospital. He read again the bronze

plaque at the door of the elevator to the pad: A GIFT OF THE
IRENE AND CHESTER MCGRAW FAMILY. He remembered that
Chester had been flown to Charlotte from the pad he funded,
and died en route.

Cutcutcutcutcutcut . . .

At 4:10, the machine lifted off the roof of Mitford Hospital
and, in the starless night, burned itself away.

Chapter
Fourteen

He had called the bishop at seven-thirty to brief him on the harrowing circumstances of last night.

'This changes everything,' Jack Martin had said. 'I'll meet you in the vestry a little earlier, say ten-fifteen, we'll celebrate together. The Lord be with you.'

According to Bill Swanson, Bishop Martin was not only never late, but known to arrive early. Now he was late by more than forty minutes. In alb and stole, he paced the confines of the minuscule room where the choir changed, the priest vested, offerings were counted, and, occasionally, an anxious bridegroom waited.

Bill Swanson's face was beet-red as he rushed into the vestry and closed the door. 'Bishop Martin can't make it, Father. He just got cell phone service. A rockslide on the mountain, quite a few people badly injured. Very serious. No cars getting through, he says.'

He stared as if the senior warden had spoken in another tongue. On every side, wreckage. Debris hurtling into the air and then falling, falling . . .

Bill Swanson's left eyelid twitched. 'Bishop says tell you to carry on. What can I do?'

'Pray.'

'Say as little as you can, would be my thinking, Father, and let the vestry handle the rest at the parish meeting. All hell will break loose when they get the details. No need for it to break loose in the eleven o'clock.'

The congregation wouldn't know what to make of seeing Tim Kavanagh in the pulpit; they would be heartily up for the flamboyance of the bishop's mitre and crozier, and for learning what Talbot had in mind for the bishop's unexplained visit. They would have the momentary shock of the old priest to work through, which would, perhaps, condition them for the blow to follow.

He could go head down into the wind and make the announcement before the opening hymn. But no, the opening hymn would give them all a chance to settle in and connect with whatever familiar words had been selected. It was a packed house, with people sitting on chairs in the aisle and standing at the rear, the usual case with a visit by the bishop. Something was up, everybody knew that much.

'I'm ready,' he said to Bill. Exhausted, strung out, wired, and ready.

Bill Swanson was reeling from this, but thumping him on the back with good cheer. 'When th' bishop can't make it, Father, God himself shows up.'

He embraced Bill and walked from the vestry into the nave and bowed to the cross and ascended the steps to the altar and the organ played and he turned to the people and lifted his hands for them to stand. They rose with a great *swoosh*, as a single body, and he opened his mouth and the words learned as a child came forth with sweet accord.

When morning gilds the skies
My heart awaking cries

May Jesus Christ be praised!
When evening shadows fall
This rings my curfew call
May Jesus Christ be praised . . .

'Blessed be God: Father, Son, and Holy Spirit,' he said.

'And blessed be his kingdom,' the people said, 'now and forever.

'Amen.'

'Almighty God, unto whom all hearts are open, all desires known, and from whom no secrets are hid: cleanse the thoughts of our hearts by the inspiration of thy Holy Spirit, that we may perfectly love thee, and worthily magnify thy holy Name; through Christ our Lord.'

'Amen.'

He felt his heart pierced through; the terrible constriction in his throat. His wife knew something had gone wrong. From the second row, gospel side, she gave the sign that she was praying—a slight raising of the forefinger of her right hand held against her cheek. And there was his dazed and sleep-deprived son sitting next to her, and thank God for his support.

'Bishop Martin is unable to join us this morning. He sends his profound regret from a scene of unthinkable tragedy on the mountain—a rockslide gravely injuring many people. The bishop is unhurt, but traffic will be delayed for some time.

'We must remember Bishop Martin in our prayers and those who, though unknown to us, are yet brother and sister in this mortal flesh. We ask God for his great mercy upon all whose lives were changed this morning on the mountain . . . and for each of us gathered here today.'

The word mercy struck a chord among the congregants. Why would they need God's mercy in the same measure as those poor souls in the rockslide?

'I am grieved to say there is more to tell you this morning. But before it is spoken, I bid you listen carefully to what our Lord Jesus Christ saith:

'Thou shalt love the Lord thy God with all thy heart, and with all thy soul, and with all thy mind. This is the first and great commandment. And the second is like unto it: Thou shalt love thy neighbor as thyself . . .

'Our neighbor and your priest, Father Henry Talbot . . .' He looked to Cynthia. *Help me.*

'. . . is in urgent need of your love, your forgiveness, and your prayers. Bishop Martin asks me to tell you that Father Talbot's duties as priest of this parish are officially ended.'

No gasping or seeming mortifications. Only stunned silence.

'Father Talbot has charged me to tell you that he is deeply repentant for not serving you as God appointed him to do, and as you hoped and needed him to do.

'He wished very much to bring you this message himself, but he could not. He bids you goodbye with a love he confesses he never felt toward you . . . until this day. He asks—and I quote him—that you might find it in your hearts to forgive him his manifold sins against God and this parish.'

He felt the tears on his face before he knew he was weeping, and realized instinctively that he would have no control over the display. He could not effectively carry on, nor even turn his face away or flee the pulpit. He was in the grip of a wild grief that paralyzed everything but itself.

He wept face forward, then, into the gale of those aghast at what was happening, wept for the wounds of any clergy gone out into a darkness of self-loathing and beguilement; for the loss and sorrow of those who could not believe, or who had once believed but lost all sense of shield and buckler and any notion of God's radical tenderness, for the ceaseless besettings of the flesh, for the worthless idols of his own and of others; for those side-tracked, stumped, frozen, flung away, for those both false and true, the just and the unjust, the quick and the dead.

He wept for himself, for the pain of the long years and the exquisite satisfactions of the faith, for the holiness of the mundane, for the thrashing exhaustions and the endless dyings and resurrectings that malign the soul incarnate.

It had come to this, a thing he had subtly feared for more than forty years—that he would weep before the many—and he saw that his wife would not try to talk him down from this precipice, she would trust him to come down himself without falling or leaping.

And people wept with him, most of them. Some turned away, and a few got up and left in a hurry, fearful of the swift and astounding movement of the Holy Spirit among them, and he, too, was afraid—of crying aloud in a kind of ancient howl and humiliating himself still further. But the cry burned out somewhere inside and he swallowed down what remained and the organ began to play, softly, piously. He wished it to be loud and gregarious, at the top of its lungs—Bach or Beethoven, and not the saccharine pipe that summoned the vagabond sins of thought, word, and deed to the altar, though come to think of it, the rail was the very place to be right now, at once, as he, they, all were desperate for the salve of the cup, the Bread of Heaven.

And then it was over. He reached into the pocket of his alb and wondered again how so many manage to make it in this world without carrying a handkerchief. And he drew it out and wiped his eyes and blew his nose as he might at home, and said, 'Amen.'

And the people said, '*Amen.*'

AT THE CHURCH DOOR, Buck Leeper gave him a crushing embrace.

A fellow who introduced himself as a visitor nodded and said, 'Right on.'

The soldier in Army uniform with his family from Wesley waited until others had gone through the line. He embraced the boy—so sober, so young, younger than Dooley.

'Where are you serving?' he asked.

'Armageddon,' said the boy.

Eileen Douglas threw up her hands and shook her head with wonder and said nothing.

Which, God knows, was saying a lot.

Chapter
Fifteen

On Monday, several of the parish communicated their thoughts as they had when he'd served at Lord's Chapel. Skipping the amenities of the USPS, they posted their envelopes directly into the mail slot of the front door.

Dear Father Tim.

It was so nice to cry in church yesterday. There is so much to cry about in this world, thank you for the opportunity.

Your friend,
Dottie Holzclaw

Father,

I have heard about the laughing thing that breaks out in churches but this is the first I ever knew of the crying thing. Wish I could have been there and wish we could have you back if only for the innovations! (What next, ha ha!)

Sincerely,
Zack Clemmons

(I played first base on our Mitford Reds team— those were the days)

GREEN FAMILY
PLUMBING & ELECTRICAL

Dear Father Tim,
    Maybe it's because we used to be Baptists but we
have never liked Fr Talbot AT ALL, though now we
do because we cried for him and we forgive him and
will try to stick with it.
    God bless you.
    Connie and Elton Green

    Charles Dickens said, It opens the lungs, washes
the countenance, exercises the eyes, and softens the
temper—so cry away.
    Love in Jesus
    Beth and Jim Chandler

Father Tim
    TEARS ARE OUR HOLY WATER

He stayed in his pajamas on Monday, occupying the hours
by listing supplies for Tuesday, talking with Bishop Martin and
Bill Swanson, praying, napping, and generally recovering his
wits. He had called Harley and was assured that his neighbor
was well enough to work tomorrow, if all he did was step and
fetch for a couple of days.

After lunch, which was delivered by his wife, he mustered
the courage to cut his own hair. Did he want help? No; there
was no hair savvy in this house. Cynthia, Puny, Dooley—all
had tried cutting his hair at one time or another and it was a
worse disaster than he might foist upon himself.

Holding the hand mirror, he backed up to the bathroom mirror and squinted at the job to be done. It drove him crazy trying to hold the mirror with one hand and manipulate the scissors with the other; it was a bloody logistical nightmare that deposited hair in the sink, on the floor, and, as he lacked foresight to use a towel around his neck, inside the collar of his bathrobe.

When he went to retrieve a book from the shelves along the hall, Puny was leaving Dooley's room with an armload of sheets.

'Lord *help*! What have you done to yourself?'

'What do you mean, *done* to myself?'

'Your *hair*.'

'I *cut* it,' he said, daring further comment.

'You shouldn't have messed with th' sides, I can tell you that.' And down the stairs she went.

He was fatigued in every part and clearly in denial. All that had happened was too distressing to think about; he held it away from himself.

In the late afternoon, his wife delivered her local gazette: she had been walking in the neighborhood when she saw the moving van headed north. Slowly plowing between the rows of low buildings on Main, the van appeared monstrous, out of place. She had crawled into bed with him, fully clothed, and gone to sleep in her own grieving.

As for the proposed car deal yesterday afternoon, there had been none, of course.

They had come home from church at twelve forty-five, turned off the ringer on the house phone, and after downing two bowls of chicken soup, he'd gone straight to bed. Dooley slept for three and a half hours and headed out with a truckload of clean laundry and a container of egg salad on ice. Three and a half hours' sleep for a five-and-a-half-hour drive was clearly insufficient, but what could be done? He surrendered his parental concerns to an All-Sufficient God and waited for the marching band.

The woodwinds, brass, and percussion kicked in at ten-thirty p.m.—Dooley was safely in Athens.

On Monday evening, they turned on the ringer; the phone bleated at once. His wife lifted the receiver as if handling a snake.

'That was Emma. All sorts of rumors have leaked out.' His wife looked older, exhausted. 'She says our voice-mail box is full.'

'Good,' he said.

The mailbox was full because people wanted answers. Just one more reason former clergy were exhorted to clear out, thereby avoiding involvement in sticky issues of the old parish.

Whatever the leaks may be, he would be hounded by questions—this one in particular:

Why didn't he, Father Tim, go back to Lord's Chapel and straighten things out down there?

After getting into bed on Monday night, he realized he had pulled the covers over his head.

FIRST LIGHT. The sun would be up a little before seven-thirty.

He walked south on Main, dressed in layers—a scarf and cap to take off, a jacket to remove, a vest to be shed when the temperature rose to the predicted upper sixties.

Nobody would find him where he was going, not for a while,

anyway. Their work would be uninterrupted, deprived of the gruesome details of Sunday afternoon's meeting.

It was morning rush hour in Mitford, largely composed of pickup trucks at urgent speed. Some flying down the mountain to greener job pastures, others flying up the mountain to glean whatever pickings the southbound left behind.

He quickened his step. This was the week that fall color would be at its peak. And the week he was finally to become what he'd so long hankered to be:

Full-time.

'Hallelujah!' he exclaimed over the backfire of Ned Colby's gravel truck.

SHE CAME AWAKE, but only enough to realize she had survived the night; that the kiss on her cheek acknowledged her as alive and sentient.

More than anything, she wanted to see the face of her husband, but she could not or would not open her eyes. There was something inside that needed to be tended first; something remote—she would have to travel to get there.

Scott was praying for her. His voice resonated in her blood as plucked strings in the sound box of a lute.

'Amen,' he said.

Still, she could not open her eyes; the membrane of her lids had come down like a shade, leaving the tears to find an exit on their own.

'Everything is going to be all right,' he said, sitting on the side of the bed. 'Hold on to that, Hope. Everything is going to be all right. I promise.'

God had promised, her husband had promised, Father Tim
had promised when they spoke on the phone yesterday. What
more could she possibly want or need? 'Live up to your name!'
her mother had liked to command.

She felt a type of shame. Her body was growing something
she had no wish to grow. It could not be surgically removed, nor
could she wish or pray it away. She was without power to do
anything at all, though she knew with terrible urgency that
something must be done.

'YOU AIN'T TH' B-BOSS OF ME.'

'True. God is the boss of you, with Harley a close second.'

'Ain't nobody th' b-boss of me.'

'Here are your pruners. When Harley gets back with supplies,
we need to be ready for new topsoil. You take that bed, I'll take
this bed, as previously explained. We must cut back the vines,
pull 'em off the building, dig out the rootstock, and remove the
old debris.'

'Ain't nobody gon' mess around back here, so why're we b-
bustin' ass to fix it?'

'If we fix it, people will mess around back here.'

Church suppers. ECW events. Cake sales. And perfect for
small weddings. A bench there, or perhaps under the old service-
berry, and maybe next spring a stone walkway from the side
entrance of the church to the door of the moderately refurbished
Sunday school. It was thrilling.

He shared this vision with Sammy, who stared into the
middle distance throughout the dissertation.

'I'm just going to love him,' he had said to Cynthia. Famous
last words.

. . .

THE MORNING WARMED UP QUICKLY.

They had off-loaded the contents of Harley's truck into the Sunday school building. Rakes, tarps, a mower, two ladders, and other tools of lawn care and home improvement. The supplies Harley was shopping for this morning would also be stored in the building. Good deal.

'Looks like there might be a hole in th' roof.' Sammy spit into a bare bed. 'I stood on that rock over yonder and seen it!'

'Where's the hole?'

'Up by th' bell on top.'

He followed Sammy inside, burrowing beyond the rakes and other gear, into the realm of disabled school furniture and musty banners.

Sammy was using Red Man, he saw the package sticking out of his jeans pocket. A better thing, maybe, than the cigarette, but with its own calamities.

They moved about, looking up to the rafters. No light filtered through the roof decking.

'No hole,' he said.

'There's water c-comin' in somewhere, I can tell y' that.'

'We can't see light through the decking.'

'It smells damp in here, 'at's enough for me.'

'First things first. Let's get the job done outside and we'll come back to this.'

In the dim light, Sammy turned to him, sneered. 'You ain't G-God, you know.'

.   .   .

HE LEANED ON THE HANDLE of his shovel, feeling decrepit. His upper body had enjoyed no useful benefit from running. He took the hat off his sweat-drenched head and hung it on the doorknob of the school.

Sammy looked at him with disdain. 'Somebody must've used a r-rusty s-saw blade on you.'

It might be a bad haircut, but he felt the heat in his face. Sammy Barlowe was absolutely, totally committed to getting his goat. He would need to be careful where he stepped with this.

He stood his shovel against the wall. He had no idea what he would say. He gave Sammy a steady gaze, prayed, and opened his mouth. Out sailed a quote from Absalom Greer.

'I'm not goin' to preach long,' he said in a remarkably even tone. 'Just 'til we get done.'

'Yo, Rev'rend!'

A grinning, toothless Harley flapped his arm out the window of the truck as he scratched into the drive behind the school building.

Harley Welch had saved Sammy Barlowe's hide.

'Where are your teeth?' he asked Harley as they unloaded a bag of organic fertilizer.

'I don't wear 'em to work. I save 'em for dress-up.'

'They're history,' said Sammy. 'He lost 'em.'

'They ain't lost, I jis' don't know where they're at.'

'If they ain't on th' windowsill in th' kitchen, they might be in th' g-glove compartment with th' ice scraper, an' if they ain't r-rollin' around with th' ice scraper, they might be in th' m-mulch pile over at Miz Baker's house—'

'Whoa,' said Harley. 'Whoa, whoa, whoa, dadgummit.'

'How 'bout on top of th' toilet tank—'

'I don't care if they never turn up,' said Harley. 'They's way too many of 'em, anyhow.'

'So send them back to Kentucky and ask your dentist to remove a couple.'

'They costed me too much to be givin' any back.'

'Lunch?' he asked Harley. 'Did you pick up lunch in Wesley?'

'Lord help! I plumb forgot.'

'Go up the street to Feel Good around eleven-thirty. We'll buy local.'

'Let me go,' said Sammy.

'I need you here.'

Sammy spit into the grass. 'You don't need me, you got Harley. I'll go up th' street.'

The punitive didn't come naturally to him, but really—he could punch this kid in the mouth and not think twice about it.

THE CAFTAN OF THE DAY was decorated with images of hot air balloons. Red, yellow, orange, green. A blue sky full. Definitely a stand-out in the produce section of the Local.

'I levitate toward bright colors,' said Shirlene, noting his interest in her garb. 'I'm in here buyin' supper; I'm *way* too tired to cook anything fancy.'

'I hear you. How's business?'

'Pickin' up a teensy bit!'

'Great! Glad to hear it.'

'I've decided to give ten percent of all spray tan sales to th' Children's Hospital in Wesley. They say you're a real good customer—or whatever you call it.'

'We'll be donors together. That's wonderful, Shirlene. Thank you.'

'Plus—I've decided to do it whether business is good or not.'

'That's the ticket! You'll be richly blessed.' He seldom encountered this especially insightful style of philanthropy.

'An' since y'all won't give me any help to meet a nice man, I have taken on th' job myself.'

'It's come to that!'

'I went online.'

He put a gentle squeeze on an avocado.

'They give you five free samples to lure you in, but listen to this—they all looked like my granpaw! Th' first one could have been on th' ground at Iwo Jima, but still very jaunty according to his bio, which I think his great-great-granddaughter wrote. I could pay respects for his service to our country, but as far as—'

The price of lemons these days . . . unbelievable. 'How were the other four?'

'You should have *seen* th' next one, he was from Memphis. His guitar was in the shape of a crocodile plus all his fingers were tattooed and he had more wrinkles than a Georgia road map. Then one had this huge dog—in the picture he was bundled up with that thing, it was big as a house. His bio said it was *th' light of his life.*' She shivered. 'Think about *that.*'

Oh, for a homegrown tomato, but their prime had come and gone. He squinted at the offering of beets.

'Then there was one with facial hair, I cannot stand facial hair. For one thing, way too much upkeep.'

He passed on to the limes. 'What about the other fellow?'

'They wouldn't give me a picture of him.'

'Not a good sign.'

'Delete, delete, delete, that's today's courtin' for you. So they gave me this bonus offer to keep me on th' hook. One last chance to make up my mind and put thirty-four ninety-five on my card. This one had a motorcycle with a sidecar—they showed his picture and he wasn't too bad. But—and here's th' kicker—eighty-five years old! What do you think is goin' *on*?

'When I was fillin' in th' application, I clearly remember typin' in fifty-eight as th' max age.' She paused, startled, smacked her forehead. 'Oh, *please*! I just realized—I'm dyslexic! I prob'ly typed in eighty-five!'

'That'll do it.'

'All this is happenin' 'cause y'all won't give me any *help*.'

'Shirlene, Shirlene, there is no help to *give*. This is *Mitford*.' He liked nothing better than offering help to one and all, but the Cupid business was totally out of his precinct. He felt mildly guilty. 'Thanks again for what you're doing for Children's Hospital. Ride over sometime with my wife and me and see your generosity at work.'

'Great. Okay. Will do. So I better get out of here. I'm playin' Scrabble tonight online, an' whippin' up a few Brussels sprouts. Do y'all ever do that?'

'Not terribly often,' he said.

As he headed south toward home, J.C. was hoofing north.

'I've been lookin' all over for you. Nobody answers the phone at your place, nobody comes to the door. What's th' deal?'

The bag of groceries was heavier than he intended. 'Have to keep moving. Perishables.'

'I hear you saved Henry Talbot's life.'

'I have nothing to say.' He walked on.

'There's a rumor you checked him into ER Saturday night.'

He took the Fifth.

'I'll talk to Wilson.'

'Wilson will have nothing to say.'

'Adele and I just got back in town; I've got to put this thing to bed for Thursday. You may as well cooperate—I'm headed to the MPD.'

'There was no police report, so the MPD will have nothing to say.'

'The night shift at the hospital, they'll tell me plenty.'

'As you know, hospital staff can't speak on private health matters, except anonymously. Which reduces any possible story to hearsay, gossip, and rumor.'

'You could help me out here, dadgummit—did Talbot try to kill himself?'

'What he did or didn't do is nobody's business but the Talbots'. The only news here is that he left Lord's Chapel under whatever circumstances the vestry cares to disclose.'

'People love to talk in this town. One way or th' other, I can get a story.'

He stopped for a moment, shifted the bag to the other arm. 'I read a line in the *Muse* recently. It stated, with some pride: *We print good news.* Enough damage has been done, J.C. Leave it alone.'

He walked on.

Debris hurtling into the air and falling, falling.

'MELITA, DOMI ADSUM!' he shouted as he came in the side door. Cynthia waved from the kitchen.

'Or, to translate: Honey, I'm home.'

'How was it on the job site?' she said.

He set the bag on the counter, gave his good dog a scratch on the head. 'I didn't kill him.'

'Good. What's this?'

'Among other things, fresh pasta. Free sample. Avis says let him know how we like it. He's setting up a pasta station on Wednesdays and Fridays. Homemade on the spot.'

'Proof that Mitford takes care of its own.'

'Cook five to six minutes, toss with olive oil, grate a little parmesan, and we're done.'

'I'll cook, toss, grate, serve, and try to make interesting conversation.'

'And I'll wash up,' he said.

She gave him a hug. 'How does it look so far?'

'It'll be beautiful, I think, though more work than I had in mind. If nobody else enjoys it, you and I will. We can walk down there on summer evenings—sit on a bench, make out . . .'

'My favorite.'

'How did your work go?'

'Still hard.' She rubbed her eyes in that way grown too familiar. 'I would love this book to be more than a book, somehow. Flaps and pop-ups and sounds, things going on. But maybe just being a book is enough. You look exhausted.'

'Mostly mental.' He climbed onto a stool at the kitchen island. 'I'm trying not to censure or chastise, just walk out something he needs, just stand with him as best I can. I don't want to go the tough-love route or any of the other stuff that probably makes more sense.'

'Drink some water,' she said, handing him a glass.

'In the end, grace may not be something the fallible human can extend. We can make each other happy for a minute or two, but I don't know about grace, maybe all we can deliver is mock grace.'

'I would take mock grace over no grace at all,' she said. 'Consider mock turtle soup. Not half bad, really. Then there's mock apple pie.'

'How can you mock an apple?'

'With Ritz crackers.'

'Surely not.'

'It's true. You can Google it. We had a call from Lace. She says don't do anything fancy. No picnic in Baxter Park, just my grilled pimiento cheese for lunch in the kitchen. She says she wants nothing more than to be with us. She misses us.'

'We miss her.'

'She and Olivia are staying put in the evenings and Skyping Hoppy.'

'A good plan,' he said, heading upstairs.

WEDNESDAY MORNING was one for the books. He was so stiff and sore he could hardly get out of bed and sincerely wished he didn't have to. He borrowed her keys and drove to the church.

When Harley went to pick up lunch at noon, the stiffness had improved, and the project lay before them in its own astonishing improvement.

Wearing bandannas, he and Sammy leaned on their shovels, eyed their work.

'What's it going to need, Sam?'

'Red maple. About four yards to th' right so it d-don't grow onto th' roof.'

'Excellent. I agree. What else?'

'Bench.'

'Two, maybe?'

'Yeah.'

'What about topiaries in urns, either side of the door? What do you think?'

'S-seem like more climbers would work. I'd run 'em on a trellis.'

More spraying and pruning. Nobody could ever again call him retired.

'What else?'

'Needs a wall back there to like frame things.'

'A wall! Good thinking.' This kid was born with an eye. The space just wandered off into Earle Johnson's yard, which was appointed with whitewashed rocks lining the driveway and an early Buick on blocks.

'Stone, of course.'

'I don't lay no stone.' A stream of Red Man into the bushes.

'Me, either. But we probably could, don't you think?' He had always wanted to lay a stone wall. 'We could get a book on how to do it. Dry wall, like in Ireland.' He'd be on this job 'til he was as old as Methuselah.

'Yeah. We don't need to be m-messin' with no mortar. Har-ley's laid stone walls.'

'Okay, great, we have a plan. But that's it, we're done. We'll go soon.'

'Where?'

'Big Mountain Nursery. We'll look at their maples and check out the stone.'

Color rushed to Sammy's face. 'I always wanted t' g-go there.'

. . .

THEY SAT ON THE STUDY SOFA and watched the news. Cold weather coming, as cold weather does, it was October. Bundle up. Bring in the plants. The usual.

He was thankful for the burning logs, his dog, their cat, the whole caboodle.

She patted his knee. 'How are you feeling?'

'Pretty beat. But I've scarcely ever been so . . .' He thought about it, making sure he had the right word.

'. . . happy,' he said.

> Dear Henry,
>   This will be a mighty short letter, utterly undeserving of your recent three pages which Cynthia and I savored. I will most definitely do better next go-round.
>   Now to it—you could never guess what scrapes I've gotten into since we talked . . .

On Thursday morning, he posted a couple of quotes on the board.

> It's what you read when you don't have to that determines what you will be when you can't help it. Oscar Wilde

> People say that life is the thing, but I prefer reading. {Logan Pearsall Smith

A calm, slow morning. The trees ablaze, Barnabas dozing in a patch of sun in the display window. To borrow a word from

Abe, the morning was a *bracha*. At ten-thirty, the *Muse* skidded to the door.

Good grief. A front-page photo of him trying to decode the lock, and his nose looking like a turnip.

Mitford Still Takes Care Of Its Own. Yayyy!

by VANITA BENTLEY

And here's LIVING PROOF, people!!
Father Tim Kavanagh opened for business last Thursday at Happy Endings, where he is working two days a week for Hope Murphy . . . for FREE. For free, can you believe it?

Which brings up the good news that Marcie Guthrie, the daughter of our former mayor, Esther Cunningham and the mother of our soon to be police chief, Joe Joe Guthrie, ALSO volunteers at Happy Endings. All to help out a person who has helped US so much by bringing a BOOK STORE to our little town.

Just think—if not for Hope we would have to DRIVE TO WESLEY at $3.65 a gallon and try to find a parking spot on the campus and by a perfectly innocent mistake park in the wrong place and then walk two blocks to the college bookstore possibly in a driving rain and back again to your car which you find has been very unkindly decorated with a PARKING TICKET!!! Go, Bears!

Come in on Wednesdays and say hello to Marcie
or on Thursdays and Fridays to say hey to Father Tim
and check out the O for October sale. 10 til 4:30.

And remember—Marcie and Father Tim cannot
do our job FOR us. We have got to get out there and
take care of our own OURSELVES!

Send a photo and let me know what YOU are
doing to take care of our own, OK? And thanks for
praying for Hope##Scott says Dr Wilson is very
pleased nd more later!!!

Vanita had discovered all-caps, which was news right there.
Mule's real estate ad was once again cheek by jowl with the
Wesley funeral home ad—somebody needed to speak to Mule
about this. The weather prediction for the coming week was
mixed, and there was the latest Leading Citizen countdown,
which he chose to skip . . .

A Delicious Way To
Fade Your Freckles

He read the Hint with absorption. How amazing. He did
like to learn something, however useless, when he invested
time in reading a newspaper.

Wanda's Feel Good Café Caves to Local Demand

Wanda Basinger is breaking her rule of NO BREAKFAST!!! Yayyy! But with reservations.

Breakfast will be served on SATURDAYS ONLY, starting at eight o'clock through ten-thirty, which seems a pretty short time frame but since lunch starts at eleven thirty they have to get the tables cleared.

To celebrate, Ms. Basinger will be serving a Mexican dish which she hopes we will all like. Caution: SPICY!

As for giving in to local demand, we asked Ms. Basinger how she feels about it.

"I feel good." she says//8%

THE CLOCK OVER THE SALES COUNTER read eleven-fifteen. His nose had been stuck in the *Muse* for . . . how long? A good half hour. *It's what you read when you don't have to that determines what . . .* Too late now.

'I HAVE A CONFESSION to make,' said Vanita.

He thought the tortoise frames of her eyeglasses imparted a very owlish and wide-awake look.

She leaned over the counter. 'I'm Anonymous.'

'You, Ms. Bentley, are anything but anonymous.'

'No, I mean, in th' paper I'm Anonymous. By bein' Anonymous, I can say what I really think and don't have to be politically whatever. Do you think that's okay? I mean, is that just another type of media cover-up?'

'Well . . .'

'Like, Coot only got one vote and that was a mean joke, so anonymously I've given him nine more for two reasons. One, because his great-great-great-granddaddy, Hezekiah, founded this town, and two, I knew it would make him feel wonderful. Surely there idn't anything wrong with makin' people feel wonderful.'

'I'm with you there,' he said.

'I needed to confess that to somebody besides my husband, I drive 'im crazy tellin' 'im stuff he says he doesn't need to know.'

'I'm inclined to that same behavior. My wife is very patient.'

'I just really admire you, Father.'

'Well, thank you. Good gracious.'

'I hear you cried in church and people cried with you.'

'True.'

'It is so nice when men cry.'

'I read that according to a study of over three hundred adults, men cry an average of once a month, and women five times a month.'

'Y'all were runnin' way behind and caught up all at once! Like, yay-y-y!'

They had a small laugh, which he managed to enjoy.

'I know Mr. Hogan wanted to run a story about Father Talbot an' all, but he couldn't find any real facts to report, just mean things people are sayin'. I'm so glad you wouldn't tell him anything.'

'Nothing to be told.'

'Anyway, here's another secret an' I'm done. If I ever run

for mayor, which I prob'ly won't, I have my campaign slogan already picked out. I wouldn't want anybody to steal it for their campaign, so you wouldn't ever tell, right, because you're clergy?'

'Right.'

'It's th' sort of thing we all have to do if we're goin' to keep takin' care of our own, okay? Imagine this on a bumper sticker . . .

'Get off your butts, people!'

Barnabas sat up, looked around.

'That'll work,' he said.

'As for the plaque you were goin' to write . . .'

'Nobody ever asked me.'

'We printed it in th' paper, that was asking,' she said.

'Okay, when is the deadline?'

'Tomorrow. It takes a lot of time to get something *engraved.* On *bronze.*'

'There is no balm in Gilead, Ms. Bentley, did you know that?'

'I know all about that. You can email me or I can come pick it up.'

'A very quick turnaround.' He sighed without meaning to. 'How about Monday?'

'I can't do Monday,' she said.

RON MALCOLM WHEELED IN as he was having a cup of yogurt and fruit. Ron had twice been on his vestry; they'd been around the block a time or two.

'Good job on the Talbot announcement,' said Ron. 'It's been hell to pay down there. Along with everything else, I hear he was dipping into th' till . . .'

'I have to tell you, Ron, I can't discuss it. I know the parish has a lot to deal with, and talking about it is one of the ways to move ahead. But I can't participate. I hope you understand.'

He was no goody-two-shoes; he had entertained more than one morsel of babble and hearsay in his time. But this was strictly off-limits.

PERCUSSION. WOODWINDS. WILSON.

He felt the odd thump of his heart.

'Sorry to be late getting back to you, Father. I've finally been able to talk with Talbot's physician. Talbot's going to make it.

'The N-acetylcysteine worked—that's an antidote for aceta-minophen poisoning—and the liver tests have improved. They expect a full recovery, with no long-term complications.'

'None?'

'None.'

'Thanks be to God.'

'They're sending him home in a couple of days.'

He sank onto the stool, lifted a petition, wondered where home might be.

'WHAT'S AN ALB?' SAID ABE.

'A white vestment worn by priests.'

'That's what I thought. They said Talbot's license plate was ALB1954. With a license plate like that, what priest in his right mind would park his car at a motel? Twice a week? Regular as clockwork? Monday and Saturday, to be specific.'

'No more,' he said, throwing up his hand.

Abe leaned against the counter. 'So, okay, did you hear the one about the priest and the rabbi who bought a car together?'

. . .

Business was slow today.

He pulled out his phone and sat at the sales counter. There had been no time for Dooley to finagle the ringtone, maybe he could do it himself. He knew to go to Settings, but that's all he knew. He scrolled the list:

People Laughing. Crowd Cheering. Rooster Crowing. Baby Crying. Thrush Singing. Piano Playing.

He selected Piano Playing but somehow ended up with People Laughing. Way more hilarity than he cared for, but he couldn't get rid of it.

He had been born in the wrong century. Worse still, he realized he would miss the cheerful woodwinds of Band Marching.

To distract himself from utter nonsense, he called Dooley and left the good news about Talbot.

Sadie Eleanor Baxter

He penned her name and remembered her small hand in his, the hand of a child willing to be led and yet completely capable of leading. He remembered dancing with her at the Fernbank reception for Hoppy and Olivia; she had floated in his arms like the seed head of a dandelion.

He entered her birth and death dates, which he knew from memory. He had gone, himself, to have the small stone engraved with these dates, her name, and the simple tribute, *Beloved.*

She wouldn't wish to be venerated for her gifts, nor have them itemized like a laundry list of two shirts, one pair trousers, three handkerchiefs. There would come a time, of course, when no one would be left to remember who gave the town museum, the state-of-the-art nursing facility, and the real estate known as Baxter Park. The joy taken in these gifts would be thanks enough for Sadie Baxter.

> *She gave the museum in which you stand to read this plaque, so that you might learn about the town she loved. She gave us a house named Hope, so that our elders might know a blessed hope of their own. She gave us more than we can acknowledge, but here is what she gave most freely:*
>
> *Herself.*
>
> *Whether we be friend or stranger, let us honor Sadie Baxter for this:*
>
> *She loved us well.*

'Hey, Ba!'

'Ba! It's us!'

Puny's twins jangled through the door at a trot.

'We haven't seen you in *ever*!' Sassy thumped her backpack on the counter.

Sissy dropped hers to the floor. 'We love th' wooden jigsaws you brought us from Ireland.'

'We hadn't had a good jigsaw in *ever*,' said Sassy.

Mighty like their dad, Joe Joe, but with Puny's red hair. They had a group hug.

'How did I come by the pleasure of your company?'

'Miz Hicks couldn't drive us home from school today . . .' said Sissy.

'. . . so Dad told us to come to th' bookstore,' said Sassy, 'and he'll pick us up when you close.'

'Good thinking!'

Sassy grinned, revealing a small fortune in braces. 'We like your job at the bookstore better than your job at the church.'

'Why is that?'

'More books!' said Sissy, who had her own orthodontic display going on. 'May we do our homework in the Poetry section and look at some of the books after?'

'We'll wash our hands first!'

'Have at it,' he said.

Borrowed grans who love books—an apt definition of felicity.

PEOPLE LAUGHING. He pulled out his cell phone and looked at the caller ID.

'Is it time?' he asked Scott.

'Please, Father. A really tough day for her. She's asking for you. If it's possible . . .'

'As soon as I close up and go to the bank.'

'So sorry there's no time for me to pitch in up there. You know how Hope House runs . . . full tilt, and then I spend every extra moment with Hope. People come and go and do what they can, but I find . . .'

'No need to explain,' he said. 'And you're doing the cooking!'

Today's sales were small, and there was less than an hour before closing. But he felt content with the day's offering, and Hope would be glad to have it.

The bell jangled; he was astonished all over again at the sight of Esther Bolick, who looked as if she'd just flown in from the Keys.

'Here,' she said, plopping it on the sales counter.

Clearly, it was a cake, he could see it through the plastic container. 'Very, very generous of you, but you know I can't do it, Esther. I hope you understand.' How many times in one brief life did he have to impress this miserable reality upon Esther Bolick and people in general?

'It's not for you,' she said, 'it's for Hope and Scott.'

'Great! An OMC?'

'Correct.'

'I thought your agreement prohibited you from putting OMCs out there.'

'I'm breakin' th' law,' she said. 'It's th' Wild West all over again. Turn me in, lock me up, throw away th' key.'

What was in spray tan, anyway? People should ask for an ingredients list.

'I just happen,' he said, 'to be going to the Murphys' after I close.'

'That's what I heard, that's why I'm droppin' it off with you.'

'How did you hear? I found out myself only two minutes ago.'

'I saw Scott at th' bank. He was talkin' to you on his cell phone and said you were goin' over to see Hope while he went to a meeting up th' hill. I had th' cake on th' backseat, so I thought why not save my gas and use yours.'

'Well, there you go,' he said. 'How about a book today?'

'I don't need to buy a book to help th' cause. I am *sendin'* a *cake*. Do you know what it costs me to bake an OMC?'

'Afraid not.'

'Including my time, which should be worth *something* . . .'

'Absolutely.'

'. . . forty-five dollars. More than they're askin' at Sweet Stuff.'

'Holy smoke.'

'I hope you notice I'm not in here yammerin' about Father Talbot like everybody else in town. I like gossip as well as th' next one, but you asked us to forgive him, so that's what I'm tryin' to do.'

'Good, Esther. Good.'

'It's not easy.'

'No.'

'I cried in church on Sunday, but not for Father Talbot. It was for Gene, who'd be heartbroken about this mess.' She drew herself up. 'It's a struggle to keep my opinions private.'

'I understand.'

Esther gave him a dark look. 'High and mighty, stuck on himself, and God only knows what he brought home to his wife. Which is all I have to say about it.'

HE STOOD ON THE SIDEWALK with the cake box, looking up. There was Omer, flying like a Jack Russell. He and the twins threw up their hands as the yellow ragwing rattled south over Main.

'THE BODY OF OUR LORD JESUS CHRIST, which was given for you, Hope, preserve your body and soul unto everlasting life. Take and eat this in remembrance that Christ died for you, and feed on him in your heart by faith, with thanksgiving.'

The throbbing purr of Margaret Ann at her side; the wafer on her tongue and the slow, sweet dissolve . . .

'The Blood of our Lord Jesus Christ, which was shed for you, Hope, preserve your body and soul unto everlasting life. Drink this in remembrance that Christ's Blood was shed for you, and be thankful.'

She allowed the wine to touch her lips but did not drink. 'Amen,' she said. And there was the warmth, so long gone from her, and some sense, at last, of her own living presence.

He packed up the communion box, and brought the cake to her and lifted the cover.

'Oh,' she said. 'I can't imagine making something so beautiful.'

'Esther Bolick cares about you, she's praying for you. So many are holding you fast in prayer.'

'It's embarrassing, all those signs saying "Pray for Hope," and the stir in the newspaper . . .'

'Why is it embarrassing?'

'It seems to ask so much of people. Why should they pray for me when they have tribulations of their own?'

'All the more reason to pray for you—it's a healing exercise for us as well as for you. Further, you gave us a bookstore, which should be reason enough. Here's an idea. Why don't we pray for those who're praying for you? Sort of a back-atcha that has its own loveliness in God's eyes.'

He placed the cake on the chest of drawers and sat by the bed and took her hand. 'What do you think?'

'I would never . . . yes, let's do it, yes.'

'Thank you, Father, for every soul who lifts a petition for Hope, for Scott, and for this special child you're giving into our lives. Bless those whom you call to pray for Hope, that they would be comforted in their own hard circumstances and shielded in their joy. Thank you for the supernatural connections that prayer creates among us, for the ties it so strongly binds. In the name of Jesus who is all hope, Amen.'

She felt composed enough now to speak it, to force the words out to someone who should know it was life or death.

'Scott and I have done extensive research, as you might know we would. The doctors could lose us both. Not in days or in hours, but in minutes.'

'That may be true, but I choose to believe otherwise.'

She smiled a little; he saw the light in her eyes. 'You adimpleate my spirit,' she said.

'That's the first arcane word you've given me in many moons.'

'I haven't been lolling about eating bonbons,' she said. 'I searched for that one.'

'I have no idea what it means.'

'Good! It will send you to the dictionary. Or the Internet, whichever comes first.'

'Interested in a sales report?'

'Always,' she said, struggling to be cheerful.

'I'm learning the hard realities of retail. Not every day can be a five-hundred-dollar day. A hundred and seventy-two plus change.'

'Perfect. Thank you, Father. I miss my customers.'

'They miss you.'

'Will you thank them for all they're doing?'

'I will.'

'I was happy to see Coot get a mention in the *Muse*. Coot loves books, did you know that? I've been meaning to say you can hire him to vacuum, I'm sure we need it, and dust, and anything else you and Marcie can think of.'

'Consider it done. And you must call me anytime. Okay?'

'Okay.'

'I have just four words to leave with you. Four words that have spoken volumes of truth into my life.'

He wanted the words to stay in the room, to remain long after he had gone. Though no one wished to hear Paul's radical injunction, it had to be told.

'In everything, give thanks.'

That was the lifeboat in any crisis. Over and over again, he had learned this, and over and over again, he had to be reminded.

'In everything, Father?'

'In everything.'

THE NIGHT WAS ALIVE with the scent of rain. He sniffed it like an animal as he carried the trash to the garage around ten o'clock.

He dumped it in the bin, making sure the lid was tightly closed against incursions from the wild. There were several loose boards through which raccoons made frequent calls, especially on evenings when Cynthia scented the air with roast chicken.

What was different out here?

The Mustang was missing.

HE RANG HARLEY.

'Is Sammy home?'

'Let me step in there an' see if he's back.' Static, rustling. 'Nossir, he ain't. He went out a while ago, said he was goin' down th' street to Lew's.'

It could have been anybody, the garage door had been left open for days because the remote needed a battery and he hadn't gotten around to it. But he knew the truth and it made him sick. Literally.

'Does he have a license?'

'Yessir, he has.'

'The Mustang isn't in the garage. I'll keep you posted.'

He walked out to the garage again and stared at the empty

space beside the Mazda, as if his car might reappear, as if he'd only imagined it missing.

Should they go looking? Kenny was working tonight; he could drive around with Harley. But why? If the car was anything like the cue, the Mustang would be back in place at some point, and what would he, Tim, do then? His stomach did the churning thing it had done when, as a boy, he was faced with crisis.

Sammy had kicked it up a notch. It was the way of rage and woundedness to keep making things worse. The third-born of the Barlowe boys was clearly begging for punishment, and the whole scenario was skidding off the cliff.

He wanted to call Dooley, but wouldn't, of course. His wife, so fond of the early bedtime, sat up with him. Kenny and Harley arrived at the side door at eleven-fifteen, in a downpour.

Alerting police about a teenager in a stolen car didn't seem a good idea, but they were changing their minds when the doorbell buzzed at half-past eleven.

They bolted along the hall as a group.

Joe Joe.

'He's all right.'

'Thanks be to God.'

'But your Mustang's totaled.'

Rain drummed on the porch roof.

'Where and how?'

'He ran it down a bank on the bypass, comin' around th' curve there at th' lawn-mower repair. I'm a man short tonight and had to be on call, I happened to come around th' curve right behind him.'

'Where's he at?' said Harley.

'In my car yonder with Officer Greene. A little banged up, a cut on his forehead. I offered to get medical assistance but he

didn't want any. He looks okay, but I have to tell you it's a miracle. Did you let him take th' car, Father?'

'It was in bad shape. Transmission. Clutch. You name it.
That could have been the cause . . .'

It was a blowing rain, slanting onto the porch.

'Will you step in?'

'No, sir, I'll track up your floor, I've got to keep movin'. Did
you know he was takin' your car?'

'He was not authorized to take it. No.'

'Things could have been worse. We've lost two down that
bank a little farther up. He said he didn't care one way or th'
other if he killed himself.'

'Lord A'mighty,' Harley said, stricken.

'Seat belt?'

'Yes, sir.'

'Was he speeding, what was he doing?'

'Went around th' curve left of center, looked like he lost control, maybe hit a slick spot. No alcohol or drugs found in th' car.
He's clean as far as I can tell. Do you want to press charges?'

'I don't want to press charges. No.'

'He's free to go, then. But I'm givin' him a citation.'

'That's th' ticket!' said Harley.

'You'll need to keep an eye on 'im, Father. That goes for you,
too, Harley. I believe he lives with you.'

'He does. Yessir.'

'Y'all can walk out with me,' said Joe Joe. 'As for th' wrecker
service, we work on rotation or you can give me a name to call.'

'Lew,' he said, taking an umbrella from the stand. 'Call Lew.
Will you file a report?'

'We will, but we'll try to keep it quiet.'

They processed to the curb, soaked. Joe Joe opened the car

door. Sammy climbed out, eyes down, a smeared gash on his forehead.

'I don't want to see you out here again doin' anything you shouldn't be doin', said the chief. 'Not even once. You got that?'

Sammy gave a curt nod without looking at Joe Joe.

An old liquor-runner eager to please authorities, Harley shook Joe Joe's hand. 'An' congratulations on bein' chief!'

Rain hammered the umbrella; he watched Sammy and Kenny and Harley make a run for it as the patrol car pulled away.

Curious that a boy who didn't care if he lived or died had buckled up.

Chapter
Sixteen

He turned the sign around to OPEN and posted a quote.

No two persons ever read the same book.—Edmund Wilson

'Nor does any one person ever reread the same book!' he said to his dog.

He was grinding coffee beans when his backpack whooped with laughter. Would he ever remember to ask somebody to change the blasted ringtone?

'Hey, buddy.'

'Hey, Dad. Just talked to Kenny. What are you going to do about last night?'

'Nothing,' he said.

'Nothing? How can you do nothing?'

'He's expecting something, but I'm going to do nothing.'

'No disrespect, Dad, but that doesn't make sense.'

'Agreed.'

'Man. I don't know what to say.'

'Me, either. I'll appreciate your prayers.'

'Okay, so I don't know where you're going with this, but you know. Right?'

Dooley sounded hopeful, even confident that his dad, the priest, was on top of things.

'Actually, I don't know.'

'I hate that he did this, this is nuts, he knows better. I'm sorry.'

They each had their own kind of astonishment to deal with. 'I'll ask Sammy to come with me to Lew's tomorrow morning. It'll be good for him to see the car. Besides, I need to get my hog-ring kit out of the glove compartment.'

'Your what?'

'Don't trouble your mind,' he said. 'Everything is going to be all right.' He was grabbing at straws, he was trusting in God, he was hanging on. 'How was rehearsal Monday night?'

HESSIE MAYHEW JANGLED IN, white as a sheet. It was refreshing to see somebody without a tan.

'Father, I need to talk.' Hessie peered around the store, which was empty of customers, leaned over the counter, and spoke in a voice so low he had to lean toward her.

'I think I'm losin' it.'

'In what way?'

'You know my Lady Spring pieces for th' *Muse*.'

'Of course. You're always good to remind us not to plant 'til May fifteenth.'

'That's exactly what I need to talk about. I couldn't say this to Reverend Browning—he's the nicest man in th' world, but he's my preacher.'

She looked around again. 'I need to talk to somebody else's preacher. Because I wouldn't exactly want Reverend Browning to think I'm losin' it.'

Hessie was clearly distraught. 'I was writing a story on Mitford School and how they're givin' an art show at Hope House.'

'Wonderful!'

'But I ended th' story by typing, Don't plant 'til May fifteenth.' She looked aghast.

'Always good advice,' he said.

'But not in mid-October, Father, *not* in mid-October.'

'Ah.'

'And *not* in a story about children's art.'

'Yes, well . . .'

'What I'm wondering is, what do people *do* when they're losin' it? I thought you might know if there's a test people can take.'

'If I knew of such a test,' he said, 'I would take it immediately.'

'I read that if you can recognize the smell of cinnamon, you do *not* have Alzheimer's.'

'I read that, too,' he said. 'I headed straight to the spice cabinet.'

'And what happened?'

'I recognized the smell of cinnamon.' He had been very happy with that outcome.

'Same with me, but maybe that's not the best way to tell.'

'Actually, I'm not so sure you're losing it. I misplaced my glasses the other day and for some reason opened the toaster oven and there they were.'

'No! Was it on?'

'It was not. Why they ended up in there is a complete mystery.'

'You were thinking,' she said.

'That's right. I was.'

'Our minds stay so cluttered.'

'They do.'

'It's modern times,' she said.

'True.'

'I always feel better when I talk to you, Father. Reverend Browning is th' nicest man in the world, but . . .' Hessie sighed. 'Actually, that isn't the only confession I need to make.'

He didn't know Presbyterians made confession, except as outlined in James 5:16.

'Are you sure there's nobody else in here?'

'Just Barnabas.'

'It's Vanita Bentley,' she said. 'I could wring her neck. There!' Hessie's breathing was rapid; her face colored. 'I said it and I'm glad.'

'Why don't we sit down?'

He led her to the Poetry hideout, where a single wing chair resided. For himself, he pulled in a chair from the Children's section.

'One thing you can say about Hessie Mayhew, Father—I am as honest as the day is long. A very desirable characteristic, if you ask me, considering th' people in today's media.

'Vanita's young and I'm old, so maybe our ages play some part in this, but look at Mike Wallace, he was a hundred if he was a day, and he kept his audience, people just loved him to death in a manner of speakin'. So you don't have to be young to be great, Father, right? You must surely find that true for yourself in your golden years.

'But here's th' thing. She can't spell for shoot, I mean for *shoot*. Plus she can't write for love nor money and all those exclamation marks drive me up the wall. Don't they just drive *you* up th' *wall*? If I had a nickel for every one, I'd be rich as cream and on a cruise to the North Pole to look climate change in the eye.

'As for news material, she jumps all over the big stories before you can have your coffee in th' mornin'. Up an' down th' street with that bloomin' microphone stuck in every face an' if there's not a big story, what does she do? She makes one up! Like th' Leading Citizen angle, it just came out of her tiny little head! Lord knows, I'm goin' to hell in a handbasket for thinkin' that, much less sayin' it out loud.

'But Father, I have read Cowper and Wordsworth and all those people you're so fond of, and tried to educate my mind and venerate beauty and lead people to think higher thoughts as in my Lady Spring columns. But Vanita? Th' highest thought she ever had was how to dye her old go-go boots black so she could wear 'em to a funeral.'

Hessie's blood pressure must be through the roof. He sprinted to the coffee station for a cup of water. 'Drink this,' he said, using his wife's directive. How fast could the ambulance get here if needed? Ten minutes?

'So you see,' said Hessie, looking tearful, 'after fifteen years of faithfully reporting th' *facts*, th' *truth*, th' *verities* of this mortal life, Vanita gets all the good stories . . .'

And there they came—the floodwaters.

'. . . without even knowin' where to put a comma!' she bawled.

He trudged to the counter and returned with the box of Kleenex.

He was not retired from his old job, not by a long shot. He had merely moved his business up the street. Actually, there were only a couple of differences between priesting and his new occupation—he didn't have to vest for this, or fool with the weekly pew bulletin.

'OUR SEXTON WAS COMING HOME from Wesley late last night.' Bill Swanson was calling on the bookstore line. 'Said he saw a wrecker towin' your Mustang. Are you all right?'

'Oh, yes,' he said. 'Just fine.'

'Must have been somebody else's, this one was totaled,' he said. 'Speaking of totaled, Bob Duncan's boy, you know Bob, just had a bad accident on his bike, they took him to Children's, but they're out of beds and sent him to the hospital over here. The parish is going to get behind the new wing with you; I know you've been a big part of Children's for a number of years.'

'Not so big, Bill, but thanks. Thanks for anything you can do. This will be good medicine for the parish.'

'Called to say you're making a world of difference in the gardens. Can't thank you enough.'

'We're just getting started.'

'We could have the Youth Group give you a hand, but they're pretty scattered.'

'It's my contribution to the plate.' He wanted to work one-on-one with Sammy for a time, then maybe they would rouse a group.

'Just so you know, Father—the parish is grateful.'

People on benches, talking, resting, looking up at the lace-work of branches . . .

He tried to resurrect his earlier pleasure in that prospect, but could not.

. . .

'I HAVE A WHOLE HOUR TODAY. I'm actually goin' to read a poem.'

'Congratulations!'

'It's sort of a payback,' said Winnie, 'for usin' that space all these years.'

He was wiping off the sales counter, dumping extra change into the cash box, going through the motions.

'Somethin' I've never understood,' she said, 'is why bookstores let you read their books and magazines and put 'em back on the shelf like nothin' ever happened. What if I let people sample my stuff? Like take a big chomp out of a jelly donut an' put it back an' keep movin'?'

'You have a point,' he said, smiling at Winnie—he could never resist smiling at Winnie. 'You're in early.'

'They went through four trays of Danish this mornin' an' I don't know how many cinnamon buns and turnovers, not to mention crème horns. Now they're all out there clutterin' up th' parkway—it's th' leaves, you know. Leaves are really, really good for business.'

A kind of haze hovered about his spirit, like particulate matter over a valley.

'I have a great idea,' said Winnie, 'but don't tell Thomas. Our anniversary is comin' up soon. Not our weddin' anniversary— this is th' anniversary of when we met on th' cruise.'

'Ah, yes.' Winnie had taken off on a cruise with Velma Mosely and returned to Mitford with Thomas, a crackerjack baker now her husband.

'Remember that great tan I came back with?'

'Maybe. Sort of.'

'An' Thomas, he was totally bronze when I met him. So, I'm gettin' us a spray tan package in honor of that wonderful time of our lives. It's a two-for-one, this week only.'

It was viral, no stopping it. 'And how many years?'

'Five great years. Or eight thousand two hundred and fifty lemon squares. Give or take.'

'*Tempus fugit!* Does Thomas ever get a break? I don't see him hanging out up here.'

'I cover for him every single Tuesday,' she said. 'Golf! He's a golf maniac!' And off she hasted to the poets.

He'd lain awake until two this morning and hadn't run since Saturday, he was a wreck. There was the momentary image of turning the sign around, going home, sleeping. He stared out the window, checking the street, as the limousine glided into the parking space in front of the store.

He instinctively made the sign of the cross.

'Father Kavanagh?' The driver stepped inside, removed his cap.

'Tim Kavanagh. Yes. Good morning.'

'Wade Truitt.' The driver walked to the sales counter, extended his hand.

'A pleasure, Mr. Truitt.'

'There's someone in the car who would like to speak with you, sir.'

'Who might that be, may I ask?'

'Would you have time to step outside?'

There was the sense of being poised to dive without knowing if there was water in the pool. He had history with a black car with tinted windows, the kind of history that had soured him on the notion of fancy automobiles in general.

'Winnie,' he called. 'I'm stepping out a minute.'

'Take your time,' she said, 'you're covered.'

It was as if he hadn't quite seen the street before, or had seen it a very long time ago. Everything was clarified, as after a washing rain.

The driver opened the car door and he stooped and looked inside.

Irene McGraw.

'Please,' she said. 'Come in. And thank you.'

He climbed in, feeling foolish, as if this might be a joke and he the butt of it. He sat at the extreme end of the leather seat; the driver closed the door with a subtle click.

'Who am I, Father?'

'Why . . . you're Irene.'

'Irene who?'

'Irene *McGraw*. I don't understand.' The voice, the clothes, the jewelry . . . not Irene, and yet . . .

She looked at him with an odd gravity. She was somehow more Irene than Irene; he was profoundly struck by her beauty. 'This is life-changing for me. You have just acknowledged . . .' She drew in her breath. '. . . something I've tried to confirm for several months—all my life, really. It is a great shock.'

He became aware of an insinuating fragrance—jasmine, perhaps—the interior of the car was infused with it.

'Such a deluge of feeling,' she said. 'One wants something so fiercely, and when it comes . . . I've spent most of my life giving expression to the emotions of imaginary characters, now I must feel all this, own all this, for myself. It's overwhelming.' She bowed her head and put her hands to her face, weeping, yet silent as stone.

He was stunned by having moved from the airy vault of the bookstore into a confined space shared with someone he knew and yet didn't know at all, only to be jarred awake by this hushed and visceral suffering.

What appeared to be an open script of some sort lay on the facing seat with a copy of this week's *Muse*, a few magazines, a box of chocolates, a blow dryer . . .

'I'm sorry, Father.' She rummaged through a large bag. 'My tissues . . . I don't know. I've surely called you out of something you need to be doing.'

'Not at all. May I ask . . . who you are?'

'I'm Kim Dorsay.' She extended her hand, and he took it. 'From Los Angeles. Thank you for your kindness. I've been reading about you in your newspaper.'

'Not that!' he said.

She smiled a little. 'I've been a subscriber for several months, since we found information that led to Mitford. I've even thought how I'd love to live here, how peaceful it must be. I've been seeking peace for a very long time.'

She searched again in the bag. 'Do you know Irene well?'

'Not well, but for some years.'

'Is her husband Raymond or Chester?'

'Chester. He died last February.'

'Chester! All the pieces of the puzzle have come together, then.' She closed her eyes briefly. 'All the pieces. Do you have time . . . to talk?'

'My time is yours.'

'I was twelve days old,' she said, 'when my father gave me away.

'My mother died when I was born. The woman who took me in was Norma Hudson, my father's secretary. Norma was a girl who came out to Hollywood from Idaho in the forties, to try and make it in that treacherous world.

'She was very beautiful, but by her own account had no acting talent—a minor role with Gregory Peck was the great highlight of her career. My father was a famous casting agent, the only child of immigrant parents from Warsaw. He rescued Norma from near-starvation, and she repaid him with ferocious loyalty. She would have laid down her life for him, really. Instead, he asked her to raise his daughters. There were two of us, you see.'

She tried to say more, but could not. She looked away, wiped her eyes with the back of her hand.

'I thought all the tears might be gone, Father. But they are never gone.'

He reached into his pocket and withdrew the handkerchief. She took it, surprised, somehow, and grateful.

'My mother hemorrhaged to death giving birth to twin girls. But Norma couldn't raise two children—she could scarcely take care of herself. I was older than my sister by four minutes. As much as Norma wanted to please my father by taking us both, she chose the firstborn.

'Our father consented to letting Irene go, you see. Norma called our mother's brother, the only family we had, and he and his wife came for her when she was two months old. Norma didn't tell them that Mother had had twins. She said no one knew, really, our parents had few friends—Father did all his socializing away from home.'

The uniformed driver stood by the limo, hands behind his back, a minor spectacle that caused traffic to slow.

'I didn't know I had a sister until just before Norma died in March. I was stunned by this news. Devastated, really.

'There had been a barrier between Norma and me all those years, I felt it keenly. I think now it was because of her guilt for taking part in separating us. Norma's life had been all about separation and grieving, and she passed that along to others.'

'Your father?'

'Daddy provided a great deal of money. I had everything the other girls in our convent school had, but something was missing, always missing. All my life, there's been a kind of ache, a void of the worst sort. I thought the yearning was for my mother or for God, or a marriage that might actually work or the children I couldn't have.' She closed her eyes. 'Or all the above.'

There was the oddly distracted look that he had seen in Irene.

'Didn't Norma tell you how to find your sister?'

'She didn't know. There was no contact with my uncle all those years, and when we searched the phone books in Illinois . . .' She shrugged. 'Nothing. As it turned out, they had moved to La Jolla when I was fourteen. Irene was living just two hundred miles from me.'

She pressed the handkerchief to her eyes.

'Norma said my uncle despised my father, who was a man for the women. When they took Irene, he promised legal action if Daddy ever tried to intervene in any way. Norma told me that Daddy was relieved, though he did offer financial help. Financial help was refused, and so Daddy left it alone. I think he quite forgot about Irene, actually, as if she never existed.'

He wondered if his father had forgotten about Henry . . .

'Norma felt that Irene may have lacked for a great deal when she was growing up. My uncle had more pride than money. It's another reason I've felt unsure about doing this. How would Irene feel if she knew I was chosen for the so-called good life?'

'I see.'

'And would it be frightening for her if I showed up out of the blue, starved for family as I've always been, and perhaps wanting too much? Or what if she's somehow known about me all along and decided not to make contact?'

Henry had alluded to feelings like these.

'Coming to Mitford a few weeks ago was as much a hunch as it was a strong lead. I've had a team of investigators working on this for months—we didn't know whether my sister was permitted to keep the name our mother chose—Irene Elizabeth. And when we finally got the lead to McGraw, we found quite a few Irene McGraws. That took a lot of time to sift through, and we were confused by the several addresses—the home in Florida, a property in Montana, the home here, and no pictures of Irene on the Internet. All we could find were of Chester in his many philanthropic activities, and only one of his wife, who had turned away from the camera.'

And there was a customer going into the bookstore, someone thin and slightly stooped.

'I was out running a couple of weeks ago,' he said, 'and saw your car head down the mountain. You seemed in a hurry.'

'My director had just died. We were very close; I did four films with him. I felt I was really getting on to something in Mitford; we had stopped by your house when the call came. I was relieved, in a way. I felt I was close to the truth at last, and it frightened me.'

'I understand that.'

'I thought about calling Irene from L.A., but that seemed impersonal, like news from a government agency. I wanted to see her face when she learned the truth—and if we were really sisters, I wanted us to experience the joy at the same moment.' She smiled at him now. 'Just the thought of it takes my breath away.'

'And mine, too, I have to say.'

'So when the *Muse* ran the little piece about her return from Georgia, I decided to come again.'

J.C.'s labors in the publishing vineyard had wrought a cup of good wine.

'In reading about your generosity to others, Father, I thought perhaps you would help me with this. Perhaps you could arrange a meeting somehow?'

'Of course.'

'Because I can't simply show up at her door. I mean, what would you do if you found after so many years that you had a brother?'

He laughed, astonished. 'Funny you should ask.'

'Gotta go. I won't ask what you were doin' in that limo. Aren't you glad I'm not nosy like everybody else in this town?'

'Very glad,' he said. 'Sorry to be so long. Who came in?'

'A professor from Wesley. Grumpy as heck. Somethin' about a book you gave his son. I told him you were out for a few minutes. He said he'd go across to the Local an' stop in later. Anyway, I did it, I read some poetry.'

'That's what comes of secluding yourself in that section.'

'It was Billy Collins.'

'An Irishman! A very enthralling fellow, once our poet laureate.'

'Poetry always scared me,' she said.

'It can be scary, all right.'

'I remember in school we had to memorize a poem about an urn. Somebody wrote an ode on an urn, or maybe it was about an urn with an ode already on it. In my understanding of urns, it is a flowerpot. Why would you write an ode about it?'

'Beats me,' he said.

'But this Billy Collins, he writes like we live.'

'There you have it.'

'Although I don't know about flying around a room.'

'Sailing,' he said. 'Sailing, I believe it was.'

'WAIT 'TIL YOU HEAR THIS, KAV'NA.'

'I know, I just got around to reading the *Muse*. You didn't tell me you have a hundred and twenty-five votes. And Coot has seventeen! This is fun.'

'Irene McGraw has a twin sister.'

'What?'

'I've just talked with her. It's Kim Dorsay—the film star Irene is said to look like. Remember the limo a few weeks back? She's here again. In Mitford.'

'The little girl in the paintings!'

'It looks that way.'

'Does Irene know she's here?'

'Not yet.'

'I have chills.'

'Me, too,' he said. 'And I need you to do something right away.'

THE AFTERNOON LIGHT WAS BEHIND the man as he came through the door. Tall, thin, hunched, a kind of Ichabod Crane in silhouette . . .

'Kavanagh?'

'Yes. And yourself?'

'Professor McCurdy.'

McCurdy laid the Wordsworth paperback on the counter. 'I'm returning your book.'

'Hastings! Who saved his money!'

'Hastings McCurdy is my son.'

'But I meant for him to keep it. It's a gift—though much used, as you can see. A fine and curious boy, your son.'

'The margins are littered with references to God.'

'Well, yes, I am prone to scribbling in margins. I study the books I especially care for. This was a favorite in my seminary days.'

'Why did you find it necessary to speak of God to him?'

'I spoke of God?'

'I find such a reference completely unnecessary in a commercial enterprise, particularly involving a child who can't discriminate for himself.'

'I'd be interested to learn what I said to your son.'

'You said, God bless you. Leading him to question the meaning of such a remark. Should his class come in again, I would ask you to refrain from religious allusion in future.'

'I will honor your request as far as Hastings is concerned. Beyond that, I can't promise to keep the lid on when it comes to the mention of God.'

The man appeared to be trembling. Nearly imperceptible, but yes.

'Do you always wear a collar to administrate the workings of a bookstore?'

'I do.'

'Why?'

'Because I am a priest, bookstore or no.'

'Must you push it in one's face?'

'It shows there's a place to run, if need be.'

'Many have run to the collar with disastrous results.'

'That's not my affair, Professor.'

'It seems a cliché to wear it outside the pulpit . . .'

The collar was clearly a sticking point with the professor, who stood before him in the cliché cardigan with elbow patches.

'. . . unless, of course, you're using the bookstore as your pulpit. A clever notion, but I am not charmed.'

'This is who I am. There's nothing to be done about it—I belong to God.'

'While I, sir, am my own.'

'George McDonald called that notion the guiding principle of hell. Have you read McDonald? He was a great influence on C. S. Lewis.'

Yes, the professor was trembling. McCurdy turned abruptly from the counter and walked toward the door.

'Just curious, Professor McCurdy—are you Irish?'

The door jangling open, then closing.

HE SAT ON THE STOOL, depleted, his dog at his feet.

'Thank heaven for you, Buddy.'

He remembered a fragment of an epitaph written by a fellow named Hobhouse, for his dog.

'". . . one who possessed Beauty without Vanity,"' he said aloud to Barnabas.

'"Strength without Insolence, / Courage without Ferocity, / And all the virtues of Man without his Vices."'

'That's you, my friend, and God bless you for it.'

He went to the yellow backpack and pulled out a dog biscuit. The Old Gentleman took it with great delicacy.

He needed to run. He needed to visit Louella. He needed to get in touch with Coot about a cleanup. He needed to get after the privet at Children's Hospital—this was the last and best chance for pruning. He needed to rest. He needed a car. He needed to work on his Latin.

As much as anything, he needed a break. Any break would do.

He left a message in J.C.'s voice mail and called Mule. 'How about checking out breakfast at Feel Good in the morning? Eight o'clock. Be there or be square.'

CYNTHIA ARRIVED with a shopping bag from Village Shoes, to buy a birthday card for Olivia Harper.

'The economy booms when you come to town,' he said.

She gave him a hug. 'Irene said Sunday after church would be best for her. I told her it isn't Children's Hospital business, there's somebody who'd like very much to meet her. Somebody special, I said. It was hard to find the right word.'

'Special definitely works.'

'She didn't seem crazy about the idea of meeting a perfect stranger—Irene is shy. Anyway, two o'clock. And we can't meet there, she said, because her house is given over to ladders and drop cloths. I think we should do it at Happy Endings, on neutral ground.'

'Good.'

'I'm jittery. What if this doesn't work? I'd hate for us to be the ones . . .'

'"For God has not given us the spirit of fear,"' he quoted from Timothy, '"but of power and of love and of a sound mind."'

Because he was feeling anxious himself, the scripture was mostly for his own instruction.

'You're worn out, Timothy. I don't like this.' She stood next to his stool and rubbed his back. 'You had your shot this morning?'

'I did. I'm fine. Don't worry.'

'I love you.' She looked down at him with that small pucker of her forehead; he felt wasted, somehow.

When she left, he remembered he hadn't turned on the music today. He selected something from Mozart's 'light and happy pen.'

The thought of calling a movie star on her private line made his knees weak. Realizing that he couldn't do it standing, he went to the Poetry section and dialed her cell number from the wing chair.

'Two hundred and sixteen dollars and ninety-five cents.'

Why weren't the receipts better, especially with the O Sale in effect? What did they need to do to get paying customers in here?

'You sound weary,' said Hope. 'I think I should pray for you.'

'Thank you,' he said. 'That would be good.'

    <Want to add time to your busy schedule?

    <Call Emma!

    <Punctuation & spelling still spotOn

No balm in Gilead.

From the window by his desk in the study, he saw Harley's truck lights bob into the driveway. In the gathering dusk, he could see that Harley was alone in the cab. Good. He had no stomach for a surly Sammy Barlowe.

'Yo, Harley!'

Harley, he reckoned, would rather not see him. Harley felt

responsible for Sammy, was shamed that he couldn't manage the boy's behavior.

'How about if I borrow your truck tomorrow? I'll pay your rental fee, of course.'

'You won't pay no rental fee, I can tell y' that. It's yours all y' want.' Harley took a deep breath. 'What you gon' do, Rev'rend?'

'Prune a hedge, put down a little mulch.'

'Nossir. About Sammy.'

Harley was waiting for the other shoe to drop.

'Nothing.' He looked at his watch. 'I need two pruning shears with your sharpest blades and three yards of mulch. Can I get three yards of your best stuff?'

'What time d'ye need it?'

'Ten o'clock on the dot.'

'I'll git it loaded an' be back before ten. How's that?'

'That'll work. Can Sammy use a little extra cash?'

'Yessir, he can. That citation costed him a hundred an' fifty dollars.'

'Ask him to be ready when you bring the mulch. We'll stop at Lew's to see the car; I need to get my hog-ring kit out of the glove compartment. Then we'll run over to Children's Hospital to the hedge project. We can knock it out in maybe four hours.'

'Yessir, this is y'r last chance to prune before winter. I can go over with ye, I can give a hand.'

'Thanks, but I want him to be stuck with me for a while. Just the two of us. It'll be good punishment for rotten behavior.'

Harley cackled. 'I ain't never knowed nobody like you, Rev'rend.'

'An' I ain't never knowed nobody like you, Harley.'

How was he really feeling about all this, about some out-of-control kid stealing his car and wrecking it?

He went deep and discovered the truth. He was furious.

Chapter
Seventeen

We should have a Main Street Grill reunion,' he said.

'Great idea,' said Mule. 'I'll give Percy a call after church tomorrow—invite him to join us at Feel Good. Maybe Tuesday.'

'Save your breath,' said J.C. 'Percy and Velma are out of town.'

'Where?' he said.

'On a cruise in the Bahamas.'

'On a cruise? In the *Bahamas*?'

'He deserves it,' said J.C. 'For forty-some years, he got up at four o'clock every morning so he could open at five.'

'For forty-some years, I've gotten up at five, and I've never been on a cruise.'

'If you get up at five instead of four, you don't get a cruise. You get a road trip in a '49 Chevy Cabriolet.'

Mule stirred his coffee. 'Anytime you say, boys, y'all can look like you've been on a cruise in th' Bahamas.'

'Here it comes,' said J.C. 'He gets ten percent every time he drags some poor geezer up to A Cut Above. They put th' guy in th' box, hit th' spray nozzle, and out walks George Hamilton.'

'Who's George Hamilton?' said Mule.

'I know what I'm havin', said J.C. 'Two eggs over easy, pep-pered bacon, a buttered biscuit, cheese grits, and, out of respect to my wife, the captain, a fat-free yogurt.'

He studied the bill of fare.

**Welcome to our new Saturday morning
breakfast menu**

Special today only:

Huevos Rancheros

For restroom key, ask Mindy.

He thought that might be poor positioning for the restroom key alert.

'They have a special,' he said.

'What is it?' said Mule. 'I love specials.'

'How quickly you forget,' said J.C. 'You hate specials.'

He turned the menu over. 'And look here. A new lunch item. Baked potato with cheese and chipotle.'

'Baked potato with what?' said Mule.

'Cheese and chee-*pote*-lee,' said J.C.

'What kind of language is that?'

'Here's Ms. Basinger, you can ask her.'

'I thought you weren't servin' anything people can't pro-nounce,' said Mule.

Wanda was wearing a cowboy hat and didn't look too happy this morning. 'Most people can pronounce chipotle.'

'Not th' people I know.'

'That figures,' she said, topping off their coffee.

'So what is it?'

'Smoked chili pepper.'

'Smoked chili pepper,' said Mule, aghast. 'Why?'

'Because I like it, Mr. Skinner. I used to live south of the border.'

'Which border?'

He thought Wanda's eyeballs were capable of rolling pretty far back.

'Look who just flew in,' said Mule.

Omer Cunningham walked over, grinning. He'd always liked Omer, a big, easygoing guy whose perpetual grin displayed teeth as big as dimes. 'Piano keys!' someone had said.

'Any room for me, boys?'

'Always,' he said, indicating the chair next to his own.

'How y'all doin'?'

'Anybody we can,' said Mule.

'Nice day up there. Not bad down here, either.'

'I see you flying south a lot,' he said.

J.C. toweled his face with a paper napkin. 'Yeah. Always headed south. You goin' someplace special?'

'Real special,' said Omer. 'There's a halfway house in Holding. I take corporate clients up every two weeks to raise money for th' place. A hundred and fifty bucks a head an' I've got a waiting list. I fly in and out of a little grass strip down there.'

'I've heard of that halfway house,' he said. 'They do a good job.'

'It'll break your heart,' said Omer. 'What I do don't help much, but it keeps me out of trouble.'

Mule looked depressed. 'If I had a plane, Fancy wouldn't let me take it out of th' yard.'

'I hear your sister-in-law might run for mayor next time,' said J.C.

'She's not talkin' about it,' said Omer. 'I believe that's a rumor.'

'I might run a piece on that.'

'How can you make news out of a rumor?' said Mule.

'People do it all the time, buddyroe.'

'I don't get it. Here's your headline: *Esther Cunningham Is Not Talking About Running for Mayor*. That's not news.'

'I've been busy gettin' my potatoes out of th' ground,' said Omer. 'So what *is* news around town?'

'Spray tan!' said Mule.

J.C. let a word fly.

'The biggest news in th' high country is right here under our noses,' Mule informed the table. 'The revolutionary, widely popular, affordable way to look young and carefree!

'You know what one of those booths can cost?' he asked J.C. 'Up to a couple hundred thousand. I'm not sayin' that's what Shirlene paid, but right here in Mitford, you've got Los Ange-lees goin' on.'

'Bull.'

'An' are you takin' care of our own by helpin' her get started in this town? No way. And listen to this, *she's* takin' care of our own by givin' ten percent of every sale to the Children's Hospital—and she's a dadblame newcomer! That's a story right there.'

Mule was ticked; this had obviously been building up.

'Are you nuts?' said J.C. 'We announced she was coming. We gave her a nice intro. If she wants to educate th' public, let her run a paid ad.'

'She didn't have to invest her future in Mitford, she could have set up business in . . . in . . .'

Mule was stuck for a town.

'Charlotte!' said Omer, naming the first town that came to mind. 'Go, Panthers.'

'Right. You ran a story on Feel Good changin' its name, what's th' difference? No wonder people fight over th' *New York Times* up at th' bookstore, they're starved to death for somethin' to get their teeth into.'

Mule had never read the *Times* in his life; he was lining up all the artillery he could muster.

'If y'all want out of here before th' lunch crowd,' said Wanda, 'you need to tell me what you're havin', pronto.'

J.C. glowered at the proprietor. 'What's with th' cowboy hat?'

She glowered back. 'Yippee-ki-yay. Bad-hair day.'

'You go, Omer.'

'Two poached eggs, medium, please, ma'am; whole wheat toast—hold the butter—and turkey sausage.'

'I'll be darned,' he said. 'That's what I'm having. Make it two.'

'Make it three,' said Mule.

'I don't have all day,' said J.C. 'Make it four.'

Mule gaped. 'Amazing. That's th' first time in twenty years we've ordered th' same thing!'

'It's th' turkey sausage,' said Wanda. 'A no-brainer for this table.'

HE WAS ALWAYS STRUCK by how much Sammy looked like Dooley. The optician said he was definitely ready for an upgrade on his prescription, but still . . .

There was nothing to say.

He drove; Sammy looked out the passenger window and jiggled his right leg. The old, inflamed scar on Sammy's cheek, the fresh cut on his forehead—the boy's face was raw history.

Sammy Barlowe knew right from wrong, no question about it. Yet he was pressing them all to the mat, especially the old guy he couldn't make angry enough to come after him.

Lew's wrecker was parked around back, the Mustang still in tow. He wasn't prepared for seeing it, not at all. Dear God.

Sammy breathed a four-letter word, which pretty much expressed his own astonishment.

'Is it true you told Chief Guthrie you don't care if you live or die?'

'Yeah.' Sammy spit into the gravel.

'I care that you live. Harley cares. Kenny cares. Cynthia cares. Dooley cares. Your little brother and sister care. But you don't care—you can go either way?'

'Yeah.'

'Baloney.' He turned and walked to the front of the station. 'What do I owe?' he asked Lew.

'Here's your bill, it's a whopper.'

'I'll say.'

'Tough haulin' it up th' bank. That's a ruined piece of machinery, all right. When I seen it, it scared me pretty bad, I thought it was you. Anyway, it's hid out back 'til I can get shed of it. No use for bad news to get around worse'n it has to.'

'Amen.'

'Here's all th' stuff that was in it.' Lew handed over a plastic bag. 'Me an' my wrecker's seen a few close calls, but this broke me out in a sweat.'

Sammy walked up, shrugged. 'It ain't nothin'.'

Lew shot Sammy a cold look. 'God is good, but he ain't Santy Claus. You definitely won't be gettin' another chance like that.'

FOUR HOURS ON THE MONEY, including a packed lunch they ate in the cab with the heater going.

Sammy had worked hard, they'd made it happen. They were in under the wire of a cold front moving in tomorrow. He felt a certain lifting of his spirit.

'Well done,' he said. 'Come in with me.'

'I'm too d-dirty t' come in.'

'Come in anyway,' he said.

'I don't want nothin' to do with hospitals.'

'Come in anyway,' he said, agreeable.

They walked along the hall to the men's toilet and washed up, then headed to ER. There went Dr. Young, living up to his name by literally racing along the hall.

'We've been working on the hedge out front, we're pretty dirty,' he said to the charge nurse, Robin Presley. 'Who can we see today?'

'Father Tim! Thank goodness you're here. It's a boy from Dyson County.'

Robin wiped her eyes. 'He's th' age of my baby brother. We admitted him a little bit ago, it's very bad. Is your friend comin', too?'

Sammy looked suddenly older, the way Dooley used to look when he felt threatened. 'I ain't d-doin' it.'

'Let's go, y'all,' said the nurse. 'It's real busy in there, so stand back. And no contact with th' patient.'

When they reached the double door of the emergency room, he looked around. Sammy was coming, anyway.

'Caught in a garbage truck compactor. They're gettin' ready to fly him to Charlotte. He's seventeen years old.'

Robin opened the door and, even with staff moving about the bed, he saw the patient clearly. The room dipped. He reached for the doorjamb, held on; Sammy turned and fled.

He repositioned a few of the larger branches in the truck bed, needing time. He had prayed for the boy, the doctors and nurses, all of it masking a kind of interior howl. Hospital patients had come and gone in his life, but nothing had rocked him quite like this. 'Jesus,' he whispered, opening the truck door.

'Why'd you do that? Why'd you make me do that?' Sammy shouted.

'I didn't need to see that, they won't any reason t' make me see that. That's some kind of God that'd do that to somebody, that's some kind of God you think so much of. No way would I do that t' nobody, hurt somebody like that!'

Yelling, sobbing, then opening the passenger door and getting out and shouting into the cab.

'Is it all jis' lies? I thought you was all about th' truth. Dooley says you're about th' truth, but how can you be about th' truth if God is all about lies? I don't git it, I don't want t' git it, I ain't goin' t' git it!'

And there came the stream of vitriol the boy had grown up with.

'An' him bein' seventeen—was that some kind of setup t'

teach me a lesson about bein' good like Dooley, or good like Kenny, or good like you? I don't see why I ever ended up with you, anyhow, how come I had to end up with you?'

Uncontrolled weeping.

He held the anger away from himself and did not enter into it; he could not enter into it. 'My dear brothers,' Saint James had written, 'take note of this: Everyone should be quick to listen, slow to speak and slow to anger.' He had listened, and he would say nothing.

Then Sammy, slamming the door and storming away, headed for the highway.

Probably for the first time in his life, Sammy Barlowe had started to feel something more than his own pain.

HE SAT VERY STILL for what seemed a long time, trying to collect the pieces hurled into the air and falling.

Then he started the truck and drove out of the hospital lot and onto the highway.

Grace may be a no-brainer for God, but for him it was clearly impossible to deliver. If mock grace was going to bring anything to the table, the heart must be kept free of malice. But how? Yank out the bitter weed, and in a flash, back it comes, and more of it. He found there was even a type of repulsion to be rooted out of his feelings, this having to do with Sammy's general hygiene and the way spitting was used as a nonverbal form of in-your-face loathing. And yet this was the package that had been set before him.

He didn't know how to help Sammy make something of himself in the competitive world of pool. It was beyond his powers. All he and Sammy had was the card currently dealt: the restoration of a garden gone wild. Together, they were making a place for the human spirit to find ease, if only for a fleeting moment. He'd learned that even the fleeting moment counts for something, counts for much. In a fleeting moment, Paul was convicted on the road, John Wesley's heart was strangely warmed, Lewis's 'land of longing' was left behind at the moment, Lewis said, 'when God closed in.'

Who was he, anyway, to tamper with the damage of a young life? All he knew to do, for now, was keep his mouth shut, and in the silence let the Holy Spirit do the talking.

Outside Wesley's town limits, he pulled off the highway a few yards ahead of Sammy; left the motor running, waited. Sammy climbed back in the truck.

There was nothing to say. He drove, kept his eyes on the road.

They rounded the curve across from the lawn-mower repair.

'God A'mighty.' Sammy slumped forward, elbows on knees, his face hidden.

The trees a riot of color; the brilliant red of the staghorn sumac . . .

Chapter
Eighteen

I 've been wondering how to tell Irene,' said Cynthia. 'What do you think?'

'I suggest you keep it simple and make sure she's sitting down. Irene, you have a sister. Don't hurry to the next piece of business, but don't tarry, either. Then say, A twin sister. One piece of information at a time. Things will develop from there.'

'Easy for you, darling. You've been delivering surprises to people for decades.'

'Let's catch our breath,' he said, 'and pray the prayer that never fails.'

They held each other and spoke the few and familiar words, and she drew back and looked at him and smiled. 'That's better.'

'All will be well,' he said.

'I regret never seeing any of her films. I did a search, she's a three-time Oscar nominee. We could be the only ones left standing who don't know her work.'

He was busy getting out of his lace-up church shoes and into his loafers. 'She may find that refreshing.'

'I wouldn't think so. This dress is so dowdy, I have no idea why I bought it. How's my hair?'

'Perfect.'

'But you didn't really look.'

'I don't have to. Your hair is always perfect.'

Wrong word. She liked her hair to appear 'tossed by a breeze,' she once said.

He went to his sock drawer, which shared space with his handkerchiefs, and took one from the pile of fresh inventory.

'I hate to wear a coat over this dress, it will smash the collar, but it's freezing out there.'

'Wear a coat,' he said.

The bookstore had tissues, a staple item that went wherever a parson set up shop—but a little backup never hurt. He took another handkerchief, this one a gift from Walter, and monogrammed; he would make sure it didn't stray. 'Your green coat would be good.'

'My green coat? With this? Ugh.'

His wife was beside herself. Moving from the quiet domestic life into the private drama of a three-time Oscar nominee was disconcerting. How did they manage to have such a big life in such a small town?

HE WOULD HAVE ROUGHLY fifteen minutes with Kim, something she requested, before Cynthia arrived with Irene.

Because Kim could be recognized, he hurried her into Happy Endings as the limo drove away. He switched on a single lamp in the Poetry section, choosing not to use the main store lights.

She was dressed simply. Dark pants, dark sweater, gold earrings. In truth, much like Irene often dressed.

They situated their chairs so he could see the door. 'Is your father living?' he asked.

'He's in skilled nursing and doesn't know me. Division in our family has had, if you will, a way of multiplying. Our mother divided from her children, the children divided from each other, my father now divided from his mental powers.'

'You have no children, I believe you said.'

'No children. And no husband after three marriages. I am by nature impulsive. I've often acted in haste and regretted it—another reason I've taken my time in following through about Irene. I'm shaking, Father. Completely undone.'

'Let me pray for you.'

'Please. I need help of any kind. I was raised Catholic, but somehow it never stuck. I couldn't imagine that God would be interested in me.'

'He's more than interested in you. It's a pretty radical notion, but he actually made us for himself, for his pleasure. He wants to hear from you anytime, about anything. Try to know that.'

He took her hand and prayed then, against the fear he felt throbbing in her palm.

As he looked up, he saw Cynthia and Irene walk by the display window.

'God be with us,' he said. He didn't let go of her hand as they went to open the door.

He heard Kim's sharp intake of breath, saw the incredulous expression on Irene's face. The glass door between them became a kind of mirror in which each of the two women saw herself in the other.

HÉLÈNE PRINGLE. Eight o'clock in the evening. Hélène never called in the evening.

'Hélène!'

'Yes, Father. Are you and Cynthia well?'

'We are. And you?'

'Very well, thank you. I was wondering if we might arrange to have a . . . *conversation privée*?'

A private talk, he knew that much French. 'Would this be a good time?'

'*Oui*, if you can be spared at home.'

'I'll pop over now if that works.'

'Come to the rear porch—would you mind coming in by the rear porch?'

'Not in the least.'

'We'll have tea in your pleasant old kitchen. I'll put the kettle on.'

They sat at the same table, in the same chairs he'd used all those years in another life.

There was the stove where he made dinner for his new neighbor with the great legs; where he'd fried bologna for Dooley and baked a Christmas casserole on the morning Dooley found a red bicycle beneath the tree.

This was where Miss Sadie's letter about Dooley's inheritance of a million-plus had been read with such grave astonishment, where his brand-new wife had travailed over the first Primrose Tea, and where Barnabas and Violet had at last made their peace and lay down together, lion and lamb. The rectory on Wisteria Lane was a museum of memories.

She filled their cups with Earl Grey and passed him a small plate of lemon slices. 'I've been thinking, Father. Quite a lot.

'Teaching piano is the only great thing I have ever done for anyone. But I'm paid to do that. I want very much to do something I'm not paid to do. I wish to do something from the heart, Father. Ever since he came out from behind the curtain . . .'

She gave him a shy look. '*Comprenez-vous?*'

'Oh, yes.'

'A few of my pupils have grown up and moved on to other interests and I have a bit more time. Time is something that must be managed, *tu vois ce que je veux dire?* One must get it firmly by the neck!'

She leaned toward him, confiding. 'I believe he has asked me to give a day to the bookstore.'

'*Formidable!*' he said in the French way.

'I'll take . . . Tuesday!' she said, as if choosing a chocolate. 'I'd like to begin right away, if that would be *opportun*.'

'Absolutely,' he said. 'I'll show you the ropes tomorrow.'

'I shall be the first to read the Sunday *Times*! After Hope and Scott, of course.' His neighbor had a very agreeable laugh. 'And Tuesday gives us an unbroken succession of days—Tuesday, Wednesday, Thursday, Friday. Good for business, I should think.'

'Wonderful news. Hope will be thrilled, as am I. Thank you, Hélène.'

'There is, however, a problem of some concern.'

He sipped his tea.

'I have no idea how to sell a book.'

'Books sell themselves, I've found.'

'And you would have to show me how to use the . . . *machine á carte de credit*.'

'I can certainly show you that. *Trés simple!*' He was quickly exhausting his French. 'There's only one true requirement in this job. Can you make coffee?'

'*Oui, oui!* Since childhood. And very strong!'

He doubted he could show her how to unlock the door, but they would cross that bridge when they came to it.

She fidgeted with her napkin, her chin trembled.

'And now, Father, may I bring before you a most unpleasant subject?'

'Please.' The other shoe was falling.

'I am a *romantique*, Father, I do not deny it. I had thought we might all live together under one roof as a type of family, each with their own strict privacy, of course. Having someone down there has been so . . . *satisfaisant* until . . . until things began going wrong with Sammy.

'I teach innocent children, Father, many of them young women, and word is getting round that he lives downstairs. He has a very, shall I say, *sale bouche*, and some very indelicate habits. You take Mr. Welch, Father—an uneducated man, but with delicate habits—clean, a fine cook, very courteous and thoughtful always. But Sammy—he smokes, you see. He leaves the house to do it, but there he stands beneath my cherry tree, smoking like a *cheminée* as people go by, and throwing his . . . um, *mégot de cigarette* into the grass.

'And if he isn't smoking, he is spitting. I have never seen such a lot of spitting. We got through the business of Mr. Welch being a former . . . *prisonnier* . . . and then there was Mr. Gaynor, and now here's another piece of business to go through—but I don't wish to go through it.'

'You'd like him to leave.'

'It would break Mr. Welch's heart, I'm sure of it, and with young Kenny going away the first of the year, Mr. Welch would be, how do you say, an empty nester. But I don't know what else to do. This is my livelihood, Father, my livelihood, and I am no longer young. Mother's estate is useful, but it does

not solve the day-to-day issues of keeping body and soul
together.

'Mr. Welch assures me that he frequently speaks to Sammy
about such behavior, but . . . *en vain*, Father, *en vain*.

'I saw the authorities parked at your curb the other evening.
I thought something may have gone wrong in your household,
and asked Mr. Welch about it. Being an honest man, he told
me the terrible truth.'

He didn't know what to say. He had never developed a Plan
B for Sammy. He didn't remind Hélène that it was she who had
found Sammy. She had seen him coming out of a drugstore in
Holding and thought it was Dooley. When he heard this, he
knew at once what was up. They had taken off in her aging car
with the very bad brakes, and gone searching. It had been the
ride of his life.

'Would you be willing to . . . give us a bit of time to settle
things?'

'But only a bit, Father. I'm so sorry. I would do anything to
please you and Cynthia, but this . . .'

She looked done in. '. . . this is frightful.'

Frightful.

A truer word was seldom spoken.

'IT HASN'T BEEN CALLED the *little* yellow house for nothing,'
said Cynthia. 'It can't contain the very big issues of a hurting
boy. I simply can't do it, Timothy. If you feel you must, then I
will comply in whatever way I can. But no, I cannot volunteer
for this.

'I'm sorry for many reasons, not the least of which is that I may look mean-spirited to others, and only you will know that I am not.'

The talk had been stressful for both. He put on a heavy jacket and a wool hat and walked with Barnabas to the bench under the maple. A nearly full moon was setting over the mountain. Its light silvered the trees, the lawn, the fence.

He sat until the chill overtook him, and walked his silvered dog back to their silvered house.

HE LAY ON THE SOFA in front of a fire gone to coals, Violet at his side. He was wiped, as Dooley would say. An emotionally rousing day, at the very least, albeit with happy consequences for Irene and Kim. Today's meeting was beyond any joy he'd witnessed in years. He had bawled like a baby, as had his wife; his handkerchiefs were two too few.

He stroked Violet's head, listening to the thrumming in her throat. 'What a good job you're doing. Just wanted to say thanks.'

He felt an unexpected peace but for one thing—something was nagging him, he couldn't put his finger on it.

'HEY, DAD.'

'Hey, yourself.'

'Just checkin' in. I know it's late.'

'Never too late to hear from you.'

Dooley wanted him to do something about Sammy's behavior, he could feel the pressure, but he would avoid that subject at all costs. Nor would he mention the talk with Hélène Pringle. Not tonight.

'I've been thinking about a vehicle,' he said.

'Great!'

'I don't want a car. I want a truck. A man needs a truck.'

Dooley laughed. 'You're full of surprises. What kind of truck?'

'Stick shift. Long bed. Two or three years old.' He had never been so sure of himself in the automotive realm. 'Red.'

'You've come to the right place,' said Dooley, who would rather turn a vehicle deal than eat when hungry. 'But you need to consider new, really. Break it in yourself, like a pair of farm boots. You don't want another guy's truck, people can be hard on trucks.'

'I don't have time to break in a truck.'

'Trust me—buy new. Leather seats. A really good sound system. Chrome-clad aluminum wheels . . .'

'Those are things. Things don't matter in the end—they wither like grass; the soul lives on.'

Dooley cackled. 'Hey, Dad, this is a truck we're talkin' about.'

HE WOKE AT THREE. The thing that nagged him was like a barely audible movement in a room at the back of the house.

Now he knew what it was.

During his rant on Saturday, Sammy had not stuttered.

He got up and went downstairs and gave his dog a scratch behind the ears and fired up his computer and Googled what he thought may be a phenomenon.

Sudden onset of stuttering is common. A sudden end to it is rare, but it happens. Why it happens is a mystery. Maybe the blow to the forehead? No search gave credence to this. And maybe it wasn't the end for all time, maybe Sammy had simply forgotten himself in his anguish for the boy in the hospital bed.

He went to the kitchen and poured a glass of water and drank it down, his wife would be proud.

Monday, six-thirty a.m., the phone.

'Good morning, Harley.'

'Yessir, good mornin', hit's twenty-eight degrees.'

'Right.'

Silence on the other end.

'You called to give me a weather report?'

Harley cleared his throat. 'Sammy wants to come t' work later, when it warms up. Or work tomorrow when the temperature's more like fifty-two.'

'He told you to say this?'

'Yessir, he did, I cain't git 'im up.'

'Tell him to get himself out of bed and I'll see you at seven-thirty sharp. Did you pick up the trellises?'

'Yessir. Nice. Real nice.' Harley did the throat-clearing again. 'I cain't git 'im up for nothin'.' Harley Welch had rather taken a whipping than make this call.

'We won't be working outdoors. We'll paint trellises in the Sunday school. Bring your sawhorses.'

Another tense silence.

'You might mention to Sammy that I have the capability to change my mind about pressing charges.'

An intake of breath. 'Yessir. An' I'll bring m' other oil heater. You want to ride down with us? Not havin' a vehicle . . .'

'I'll walk, thanks, and see you there.'

'Yessir, Rev'rend, seven-thirty.'

'Sharp.'

'We'll be there sharp.'

His tolerance for a stolen cue?

Generous.

His tolerance for a wrecked automobile?

Beyond generous.

His tolerance for not showing up for work on time?

Zero.

'WHAT Y'UNS WANT FOR LUNCH?' said Harley.

'The usual,' he said.

'Reu-reuben,' said Sammy. 'An' f-f-f-fries.'

Not only had the stuttering not stopped, it was worse.

He'd given the matter into God's hands; he had other fish to fry.

With a table contrived of two sawhorses and a sheet of plywood, the occasional sound of rain on the tin roof, and their heaters going at full gallop, the old Sunday school was a pretty tolerable winter headquarters. Today the trellises, tomorrow the benches—which they had decided to build themselves.

After lunch, he walked up from the church and met Hélène for a run-through. He dreaded the possible street theater with the lock business. He gave her fair warning and handed over the key.

In went the key, click went the lock.

'C'est merveilleux!' she said.

From: Emma Newland
To: Fr Tim Kavanagh
Tuesday, 7:15 p.m.

<Cannot keep Tuesday open for all eTernity

<Let me organize your filling, run your calendar, pick up
your cleaning, streamline your computer system and
make life easier~as of yore!!!

<This offer ends soon.

'Not nearly soon enough!'

'What did you say?' Cynthia asked from the kitchen.

'Just talking to myself.'

'It's come to that,' she said, popping chicken in the oven.

'What's Olivia's report on Hoppy?'

'He's been sick, but improving. It's not malaria, as feared. Home in November, then off again to South Sudan and home for Christmas.'

He called Hélène.

'How did it go?'

'*Trés bien*, Father, *trés bien*! I was nervous as a cat, but can't recall when I've known such enjoyment. *Pur plaisir!* I feel I have stood at the crossroads of the world!'

That would be one way of looking at it.

'Two people from Canada, three from Missouri, and someone from Franklin, Tennessee. The last of the leaf peepers, says Winnie.'

'And all went well at the bank?'

'Oh, yes, one hundred and ninety-six dollars, I put in four of my own to make an even number.'

'Well done, Hélène! Well done! I'll let Hope know.'

'Sometimes we go too long, do we not, Father, for want of refreshment of our souls? I love music, but I had forgotten how

I love words. And people can be rather enjoyable, as well, *vous ne pensez pas?'*

LIGHTS. COFFEE. And the roar of the Hoover.

Coot was a regular German hausfrau. In the corners, tight to the baseboards, under chairs and tables. All this preceded by the beating of chair cushions and the dusting of a grim rubber plant from a customer relieved to be shed of it.

"At's done,' said Coot, wiping his hands on a rag. 'Now, let me show y' somethin'.' Coot held up a book, grinning to beat the band. 'Looky here!' he said, pointing to the second word in the title. 'C-A-T. *Cat!*'

'Yes! Wonderful!'

'Now, looky here.' Coot pointed to the fifth word in the title. 'H-A-T. *Hat!*'

He whistled, gleeful.

'But I ain't got them in-between words yet.'

'You'll get 'em,' he said. 'You'll get 'em.'

THE MUSE TRUCK WAS RUNNING LATE this morning. He stood at the window, looking for the truck with the avidity of a *Christian Science Monitor* subscriber. Had his brain ossified? Was he carrying around a rock up there?

When he saw the truck coming, he stepped outside and caught the delivery in midair.

Two for One:
Today's Helpful Hints

We are big into clean, happy air, how about you??

One: To make your rooms smell fa-bu-lous, try a few drops of lavender oil in a glass of really hot water and yayyy, you have destroyed unwanted cooking odors and doggie smells if you have a dog&^.

Two: to clean your bottles Cut up a raw potato and put the pieces in the bottle with a tablespoon of salt and two tablespoons of water and shake. Every stain gone in a flash! You will not believe it!

Susan, Joe, Avice and
Wilma Faye Are Taking
Care of Our Own.
Are You?

Dear Vanita, here is a pic of a bag of trash I picked up on the road to Farmer. I power walk out there which is crazy because I could get killed in a heartbeat. If people are not driving on the shoulder they are driving in the middle of the road and saying it's because they pay taxes on both sides!

Anyway, by the time I get home I have usually picked up about seven pounds of garbage thrown out by cretans (I looked this up, it fits exactly), otherwise known as rednecks. Yours sincerely and go, Panthers! Susan Glover, age 56, Rural Route 4

Hi I am Joe Zwieback like the toast. Here is a picture of me from last year's two-foot powder blowing snow off the walk of somebody who did not have a shovel, a blower or even a job. You cant see me for the snow flying but that is my dog Howdy a real trooper—me and him moved down here from Minnesota for the climate ha ha. Thank you.

Vanita honey

I am setting here on my loveseat with little Lisa May who is two. I am taking care of Mitford by taking care of Lisa May whose mother my next door neighbor on route four has to work two jobs. My great grandson Buddy who is twelve took this picture on his phone and printed it out at school. I am also taking care of Buddy for my DIL who is PG and works for NCDOT. So that is my 2 cents worth. Thank you and God bless you. Avice Porter

I am nine yers old and taking care of Mitford by being nice to people who don't even deserve it. My Sunday School teacher says don't worry about being nice to people who deserve it—that is easy. So here is a picture of me being nice to somebody (he is the blur on the right) who threw his stupid YUKKY lunch bag in our yard. I very nicely asked him to pick it up but when he didn't I chased him down and gave him a whipping he will NOT forget. Yours truly, Wilma Faye Barkley, Dogwood Lane

Hessie Mayhew opened the door and stuck her head in.

'Just wanted to say that is not *my* Helpful Hint in today's paper, I hope you know that.'

'I figured,' he said.

'While my Hints come from personal experience, she gets hers from a book. Who washes their bottles anymore? Do you wash your bottles?'

'I don't really have any to wash.'

'You see? Useless, outdated information!'

The door jangled shut, and opened again to admit Esther Cunningham, who had broken out in a smattering of her old blotches.

'When you were down at th' church,' she said, 'we mostly saw you in th' pulpit and out runnin'. Now you're right here in one spot where we can get at you—in a manner of speakin'.'

He grinned. 'I feel pretty gotten at, all right. How are you, Esther?'

'I'm thinkin' of pitchin' my hat in again. What do you think?'

'Do you really want all that commotion?'

'I like commotion. I miss commotion. I operate on commotion.'

'What does Ray think?'

'He thinks I'm a nut case—what else is new? You reckon there'd be any opposition? Andrew Gregory says he wouldn't run against me, provin' what a brilliant thinker he is, after all.'

'You were certainly one of the best . . .'

'*One* of th' best?'

He laughed. 'You're tough.'

'I am not tough. I'm soft as th' inside of a cathead biscuit, that's why I was a good mayor. I don't want you to talk about this, you hear? I want to keep it off th' street 'til I'm good 'n ready.'

'Got it. What would be your platform?'

'Lord only knows. You think th' old one still works?'

'In my opinion, it's working as we speak.'

'We might need somethin' fresh. Ray's messin' with it, he's good at that. You know I'd have to hammer th' merchants. They're goin' to sleep at th' wheel.'

'Hammering the merchants is your long suit.'

'Can I count on you?'

'I'll do what I can,' he said. In truth, he was perfectly happy with Andrew Gregory's administration.

'What improvements do you think we need? I'm doin' a limited survey. Very limited.'

'The trail behind the hospital,' he said. 'A waste of good real estate. Overgrown, littered with debris. Isn't that town property?'

'It was deeded to th' town in 1927. Twelve acres. The American Legion laid out th' trail in '52.'

'Needs attention. That done, people will use it for the right reasons.'

'I think it's time to raise taxes. I promised I'd never raise taxes, but that was then, this is now. That dog won't hunt anymore.'

'What will we do with the tax dollars?'

'Parkin', for one thing. We've got to have it.'

'Where would we put it?'

'I say tear down Evie's old house, put it on Main.'

'I don't know, Esther, you'll have a fight on your hands.'

'No pain, no gain.'

'People are getting interested in the plan for an inn on that spot.'

'Do we need parkin' worse than we need six rooms with smelly potpourri and four-poster beds? I ask you! Main is th' only place that makes sense. Otherwise parkin' has to go to th' old shoe barn—too far away, then we have to provide shuttles.'

'There could be some traffic congestion if you put it on Main.'

'We'd run 'em in on Main and out on Maple.'

'Maple is a mighty narrow street. And what about charging for parking? You know locals don't want to pay for parking.'

Esther gave him a look for which she was noted. 'You let me handle it, Father.'

'Glad to!' he said.

'DARLING! Any business up there?'

'Spotty,' he said.

'You have a hundred and seventy-four votes.'

'Never-ending.'

'I need peppermint tea. Can you stop by the Local?'

'Absolutely. What else?'

'Two lemons. Lace will join us for lunch on Saturday. Peppermint is her favorite. Now. I have two great surprises.'

He had never enjoyed surprises, but people continued to foist them on him.

'Guess who has a kitten?'

'Not Violet.'

'We do. Sammy brought it over. Wait 'til you see it.'

'Sammy? A kitten?'

'He said it needed a good home. Sammy seemed different, somehow. More . . . thoughtful, maybe. Something . . . I think it was the kitten, he was very tender with it.'

'What kind of kitten?'

'White as chalk with one black ear. Adorable. I was making the pimiento cheese for Lace's visit and Sammy brought it over in a box. So I gave him a grilled cheese and we closed the door to the hall and put the kitten on the floor and he was perfectly at home.'

'It's a he? How does Violet feel about this?'

'We don't know yet. She's on top of the refrigerator, where she goes to think things through.'

'Do I need to drop by the hardware for a litter box?'

'Sammy brought one.'

Sammy Barlowe had put two and two together? In this life-time? Unbelievable!

'I named him Truman.'

'For Harry?'

'For Truman Capote, who threw a famous Black and White Ball.'

'Aha.'

Their big life was getting bigger by the minute.

'So here's the other surprise. Someone I think you will like very much is walking up to see you right now.'

'Who?'

She laughed. 'It's a surprise.'

'FATHER TIM?'

The priest held forth his hand. Blue eyes. A dazzling smile. Ruddy cheeks. Muscles, even.

No introduction needed. He threw his arms around Father Brad and slapped him on the back, jubilant.

'Are we ever glad to see you!' he said.

Chapter
Nineteen

Snow.

He stood at the window and watched it fall, listening to Vivaldi's 'Winter.'

Unpredicted precipitation had begun around ten this morning—a thin offering which he thought would soon be over. But it had increased in volume and beauty and at eleven-thirty the town was vested in white.

Abe sailed by the window, threw up his hand, headed across to the post office. Mitford School had closed an hour ago; he saw buses ferrying home those they had recently delivered. He wondered whether the inveterate reader runs for a book when it snows, or if snow itself is entertainment enough.

A car nosed into a parking space across the street. Someone with mighty long legs was getting out, then waiting for traffic to pass. Beautiful, he could see that.

Good Lord! It was Lace.

Flashbacks of Lace teaching Harley about buffalo, and bark canoes. Lace bleeding from the lacerations to her back. Lace kneeling in the street beside his badly injured dog . . .

He hurried to the curb, glanced both ways, and met her halfway.

'Thanks, Father! What a welcome committee!'

Snow in her hair, on the shoulders of her coat.

'I left at six this morning,' she said. 'I'm so happy to be home. It's lovely—like a Christmas card.'

Inside, he helped her out of her winter wrappings—coat, scarf, gloves—as proud as any father. Lace Harper wasn't a girl anymore; she was a young woman at ease in her skin.

'I decided to stop and see you first, Olivia's in a meeting 'til one.'

'Great to have you home. How about a cup of tea?'

'Tea! You have tea!'

He had bought two boxes of peppermint—one for Happy Endings, just in case. He plugged in the kettle.

'Do you like running the bookstore?'

'Absolutely. And all for a good cause.'

'Dooley says you and Sammy and Harley are redoing the rose garden at church.'

'Can't wait for you to see it next spring. We're pretty excited.' He put a tea bag in a cup.

Barnabas got up and made his way to the one who, with Dooley, had saved him from certain death after the hit-and-run incident.

'Barn! You look so handsome in your bandanna. I've missed you.'

Barnabas received her affections, sniffed her boots, sprawled at her feet.

'How did you know what you wanted to do with your life, Father? I'm constantly trying to figure that out.'

'I'm not sure I figured it out. I was chiefly motivated by the notion of changing my father's heart if I became a priest.'

'Did you change his heart?'

'I don't think my priesthood ever mattered to him in the

way I hoped it would. God knows. What do you want to do with your life?'

'If . . . Dooley and I get married, I would like to work in the practice with him. But would that be . . . I don't know, enough?'

'How do you mean?'

'I wonder about making a commitment to the practice and then discovering it isn't enough. I love art, I feel I chose the right major, but I don't feel I have the luxury of becoming an artist. I should probably just learn to make a mean roast chicken with fingerling potatoes.'

'You can make roast chicken and pursue your art, one doesn't exclude the other.'

She smiled. 'But if I pursue my art, would there be money for roast chicken?'

'You have a point.'

'I don't know. I hope I'm not wasting my time in this major.'

'God will use it for good, is my guess. He doesn't like to waste anything; he's thrifty as a New Englander.'

'If . . .' she said again, but didn't finish the thought. 'We'd like to have children. Four, actually.' Her cheeks colored. 'There would be geese and goats and chickens—and Dooley is talking about cattle and the children could have horses. Think of all the fertilizer for the fields and garden! And there's that wonderful pond and the big creek and the woods . . . we want the whole hundred acres to be chemical-free. We know we can't save the world, but we can be kind to our hundred acres.'

Here was a veritable cornucopia of information. Clearly, Lace was the go-to on such matters of the heart, not Dooley.

He was grinning like a kid. 'If anything were ever enough,' he said, 'that should be it right there.'

'In the end, it all seems too much to contemplate. And it's

such a long time to . . . finalize things. Dooley has to finish college, then four years of vet school, and I have two more years . . .'

She put her hand to her forehead. 'I just don't know . . . the world is so big and the opportunities so totally endless. You and Cynthia have always helped me figure things out . . .'

'Maybe it's too soon for you to try and figure things out. Know that God has a plan for your future. Watch and wait for his timing, and when it comes, hitch a ride. You'll know.'

She sighed, gave him one of her ravishing smiles. 'You're right. I'm always fretting over something.'

'Let's have another look at your ring. Oh, yes. Beautiful!'

'It's a friendship ring.'

'Right.'

'Which leaves everything between us wide open. I really wanted a ring that, you know, said this is one thing, at least, that's for sure, we can face all the unknown stuff together.'

He had no salve for this.

'At the same time,' she said, looking brighter, 'I'm glad for it to be a friendship ring.'

'Good!'

'Because he is my best friend—most of the time. And I really work on that being enough. People tell us to wait, not to get married while he's in vet school, there's a lot of divorce in vet school. But six years . . .'

'When we were in Ireland, you and Dooley had a conflict.'

'I punched him. That was bad, I know it was bad. That's what was done to me, so it's what I learned to do, but I know it's wrong and I don't want to do it anymore. It's no excuse, but he was making me crazy with being late, sometimes for hours.'

'He and I had that issue.' He handed her the cup of steaming tea. 'Drove me nuts. Maybe it's because he never had any control over what was happening to him as a boy. Being late was somehow a way of taking charge. Is he doing better?'

'Yes. He knows that making people wait is wrong, just like I know that punching him is wrong. We struggle, Father. Instead of acting out the old stuff we were brought up with, we're trying to create our own relationship. Something . . . brand-new.' Her amber eyes were flecked with green.

'You love him, I can see it.'

'More than anything.'

That alone should be enough, he thought, but of course it never is. Courage has to come in there somewhere, and perseverance and forbearance and patience and all the rest. A job of work, as Uncle Billy would say, but worth it and then some.

IT WAS CHILLY in the store. He left the wool scarf wound about his neck.

He had just unwrapped his sandwich when an older couple came in, holding hands. He didn't often see people holding hands these days.

'Ralph Henshaw!' said the man. 'Retired from vacuum cleaner sales in Ohio to the comparative ease of the mountains of North Carolina!'

'Ralph, Tim Kavanagh.' They shook hands.

'My wife, Delores.'

'Call me Dot,' she said.

'Happy to see you. How may I help this morning?'

'Well, for several months, Dot and I have considered a move

from First Baptist in Wesley to one of your fellowships in Mitford, Lord's Chapel being a strong consideration. From what I've heard from my golf buddy, a lot of Baptists become Episcopalian, though Episcopalians strongly resist becoming Baptist.'

'I would agree with that,' he said.

'We thought a bookstore would be a neutral place to ask a few questions about your local churches.'

'Glad to help,' he said.

'One thing I'm wonderin' is if real wine at communion has anything to do with th' drinkin' those people are famous for.'

'There's a thought.'

'I certainly don't believe grape juice does the job,' said Ralph.

'Me neither,' said Dot.

'But I do wonder if a taste of the real thing at the altar is what gets them started in the first place. Anyways, Dot and I figure we're old enough to take a little vino and not let it affect our entire lives.'

'Right,' said Dot.

'I've heard those jokes about Baptists,' said Ralph, 'how they won't speak to you in the liquor store, and some of that is true . . .'

'Definitely,' said Dot.

'Truth is, us Baptists like a little shooter now and then, just not right out in your face with every Tom, Dick, and Harry lookin' on.

'Now, here's the big consideration. We've heard that Episcopalians can be more than a little on the stiff side. I have to tell you, we tried that crowd over in Sandusky, but only one time. It was the solemnest-looking bunch we ever came across. Right, Dot?'

'Really,' said Dot.

'Here's what else I heard. The other Sunday your pastor down at Lord's Chapel cried. Right out in front of everybody. Not talkin', not preachin', just bawlin'. That might be a little liberal for us. So we thought if things don't work out down there, how about the Presbyterians?'

'Talk about solemn,' he said.

HE COULDN'T STOP LAUGHING.

'What's going on?' said Abe.

'I just realized I had my scarf . . . around my neck . . . and they couldn't see my collar . . .'

'That's funny? No. You want funny, have you heard the one about Rabbi Goldman and the Brooklyn Bridge?'

He was starved for laughter; it was a feast he didn't want to end.

EACH TIME HÉLÈNE'S MANDATE came to mind, he rejected it. He had no idea what to do; it was out of his hands entirely. As for their work this week at the church, it had gone well enough. Sammy hadn't balked, nor had he talked. He was silent, did his work, took the occasional direction, gave the occasional curt suggestion. There was no indication that the scene at the hospital had happened.

Hélène Pringle's intentions may have gotten through to Harley, who watched Sammy like a hawk and demanded that any spitting be done outside the Sunday school, period, no matter if it was in 'serious bad shape.' An alpha Harley was a marvel to witness.

. . .

MARCIE GUTHRIE DID THE BOOKKEEPING, handled their online business, and ordered the inventory, which gave him time to actually read a book. He had heard of booksellers who never read, and didn't care to be one.

He had to find a book for himself, one to look up from when someone came in. 'Always read something that will make you look good if you die in the middle of it,' P. J. O'Rourke had said. He must stick that on the corkboard.

He was turning from the window when he saw the limo heading south on Main. He threw up his hand, waved, heard the horn as the car passed from view. K.D. would be going down the mountain with her monogrammed glasses case, retrieved yesterday from Lew Boyd.

After a separation of sixty-two years, Kim Dorsay had just spent four days with her twin sister. He and Cynthia had seen them last night at dinner, which Kim had cooked in the rented lodge in the hills. It had been a pretty phenomenal meal, strictly Italian, with a goodly quantity of Prosecco. He'd told Uncle Billy's basic repertoire, begging their pardon for its hopeless rusticity, and they had all done a good bit of laughing. Kim clued them in on people he'd never heard of, except possibly Dustin Hoffman.

In the end, he and Cynthia shared the odd feeling that they'd gained a sister or two, themselves.

MISS MOONEY OPENED THE DOOR and blew in with the snow.

'Just letting you know you won't be troubled with us today, Father. We are *dispersed!*' She shook out her wool cap, unleashing a tangle of curls.

'Hooray for snow days. How is Hastings coming along?'

'He loved the new book he bought and is saving for another, so we must put our thinking caps on. He's been out for a few days. Low-grade fever, I'm told, not eating or drinking.'

'An interesting boy, to say the least. I see our new reader is making progress.'

'Coot is very quick. His reading skills simply pop out and astonish me. An odd thing—he's frightened by the capital letter!'

'A candidate for e. e. cummings, perhaps?'

They had a laugh.

By teaching Coot to read, Miss Mooney had reminded him of something rather wonderful—there really was balm in Gilead.

'The Powder Pig has arrived, but no chunder and no chicken necks, please.'

'Chunder and chicken necks?'

'Ski talk! Snow does that to me. I was in such a hurry the other day, thought I'd come in and be civil.'

Father Brad indicated his gear—wool scarf, jeans, hiking boots, hat, fleece-lined jacket. 'Vestments for Rite Three. What's going on today, Father?'

'You're the most we've had going on in some time. What do you think of our village now that you've been around the block, so to speak?'

'Looks to be all apple and no worm.'

'How about a good bit of apple, and definitely some worm?'

'We'll all be human together, then.'

'I just made a fresh pot of coffee . . .'

'Half a cup, thanks, I'm meeting a realtor here in twenty minutes. Leaving for Colorado first thing in the morning, wanted to touch base again. Where's Barnabas?'

'Not in the display window, too cold. Probably on the heat vent at American History. We'll rattle his treat bag.'

Barnabas appeared, yawning. He thought his dog looked especially freewheeling in the red bandanna. Father Brad squatted, took something from his jacket pocket. 'You're a wise and handsome fellow. See what you think of this—organic oatmeal with spelt flour.'

Barnabas took it at once. Down the hatch. Two chomps.

'He likes it!' he said.

'It's what I give my girl at home; bake 'em myself. Daisy's around four years old, looks forward to moving to Mitford.'

'Her breed?'

'Mongrel, like the rest of us.' Father Brad powered to his feet like a jack-in-the-box.

'Did you find a place?'

'Not yet. I looked at a couple of rental houses yesterday, but I'm starting to think an apartment.'

'We don't have apartments in Mitford.'

They sat on stools at the coffee station.

'Just as well, parishes don't trust priests in apartments, even interims. Too fly-by-night. They prefer clergy strapped with a mortgage and a lawn to keep mowed. By the way, I hear you're doing this gig pro bono.'

'I feel I owe the owner for the experience. How did you find things down the street? I hear you're good at damage control.'

'I'm the guy with a shovel who follows the elephants.'

'I don't envy you.'

'My vision for Lord's Chapel goes beyond trying to help clean up the Talbot business. I'd like to put together a really strong Youth Group, but I haven't seen any youth around.'

'They're definitely here. I have one over at my place, he's trouble enough to be an entire group all by himself.'

'What age?'

'Seventeen.'

'I was at my worst at seventeen. I went from punching out a cop and spending time in juvenile detention to stealing a car and selling dope. I was ballistic. Finally got my act together, made it through four years of college with pretty good grades, and joined the military—I was surprised they'd have me. It changed everything.'

Father Brad peeled out of his wool scarf.

'I'll be coming to Lord's Chapel at an awkward time all around. In addition to the Talbot business, there's January— party's over, people can be a little edgy, depressed. Anyway, thought I'd make a quick reconnaissance to Mitford and get a few ducks in a row so everything doesn't hit at once. Pray for me, if you will.'

'Consider it done. And know that you can call on me at any hour.'

'Thanks, that means a lot. My wife, Kate, would have loved it here. I lost her two years ago, she was my life. So I lost my life and had a hard time getting it back. The good news is, the trauma of losing her led me into a whole new relationship with Christ, a higher place than I'd gone before. Maybe we can only go as high as we can go deep. But enough!'

'Marine Corps, the bishop says.'

'*Semper fidelis*. Twenty-three years old, saw my first action in Cambodia. Intelligence told us it would be a cakewalk—small weapons, a couple dozen enemy. We lost thirty-eight men— Marine, Navy, Air Force—in less than twenty-four hours. When I'm asked to give my testimony, I've been known to give it in two words: Koh Tang.

'When I get back to Mitford and the dust settles, I'd like to tell you how I ended up in a collar. I hope you'll give me the pleasure of hearing your story.'

'I look forward to it. So what is your Rite Three?'

'Skiing. Hiking. White-water rafting. Trout fishing.' Father Brad's smile would light up a room. 'I'm a mountain guy all the way, with two beautiful daughters and four grandkids who love this stuff, too.'

'We'll be proud to have you and Daisy,' he said.

'And seven gardenia trees in containers. I'm haulin' those babies out here personally. Tropical plants that love heat and humidity, and what do they get from me? Mountain winters.'

Father Brad rewound the scarf around his neck and gave him what was known as a bear hug. 'I'm proud to be called into the good company of this parish. He has set my feet in a spacious place.'

A brother in the cloth, somebody to hammer things out with. The camel caravan from Gilead appeared on the horizon, saddlebags filled. Balm galore.

. . .

HE WAS GOING TO CALL HOPE when she rang the store.

'Are you all right?' he said.

'A little bleeding, but Dr. Wilson isn't worried. All appears to be well, though I'm not to be up and doing.'

'What about your sister, Louise? Can she come for a visit?'

'Her work schedule is frightful. Soon, she says. I miss her.'

'Family can be good medicine.'

'I'm thankful for my Mitford family. Avette Harris is knitting an entire layette. With her left eye wandering as it does, she says she wouldn't trouble herself with such vexation if she weren't certain our baby will make it.'

'Good on Avette.'

'I must tell you that lying here has given me an awful burden of thinking.

'The first thing, Father—will you pray for where I'll stay during the month in Charlotte, before the baby comes? I've hesitated to ask because we ask so much of you already.'

'Prayer is never too much to ask. Consider it done.'

'Thank you from my heart. The other thing is . . . I'd like to do something for someone. People do so much for me that I can never repay their kindness. Scott has been given a wonderful raise at Hope House and I'd like to hire Coot. Three days a week, four hours a day.'

'Ah!' There was a beaming face if he ever saw it. 'To do what, exactly?'

'To do anything you wish . . . clean, carry out the trash, go to the store, take packages to the post office. And I'm sure the display windows could use a good washing. It would give a bit of relief to you and Marcie and Miss Pringle, but mostly, Father, it would give Coot the chance to be around books. He loves books.'

'Very useful thinking!' he said. 'Yes, indeed. We should all take to bed for a dose of useful thinking!'

THE SIDEWALKS WERE SHOVELED, the town crew was on it. The snow, however, was still coming down. He arrived home with a box of organic popcorn, to find preparations under way in the study.

The DVD player had its own remote, a notion he didn't take to.

'See this button?' said Puny. 'It says On. Now, see this button? It says Play.'

'One thing at a time, please.'

She rolled her eyes. 'Okay, see this button? What does it say?'

The type was minuscule and on a black background, no less. Did the maker not consider the buying power of the senior citizen? Was this stuff produced chiefly for small children with 20/20?

'My glasses,' he said. 'I've got to get my glasses.'

'They're on your head,' she said. 'Okay, what does it say?'

'On.'

'Great! Push it.'

He pushed it. A green light.

'It works!' said his wife.

'Next, you'll hit Play.'

'Let's see, where is Play?'

'Right here, right next to On.'

No wonder he never did this stuff, it was humiliating.

'And here's Pause. If you want to, you know, let Barnabas out or anything.'

'We'll never use Pause,' he said, decisive. 'And maybe you should leave it on so all we have to do is hit Play?'

'If you say so. Lord help!'

'Where's the movie?'

'Here,' she said, handing him the thing. 'Put it in right there.'

'Where?'

'Hit Open.'

A tray slid out.

'Now put the disc in.'

'Which side up?'

Puny was ready to pack up and go home, possibly for good. His wife appeared to be taking a nap with Truman.

THIS WAS THE COOLEST THING they'd done 'in ever,' as Sassy might say.

A forty-two-inch screen was a lot of real estate, and Kim Dorsay knew how to occupy it. They lounged on the sofa, mesmerized. How could they have just had dinner with this person who had shucked garlic like a pro?

The phone rang. He leaned to the end table and checked the caller ID. Georgia. But he didn't know how to work the Pause thing.

'Hit Pause,' he told his wife.

'Where is it?'

'Somewhere around Off and On. Hey, buddy.'

'Hey, Dad, I found your truck. Two years old, long bed, stick shift, leather seats, nineteen thousand miles, and you're not going to believe this . . .'

'Try me.'

'It's red.'

'Man!'

'Everything you wanted but crank windows. The windows are automatic.' Dooley told him the price. 'I checked that with the Blue Book. On the money.'

'Where did you find it?'

'The Internet. It's about sixty miles from you, in Hendersonville. You could ride over with Harley. But you need to move fast—the price is right, it's clean, it won't last long. I'll email photos, the owner's contacts, everything.'

'Good job,' he said. 'Maybe next week. First thing.'

The thought of buying a truck was a whole other feeling from that of buying a car. He was grinning like a mule eatin' briars.

'What did I miss?' he said to his wife, who had obviously not located Pause.

Chapter
Twenty

Saturday.

He remembered how fraught his Saturdays had been when he was a full-time priest. Wrestling his sermon into acceptable form, trying to get over the week and rest for the morrow, hammering at his personal stuff.

Then he retired, and he remembered how he dreaded trying to fill Saturdays with something worthy, up to snuff, accountable. And now here he was, maybe for the first time, really liking this day, feeling the liberty of it, the broad possibilities. Harley had said he could borrow the truck. The roads had been scraped, they could leave after lunch and be at the nursery by three o'clock.

He opened the Old Testament at random. Ecclesiastes, aka Solomon or Ezra, God only knows, chapter three.

> To everything there is a season, and a time to every
> purpose under heaven . . . A time to weep and a
> time to laugh. A time to mourn and a time to
> dance . . . A time to be silent and a time to speak.

It was time to speak.

Would it be a waste of breath? That wasn't for him to

determine. He would speak from the heart. Let the chips fall where they may.

He looked out the study window. New snow was falling on the old, though nothing heavy.

He auto-dialed, made the sign of the cross.

'Hey, Sam! I've got a little time this afternoon. Want to go buy a tree?'

HE ANSWERED THE DOORBELL and there was Jena Ivey, nearly hidden from view by a great bower of hydrangeas in a color he'd never seen.

'Holy smoke!' he said to the owner of Mitford Blossoms. 'Come in, come in.' He moved the candlesticks, the Delft bowl on the console. 'Right here.'

'Hard to get this bronze color. They would look better on the coffee table in your study, Father. Not enough light in here.'

Their voluptuous amber radiance was breathtaking against the background of falling snow.

His wife was ecstatic and, he had to confess, so was he.

Cynthia took the card from the envelope.

> *With grateful affection from one*
> *who was lost and is now found*
> *Kim*

Having told Lace the backstory of the hydrangeas, they sat at the kitchen counter, Lace in the middle. Though they asked that she keep the twins' story quiet for now, it would later be one to pass down through any family.

'So tell us again,' said Cynthia, 'what you said to that pomp-ous professor.'

'I said, If you'uns wadn't s' full of yourself, you'd be a whole lot better at gettin' people t' pay attention.'

'And what did the poor man have to say about that?'

'He was completely startled, then he laughed. He thought I was joking.'

Whooping with laughter, the three of them.

'When I get excited or happy or really, really angry, I start talkin' like I did growin' up. You know that Olivia hired a tutor to help me get over my old speech pattern. But when I went off to school, I guess I was still talkin' like a hillbilly. For a long time, nobody would be my friend; people were ashamed to be with me.

'Even now, the way I speak is just a surface thing, I can do it, but the old way is still there and I'm always trying to hold it back. Sometimes I get really tense from holding it back; it's like trying to hold back who I am.'

'And who are you?' said Cynthia.

'That is so hard. Deep down, I guess I'm the girl who grew up livin' sometimes under a house that was fallin' down, with a sick mama who turned her head to whatever my daddy done . . . see there?' Lace put a hand over her face. 'Once in a while, it just pops out.'

'We sure love that girl,' said Cynthia. 'If memory serves me, which it often doesn't, she's that amazing person who got a scholarship to one of the finest universities in the country.'

Cynthia put her arm around Lace. 'Don't ever be ashamed of that lovely girl under the house who educated herself from the bookmobile. She had grit and backbone if anyone ever had, and she'll be there for you through thick and thin.'

'Great good is written all over those hard times,' he said. 'God sent Absalom Greer to tell you about the one who loved us first; he sent Harley to give you refuge when you needed it; he sent the Harpers to give you the home you wanted and never had . . .'

'I know,' she said. 'I do know, and I'm really thankful.'

'You and Dooley have much in common,' he said.

'Sometimes too much. But if we're patient and talk things out, we can usually say, Okay, I get it, I understand why you did that. I think you know that Olivia arranged for us to see a counselor. Two whole years and we still go when we can, we even work with him on the phone. It helps, it really helps. Would you like to have your present now?'

'Yes!' said his wife. It was a day of presents.

Lace went to the outsized portfolio she'd brought along, and unzipped it. 'Don't look. Close your eyes.'

The clock ticking. 'Okay, you can look!'

He and Cynthia drew in their breath at the same moment. A Greek chorus.

Every remaining freckle. Every red hair. The light in his eyes. The crooked grin. The works. Lace was holding a life-sized portrait in oil of Dooley Barlowe Kavanagh, from the waist up, wearing a T-shirt that read LOVE IS AN ACT OF ENDLESS FORGIVENESS.

A surge of feeling. 'Well done,' he said.

'Remember the little Baptist church on the way to Meadowgate from Holy Trinity?' said Lace. 'The message on the shirt was on their wayside pulpit one morning; we all liked it.'

Cynthia embraced Lace, held her tight. 'You're so gifted, so gifted. Hard to find the words.'

'I had the shirt made for him,' she said. 'And one for me, too. It reminds us both.'

Barnabas came over to look, wagged his tail. They inspected the brushstrokes, the candor of the eyes, the facial expression which Lace found 'a little dubious.'

'Let's hang it as is, no frame to distract the eye,' said Cynthia. 'But where?'

'Over the mantel!' he said.

Agreed.

He toted in the ladder and removed the mirror.

'I think of Harley,' he said, handing the mirror down to Lace.

'Never a jot of formal education, but he wanted more than anything for you to have it. He was proud of every step you took, every book you read, and then you turned around and started teaching *him*, and it was literally life-changing. He says learning American history from you was better than going west with Lewis and Clark.'

This amused her. She handed up the canvas.

'I went to see him before I came over,' she said. 'He is so adorable. He had his teeth in; I hardly knew him. I said, Harley, who was the Indian woman who traveled with Lewis and Clark? That is really an unfair question because her name just drives people crazy trying to pronounce it and it's been years since Harley studied the expedition. He didn't hesitate a minute. Sock-ah-ja-*wee*-ah, he said. So I said, What is another name for the prairie hen? and he said, Grouse—an' they got four toes on each foot!'

They sat at the kitchen island and admired the portrait 'forty ways from Sunday,' as his mother would have said, and split one of Winnie's napoleons three ways.

.   .   .

'He don't even talk like Dooley n'more. It's like he's somebody else, like that stupid dirtbag dean's kid over at Bud's. What's Dooley tryin' to prove, anyhow, always thinkin' he knows it all? He thinks his money makes him some kind of big shot, some kind of god? He wants a truck, he gets a truck, he wants a cue stick, he gets a cue stick.'

The snow in these mountains was a lovely thing. The heater in Harley's truck was another lovely thing.

'I don't care if I live or die, it don't matter to me, I know I don't want to be like Dooley or you or Harley or nobody else, I want to be like myself.'

Come, Holy Spirit.

'I believe you're missing something here,' he said. 'You think all good things just fall into your brother's lap and are there for the taking?

'Let me tell you about Dooley. He helped raise four kids, remember? Walked you to school because there was no car to go in and no bus out that way, and nobody else to do it.

'And how about putting food on the table? He was ten years old, but he saw it as his job, and he managed that scary responsibility as best he could. Nobody starved to death, you're all still here.

'And yes, Miss Sadie provided money for his education, but do you think Dooley went off to that fine, expensive school and got by on money?

'Dooley didn't know how he was going to get by. He wanted to run away from that school, he wanted to come home where the love was. But he toughed it out with all those guys with privileged backgrounds and fast cars, who laughed at him and called him a hillbilly. He dug down deep, where most of us have to go in this life, and he found gold. He found a way to do more than just get by, he found the guts to go against all the odds and, with God's help, make something of himself.

'And maybe you think school is a piece of cake for your hot-shot brother, that he just breezes through and has a good time. You would be wrong. School is hard. That's what makes it good. And because he has two more years, plus vet school, that makes it double hard—and double good. Because when he gets through, he'll have a way to help ease some of the suffering in this world.

'You brought us a kitten. You wanted it to have something to eat, a good home, a safe place. That's what Dooley wants for the animals he'll spend his life treating. A few years ago, a pony gashed its belly on a barbed-wire fence. It was dying. Dooley helped save its life. Barnabas was struck by a car and would have died, no question. But Dooley and Lace knew what to do and that good dog is still with us.

'You said that when Dooley wants a cue, he buys a cue. And he just bought a beautiful stick for you. Is this the hotshot brother who considers himself a god? Looks to me like it's a brother who's thoughtful of your needs, a brother who wants the best for you because he loves you. Actually, you've got two brothers who fit that description. Two!'

He pulled into the parking lot of the nursery and turned off the ignition.

'I hope you're listening to me, Sam. You're about to lose your place at Miss Pringle's because you've openly defied the few things asked of you. You'll be on the street, and for what?

'Most of your life, you've been up against it, and it looks like that's where you want to stay. You didn't have a choice when you were younger, but now you do.

'Do you want to shoot great pool or would you rather be dead?

'Do you want to build beautiful gardens or would you rather be dead?

'Do you want people to love you, really love you and care about you, or would you rather be dead and miss all that?

'You can't have it both ways.

'If you choose life, if you choose to honor yourself and others, too, I'll help you get on with it. Harley will help, Kenny will help, Cynthia, Miss Pringle, a lot of people will help.

'So you've got help—and you've got talent. And better than that, you've got God. God is on your side, Sam, because he loves you. Why does he love you, why does he love me? We can't fully understand it, but that's what God does, no matter how stupid or crazy we are, God loves us anyway. He wants the best for us, anyway. You steal my car and wreck it, I love you anyway. Do something like that again, I'll love you anyway, and I'll also do this: I'll press charges, and it won't be good.

'The party's over, Sam.'

He laid his hand on the boy's shoulder, felt the flinch.

'But the fun is just beginning. Let's go in and buy a tree.'

HIS MAMA HAD NOT EAT a bite in three days.

'You want a nanner?' he'd say. 'Hit's ripe.' Good as she loved ripe bananas, she'd shake her head no. 'Read me out of that book,' she'd say with the hoarse sound she'd picked up lately.

He'd got home before dark after going over town for a special treat. Maybe that would do the job. He stomped snow off his boots and hung up his jacket on a nail by the door.

Things was peaceful as water in a spoon. The oil heater was goin' and the TV wadn't blarin' a'tall.

'Miz Ivey sent you a jelly donut, hit's blueberry, you want it?'

'Nossir, you eat it y'rself. Read me out of that book.'

He took the book off the mantelpiece and showed her the cover. To keep things new every time, they played like they had not done this before.

'C-A-T,' he spelled out. 'Cat! There's th' cat.'

'In a hat,' she said, beating him to it.

What he did was go by the pictures and make it up out of his head with what he remembered from his teacher Miss Mooney.

He sat down in his chair. 'Th' sun . . . did not . . .' He hesitated, studied the word. '. . . sh-h-h . . . *shine* . . .'

'Oh, yes,' she said. She crossed her arms over her sunken chest and closed her eyes. 'Th' sun don't shine of a night.'

'It was too wet . . . to plow. Wait a minute. To *play!*'

'That's right. Too wet.'

'Hit was stormin' pretty bad an' we had to set in th' house.'

'Set in th' house,' she said. 'That's right.'

'They won't nothin' to do but set.'

He held the book close so she could see the picture of two young 'uns settin', but her eyes were shut tight as a henhouse door.

'I remember back when Mama was livin',' she said.

The icy rain began. *Patpatpatpat* . . .

'We would set in th' house an' wait for th' rag man, he'd come by hollerin', Rag man, rag man! We was happy as a dog with two tails to see 'im, he was a little bitty man with a black mustache. He give us money for rags an' with nine young 'uns in the' house we had a-plenty to sell—thirty-cent, forty-cent worth 'bout near ever' time.'

Look like all that talkin' had wore her out. He hurried to a page where things was goin' on, where them big letters bunched together to make a loud word.

'Then somethin' went BUMP!' He jumped when he hollered that word, he couldn't help hisself.

'Good gravy!' His mama opened her eyes. 'What was that?'

'He's comin' in now! He's steppin' on th' mat, he's comin' in th' house!' He had goose bumps all up his right leg.

'Who's comin' in th' house?'

'Th' CAT! An' here's what he says.' He 'bout near remembered this word for word. 'Says we gon' have lots of fun that is funny.' Yessir, he was gettin' the hang of this.

'Fun that is funny. I sure like that,' she said. 'Keep a-goin'.'

He thought she sounded tired, real tired.

'Now here in a little bit, th' cat is throwin' a fish up in th' air. Ol' fish hollers out, says, Put me down, I do not want to fall. An' th' cat, he says, I ain't gon' let you fall!'

Patpatpatpat . . .

'You ain't gon' let me fall, are ye, son?'

He was startled by this, by the way she was breathing. 'No, ma'am, I ain't. Not for nothin'.'

She was needin' a little pick-me-up, he could tell. 'You want you a dip?' He moved her walker and got in next to her bed and looked on her night table for the snuff jar. A little dip always perked her up.

Her hands was crossed over her chest, her eyes closed, her breathing had calmed down. 'I've got all I want of ever'thing. You're a good son.'

His heart flopped around. She'd never said nothin' like that before. He didn't know what to answer back.

Nossir, she was not actin' like Beulah Mae Hendrick. She had to eat a bite, even if he had to call the neighbor woman to make her do it.

He went to the kitchen and gobbled the donut in three bites and made a bowl of hot oatmeal with sugar and the last of the milk and listened to the rain chiming in the downspout. They said over town it might turn to ice by mornin'. He cocked his head to hear it better, cupped his hand about his ear. It was as good as any music on the radio.

'Mama!' he said, carrying the warm bowl to her bed. 'Looky here.'

Her mouth was open but she wadn't snoring. He passed the oatmeal close to her pillow so she could smell it and set up.

But she didn't set up.

He remembered that he hadn't said anything about Sammy's determination to be himself. That was the very thing they all wanted him to be. He wished he had made that clear.

But he'd said enough. It was time to listen.

He got up from the chair in the study and called Henry. He had the strange sense of missing his brother.

'I talked to somebody in the doctor's office, she had acute myelogenous leukemia,' said Henry. 'A relative helped with a stem cell transplant. That was five years ago. Now she's driving a delivery truck, owns a florist business, and went on a trip to Alabama in September. That's what I'm hoping for. But maybe not Alabama.' Henry laughed.

'Maybe North Carolina.' His heart galloped when he said it.

THE SNOW HAD CIRCLED like a plane over Atlanta and come back to land again.

Early in the year for this much snow. It seemed only days ago that the leaves had turned, and now this. He felt the odd sense of captivity that he sometimes experienced in winter, in the mountains.

Eight-thirty. His wife was in bed, reading. He watched her squint at the page, but said nothing.

He had an appointment with the truck guy in Hendersonville on Tuesday. Harley knew something about buying trucks. All he, Timothy, knew to do was to kick the tires and walk around the vehicle, looking stern, which was his Grandfather Kavanagh's style.

He didn't recognize the caller ID.

'Father, I'm the Hendricks' neighbor, Jenny Thomas.'

'Good evening, Jenny.'

'Miz Hendrick passed a little while ago and Coot is asking for you. He's devastated. I know the roads are bad, I doubt you can get here, but perhaps you could give me some pointers. I'm a caregiver for forty-two years, but consoling the bereaved is . . . I do other things much better.'

'Let me think about this, Miss Thomas. I'll call you back right away.'

No way was he taking his wife's car out in this. Route 4 was three-plus miles outside the town limits. The county would be plowing that area, but not the side roads.

He rang Esther Cunningham.

'I'll get right on it and call you back.' He could hear her adrenaline pumping.

Completely confident that Esther would come through, he dressed in roughly three layers, including a hooded, oiled jacket from his first Ireland trip. But it would be the boots that mattered.

JIMMY PRESTWOOD BRAKED A PLOW at the corner of Wisteria and Main. He clambered in. 'Special order just for you, Reverend. From th' gov'nor, they said.'

At the highway, they connected with a county truck.

'Supervisor said pick you up. Where you goin'?'

'Route 4, Brush Mountain Road, third house off the highway.'

'I can't take my plow down in there.'

'I'll walk in.'

'This is some kind of weather for October. They already got three inches in Banner Elk and more comin'. You got a light to see by?'

He patted his jacket pocket. 'New battery. You're picking me up, I hope.'

'By th' time I head back this way, it'll be one, two o'clock. This is gettin' pretty bad. But I could try to make it back by one. Yeah, you bein' clergy. I'll get you at one.'

'I'll be at the highway at one. For God's sake, don't forget me.'

Was he nuts? That had certainly been said on more than one occasion. His wife had given him that worried look, something that usually kick-started a worry or two of his own.

He switched on the flashlight, jumped down from the plow, and headed into the night.

'Jesus,' he said.

. . .

SEMINARY DIDN'T TEACH SPECIFICALLY about consoling the bereaved; that was something that came with on-the-job training.

Coot Hendrick was indeed devastated.

'She said I was a good son.' Coot repeated this again and again, sobbing.

'Yes, that's what a lot of people say you've been.'

'Maybe she ain't gone. Seem like I seen her breathe. Did you see 'er breathe?'

They went into Coot's bedroom while the Hendricks' neighbor removed the garments of the deceased and did what had to be done with the body. Something was awry with the phones, the usual in bad weather, and they couldn't contact the funeral home. In any case, his walk from the highway assured him that their vehicle wouldn't fare well down here.

No, she didn't know anyone who could watch with Coot tonight, but she would stay until he fell asleep and come back first thing in the morning.

'Do you do this for all your patients?'

'Miz Hendrick wasn't really a patient. I just looked in on her, organized her medicine box, took a hot meal now and then. Coot did all he could, and the county sent someone, too. We managed.'

'I believe you must be an angel,' he said.

She shook her head no, smiled. 'I owe God big time.'

He told Coot he was sorry, which he was, and that Beulah Mae had lived a long life, which she had. Mostly, he was simply there, a warm body in a sweater with a reindeer on the front.

He found a tea bag and made tea and added sugar and gave it to Coot. Then he sat next to him on the side of the bed and held on to his old friend and didn't let go for a long while.

HE WAS THANKING GOD for the clear, frozen night and the brilliance of the stars so thickly set in the great bowl, and for the headlights of the plow coming his way, pretty much on time. He had to climb over the berm of snow kicked up by the plow at the edge of the highway.

Safely home, he emailed the news to Emma, which was as good as announcing it at a town meeting.

Two-fifteen. He was spent. Beyond spent. After a hot shower, he sat in the wing chair in their bedroom, too exhausted to get in bed.

'I will never do that again,' said his wife, meaning it.

'What?'

'Let you go off into the night in a snowplow, for Pete's sake. I have never been and never will be the clergy-spouse poster child, but heaven knows, I have tried to let you do what you feel led to do, without interfering.'

'I was *fine*,' he said.

'Quoth the raven,' she said, turning off the lamp on her side.

THE PLANNING WENT SWIFTLY.

To give the temperature time to warm up, the funeral service would be conducted on Tuesday afternoon.

As the Hendricks had no church affiliation nor funds for funeral-home amenities, the service would be graveside.

Somehow, word got around that the yellow house on Wisteria Lane was the drop-off point for food.

Early Tuesday morning, which was cold and blustery, Esther Bolick delivered an OMC. Beneath her heavy coat, she was still in flannel robe and nightgown.

'I look like Miss Rose on a bad day,' she said. 'But here you go, an' bless 'is heart. I heard his mother sing that song about killin' Yankees, she could've been in the Carter family.'

Fortunately, Puny had switched her Wednesday for Tuesday and arrived with a bowl of her famous potato salad.

'I used red potatoes 'cause that's what I had,' she said, 'but russet works better. Have a bite an' see what you think.'

Winnie Ivey made a delivery around ten, as he was putting the ham in the oven. Another OMC.

Winnie spied the first delivery on their kitchen counter.

'Esther?'

'Afraid so.'

Winnie laughed. 'She is out of control, Father! She can't help herself. But it's okay, she never sells one, she just does it as a love offering. What's that wonderful smell?'

'Esther can't help herself, and neither can I. I'm baking a ham. Previously, I did it just for weddings, my own included, but I've decided to do funerals as well.'

'Ham to die for!' she said. 'Baptisms?'

'No baptisms. Not yet, anyway.'

'Shirley Owen told me she's bringin' fried chicken.'

'Shirley's Baptist,' he said, 'it'll be good fried chicken.'

'We'll have to heat it to crisp it up.' Puny rattled flatware from the dishwasher into a drawer. 'That's an old Church of God trick when my gran'daddy was preachin'. Church of God women are all about crispy.'

'Poor Coot,' said Winnie, 'his overalls will have to be let out three sizes. What time is th' graveside?'

'Two o'clock.'

'I'll see you there,' said Winnie.

'You're coming? In this cold?'

'Of course I'm coming.'

Minnie Lomax entered by the side door. 'I couldn't get anybody to the front.'

'Come in!' said Cynthia. 'It's a circus in here.'

'Green bean casserole!' Minnie set it on the counter, proud as anything. 'And I don't need th' dish back.'

'I love green bean casserole,' said Cynthia. 'I'll try not to eat the whole thing.' She went to his desk for paper and a pen. 'Okay, I'm writing all this down so we know who did what. Where did these OMCs come from?'

'Guess,' he said.

'This one is from Esther, right?'

'And that one's from Winnie.'

Cynthia recorded this data.

'I would never make an OMC,' said Minnie.

'I'm with you,' said his wife. 'Puny once had to take a day off after making an OMC.'

Emma Newland came in through the garage bearing a platter covered with a tea towel. 'Ham biscuits!' she announced.

'Oh, glory!' said his wife. 'I'm starved. I love ham biscuits.'

'You cannot have a funeral without ham biscuits,' said Puny. 'I can tell y' that.'

If he hadn't already had diabetes for more than a decade, he would certainly have it by morning.

And there was Ray Cunningham, God love him, coming in by the side door.

'Your specialty?' he said, interested in the familiar container with the red lid.

'You got it,' said Ray. 'Pulled pork! An' keep your cotton-pickin' hands offa this pot.'

He took his cell phone from the charger.

'Who was that laughing?' said Emma.

'Hello, Miss Pringle!'

'Father, this is so . . . I don't know how to say . . . I cannot find . . . we are completely out of *papier hygiénique.*'

'Ah, toilet paper. So sorry. I'll drop some off on the way to the funeral.'

'*Merci!*' she said. '*Beaucoup!*'

Stirred by numerous crazy-making aromas, his dog came into the kitchen, followed by Truman.

He stuck the phone in his shirt pocket and looked at Violet at her roost atop the refrigerator. 'Good idea,' he said.

WHAT WOULD BE SADDER than driving alone to your mother's funeral? He fetched Coot.

'I hope they got 'er teeth in,' said Coot.

'I'm sure they did.'

'Since we never looked in there to check.'

'Right. They do a good job.'

'I told ye she was a hundred but I don't know that for a fact.'

'I believe that's close.'

'She told me I was a good son.'

'You've been a very good son.'

They rounded the curve where Sammy . . .

'Hope would like you to come to work at Happy Endings as a regular.'

'Are you tryin' to git me t' laugh? Is that a joke?'

'It's th' gospel truth. Wednesday, Thursday, and Friday, four hours a day. If you'd like to do it, you may start anytime.'

There was a small light in Coot's eyes, but his passenger didn't say anything right away.

'I was thinkin' I had to talk to Mama about it.'

For a long time after his own mother's death, he remembered thinking the same thing.

'But I guess I can start right off.'

'Ten to two,' he said.

'I'll start next day you an' y'r dog are there.'

'Thursday.'

Coot appeared thoughtful again.

'Do you think when we're workin' an' all, that maybe we could . . . have some fun that is funny?'

'I can just about guarantee it,' he said.

TWENTY-SEVEN PEOPLE GATHERED, frozen as popsicles, beneath a small tent whipped by the wind. In the old days, they couldn't bury until spring when the ground thawed. Thank heaven for the backhoe, which got the job done.

'The Lord be with you!'

'And also with you.'

The tent shuddered, creaked on its poles.

'Oh, God, whose mercies cannot be numbered: Accept our prayers on behalf of your servant Beulah Mae, and grant her an entrance into the land of light and joy, the fellowship of your saints; through Jesus Christ our Lord, who lives and reigns with you and the Holy Spirit, one God, now and forever.'

'Amen.'

He'd been pretty amazed to see Esther Cunningham and Ray out in this cold, and Esther dressed for what looked like a summer garden party.

'She's campaignin',' somebody said.

'Startin' mighty early. The election idn't 'til next November.'

'You have to start early these days.'

'Esther isn't *starting* to campaign,' said Bill Sprouse. 'Esther has never *stopped* campaigning.'

'Well, there you go,' he said.

Coot had hoped people could come to the preacher's house afterward instead of to Route 4. Thus relieved of carting the whole business to the boondocks, they trekked to Wisteria Lane and did a mighty bit of damage to the offerings.

When their party of twenty-seven gathered in the kitchen and held hands for the blessing, he was surprised by his tears. Not for the dead, no, but for the living, and for how good it was to be alive and together, and to laugh and give thanks.

Chapter
Twenty-one

Make it a rule never to give a child a book you would not read yourself.—George Bernard Shaw

He pinned the quote to the corkboard, thinking of Irene McGraw's wise and charming habit. Irene would be driving Cynthia to Winston-Salem today, for lunch and the eye doctor.

He pinned one contributed by his wife.

There are perhaps no days of our childhood we lived so fully as those we spent with a favorite book.—Marcel Proust

The corkboard was literally bristling with quotes from customers of every ilk. He stood back and reviewed their dispatches with satisfaction.

'Vanita?'

'Don't tease me,' she said. 'Everybody's teasin' me. It's th' Palm Beach, I did it in th' line of duty. You can't write journalism on a subject you don't know anything about.'

'Really,' he said. Talk about hot off the press. He could smell the ink as Vanita thumped the new edition on the counter.

'One more week and we're wrappin' up your big story! Total votes for Father Tim Kavanagh as of today's edition—one hundred and ninety-four! Yay-y-y! You're definitely goin' to be the town's leading citizen.'

'You know, of course, that I'm not the town's leading citizen, nor do I wish to be.'

'But why not? There's no responsibility that comes with th' recognition, it's not like it's a payin' job an' you have to clock in every mornin'.'

'It just feels . . . it's . . . I don't deserve the title.'

'But a hundred and ninety-four people think you do. Plus th' winner will get a free spray tan treatment! For you, I think Fancy and Shirlene would definitely do th' Palm Beach, which is their top of th' line!'

'So. I've been wondering,' he said, 'is there any way I can pass the torch to somebody else? I mean, give it to me if you must, but I'll hand it over to someone more worthy. That would be a story right there.'

'Who would you hand it to?'

'I don't know. I'd have to think about it.'

'Don't waste your time, there's not anybody.'

'Why not the mayor? That's about as leading as you can get.'

'Way too easy. Are you just bein' humble?'

'I'm not terribly humble, really. Let's figure this thing out. I mean, it took off without me being . . . in the saddle, so to speak.'

'You don't have to go through a big ceremony or anything. I mean, it's not like we have a big weenie roast on th' lawn at Town Hall.'

'So what will you do to make it . . . official?'

'Like there's not a *crown* or anything. We'll just run your picture in the paper and I'll write something really, you know . . .'

'Embarrassing,' he said.

She looked bewildered. 'So you don't like my idea that united our little town and gave us somethin' positive to focus on? An' a way to interact by writin' in our votes? An' a way to show respect and admiration for others?'

Vanita was blinking back tears.

'So, yay,' she said.

She turned and walked to the door and didn't look back.

Good Lord. He stood rooted to the spot, then sprinted out the door and down the sidewalk and caught up with her at Sweet Stuff.

'Vanita! I'm so sorry. I am really, really sorry. I was ungrateful. I hope you'll forgive me. Please. I'd be honored to, you know . . .'

Vanita beamed—the sun broke forth, birds sang. She gave him a hug.

After five years of so-called retirement, he was once again prey to the stresses of public life.

HE CALLED HIS WIFE, told her everything.

'Lighten *up*,' she said. '*Be* the leading citizen, for heaven's sake. *Ride* in the parade and wave to the crowd. You only live *once*.'

Fine. Okay. Done. End of sermon.

TO THE ROAR OF THE VACUUM CLEANER, he read Beulah Mae Hendrick's obit.

Diligent to honor the deceased, Hessie had included lyrics to the Hendrick family ballad about a Mitford ancestor who shot and buried five AWOL Yankees during the Civil War. There was a brief mention of Tuesday's graveside service and the 'wind-tossed' tent beneath which Beulah Mae 'lay in eternal rest.'

> *Dear Vanita*
>   *I am sooo glad to share what I do to take care of our own! I have given a good and loving home to sixteen cats and here they are. Have you ever tried to get sixteen cats to stay still for a picture?? That is Elvis in front see his white jumpsuit and I added the rhinestone collar!! Anyways, sorry about all the red eyes my camera is old as dirt%^*

He couldn't do this anymore. He just couldn't. As for the Hint, it was three home remedies for headaches, but he never had headaches. What they needed around here was some real news. Or maybe not, since that could be pretty frightening stuff.

On Monday, he would call the *Charlotte Observer* and sign up for a year, an act which would not only illuminate world events, but add serious volume to his stash of fire-starters.

MARCIE WAS SUBBING FOR HIM from eleven to twelve so he could have an early bite at Feel Good and a private chat with the boss.

'Don't stay too long,' said Marcie, one of Esther Cunningham's five good-looking daughters and mother of seven. 'I've got to run home and start bakin' and freezin' for th' swearin'-in, then get back to Avis and finish th' payroll. I'm leavin' you a note about th' mice.'

He didn't question this remark.

'A prayer breakfast?' said Wanda. 'How many?'

'To begin, five or six. Starting early January. I expect the numbers will grow.'

So far, he'd come up with Bill Sprouse at First Baptist, Bill Swanson from Lord's Chapel, the new Methodist hire, and Reverend Browing at First Presbyterian. He hoped Father Brad would join them, and anyone else who took a notion.

'You're goin' to pray?'

'And talk and have breakfast, of course. And yes, pray.'

'Right out in front of everybody?'

'How do you mean?'

'I mean, we don't have a back room where you can, like, go pray.'

'We wouldn't need a back room. Just wondered if we could start off with the table in the corner? Every other Saturday, eight o'clock sharp.'

'But so you're goin' to pray where people can see you prayin'?'

'Well, yes, I suppose so, that's the usual way of the prayer breakfast.'

Wanda had a concerned look. He needed Mule in on this.

'It happens all over the country, all the time,' he said. 'Wendy's, McDonald's.'

'We're not fast-food, Father.'

'I was just giving you an example of how widespread the prayer breakfast is. If it's a problem . . .'

'I don't know squat about your particular religion,' she said. 'I was raised Holy Roller. Y'all don't by any chance fall back in th' Spirit, do you?'

'Not usually,' he said.

'Hey!' said Omer. 'Any room for me?'

'I'll get back to you,' said Wanda. 'What's for th' flyboy today?'

'The usual,' said Omer. 'An' thank you, ma'am.'

'Don't mention it,' she said.

'What's goin' on in town?' asked Omer.

He slid his copy of the *Muse* across the table. 'All yours. More than you ever wanted to know. How was your potato crop this year?'

'Awesome. I'll bring a bag by th' bookstore.'

'We'll sure appreciate it. Nice shirt.' He was a longtime fan of the flannel shirt.

'Thanks. Yard sale. Two bucks.'

'Mule likes a good yard sale.'

Omer grinned. 'He's beat me out of a few items over the years.'

'You flying today?'

'Not today. I've got a project goin' at th' house.'

'What are you up to?'

'A Scrabble game. Online. Playing with somebody who's pretty good.'

'You play Scrabble? Online?'

'I'm stuck with some crazy letters, but I think I've got it figured out. Just need to get back to my dictionary.' And there were the piano keys, and maybe the intro to a little Irving Berlin.

. . .

HEADING ACROSS TO THE BOOKSTORE, he realized he was doing something he almost never did, even though he very much enjoyed doing it.

He was whistling.

> *Fr Tim,*
> *MICE UPSTAIRS!!! 3 and maybe more!!! I beg u*
> *2 do what needs 2 B done B4 next Wed. and know u*
> *wl B HUMANE. I owe u a donut. Hugs Marcie*

The note was decorated with a smiley face.

'Dora,' he said, calling down to the hardware. 'I need a humane mousetrap.'

'Sorry. When it comes to mice, we don't do humane.'

'What do you have against mice?'

'They get in th' feed sacks, eat th' birdseed, poop on th' counters, you name it. An' since you're runnin' the bookstore, I guess you know they eat books.'

'Eat books?'

'Plus chew electrical cords, gnaw through wires, climb pipes . . .'

'Okay, so . . .'

'I can give you pellets or th' old-fashioned wood trap. Or you can go th' five-gallon-bucket route. That's popular.'

'I'll get back to you,' he said.

For some reason, he could not engage with this project, donut or no.

'Coot,' he said. 'Could you step here a minute?'

. . .

THE OLD PEOPLE HAD SAID it would be a hard winter, and weren't they usually right? Four inches of snow they'd had, with leaves still clingin' to the trees, and she couldn't get warm to save her life.

Esther Cunningham backed out of the garage and headed to town. Ever since the Hendrick funeral, she had been cold as a corpse, herself. Her brother had invited her to Florida to sit in the sun on a bench in his retirement community, but no way. The sun would come back around soon enough and she had never enjoyed sitting on a bench, period, much less with old people.

Mama, you need to slow down! She had not liked hearing that from Marcie Guthrie before eight o'clock this morning. And look who was talkin'. Her daughter was a chicken with its head cut off—down at the Woolen Shop to do the books, over to the Local to get out the payroll, up to Village Shoes to do Abe's inventory, over to Lew Boyd's to help with his taxes which were a rat's nest, and now volunteerin' at Happy Endings every Wednesday, which had for years been Marcie's only day off—except Sunday, when she went to church, taught Sunday school, and cooked a big dinner for her kids and grans.

As for Joe Joe's swearin'-in next Saturday, who but the chief's *own mother* had signed up to bake three hundred cookies and two sheet cakes? Marcie Guthrie was th' pot callin' th' kettle black.

And there was that bloomin' plastic bag still flappin' around on the awning of the Wool Shop. She guessed she'd have to climb up there herself and yank it down. She despised plastic bags. Wasn't there a gazillion of the dern things out in the ocean with flip-flops and milk jugs whirlin' around in a gigantic cesspool?

When she was mayor again, plastic bags would be outlawed. The merchants would have to use recycled paper and they would not like it. What is this, a socialist state? For crap's sake, Esther, this is America. Nossir, they would fight her tooth an' nail on that little ord'nance.

'Bring it on!' she shouted.

She bent over the steering wheel, coughing. Lord help, she was gettin' a cough like nobody's business. A wrackin' cough, is what her mother used to call it. It had been so bad last night that Ray got up and slept in the guest room.

She pulled down the visor and looked in the mirror.

Blotches. Big time. And her heart bangin' around every-whichaway.

She had never paid much attention to her heart or any of her other organs, she just let 'em do whatever they had in mind, and what business was it of hers?

Lord help, it was kickin' around in there. She pulled into a parking lot and rolled the window down. She was hot as a firecracker, and where was she anyway? Was this Wesley or Mitford? She turned on the radio, maybe they would know.

'I FOUND HER PULLED OVER in front of Shoe Barn. Motor runnin', radio goin'.'

Hamp Floyd, Mitford's fire chief, had gone to buy boots for rabbit hunting.

'She was slumped over the steerin' wheel; been listenin' to Rush Limbaugh. He was talkin' about the government gettin' rid of Social Security.'

That'll do it, he thought.

'I got the ambulance to take her to ER; I'm up at the hospital 'til somebody can get here. Her preacher's out of town. One of the nurses said call you, you'd come.'

'Is she . . . ?' Was this last rites? Good Lord!

'They're puttin' her in ICU, is all I know.'

'Where's Ray?'

'Somewhere in Wesley, he don't carry a cell phone.'

'I'll be right there,' he said.

Who would sub? Not his wife, who was at the eye doctor in Winston-Salem.

'Coot,' he said, 'can you step here a minute?'

'FATHER. Do . . . o . . . o me a favor.'

'Anything,' he said. Heaven knows, a big chunk of Mitford history was lying right here, hooked to two IVs, a heart monitor, and a tank of oxygen.

'Climb up on that awnin' at th' Wo . . . o . . . ol . . . en Shop . . .'

There was a long pause, the monitor beeping.

'. . . an' get that da-a-adgum plastic bag down.'

'Consider it done,' he said.

CYNTHIA'S DIAGNOSIS: MACULAR HOLE.

Neither had ever heard of it.

She explained the fairly rare condition as best she could. 'They'll remove fluid from my right eye and replace it with a bubble of gas. I'll have to lie facedown for two weeks.'

Facedown? Two weeks? Unbelievable!

'I'd like to wait 'til after Christmas. But my vision in that eye is going fast, it's decreased from twenty/forty to twenty/one hundred. I may have to shut down the book 'til this is behind me.'

'What will it be after the procedure? Good as new?'

'It takes about six months to regain full vision.'

He found the whole prospect gruesome. He declined to ask how she would lie facedown on the post-op trek from Winston, much less at home.

Around seven, he laid out her new robe and ran her bath, then made a simple dinner, which he carried upstairs.

'The good news,' she said, 'is that Irene isn't going back to Florida for the winter. Except for Christmas, she's staying here and painting.'

It was rare for any of the Florida crowd to spend a winter in these parts. To them, snow was good only for Christmas card scenes, and ice storms were good for nothing.

'She invited me to paint with her in her studio—I'll do several pieces for the auction.' A small light in his wife's eyes. 'We can have her over for dinner and a movie!'

'What does she hear from Kim?'

'Irene will take several of her grandchildren out to Los Angeles in March. Kim is thrilled about having all these nieces and nephews. Okay, your turn,' she said, ready for his gazette.

Esther had suffered a stroke which affected her left side — droopy eye, some temporary speech impairment, arm movement disabled. This hateful circumstance was accompanied by the early stages of pneumonia.

Ray had been located at Wesley's big-box home improvement store and summoned to the hospital, where he said repeatedly to the nurses, I tried to tell her; we all tried to tell her. Wilson wrote a prescription for Ray. The daughters showed up, saying in chorus, We tried to tell her; Mama never listens.

To add to the shopping cart of health issues, Wilson suspected artery blockage, possibly valve stenosis, but these tests could not be done until tomorrow. There was a distinct possibility that Esther would be ferried to Charlotte via the copter service.

On his way off the floor, the charge nurse had caught up with him. 'She said tell you or somebody to be sure that big bag of Snickers behind th' TV in her den makes it to the swearin'-in. She wants th' kids to have that candy.' The nurse gave him a meaningful look. 'Super important, she said.'

'The swearing-in is more than a week away. Will she still be in the hospital?'

'Probably not, but she said if I don't pass that message along, I'll get plenty of time to think about where I went wrong.' The nurse thought this was hilarious, but also true.

Esther's famous candy giveaway. Even on her deathbed—and he hoped this wasn't it—Esther would be in campaign mode.

As for life closer to home, he reported that Dooley was getting in late tonight, and would visit next door before coming over around eleven. He would stay up to greet him. And here was some good news: Dooley was requesting only one family dinner, not two, hoping that tomorrow night might be good for Cynthia.

'He'll be spending time with Kenny and Sammy, anyway, so

maybe tomorrow is a good night for Buck and Pauline and Jessie and Pooh—if that works. We'll make it easy.'

He was accustomed to his wife being up for anything; it was unsettling to see her drained of the energy he unfairly relied upon.

'You'll be able to see better after the surgery,' he said. 'But there is a downside. You've always told me I'm pretty good-looking, and now you'll know the bitter truth.'

She laughed a little.

He tucked her in with a quote from Victor Hugo.

'"Sleep in peace, God is awake."'

THE FIRE HAD DIED DOWN and he didn't poke it up. The room was warm against the October night.

'Can you use a snack?' he asked Dooley.

'What is it?'

'Cynthia's egg salad, made this morning, with extra mayo on whole wheat from Winnie.'

'I could use a snack.'

He opened the container of egg salad, gave Dooley a root beer. 'Cynthia turned your bed down.'

'Five-star,' said Dooley. 'Thanks a lot. Has Sammy been nicer to you?'

'I haven't seen him since Saturday.'

'He was different tonight.'

'How do you mean?'

'He didn't try to pick a fight. Harley and Kenny say he's doing better.'

'Glad to hear it.'

'So something you did must have worked.'

'Time will tell,' he said, pouring himself a glass of water. 'I missed my trip to see the truck because of the funeral.'

'I'll run you down Saturday, it's only two hours. I'll kick the tires for you.'

He laughed. 'You're a good guy.'

'You, too, Dad. Cheers.'

Chapter
Twenty-two

In all his days in ministry, he couldn't remember fixing anybody up. Not directly, anyway. He had prayed for Puny to find a husband and she did, but he hadn't exactly brokered the deal.

'I suppose we could have them over for dinner and a movie,' said his wife.

He measured out a spoonful of honey for his oatmeal. 'What if it doesn't work?'

'They could just be friends.'

'What would I say to Omer?'

'That you'd like him to meet someone who loves Scrabble.'

'Perfect,' he said. 'But dinner and a movie? That's four hours. Shouldn't it be just coffee? I read that somewhere. Or maybe lunch at the Feel Good?'

'Lunch. I'll join you.'

His wife didn't often join him for lunch. 'Yay-y!' he said.

BEFORE STRAPPING ON HIS BACKPACK, he made a call.

'Add this to my tab, please. As soon as you can, take an extension ladder to the Woolen Shop and remove the plastic bag that's caught on the awning thingamajig.'

'That'd be y'r retractable lateral arm,' said Harley.

. . .

I<small>T WAS</small> T<small>EACHER'S</small> W<small>ORKDAY</small> at Mitford School; Miss Mooney arrived at Happy Endings at ten sharp.

'I need a great audio book,' she said. 'I have only fifteen minutes of wild liberty.'

'*Out of Africa!*' he said, trying to give her a break on an O title.

'Already have it; I'll take a quick look. If it's okay, I'll be here at three o'clock sharp. Coot's reading lesson.'

'How are the lessons coming?'

'He's very eager and hardworking. I dislike asking, but you could give a hand.'

'In what way?'

'He needs someone to read to him on occasion, it would be a great help.'

'I can do that,' he said.

'And it would be wonderful if you could ask for something in return. Something he could teach you.'

Coot's ancestor, Hezekiah Hendrick, had founded the town. He had always wanted more understanding of that family lore.

Abe jangled in around ten-thirty.

'I'm here to buy a book.'

'It's about time, buddy.'

'But only with a free coffee.'

'Always available.'

'I've just realized my cell phone is bigger than my bookcase.'

'Oy!' he said.

Abe had a laugh, poured himself a cup. 'So what's left in the O Sale? October is toast, there should be a big markdown.'

'We started with a big markdown.'

'Right. But the markdown of the markdown adds a little pizzazz in the home stretch.'

He had discussed the notion with Hope, who hadn't been averse to another five percent off a few titles at the end. 'Let's see what we can do.' He scrolled their O inventory on the computer.

'*Othello.* The play.'

'No Shakespeare,' said Abe.

'*Of Mice and Men.*'

'I have mice already.'

'*Old Man and the Sea.*'

'Not into fishing.'

'That's my best offer on markdowns.'

'Great,' said Abe. 'I'm off the hook 'til November. I've been meaning to ask, why do you think gentiles were invented?'

'Tell me.'

'Somebody has to pay retail.'

Winnie arrived with a bakery box.

'What are y'all laughin' about?'

'Not much,' said Abe.

'Chocolate donuts!' Winnie lifted the box lid. 'Two days old, but still good.'

'Thanks,' he said. 'I pass.'

'I'm in,' said Abe. 'Why us?'

'Overstock,' said Winnie. 'It's turned too cold for tourists, we have to get rid of 'em somehow. Where's Coot? He likes chocolate.'

'Buying supplies.'

The door opening, a blast of frigid air. 'I love chocolate!' said Shirlene, shucking out of her coat.

'Help yourself,' said Winnie, 'but th' one with sprinkles is for Coot.'

'What brings you three doors north?' He got an eyeful of the caftan-of-the-day: Palm trees. Monkeys. Distant islands.

'I'm thinkin' of gettin' a dog and wanted your advice. I see you out with your dog all th' time and figured you would know.'

'Here's my advice,' said Abe. 'Don't get a dog.'

'Why not?'

'Vet bills through the roof.'

'Get a cat,' said Winnie. 'You won't have to walk your legs off, go out in th' rain, or carry a poop bag in your pocket.'

'I'm single, I think I should get a dog.'

'What breed?' he said.

'I have no idea, that's what I wanted to ask you. Not th' breed of your dog, I can tell you that, he's bigger than my sofa.'

'You definitely want a barkin' dog,' said Winnie. 'But not a yappin' dog. An' somethin' small enough to sleep with, to keep you company.'

'Ooh,' said Shirlene, 'I don't think so. Where I come from, we don't sleep with dogs.'

'Me, either,' said Abe.

'Dogs are always after somethin',' said Winnie. 'Sittin' by th' table, starin' at you 'til you could keel over. I mean, dogs are so—'

'Earnest!' he said as his dog parked himself in front of Winnie and stared at the bakery box.

'See?' said Winnie. 'Is this how you want to spend the rest of your life?'

'That is th' biggest dog I ever saw,' said Shirlene, stepping back. 'Did you adopt him?'

'He adopted me.'

'So what do you have?' Shirlene asked Winnie. 'A dog or a cat?'

'Goldfish. Two, actually.'

'Not much good against intruders,' said Abe.

'A golden is a fine dog,' he said. 'Very noble and socially agreeable.'

'Could I take it to th' salon with me?'

'You could,' said Winnie, "'til it got hip dysplasia and could not climb the stairs.'

'As for a cat,' said Abe, 'if it knew you wanted it to go with you to the salon, it would not go.'

'Right,' said Winnie. 'You could not let it *know* you wanted it to go, and then maybe it would go.'

'Somebody buy a book,' he said. For Pete's sake.

'I could buy a book on dog breeds,' said Shirlene. 'What a fun idea!'

'Right this way,' he said.

'Three great books on dog breeds.' He placed them on the table next to the rubber plant. 'See what you think.'

Shirlene chose a book, thumped into a wing chair. He stood on one foot, then the other.

'Shirlene. Cynthia and I would like you to meet someone who loves Scrabble.' He was relieved to drag his wife into this.

'Really? Who?'

'Just, you know, a friend. Very nice. Has a garden. Potatoes, mostly.'

'But who?'

'You don't know this person.'

'Is it a man, is it a woman? Scrabble is totally unisex.'

'A man.'

'What's his name?'

'Omer.'

'Homer?'

'Omer. No H.'

'Are you tryin' to fix me up?'

'Well . . .'

'You are so cute to do this!' She sat forward in the chair. 'What does he look like?'

'Big. Great smile.'

'Wait a minute. Big. How big?'

'Maybe six-two.'

'Toned?'

'Um. I don't know about toned. Trim, for sure.'

'Trim is great! Handsome?'

'That's a judgment you'd have to make for yourself.'

'Okay, but I mean *really*—is he handsome?'

'Shirlene, Shirlene. Are you in?'

She pondered this. 'Big. Nice. Great smile.'

'Trim,' he said, to reprise. 'Has a garden. Loves Scrabble.'

'Wow. So, yes! Wow! I'm in!'

Lord help, he was glad to be done with it.

'You are really cute to do this, Father. I am so excited. Maybe I don't need to get a dog.'

'Time will tell,' he said. 'I'll try to put together a lunch before long. At the Feel Good, okay?'

'How's my tan?'

'Your tan?'

'Do I need a refresher? What do you think?'

'Talk to your sister,' he said.

It was sort of a cool thing to get people together, albeit a little scary. Compared, however, to the apprehension of arranging the Kim and Irene meeting, this should be a piece of cake.

. . .

DOOLEY, SAMMY, POOH, AND JESSIE blew in after lunch, smelling distinctly of pepperoni. Jessie's dog, Bouncer, brought up the rear.

Jessie was a plump, rosy-cheeked thirteen-year-old with a mane of chestnut hair and a good bit of makeup. Outgoing, loud, affectionate. A few years ago, he and Cynthia and Pauline had driven to Lakeland, Florida, and rescued Jessie from a dire situation with a relative. Pooh, sometimes plain Poo, and recently turned fifteen, had been with his mother all along. Pooh was nuts for his older brothers, and for baseball, softball, most any ball—from whence sprang the original nickname, Poobaw, after the pool ball he lugged around as a toddler.

'Buck has bronchitis,' said Jessie. 'He's pitiful.'

'So we can't come to your house to eat,' said Pooh. 'Can we come another time?'

'Absolutely.'

'We're goin' out to Kenny's restaurant tonight,' said Dooley, 'and a movie after.'

'Me an' Jess are ridin' in th' crew cab,' said Pooh. 'Mama says she's sorry.'

'We'll pray for Buck,' he said. 'Hey, Sam.'

'Hey. Your plastic b-bag's down.'

'Wonderful. Who got up there?'

'Me,' said Sammy.

Bouncer sniffed Barnabas; Sammy, Jessie, and Pooh vanished into the books.

'I checked with the trust people this morning,' said Dooley. 'Man.'

'What's up?'

'A lot. Buying out the practice, paying for college, and on top of that looking at four years of vet school. Huge. There won't be much left.'

Growing up. No wonder so many people resisted it.

Dooley stared at the floor for a time, pensive.

'There's no way we should get married 'til after vet school. Sometimes I feel like you and Cynthia want us to . . . you know . . . sooner.' Dooley's face flushed.

'We don't. Not at all. We hope you'll marry—but only if it's the best thing for you both. We agree that you should wait for the right time. We're completely with you on this.'

'Lots of people get married in vet school, then split. It's a really tough ride, a lot of work. I don't even know if I'll be accepted— sixty-five percent of applicants don't make it. I mean, think about it, Dad. Six more years of school. Man.'

Laughter in the stacks—a good sound.

'Lace and I have some stuff to work out.'

'I understand.'

'Did you have stuff to work out?'

'Did I ever. I'll tell you sometime.'

He pulled out his wallet; removed a twenty. Dooley watched him fold it as many times as the currency would allow.

As on Dooley's birthday more than eleven years ago, he placed it in his son's outstretched palm.

Dooley's cackling laugh.

'Don't spend it all in one place,' he said.

'Thanks. I'll need it. Meant to tell you, th' thing about Sammy's teeth is goin' nowhere.'

'Gunpoint. That's our only hope.'

Sammy came to the counter, book in hand.

'How much is this?'

'Sammy wants to garden with cow poop,' said Jessie.

'It ain't n-nothin' but grass that's gone through th' digestive system.'

'Grass and *bugs*,' said Jessie. 'Besides, where are you goin' to get cows?'

'Let's see,' he said. 'This book is twenty dollars. Less fifteen percent because the title begins with O for *Organic*.'

'Seventeen dollars!' said Jessie. 'I'm good at math.'

He added the tax; Sammy laid several bills and change on the counter, took the book, and headed to the door.

'Thanks for your business!' he called after Sammy.

'That's a lot of money for a book,' said Pooh.

Dooley pocketed the folded twenty; dug in his wallet and gave a twenty to Jessie. 'For ice cream.'

'Thanks, Dools!'

'See y'all back here in twenty minutes, and I'm totally lookin' for change.'

'In one pocket and out the other,' he said. 'Just what you were talking about with the trust.'

'What are you going to do, Dad?'

'About what?'

'About Miss Pringle. About Sammy.'

He was fed up with being asked what he was going to do about Sammy.

'I have no idea.'

'Could he live with . . . ?'

'No.' No explanation necessary. 'But here's what we must all do. Pray. Are you praying?'

'Sometimes.'

'Your brother needs full-time,' he said.

'He's doin' better.'

'Miss Pringle is looking for much better. We have her to thank that he's still there at all. In fact, you might thank her next time you see her. Take flowers.'

'Are you serious?'

'Remember your trip to New York with Cynthia? Remember I gave you money just for flowers?'

'I was buyin' flowers all over th' place.'

'Remember the look on her face when you gave her the flowers? Any happiness there, any delight?'

'Really. Big time.'

'Flowers don't solve anything, but they can improve most everything. Whether Sammy gets to stay is up to him. Either way, Miss Pringle has been a saint.'

'Got it.'

'Ask Jena Ivey to tie a few stems together with a ribbon, and deliver them by your own hand. Twenty bucks and not a penny less.'

'In one pocket and out the other.' Dooley hoisted himself onto the counter. 'So, Dad. I've been thinking. How about a truck better than the one in Hendersonville? Long bed, stick shift, leather seats, red. It has a couple of features you aren't lookin' for, but you can't be too choosy with used. Local owner, no traveling to pick it up.'

'How local?'

'I'll make you a really good deal.'

'Your truck?'

'It's too much truck for me. I was wrong; I hate t' say it. I don't need that much truck right now, not 'til I get th' practice. But you do, Dad. You need a truck to do your landscape stuff with. It's perfect. Crew cab for Harley and Sammy, the whole deal.

'And when I hang out my shingle, I'll buy it back. You won't put many miles on it, you'll take good care of it, and it'll be broken in for th' practice.'

'How would you get around?'

'I want to buy a truck I just saw in Wesley. Used, but it's a better vehicle for me. For one thing, I don't need a crew cab and a long bed right now.'

'I don't know . . .'

'If you don't like it, I'll take it back and sell it to th' guy who does grounds maintenance at school.'

One more thing to think about felt like one more thing too much.

'I'll run it through the wash in Wesley. Tires already kicked.'

They went out to the curb.

'What about that scratch on the passenger door?'

'You're in buyer's mode, for sure. I'll take care of that. A little touch-up with a paint stick.'

He opened the door, looked inside. Pretty clean, all things considered.

'Take it around the block,' said Dooley.

'Why the straw bales in the bed?'

'Goin' to Meadowgate this afternoon, they're fresh out of straw. I picked it up at th' feed store in Wesley.'

He remembered bouncing around in the wagon with Louis in Holly Springs. The rutted farm roads, the smell of hay and horse sweat, the creek flashing in a hard summer sun . . .

'Okay, I'll do a quick test drive. How about Barnabas rides shotgun, and you and your crowd ride with Coot on the straw bales?'

'Cool,' said Dooley.

Coot was upstairs stuffing mouse holes with rags soaked in peppermint oil, a trick recommended in a Hint. He called up the stairs. 'Coot! Let's go have some fun that is funny!'

He had never used the sign so commonly employed by fellow merchants for a quick dash up the block. He turned it around to face the street.

Back in Fifteen Minutes

He was ready for a little wild liberty of his own.

HONKING. Playing country music—loud. Laughing. Waving. It was his early run-up to the Independence Day parade.

'Country come to town!' he hollered, rolling through the gas pump aisle at Lew's.

They saw J.C. hoofing by the fire station, blew the horn. J.C. raised his camera, fired off a couple of shots. Avis threw up his hand. In the rearview mirror, he could see Coot, as excited as any country boy.

It felt good to make people happy, himself included, simply by tooling around in a truck full of kids and dogs.

BACK AT THE STORE, they hammered out the details. He would wire the money into Dooley's account on Monday. Dooley would use the truck until tomorrow when the deal in Wesley was done.

'Are you goin' to buy it?' asked Jessie.

'You should buy it,' said Pooh.

He put his arm around Sammy's shoulder, not an easy thing to do with this tall kid.

'Done deal,' he said. 'Sammy and I need a truck to get our rose garden finished. We're going to build a stone wall.' One way or another, come hell or high water.

'Yay-y-y,' said Jessie.

HE CALLED HOPE; Scott answered.

'Bleeding again,' said Scott. 'Wilson's coming over.'

'What may I do?'

'What you do best. Please.'

'Consider it done.'

'There's good news,' said Scott. 'Hope's sister, Louise, is moving back to Mitford in December. Her company is moving to Denver, so she'll be running the store starting January first. I know you're glad to hear it; you've had a long go at Happy Endings.'

'I needed a long go. Louise is a lovely woman. I'm happy for all.'

'There's something more. We wanted to tell you earlier, Father . . . we've known since the first ultrasound, but . . . somehow, we were afraid to . . .'

The chaplain paused, cleared his throat. 'It's a girl!'

HE BUSIED HIMSELF WITH LOCATING the N for November banner and cleaning the coffee apparatus. He didn't always know what to do when joy comingled with dread.

He tied a fresh bandanna around the neck of the Old Gentleman, as a kind of flag to heaven.

MOZART JOINED VOICES with Coot and Miss Mooney, hard at their task in the Poetry section.

The store phone. 'Happy Endings! Good afternoon.'

'Father Kavanagh?'

'It is.'

'Professor McCurdy was in to see you recently.'

A very professional-sounding woman.

'Yes. And I hear the professor's son, Hastings, is not well.'

'He was admitted to Children's Hospital at one o'clock today, his fever is a hundred and three.' The caller's voice wavered, she drew in her breath. 'He's very confused. Hastings is never confused. They say this is not a good thing.'

'Is there a diagnosis?'

'They believe it's meningitis. Whether viral or bacterial, they don't know. They've given him antibiotics and will go forward with a spinal tap.' The hospital paging system sounding in the background. 'This is all very serious, yet he's on a gurney in the hallway. It's a wonderful hospital, but the conditions . . .'

'We hope to rectify this soon.' What consolation was that? He disliked the sound of it.

'Can you do something, please? I'm told you're a longtime donor, could you get him into a room?'

'I very much doubt it. I know the staff and trust them to do all they can for Hastings. There's a shortage of beds . . .'

'I don't know any people of the cloth. I've read about you in the Muse. Would you . . . pray for Hastings?'

'Absolutely.'

'The professor is away. Do you think you might come to the hospital?' He heard the urgency; the cool professionalism had gone.

'I'm tied up until five. But I'll come straight there.'

'Should you see the professor again, please—don't mention that we've spoken.'

'You are Professor McCurdy's . . . ?'

'Wife.'

THE SLEEPING BOY APPEARED SMALLER still in the confines of the bed. The delicacy of the human eyelid had always astonished him—its silky thinness over such a vital organ; its bluish hue as pale as watercolor.

Hastings, it's the one who lent you the Wordsworth, he might say when the boy woke up. But the Wordsworth had been a thorn. He sat by the bed and prayed.

Sharon McCurdy stood with her back to the wall, looking shocked and somewhat fierce. She was clearly uncomfortable with the priest, but wanted him there, nonetheless.

'He's a sweetie,' said Nurse Robin. 'We're all thankful it's not bacterial.'

Twice he'd been around the block with meningitis in young parishioners, both bacterial and far more serious.

He prayed from the heart for Hastings McCurdy, a boy who might have been himself at this age—reading in advance of his learning level, interested in the classics, and smaller in stature than other boys in his class. As for the outcome, he would most likely be released tomorrow or the next day.

'Please sit,' he said. Sharon McCurdy had earlier refused the chair and insisted he keep the closer watch.

'I cannot,' she said.

'Does your husband know?'

'I try not to trouble him. He's at an important gathering of scholars.'

'There's an important scholar lying right here,' he said.

She tossed her head. 'There must be a room somewhere. All this rushing about in the hallway . . .'

'I've watched them work many times over the years. All we're missing here is three walls.'

'I thought it was flu,' she said, blaming herself. 'And then the vomiting . . .'

'Many similarities to flu when it presents.'

'The spinal tap was hideously painful.'

'Yes, but they know from the tap what to do.'

'What can you do, Father?' She was testy.

'I'm praying.'

'Is that enough?'

'That's a very good question. I often asked that in the early years of my calling. But yes, I believe it is fully enough. My common experience each and every day shows prayer to be fully enough.'

'He could have some memory loss, they say. He knows so many wonderful things by heart. One of the poems in the book you lent, he was learning by memory.'

'Which one, may I ask?'

She was close to tears. '"By the Seaside." He asked me to define bemocked.'

She covered her face with her hands and turned to the wall.

The sun is couched, the sea-fowl gone to rest,
And the wild storm hath somewhere found a nest . . .

. . .

THREE EMERGENCY ROOM ADMISSIONS and a funeral, all within a couple of weeks. While the stuff of life came in big batches for the full-time priest, the retiree was generally given the smaller batch. He certainly couldn't complain of his modest handful, though a wedding in the mix would be a pleasant distraction.

He scrolled his emails.

Even communiqués from former parishioners occasionally arrived in batches. A kindhearted message from Sam and Marion Fieldwalker in Whitecap. Agnes from Holy Trinity had come online, albeit dial-up; wonders never ceasing! And there was Liam, though not a parishioner in the strict sense, sounding in from Sligo to say Bella had won an impressive award for her fiddling. There was no gathering of his parish under one roof—his flock was scattered from mountain to shore, and beyond to an emerald isle.

> <Once more all is well. Wilson says keep doing what we're
> doing. Thanks for your mighty prayers.
>
> <Scott>

At the end, a message for which he had not waited with bated breath.

> <Tuesdays with Emma
>
> At the unheard of old rate
>
> <GOING, GOING . . .

He took Barnabas out, then checked the stove (a habit said

to be a sign of old age). As he was turning off the lamps in the
study, he heard the message arrive in his computer in-box.

<GONE.

He had thought it would never end, and yet—it had ended.
He sat down in his desk chair, oddly bereft.

SHE UNDERSTOOD AT LAST why she had felt distant from
the child beneath her heart. She had lived with an image of
the trap her body was laying, and felt the guilt of it—all this
shadowed by the sense of entrapment she'd once known, herself. In fearing the worst, she had missed months of happiness
and intimations of joy.

Not days, not hours, but minutes, they had said. But not for
everyone, only a few. She had been claiming as her own the
tragedy of the certain few.

She turned her head on the pillow and searched the face of
her sleeping husband. It was charted territory, this face she
had been granted before the beginning of time. Their daughter must come into the world and know the benediction of her
father's deep tenderness—it was that simple.

She would choose happiness and, in the mysterious way of
blood, share it with their daughter, beginning now.

Chapter
Twenty-three

A cold rain began at first light on Monday, and showed no sign of abating. The heaters weren't much help; they were painting with gloves on.

He and Sammy would work only a half-day, after which he'd run to the bookstore and put finishing touches on the N Sale.

They took a break and sat on opposite sides of a pew missing its end pieces. Sammy was digging into a bag of Cheetos; he was finishing a pack of raisins.

'Thanks,' said Sammy, not looking up.

It took a moment for this to sink in. 'What for?'

'Everything.'

Sammy rose abruptly, stuffed the bag in his pocket, and returned to putting a second coat of paint on the trellis.

'OH, MY, not a soul stirring up here,' said Hélène Pringle of her Tuesday vigil. 'It's the dismal weather, *vous ne pensez pas*? But Christmas is coming, Father, and things will pick up, I'm sure of it. I've a grand idea for December's display window.'

'Wonderful.'

'I believe you do not have a D for December Sale?'

'That's correct.'

'So the window would be quite free for a live Saint Nicholas! Sitting in that wing chair, reading a book! *Très charmant, oui?*'

'Live?'

'Yes, people would stop and peer in to see if he's real and then they would come in and—don't you see?—buy books!'

'Hélène, you're a marketing genius. Can you get home safely this evening?' He heard what he thought to be Grieg in the background.

'*Oui.* I walked up in my good boots; I shall be warm as toast. And I did have a sale this morning. Mrs. McGraw ordered three books by phone, to be mailed to her grandson in Germany, it's his birthday. I've sent them across to the post with Mr. Hendrick—he is very handy.'

'So you're happy selling books? The honeymoon isn't over?'

'Oh, no, and I'm listening to *Peer Gynt*. Do you care for Grieg? I always found him very agreeable.'

'Good,' he said, not caring for Grieg.

'He died peacefully in his sleep,' she said. 'I'm so glad for him, he deserved that.'

If he were a better person, he might have asked how things were going with Sammy. But no—as far as that was concerned, he was staying in the tall grass.

BEFORE DARK, he was sent on an errand by his wife.

'Mac and cheese,' he said to an astonished Coot Hendrick, who came to the door.

The dish was still hot.

He loved flinging carbs around.

. . .

'I'M PAINTING WITH IRENE tomorrow and Friday,' Cynthia said over dinner. 'The auction will be here before we know it.'

Each time the auction was mentioned, he felt the guilt he'd already thoroughly wallowed in. Quite likely there was some ego involved here—he had been a donor for nearly twenty years. Nothing extravagant, merely steady; they counted on him. But now he had nothing significant to give, nor any contribution to make to the auction.

He had gone about the house looking for a desirable donation, but there was nothing he could part with. He considered the elaborate needlepoint of a verse from Proverbs, worked by Nanny Howard, *Blessed be the Lord who daily loadeth us with benefits.* That would fetch a good sum from a needlework collector, but no, he had nothing to give, selfish man that he was. Perhaps Dooley and Lace would want it when . . . if . . .

Edith Mallory was the only person he knew with a serious profile for philanthropy. Why couldn't he call her? He couldn't, that's all. Given their history and the crucifying injury to her brain—even considering that she was now a believer—he could not do it, though he occasionally stared at the phone with good intentions.

On the upside, Hastings was home; Nurse Robin had passed along a favorable report. He needed to come up with the perfect book for Hastings, but nothing from his own shelves, of course. *All Creatures Great and Small* would be commendable, or perhaps *The Chronicles of Narnia.* He must give his selection a good deal of thought and consult with Miss Mooney.

Petronius woke only about midday, and as usual, greatly wearied. The evening before he had been at

*one of Nero's feasts, which was prolonged till late at
night. For some time his health had been failing. He
said himself that he woke up benumbed, as it were,
and without power of collecting his thoughts . . .*

At last, he was a bookseller reading a book. He would take
it with him tomorrow to Happy Endings.

Cynthia busied herself with two trays of lemon squares for
the swearing-in. Barnabas snored and their cats slept, as he
settled into his chair by the fire and let the visceral power of
Quo Vadis flow into a second reading of Henryk Sienkiewicz's
novel set during the reign of Nero.

THERE THEY WERE on the front page, a bunch of hillbillies
out for a joyride in a pickup truck—Barnabas hanging his
head out the window after the fashion of dogs in trucks, and a
number of arms wagging from the truck bed. Photo credit:
J. C. Hogan.

Can you Spot
Our Leading Citizen
In This Picture??

**Yes, that is Father Tim, our Leading Citizen, driv-
ing his new pickup truck (an older model, but new
to him)! Riding upfront is Barnabas, his Irish wolf-
hound/Bouvier (JCH check splng) mix, and Dooley
Kavanagh, Sammy Barlowe, Pooh Leeper, Jessie
Leeper, Coot Hendrick (a Leading Citizen semi-**

finalist!) and Bouncer, a sort of corgi like the Queen
is crazy about or maybe a dachshund >>

'We were just having fun,' said Father Tim Kavanagh, who received 236 votes!

Are you having fun? We hope so. Life is short, right?

cONGRATUlations to Father Tim Kavanagh!!!

Following this journalistic debacle, in which he was quoted as
saying something he had never said, was a twenty-year-old photo
taken soon after he came to Mitford, in which he had no wrinkles, no wattle, no bifocals, and considerably more hair. This
piece named him the winner of what was to be an annual contest, herein called 'an election by the People and for the People.'
He learned that he was to claim his prize of a free top-of-the-line
spray tan treatment by December 15, or forfeit the prize.

A Revolution
On Mitford's
Main Street!!

He scanned the piece.

". . . *cost between '$100k and $200k.*" *The tanning solution*
"*made from beet juice and walnut extract.*" Amazing. Blah, blah.

"*You could watch a video except they lost the video in the move
from Bristol.* "*You do NOT need to watch a video to have a successful
spray tan experience,*" *says Fancy Skinner, who is wearing Tan Number 74 or the Palm Beach. Number 74 is somewhat darker than the
West Palm Beach but* . . . blah, blah, blah . . . a total revolution . . .

Interviews with spray tan customers. "*You just go in and take*

your clothes off and press the green button," says Ms. Esther Bolick, "and after you get sprayed,, a machine blows you dry."

"When asked how the experience made her feel, Ms. Bolick
said, "It made me want to go shopping."

Esther Cunningham
Returns Home Yayyyy!

Here was a photo, obviously vintage, of Esther with a bee-
hive hairdo and an astonishing resemblance to Carol Burnett
back in the day.

> Former Mitford mayor Esther Cunningham returns
> home this afternoon from Charlotte where she was
> outfitted with not one but TWO stenTs!^&
>
> She is also recovering from pneumonia and will
> need a lot of rest so back off, people and let her GET
> WELL SOOn.
>
> If you send flowers remember Ms Cunningham
> CANNOT tolerate lilies unless you cut the stamens
> off. BTW stamens can be harmful to cats did you
> know that? So cut them off no matter what OK? It is
> actually the anthers not the stamens but the anthers are
> ON the stamens. Use scissors or take a vacuum cleaner
> upholstery brush and suck up the anthers. This is hard
> to describe so call me if you have to,—7615, Ext. #3.

'Hello, Vanita?'

'Hey! Congratulations, Father! People are so glad you won!

I'll bring you a ribbon kind of thing to wear. I hope you'll wear it proudly!'

'I see I was quoted as saying we were out having fun—in the truck. Did I say that?'

'Mr. Hogan said that if he was you, which he isn't, that's what he would say.'

'So Mr. Hogan spoke for me, correct?'

'Yessir, he did.'

'Aha. Well. And nice job, Vanita.'

'Oh, thanks. I really appreciate that, comin' from you.'

'Keep up the good work,' he said.

Then there was the Hint, titled 'Deodorizing Woolens.' He tried to read it, but couldn't. He just couldn't.

'IT'S NOT TRANSFERABLE,' said Shirlene. 'But if Homer is really cute, like you say, it might be transferable.'

'Blackmail, Shirlene.'

'Okay, okay, it's transferable. Who do you want to transfer it to?'

'Let me get back to you on that.'

RAY CUNNINGHAM, the very personification of hail-fellow-well-met, was looking frayed.

'I'm meetin' two of my girls here in a little bit an' drivin' to Charlotte to bring Esther home.'

'Great, wonderful. I hear she's doing well.'

'I was down there with her a few days. It was tough.'

'I'm sure of it.'

'We nearly lost her.' Ray looked away, cleared his throat.

'Pneumonia, stroke, blocked artery—a cluster, is what they called it. She's not herself, Father. Nossir, it's not Esther talkin'. She said tell you she's not runnin' again.'

'Doctor's orders?'

'Just says she's over that mess. Wants to go on th' trip out West, like we planned. Says she looks forward to smokin' that peace pipe with th' Indians.'

'A change of heart!'

'She won't inhale, though.'

'No.'

'Says it's very generous that they'd sit down with us, much less pass th' pipe.'

'I'll drop by as soon as she's up to it. What's the prognosis?'

'Doctors say she'll be fine. Built like th' *Titanic*, one said; which would've been okay if wadn't for th' iceberg.' Ray looked dazed. 'I was gon' make baby backs for her homecomin' but the doc says glazed carrots, green peas, like that—no more baby backs. Glazed carrots. I don't know nothin' 'bout glazin' a carrot.'

VANITA DELIVERED THE RIBBON KIND OF THING. A discreet navy blue with a metal medallion inscribed MLC.

'Mitford's Leading Citizen,' she said. 'You will pass it on next year to your successor.'

She begged him to wear it. He said he would, but not twenty-four/seven.

ABE POPPED HIS HEAD IN. 'Mazel tov!'

On his way to a real estate closing, Mule dropped by to offer felicitations. 'I voted for you,' said Mule. 'And I think Shirlene did, but I don't know about Fancy.'

The Collar Button man stopped in for a handshake, perfuming the place with pipe smoke, not a bad thing.

His wife sent flowers from Mitford Blossoms. Calla lilies, anthers and all, which gave the sales counter a certain distinction.

At four-thirty, Esther Bolick plopped her cake carrier on the counter.

'Congratulations,' she said, sour as a pickle.

'Thank you.'

'Sick people are workin' me to death, two of my book club members are sick as cats, not to mention Miz Hendrick's funeral.'

'Why, Esther Bolick. Baking this impossibly difficult and extraordinary cake is your passion. This is your life's mission. Think about it—the merest sight of you with this cake carrier lifts the human spirit.'

'At forty-five bucks a pop, I could be a lot happier doin' somethin' else for th' human spirit.'

He looked her in the eye. 'You can't fool me.'

Esther burst into laughter. 'I never could. Gene used to say to me, You can't fool th' father.'

'Does that mean you tried?'

They had a laugh.

'So Ray's gone to Charlotte with two of his girls to fetch Esther,' he said. 'What am I supposed to do with this?'

'Deliver it to th' Cunninghams this evenin', if you don't mind.'

'Can't you deliver it to the Cunninghams?'

'I cannot. I'm goin' down th' mountain here in a minute to

spend the night with a friend, and tomorrow I am finally goin' shoppin'. I am truly goin' to shop 'til I drop, I have not bought a stitch since Gene passed. Two dresses, if I can find a dress in this pagan world. New shoes, one pair with two-inch heels to be worn only when sittin' down. And a hat.'

'You don't wear hats. I have never seen you in a hat.'

'You most certainly have seen me in a hat,' she said. 'I wore a hat to your wedding, don't you remember? Besides, times change, Father; people change. Not everybody is stuck in their ways. Don't you know that?'

'CONGRATULATIONS,' said Puny, who dropped by soon after he arrived home. 'I voted for you three times an' th' girls voted for you six times.'

'People could vote more than once?'

'There weren't any rules in that contest, which is my kind of contest. An' take this with you, if you don't mind.'

She handed him a large bowl with a snap-on lid of a smiley face.

'What is it?'

'Potato salad for Mamaw Cunningham.'

'How did you know I was going over there?'

'I saw Esther Bolick pumpin' gas at Lew's, she said you were takin' her OMC over this evenin'.'

'What am I, the new food service in town? Why can't you take it over?'

'I'm goin' to a PTA meetin' that will last 'til eight o'clock. Then I have to finish bakin' for th' swearin'-in. Plus I'd like to run up a set of curtains for Joe Joe's new office.'

'Curtains in the police chief's office?'

'They're not *tie*backs.'

'Anyway, Esther cannot have this potato salad.'

'Who says?'

'Her doctor. It contains mayonnaise and bacon. Esther is on a diet of glazed carrots.'

Puny was thunderstruck. 'Glazed carrots?'

'Have you ever glazed a carrot?'

'You're kidding me, aren't you?'

'Puny, Puny. Would I kid you?'

SINCE HE WASN'T RUNNING these days, he was determined to walk to the Cunninghams'. His wife wanted to drive him up, but no, he could do this.

'Well, then, I'm slipping something in your jacket pocket, okay? My editor sent chocolate truffles today; I'm sharing two with Esther. Try not to mash them.'

And there he went, a pack mule in a fleece hoodie, into the winter gloom.

HE ARRIVED AT THE CUNNINGHAMS' at six-thirty, feeling grumpy. Kavanagh's Schlep and Haul. Ray was overjoyed with the provender, though the entire delivery was a no-no in the new diet plan.

'We're happy to have you home,' he told Esther, who was sitting in a wing chair in the Cunningham den.

'The girls took my recliner and stuck it in the fur . . . r . . . nace room, can you believe it? They said a new study shows older people spend too . . . o . . . . o much time in their recliners and lose th' use of their legs! Too . . . o . . . k it right out from under me, and Ray Cunnin'ham did nothin' to stop it.'

'I'm tryin' to look after you, Sugar.'

She gave her husband a dark look. 'Just wa . . . ait'll they haul yours out of here!'

He removed his jacket, made himself at home. 'Did you see the piece in the *Muse* about your homecoming?'

'I'm too doped up to read. What else is goin' on?'

He felt like a schoolboy reporting to the principal. 'We got the bag down!'

'What bag?'

'The plastic bag that drove you nuts. On the awning at the Woolen Shop.'

'Why'd you bother yourself with such aggravation? Don't you have more important things to do . . . o . . . o?'

'Esther, you asked me to do it.'

'I was pre-stroke, Father, pre-stroke. I don't care if th' blo . . . o . . . oomin' thing hangs there 'til th' cows come home.'

'Really!'

'A nuisance, all of it. Let this town run itself. I always thought I was runnin' it, but it was r . . . r . . . runnin' me. I'm done.'

'I've heard that before.'

Esther gave him one of her rare smiles, she was practically beaming. 'This time I mean it. If I ever say I'm goin' to run for office again, you can have me committed. Send me straight to Br . . . r . . . oughton.'

'So, would you ride with me in the parade next July?'

'Is th' Pope Ca . . . a . . . ath'lic?' she said.

. . .

His wife encouraged him to wear the ribbon thing, which he did. 'The *dignitaries* will be there!' she said, pinning it on his lapel. She took a picture with her cell phone, thoroughly amusing herself.

It was a spread fit for a tent meeting.

Ray Cunningham indicated the two tables, fully loaded. 'Right there is what fuels this town. Premium high-test octane.'

He eyed the vast bowl of Snickers bars. There was hardly a bite in view that he could put on his blue-for-MPD paper plate. Given his morning blood sugar reading, he couldn't drink the sweet tea or the hot cider or have even a forkful of his wife's lemon squares. He took a cheese wafer and a bottled water.

'Lord help,' said Avette Harris, scornful of such meager refreshment.

He considered the swarm of notables.

Chief Hamp Floyd of the Mitford Fire Department, known also as the Worm. Mayor Gregory and his gorgeous Italian wife who not-so-vaguely resembled the actress whose name he couldn't remember, the one who said she owed it all to pasta.

Lew Boyd and his Tennessee bride, Earlene, who allowed that the swearing-in was, as her grandmother would have said, 'more fun than a corn-shuckin'.'

His buddy Bill Sprouse, of First Baptist. Percy and Velma Mosely, former proprietors of the Main Street Grill, wearing natural tans with no walnut extract called for.

Two stray dogs foraged through the crowd.

Chief Guthrie's mother, Marcie, in a mother-of-the-bride lace dress with corsage, attended on every side by Guthrie and

Cunningham kin as numerous as Abraham's stars. And over there was Abe Edelman with his wife, Sylvia, and here was his old friend Buck . . .

'Buck!' He loved this big guy who, in a drunken rage, had once thrown a couple of chairs at him but was now as peaceable as the proverbial lamb.

'Lord bless you, Father. And congratulations.'

An embrace, hard and warm, from the man married to Dooley's mother. He and Buck had gone down the mountain a couple of years ago, following an elusive trail that led to Sammy.

'Feeling better?'

'A whole lot, but now Pauline has whatever it was. How's Sammy?'

'He's . . . all right.'

'What can I do?'

'Maybe take him to the construction site with you one day. He has a curious mind, and is pretty savvy about the way things work.'

'I'd like to do that. An' Kenny?'

'A wonderful young man. We'll miss him greatly when he leaves in January.' A Barlowe gained, only to be lost—though not for good, as it once seemed.

Buck nodded, sobered by the way of things.

'Time,' he said to Buck. 'It does heal.'

And there was Doc Wilson in his running gear, and J.C. with his Nikon and fancy photographer's jacket, and Olivia Harper talking with Cynthia, who was decked out in a dress the color of cornflowers.

Across the room, Tad Sherrill, Betty Craig, Puny brushing

something off the lapel of the chief's new uniform, the rowdy crew from the waterworks, Ron Malcolm, Mule and Fancy, Coot in what appeared to be overalls ironed with a crease in the pant legs . . .

Captain Hogan tucked her thumbs in her gun belt and surveyed the room. 'It'd be a great time for somebody to come in an' rob th' town.'

And there went Sissy and Sassy pushing Timmy and Tommy in an all-terrain vehicle resembling a double stroller, and here was Shirlene in a caftan picturing indigenous tribes in a rain forest, with parrots.

It was as good as a coronation.

On Sunday afternoon, he glanced out to the deck to see whether he'd put the cover back on the gas grill.

Sammy was sitting on the top step, holding Truman. Sammy's back was to the door, but he could see the boy's face in partial profile. Sam was talking to the black-and-white kitten and stroking its head and saying something.

He went to the study, where Cynthia was lying on the sofa, eyes closed.

'Are you awake, Kav'na?'

'Just resting my eyes.'

'Let's invite Sammy and Kenny and Harley over for burgers and pool this evening. What do you think?'

She smiled, eyes still closed.

'So amazing. Puny was going to make chili tomorrow, so we have two pounds of Avis's best. And I just bought a head of cabbage for coleslaw.'

The little miracles. Those were the ones to watch for in this life.

'I'll chop!' he said.

'I AIN'T NEVER F-FIRED UP A GRILL,' said Sammy, who proceeded to fire up the grill, as demonstrated.

'What if I burn th' burgers?'

'Not allowed. Besides, I'll be standing right here; I won't let it happen.'

'Okay, what next?'

'Next we wash our hands.'

They shared the deep sink in the garage, one of the relics installed by Cynthia's deceased Uncle Joe Hadleigh. Very handy for a man who changed his own motor oil, which yours truly never did.

'You might want to use more soap,' he said.

This would be 101 all the way. He was pretty excited.

They went to the kitchen, where the goods were laid out—spatula, room-temperature ground beef on a platter, salt grinder, pepper grinder, sliced cheddar, et al.

'Number one,' he said, 'is to start with beef that's eighty-five percent lean. Any leaner than that, the burgers are dry. Avis grinds it coarse for us, not fine. A fine grind can get a little soft and fall apart on the grill. So, eighty-five percent lean, coarse grind. Next thing is, we're not going to handle the meat too much.'

He ground salt and pepper, lightly worked it into the meat, scooped a handful, and slapped it into shape. 'Give it a try.'

His sous chef stood transfixed for a moment, took a deep breath, and deftly shaped a thick burger.

'Perfect.'

Sammy exhaled.

And there was Dooley, albeit above the mantel, seeming nearly present in the flesh.

They carried the platter to the deck. A biting cold. The grill was their fire pit in the heart of the cave.

For him, this was the hard part—when raw meat hits the grate, it sticks. The trick was to flip the burger the moment it released from the grate, and not before.

'By the way, no pressing down with the spatula. The juices run out, the burger gets dry.' He was Julia Child in her heyday, he was the entire Food Network.

'Man.' Sammy shook his head.

'Not to worry. It gets easier every time you do it.' Maybe that wasn't completely true, but . . . somewhat.

HE HEARD THE CUE strike the ball, the sound sharp and clean to the ear. He heard Sammy whoop, heard Kenny and Harley laugh. Sam was doing what he loved, in a house with people he could almost trust.

He didn't need to be in there pretending to learn the game. He was doing something he loved, too—cleaning up the kitchen with his wife.

CYNTHIA TURNED OFF her bedside lamp. 'Your Burger Boot Camp was a hit.'

He lay with eyes closed, grinning.

'A very happy party,' she said. 'I'm glad we invited Hélène.'

'He did a good job, Sam.'

He didn't want to think beyond that simple and wondrous fact.

.   .   .

IN THE MURPHYS' SMALL COTTAGE three blocks away, Hope sat in bed with a book from Happy Endings.

'Catherine,' she said.

'Umm,' said Scott.

'Hannah.'

'Close.'

'Rebecca?'

'Ah.'

'You have a try.'

A long silence, the small wind at the shutters.

'Laurel!' said Scott.

'Pretty.'

Another long silence.

'This is hard,' said Scott.

After the long lying-in with fear, a certain joy had come, was a whole new presence in the room. They were praying about the name, of course, so no hurry, it was ready and waiting to be found. And yet she felt the mounting pressure to know their daughter's name. They were yearning for it, really.

'Elizabeth is always good,' he said.

'True.'

Naming was a peculiar exercise. One headed off in so many directions at once. In some cultures, the child wasn't named right away, and certainly not before it was born. She spread her hands over the globe of her belly—felt the pulse of her heart beating in the waters of the gulf beneath.

The gift of this child was so miraculous, so out of proportion to human understanding, that . . . who could label such profound mystery with a name?

Chapter
Twenty-four

They all felt the reward of having made great advances on the rose garden job.

Not the least of their satisfaction was the maple. Breaking new ground, even with the snow melt loosening the soil, brought the sweat, but he and Harley and Sammy got it in and tamped down the earth and spread the mulch and edged the ring and looked at each other in a way that to him seemed oddly parental.

Even so, it was time to halt their efforts 'til spring; it was too frigid to work productively. Sometime in the next few months, they would choose the stone and have it hauled to the site in May.

Harley and Sammy would have to do in winter what others did in these parts—hunker down and be glad for slim pickings. He noodled his noggin, as Uncle Billy would say, for a project that might give them income.

He pondered this on Thursday morning, as he went upstairs to Happy Endings' second floor, to the rooms where Hope had made a home when she bought the business.

She had hung curtains at the windows facing the street and set a lamp there. When walking Barnabas to the monument in the evenings, he had relished seeing the glow above the store, had felt a certain gladness. *We are not alone in this world; there is a light in the window.*

And at Christmas, there was Hope's shining tree where the lamp had been. It was nothing more than a lighted tree in a window—but in a window long dark. That had been the joy of it.

He found the printer paper and tucked it under his arm and went to the stairs. The upper floor smelled of peppermint oil, a good thing.

HE WENT ALONE to the Feel Good for a quick lunch, hoping to connect with Omer while he was at it.

'Any thoughts?' he asked Wanda.

'I'm still thinkin',' she said, filling his tea glass.

She was wearing the cowboy hat again—not a good sign as far as her disposition for the day was concerned.

'How could something so simple require so much thought?' he said. 'Six or seven people come in, behave decently, sit in a corner with relative privacy, and order breakfast. At an average cost of, say, seven bucks, that's roughly fifty dollars' worth of business, plus tips.'

The arched eyebrow. 'Mighty few preachers leave tips.'

'We're a thrifty lot, all right.'

'Cheap,' she said.

'Okay, okay.'

'Why don't you use a church for your prayer breakfast?'

'There is a serious problem with using a church for a prayer breakfast.'

'What?'

'Churches do not serve breakfast.'

There was her lopsided look that passed for a grin. 'All right. But no shoutin', Bible-thumpin', or altar calls.'

'Not from me.'

'And thanks for th' business. While you're at it, maybe you can pray for this place to keep runnin' a black bottom line. Everything's goin' sky-high and nobody wants to do a day's work.'

'I will pray for that.'

'So it's okay to pray for a bottom line?'

'Absolutely. God allowed this business to come into your hands. He gave you the gumption to work hard and give your customers honest value. He wants you to succeed.

'So, there's every reason to ask,' he said, 'and—to give thanks for his continued good favor.'

Wanda's spirits appeared to brighten.

In breezed Omer, with his piano-key grin lighting up the place.

'Flyboy!' someone called. Omer threw up his hand, removed his cap, and turned to greet the proprietor. 'The usual, please, ma'am.'

Wanda brightened a good deal more.

Why tarry? As soon as Wanda brought Omer's glass of tea, he launched.

'Omer. You've been single for a while?' He was nonchalant as anything, eating his salad with grilled chicken.

'Twelve, thirteen years.'

'Any children? I can't recall.'

'No kids. Just a couple of ragwings.'

'Would you be interested in meeting someone who plays Scrabble?'

Omer gave him an uncharacteristically dark look. 'Who?'

He realized he should have talked to Omer before he said

anything to Shirlene. What if Omer had enough Scrabble in his life and wasn't interested?

'Fancy Skinner's sister, Shirlene. From Bristol.' He was suddenly, mortally, uncomfortable.

'Bristol,' said Omer, staring at his tea glass. 'Th' woman with th' spray gun who moved here?'

'Right. There's a story in last week's *Muse*.'

'I don't know. I'm not handy at women.'

He hadn't been handy at women, either, and look at him now. An old married guy trying to fix people up.

'Guess it's been too long. I'm just a gnarly 'Nam vet livin' on four acres with a patch of potatoes and a dog. Not much goin' on with me—a few yard sales, a little Scrabble online.'

The perfect demographic! Nailed! How often does that happen in life?

'Pretty dull,' said Omer.

'Dull? Not in the least. How about your halfway house ministry? I wouldn't call that dull. So maybe we could have lunch. With my wife. And Shirlene.'

'Lunch,' said Omer. 'I don't think so, Father.'

'Coffee?'

'I don't drink coffee.'

This was a nut to crack.

'What kind of dog?'

'Mutt. Named Patsy.' And there was Omer's smile again.

'I believe Shirlene is currently looking for a dog.'

'Good for the head. By the way, I've been meaning to bring you some potatoes. I'll drop 'em by th' bookstore, guaranteed. Yukon Gold or russet?'

'Either way. We like both. And thanks.'

This wasn't going terribly well. He would have to ask Cynthia to give a hand here.

'I DID IT BACKWARDS,' he said. 'I don't know how I get myself into these things.'

'Meddling, sweetheart, that's how. You have a special knack for it.'

'What to do?' he said.

'Leave it alone for a while. You didn't name a time for lunch. You were vague, right?'

'Vague. Yes. Which reminds me, I never told Shirlene that he's over her maximum age limit.'

'By how much?'

'I don't know. Five or six years. Maybe more.'

'Hmm,' she said. 'You trump me by six years and I don't think any damage has been done. Not yet, anyway.'

'It's not over 'til it's over, Kav'na.'

They were lying in bed, his favorite tryst for plain talk.

'Your book. Is it ever going to end?'

'I just began it in September. Really, sweetheart, it's only November. This is what I do.'

'Will you ever . . . retire?' A disgraceful word, but there it was. 'It is very consuming, your work.'

'True. But why have work that isn't consuming?'

He had no idea what to say to this. 'You're definitely worse than I am.'

'In which of many ways?'

'You never want to go anywhere,' he said, 'yet I'm the one with the reputation for never wanting to go anywhere.'

'I told you I would love to take the RV trip. When everything is done here.'

'What is everything? And what do you mean by done?'

She couldn't answer this; she simply didn't know; she would have to play it by ear, she said.

He switched off his bedside lamp and held her hand, and prayed something best suited, in his opinion, for early morning, though indeed it was never too late in the day for these ardent petitions.

'Almighty and eternal God, so draw our hearts to you, so guide our minds, so fill our imaginations, so control our wills, that we may be wholly yours, utterly dedicated unto you, and then use us, we pray, as you will, and always to your glory and the welfare of your people, through our Lord and Savior Jesus Christ.'

'Amen!' said his wife.

WINTER COULD GET plenty long up here. In a few short months, they usually saw all of Mark Twain's storied hundred and forty-nine weather modes.

After Christmas, the bookstore would be 'quiet' according to Hope and 'dead' according to Marcie. And he was at a standstill on the rose garden.

He didn't want to 'snuggle in' for the winter. He wanted to do something that got his blood up and skip the depression he sometimes suffered when 'earth stood hard as iron.'

There was the trail behind the hospital. Though he expected to be done at the bookstore when Hope's sister came on in January, it could be May before weather was good to work outdoors. As for the planning and organizing of a project like this, he could work on that anytime—preferably right away.

He had swung into the trail when he was running on Tuesday. One had to be especially adroit to run back there. The many exposed tree roots and general wear and tear were dangerous for walkers and runners alike. Those were issues the town crew could work on. As for the trash, it wasn't conveniently confined to the perimeter of the trail, but meandered far into the woods. He would crew that job himself.

He had made it to the turnaround, which seemed a popular spot for trash disposal, then got out of there. Was he nuts? Maybe, but he still wanted to see the place redeemed.

The town wouldn't spring for amenities; he would need to provide appropriate trash bins and signage. Signage was important. A few hardy shrubs, topsoil, mulch. And later, way later, a couple of iron benches.

He and Sammy and Harley could walk the trail together, then spend a few evenings by the fire, thinking it through. Hadn't Sammy's woodland shade garden, which he saw the day he first met the boy, been something to marvel at?

Philosophy wasn't his long suit. But in the scheme of things, of what real importance was a ruined walking trail or a neglected rose garden? Yesterday, he had selected a book at random and discovered this by Abraham Verghese in *Cutting for Stone*:

'We are all fixing what is broken. It is the task of a lifetime.'

Only one problem. He was running out of money. There were a few CDs lying about and earning a drop in the bucket, but nothing was due to roll over anytime soon.

TRUMAN HAD DONE all in his power to move the imperial heart of Violet Number Four—or was it Five? Violet was having none of it. She was still offended, and still using the top of the refrigerator to remove herself from the rabble below.

The Old Gentleman was another matter. He had adopted the black-and-white stray after a considerable trial period, and life was good.

However—and there was always the however—Truman enjoyed getting out and about. Soon after the adoption, he and Cynthia had driven the little guy to Meadowgate, where Hal put an end to any future patrimony. The thorn of venturing through their neighborhood had been removed.

'Toys,' said his wife. 'Something to do with all that energy. Maybe a windup mouse.'

'We don't have time to wind up a mouse,' he said.

'A cat door,' said Sammy.

'How would we get one?' she said.

'Me an' him could m-make you one.'

He had never been anything at all to Sammy. Not 'this guy' or 'that man,' and certainly not Dooley's 'dad.' Now, at least, he was 'him.'

AT A LITTLE PAST FIVE, he was rummaging around at his desk, still hoping to find the missing love letter. Talk about a complete and aggravating mystery . . .

He answered the knock at the side door.

'In you come!' he said to his French-born neighbor. 'A cup of tea?'

'No, thank you, Father. I smelled something cooking and knew you were home.'

'Cynthia is painting with a friend and won't be here 'til six. Will you sit at the counter while I stir the pot?'

'The aroma drifted all the way to my porch—I pursued it through the hedge!' She popped herself onto a stool.

'Soup,' he said. 'Full of scraps, as soup must be. I'm using chicken, lamb, and beef bones for flavor.'

'Very wartime,' she said. 'My grandmother fled Paris when it fell to the Germans. She went to Vichy, where she learned to cook like a *paysan*, the bone being always the chief ingredient of good soup.'

She watched him stir in the rice, positively mesmerized. If her news was bad, he wished she would get along with it.

'Congratulations, Father, on being voted our leading citizen. A designation of great merit!'

'Thank you,' he said. His wife had advised him not to rattle on with self-conscious modesties.

'You remember how I said I wished to help someone.'

'I do remember.'

'Thus I am going to the bookstore on Tuesdays and for my small effort, I have been revitalized, quite *nouveau-née*. Now I wish to do something more.'

He put the lid on the pot, and went around and sat at the counter with her.

'Your Dooley brought me a bouquet. *Trés charmant*, Father! I suspect it was your idea, and a very lovely one. But that did *not* influence what I have to tell you.'

The other shoe was being dropped.

'Sammy may stay, Father.'

'Ah!'

'But only as long as he minds the rules that must be laid down.'

'Thank you, Hélène. You've been more than generous as it is. What are the rules?'

'He may not smoke in the house at any time; he may smoke only at the rear of the house in the old garage—and he may *not* burn it down.'

'Fair enough.'

'He must keep current with his *loyer*.'

'That's rent, I believe?'

'*Oui*. He may not leave any clutter of any kind on my porches.' She took a deep breath. '*Finis!* But what if I have forgotten something he must not do and wish to add it later?'

'Always good to have rules known beforehand. I'll help you think.'

'Perhaps I am acting too quickly in this decision, perhaps I should wait for further proof of good intentions. But Mr. Welch and Kenny seem to think there is . . .' She sought words. '. . . *un changement véritable en lui*.'

'He might easily have been killed when the car went down the bank. The police have seen people walk away from such accidents, but rarely. Perhaps, in some way, it waked him up.'

'You have reminded me of another rule,' she said. 'He may not be arrested or have anything at all to do with violating the law.'

'Yes. Good.'

'If,' she said, gripping her hands together, 'he defies any one of these rules, Father, he will be . . . he will be . . .' She looked to him.

'Dismissed.'

'At once,' she said.

They were both relieved to have done with it.

'I'm pleased for you that he's doing better.'

'Quite a bit, yes. He took it upon himself to go to the old garage for his tobacco doings, and removed his clutter from the porches. Kenny is a sensible influence, of course, so mature and wise. And Mr. Welch has done his utmost. Only yesterday, Sammy thanked me for the roast *poulet* I made for their supper.'

'Highly deserving of thanks.'

'If he is merely buttering me up, as they say, and such courtesy is soon to be ended, then—pardon me for repeating—he is *poof!*'

'Understood.'

'I always felt I owed you something because I stole your angel.'

'You owe me nothing, Hélène. Please never think that again.'

'You gave me a second chance, and I wish to do that for Sammy.'

'Thank you. God bless you.'

'Well, I must be going.' She got down from the stool and made her way to the side door. 'Please give my fondest greetings to Cynthia.'

'It's dark out there, Hélène. Let me walk you through the hedge.'

'*Non, non, merci.* I left my flashlight on your stoop. Oh, and Father . . .'

Hélène had a particular gift for looking as if the sky might fall.

'Could you loan us another roll of . . .' She blushed.

'Out again?'

'When I send Mr. Hendrick to shop, we buy but one roll at a time—for the sake of frugality.'

'No, no,' he said, amused. 'You must buy the large economy-size packs. We are operating a business for the public!'

HE WAS AWAKE AT FIRST LIGHT.

Hearing the patter of rain, he remained in bed, drowsing, dozing, a rare gift. He didn't need to be early at the bookstore this morning, he would arrive a little before ten. Coot would be sitting in his truck around the corner, eager to begin.

At eight, he raised himself on one elbow and watched her sleep. He loved this woman.

She opened her eyes, smiled. 'Hey. Was I snoring?'

'Never. I'm here in an official capacity.'

'And what might that be?'

'I'm making a cold call.'

'On who?'

'You.'

'What for?'

'We're going to need money for trash bins, signage, a few shrubs—and greasy fast-food for the crew.'

'How much?'

'Maybe two thousand.'

'Two thousand?'

'Trash bins have to be heavy-duty. Signage has to be on metal. With lag bolts.'

'Lag bolts.'

'Then there are the gutter guys at the Sunday school.'

'The gutter guys. How much total?'

Probably three thousand. Then again, nothing ever came in on budget. 'Thirty-five hundred.'

Like everybody else who was hammered for money, she looked grim.

'All deductible!' Just a reminder.

'Four thousand,' she said, 'and not a penny more.'

More than he asked for. He had just experienced every development director's dream.

Chapter
Twenty-five

In the second week of November, here was weather so ardently wished for in October—Carolina-blue skies, the intoxicating dose of clear, keen air, and, though the planet had tilted some weeks ago, finally the slanting golden light and plangent cries of geese along Mitford Creek.

After long rains and snow muck, it was a delayed harvest of pure pleasure. Yet there were a number of people not inclined to enjoy the moment, preferring instead to noodle their noggins with the prospect of snow for Christmas.

Local fire chief and weather guru Hamp Floyd was number one of the above number. Amazingly, Hamp was generally more accurate than the woolly bear caterpillar so fondly celebrated in local folklore, albeit for different reasons. While the width of the woolly worm's stripes were believed to forecast winter weather in general, Hamp's predictions were for Christmas snows in particular.

Indeed, he had nailed three out of five Christmas snow forecasts in recent years, including one forecast of 'no snow, zero,' and had become known simply as the Worm—a distinction quite apart from the woolly worm itself, or the good fellow called Mr. Woolly Worm, a zealous aficionado of the aforesaid actual *vermis*.

Though Hamp's Christmas forecast was usually announced around Thanksgiving, he said he felt 'led' to declare early this year.

On Saturday, his soothsaying was recorded on a chalkboard at Lew Boyd's, next to a display of locally crafted deer jerky.

Get Out Your Shovels!

The Worm's

Christmas Forecast

Is In!

~~

Snow Start Dec 24

End 26

12 3/4 inches

You heard it here first!

As was the custom when Hamp's forecast hit the street, there was a mild flurry of bets placed around town, though nothing so serious as to alarm authorities.

Generally speaking, there was a good bit of aggravation at the prediction, as most people preferred two or three inches, max, just for the seasonal look. A foot-plus would stall traffic, force everybody out with shovels, and generally make a mess.

Apprised of this news while filling up with regular, J. C. Hogan could not believe that a gas station had scooped his newspaper. He would talk to Hamp—would he ever. In the meantime, he gave Lew a look that would kill and scratched off from the pump in his 1997 Toyota hatchback with the rusted rear fender.

The Worm had never revealed his method of forecasting—it was as secret as Esther Bolick's OMC recipe had been in days of yore. Did it come to him in dreams? Was he ripping off the *Farmer's Almanac* and claiming such wisdom as his own? Did his joints ache that far in advance of a snow event six weeks out?

He had been asked these questions for years, and for a fact could not tell anybody his method because he didn't have one.

In his particular case, weather forecasting had begun a few years ago while getting a haircut in Wesley.

As he recalled, they had been talking baseball—he rooted for the Yankees—which was common even in football season. He was just getting a dose of his barber's rant on the Red Sox when in walked some character in a woolly worm costume, promoting the annual Woolly Worm Festival everybody was nuts about.

'Just a little off th' sides,' said a muffled voice from within the costume.

Everybody wanted to know would it be a long winter, a warm winter, a hard winter—how would the woolly worm describe what was coming?

'A long winter with plenty of snow,' was the best the guy could do.

'Yeah, buddyroe, but when?' said the barber. '*When's* th' snow comin'? That's th' trick.'

Whoever was in the costume did not have a clue.

Just to hear his head roar, Hamp rattled off a couple of dates and precipitation levels specifically for Christmas, the only time anybody in their right mind, except ski slope owners, wanted snow. And boom, two and a half months later the weather did what he said it was going to do.

This scared him to death. The *Muse* had credited him with an 84.5 percent accuracy rate, which was two points ahead of the actual woolly worm.

Who Needs The Woolly Worm When We Have Hamp?

The headline had run on the front page of the *Muse*, along with a picture of the fire chief standing by the department's new yellow truck. His wife, Jeanette, had the page blown up to ridiculous proportions, mounted, and screwed into the wall of their den for his sixtieth birthday. When he passed, it was his wish that it be installed in the engine room of the fire station, though God knows, everybody there hoped that such an installation would be a long time coming.

'THIRTEEN INCHES!' SAID ABE, WHO refused to own a snow shovel. 'Oy!'

'Somebody said fourteen or fifteen inches!' Winnie looked positively distraught when he dropped by on Saturday for a loaf of whole wheat.

'Only a foot and three-quarters,' he said, pacifying. No matter— Winnie and Thomas had a very steep driveway; this was not a good thing.

The news swept along Main like a brush fire, picking up several inches along the way. By the time it reached the Oxford Antique Shop, the forecast was for a couple of feet.

More than a few were ticked at Chief Floyd. Lew Boyd, to name one. 'Anything over two inches,' said Lew, 'an' th' only business through here is snowplows.'

'It's only a *prediction*,' he said to those, Cynthia included, who appeared to take the emanation as gospel truth.

HE WALKED HIS DOG around Baxter Park, threshing it out.

Did he really want to do this? Nobody had asked him to do it, or even hinted that he should.

It would make sense for everyone else, but did it make sense for him? He wasn't accustomed to considering things in this way.

Bottom line, he had only so much get-up-and-go left in this life. How best to spend the remains, as it were? More to the point—if he didn't do this, what would he do? Sit in his chair by the fire reading *Quo Vadis*? Books had to be read, and since when could reading a classic be considered an unwise use of time?

In the end, three questions:

What time of year was best for bookstore sales? Christmas— which started before Thanksgiving these days.

What day of the week historically showed the best sales numbers?

Saturday.

How could they afford to miss the biggest hurrah of the year? They couldn't.

'I WANT YOU TO BE HAPPY,' she said. 'If you're happy, I'm happy.'

'That simple?'

'Pretty much.'

'You're absolutely certain?'

'Cross my heart.'

Maybe he wasn't absolutely certain. But since she was certain, well, okay, he felt more certain.

On Sunday evening, he walked the three blocks to the
Murphy cottage to deliver the news. He gave the prescribed
loud knock so it could be heard all the way to the bedroom.

'MY DEAR MISS PRINGLE. Lest you forget, I am Sales, not
Marketing and Promotion.'

On Thursday, Hélène had come by to say hello, and was
saying more than he cared to hear.

'But Father, being the good Saint Nicholas *is* Sales. Don't
you see? With you sitting in the window in that novel costume, people will flock inside!'

He studied the cash drawer.

'Saint Nicholas was a very lovely person,' she said. 'His family was wealthy and left him everything, and what did he do?
He gave it all away. Do you think those poor, malnourished
children would have had a single nut or sweet if it hadn't been
for this godly man? He was no *poulet de l'anée*, and yet there he
was, a lowly bishop journeying about in the snow with his
heavy sack . . .'

She was looking at him intently.

'. . . *all* for the happiness of others.'

He tried to appear absorbed in opening a roll of quarters.
She pressed on.

'He is, you understand, the *patron saint* of *children*! And I *know* . . . how you *care* . . . for *children*.'

He felt his pulpit voice coming on, but had no idea what to say. Leave off, Hélène! *Arrête!*

Pushy Frenchwomen!

HE HAD NO EAGER DESIRE for a helpful hint, no curiosity as to how J.C. handled Hamp's crossover to the enemy. He was in agreement with Esther Cunningham—he was tired of this town running him, albeit via the *Muse*. He was a free agent.

'Take that,' he said, tossing today's edition into the waste-basket.

Barnabas looked up, blinked.

BUT WHAT TO READ TO COOT? He had failed to ask; Miss Mooney had failed to say.

He sat with her eager pupil at the coffee station.

'"*Tom!*"' he read.

'No answer.

'"Tom!" No answer.

'"What's gone with that boy, I wonder? You, Tom!"'

ONE NEVER KNEW who was coming through the door in the afternoon, for the light from the west was behind . . .

Talbot.

Or was it Talbot?

He stood, and remembered to close his mouth. It was Talbot.

Without hair, without much flesh on his bones. The shock of seeing him sent blood pounding in his temples.

Talbot walked to the counter with a kind of frailty he'd never seen in the man. 'Greetings, Father. I'm on the street for the afternoon. Running the gauntlet, you might say.'

'Henry . . .'

'I've been spat at twice, called a name that shows no favor to my mother, and shunned by all the rest. It was the stoning I came for, though lacking in the zeal I feared.'

The beating pulse in Henry's hand as he clasped it in both of his . . . He was thoroughly startled.

'I just emptied my warehouse—I'm about to depart Mitford for the last time.'

'Come,' he said. They walked into the refuge of verse, and sat in the wing chairs, one of them added recently by a customer. Henry Talbot seemed somehow distilled, as if flesh had been exchanged for sinew. 'I parked the U-Haul on Church Hill to force myself to walk here.'

'Are you all right?'

'I'm all right enough to take off the rug, the wig, the piece, the sham. My head is bare. And there you have it.' Talbot gave him something like a smile. 'How are you liking your bookstore parish?'

'Small, but rewarding.'

'How did you know where to find me that night?'

'It was a hunch. You once said you ran back there.'

'It's no fit place for running, of course. I more often used the school track for running, and used the trail to hide. Why do you think God allowed it all?'

'Why did you allow it?'

'I wanted to do what I wanted to do and figured it was his job to stop me.'

'He was the policeman.'

'And I was the truant who demanded no rebuke, nor any disgrace.'

'Some weeks ago, he stopped you. What now?'

'I wish he had taken me, and yet here it is, a life to be lived. I have no answer to what now. He spoke to me on the trail that night and said quite plainly, You're mine.

'It made me angry. Why would he speak to vermin? It didn't make me feel chosen; it made me feel he would speak directly to anybody, a cheap thing. And if I were his, for what was I his? What use could I possibly be?'

'Give yourself time, let him show you.'

'That night was a foxhole. One might suppose I'd gotten, at the very least, a religion out of it, but I did not. There were all the bells and whistles, and yet I was not transported beyond my sense of ruin.

'I'm thinking that I missed something, that when he said I was his, I failed to respond in an acceptable way, I blew it. Because now I feel I might really wish to belong to him. But I don't know how, and even so, maybe it's too late.'

'It's never too late. Watch and wait.'

'You know how to cut through the bull, Father, and I have a lot to cut through. On the walk over here, I stepped behind the school gym and wept for myself, that I could summon the courage to expose my worthlessness to all eyes. I've always felt worthless. Perhaps I became a priest to veil that notion of myself, but it didn't work. I was all the more aware of my little value.

'On the street just now, I was grateful for the spittle and

cold looks. Grateful, because in facing their scorn, I felt a certain worth, after all.'

'Thank you for coming to see me, Henry. It means a great deal.'

'I came to thank you. But for you and your son, I was gone from this world. You were part of what forced me to this.' He touched his bald pate. 'Some actually call it fashion, I call it penance . . . though in the end, maybe that's just more bull. Who knows?'

'Mary?'

'Gone from me completely. The wonder is that she stuck it out so long. I feel utterly naked, she was my shield and defender. If I'm to have any shield now, it must be God himself. There's no one for me and everyone against me.'

'I'm for you.'

'I guess I believe it or I couldn't be here. I've been sick, and I'm not well yet. I don't know if I was ever quite well or ever can be.'

'I remember,' he said, 'not knowing if I was ever well or ever could be. I was ordained, and yet all the seasons were Lenten; there was no relationship with him. I was a soul in prison, bound to stick it out and go on with the show of being his man.'

'What changed?'

'I think you could say I came to the end of myself. I really did want a show all my own, and he had to hammer me pretty hard to make me see that it was all his. We don't like relinquishing the power we never had anyway, even though running the show ourselves never works.

'I surrendered everything to him. What did I have to lose? What I had to gain was—believe it, Henry—everything. It's so simple that it baffles us; we're more enamored of what's grinding and hard.'

'Grinding and hard. Yes. Pray for me.'

'I do pray for you. I believe quite a few in this town pray for you.'

'I could never have said this a few weeks ago. But I want what you have.'

'What I've come to have—out of all that was grinding and hard—is a relationship. Bonhoeffer said it's not about hero worship, but intimacy with God.'

'No. I can't do the relationship business.'

'From the *Miserere Mei, Deus*. "Make me hear of joy and gladness, that the body you have broken may rejoice." You can have joy and gladness just as I got it, by petitioning God in a simple prayer delivered with a full heart.'

'I'm not ready for . . . intimacy. I want it, but it terrifies me. What is close and visceral has always terrified me.'

'It terrified me,' he said. 'Stood my hair on end—back when I had any to stand.'

It was mighty good to laugh.

Chapter
Twenty-six

Their turkey order was in at the Local, the side dishes planned, the invitations out. All but Louella's.

CNN was busy covering the world on Louella's big-screen TV. He sat on the stool and took her hand.

'You're the gravy on our biscuit, Cynthia says. And we don't see you half enough. Dooley will be home at Thanksgiving—could you come for dinner at our house? I'll pick you up and deliver you back no worse for wear.'

'Only place I go to supper these times is down th' hall or Room Number One. I would sho' like to do it, honey, but I'm past all that.'

He rattled off the menu. 'I could bring you a plate.'

'No, no, y'all go on an' have a happy time an' bring Dooley up to visit when you can. He'll be good medicine for me an' everybody else.'

'I'll see what I can do.'

She glanced at CNN, writ large on her wall.

'What you think about these politics goin' on?'

'We must pray for wisdom,' he said.

She leaned forward, cupped her ear. 'Who's William?'

. . .

THEY WOULDN'T ATTEND the All-Church Feast this year, they would have their feast at home. Dooley, Lace, Sammy, Kenny, Olivia, Hélène, Harley, Coot—the democratic system at work. Ten of them around the table set up in the study, with take-outs for the Murphys and Coot.

Dooley would actually have three Thanksgiving dinners. One at the yellow house; one with his mother and Buck, Jessie and Pooh; and a third with Marge, Hal, and Rebecca on the following day at Meadowgate, a feast to which he and Cynthia and Lace and Sammy and Kenny and Pooh and Jessie were also invited, along with his proffered ham.

So, okay. For the dinner on Wisteria Lane, he would pick up the turkey from Avis and the yeast rolls from Winnie; Puny would make a sweet potato soufflé; and Cynthia would do a classic green bean casserole and two pumpkin pies, sweetened with something parading as sugar.

Oh, and the cranberry relish, which he would concoct, and so forth and so on.

His head was spinning.

'DARLING, please deliver yourself to the Collar Button man at three o'clock on Tuesday.'

'Whatever for?'

'He's going to measure you.'

A startling thing to be told. 'I don't want to be measured.'

'And wear your leading citizen ribbon.'

'Why?'

'Because it sets an example for your successor next year. It's a lovely thing to be seen wearing. It gives people an uplift, I should think, knowing that we even *have* a leading citizen.'

'What am I being measured for? A clown suit?'

'That's close,' she said.

THE COLLAR BUTTON MAN lit a match, applied the flame to the bowl of his pipe, and there went the fond habit of puffing away to get the thing going.

'Mrs. Kavanagh wants you to have an especially nice suit, Father.'

'I have a nice suit.'

'Where did you get it, may I ask?'

'At the Suit Barn.'

'That is not a nice suit. Trust me.' The tobacco kindled, glowed. The Collar Button man smiled as if transported.

He had never taken a vow of poverty, but a bespoke suit? Throwing dollars down the drain. And what if he gained an ounce or two? Or more to the point, lost five pounds as he was hoping to do before Christmas?

There was no wiggle room in any article of bespoke clothing. It was made to fit the person one is right now, at the very moment of measurement, when only moments later, one would no longer be that same person.

'Surely you won't be tailoring it?'

'Surely not! It will be done by a distinguished tailor in New York City, which will take rather a long while and be completely worth the wait.'

The Collar Button man drew on his pipe, exhaled. The cherry-scented smoke formed a minor halo above the proprietor's head. 'It will last a lifetime, and make your wife very happy into the bargain.'

'Well, there you go,' he said. 'Measure away.'

THE CORKBOARD WAS EXPANDING its subject range.

'The happiness of life is made up of minute fractions—the little soon forgotten charities of a kiss or smile, a kind look, a heartfelt compliment, and the countless infinitesimals of pleasurable and genial feelings.' Samuel Taylor Coleridge

The countless infinitesimals. He had enjoyed these with great thanksgiving, and if preference could be had in this life, he would take infinitesimals any day.

Coot was dusting the rubber plant—a bloody nuisance which he would like to toss out the door. The garbage guys would be amazed to see the monstrous thing sitting on the sidewalk.

He called Hope. 'I was wondering . . . what do you think . . . could we get rid of the rubber plant?'

'The customer who gave it to me is still living,' she said. That was a no.

'So she visits the bookstore regularly?'

'Only on occasion. She calls in her order and Scott delivers it to her door when he goes down the mountain.'

'So . . . ?'

'I think it's not yet safe to give it away.'

'Actually, we couldn't give it away. Trust me.'

She laughed. 'Whatever you decide, Father. I'll leave the dirty work to you.'

While popping a few raisins, he had an idea. The red paint left from doing his basement door would give the faded pot new life.

'If you could put a little polish on the leaves,' he said to Coot.

He queried Marcie when she came in to place an order with their distributor.

'I don't know, Father. It's not that bad now that Coot shined it up. It looks almost real.'

'You think someone would give money for it?'

'I wouldn't go that far, but you never know.'

'One man's trash,' he said, quoting a sign on a Wesley junk shop, 'is another man's bling.'

BRAHMS WAS THE COMPOSER of the day. Not the best pairing for *Quo Vadis*, but such was life. He dug the book out of his backpack and put it on the counter. Winnie had just arrived with a sugar-free cookie for the bookseller, ready to spend her fifteen-minute break with the poets.

'Lord help,' she said, 'here comes Shirlene. It's forty-eight degrees out there, she'll be a popsicle.'

The caftan of the day was azure, as he believed his wife might call it. Printed with foaming waves washing onto a sandy shore and a random display of seashells. Somewhere around Shirlene's equator were distant islands with palm trees.

'I don't know, I just don't know,' Winnie said to him, sotto voce. 'Aren't you freezin', Shirlene?'

'No, I'm burnin' up. Flashin' all over the place. But you know what I want, more than anything? For people when they see me to be reminded in their hearts . . .' She lifted her arms;

mountains rose from a tropical sea. '. . . that somewhere on the planet the sun is shinin', the waves are breakin' on the beach, and all is well with this troubled world. That is so important.'

'Well, there you go,' said Winnie. 'You're doin' a service. Which I myself will be doin' shortly by goin' back to work.'

'What's up?' he asked Shirlene.

'Look at this, Father, an' see what you think.'

She opened her book on dog breeds and laid it on the counter. 'I can't really find a picture of th' dog I have in mind, I don't know what breed it is. But here's one I guess would be okay. I might go look for one like this at th' shelter. What do you think?'

'You will never find this breed at the shelter. Not the Wesley shelter, anyway.'

'Why not?'

'This is an expensive dog, not the sort you'd find in these hills.'

'Expensive dogs get lost and run away, too.'

Winnie peered at the photograph. 'You would have to go to Los Angeles, California, to find that poor thing wanderin' th' street. Maybe you should just go to the shelter and see what they have.'

And in swung Omer Cunningham in his aviator cap with earflaps, and Patsy on a leash.

'Ooh,' said Shirlene. 'That is exactly th' dog I am lookin' for!'

'This dog is taken,' said Omer.

'What's its name?'

'Patsy.'

'Patsy! This is exactly the dog I would love to have. Look at its face.' Shirlene stooped to pat Patsy—palm trees swayed. 'Patsy, Patsy, I would sleep with you!'

'She's sleepin' with me,' said Omer.

Shirlene looked up and smiled. 'Well, she is one lucky girl.'

'Whoa,' said Winnie. 'I gotta get on my break.'

He was staying in the tall grass. He wouldn't say a word, no, sir. Let them figure out the yard sale and Scrabble business, he was glad to get this thing off his hands.

'Here you go, Father.' Omer thumped a bag on the counter. 'Russets and Yukon Gold.'

He examined a russet. 'Beautiful! Prizewinning! My goodness, look at this.' He said what people in his Mississippi childhood always said when given a worthy gift. 'What do I owe you?'

'Free as th' air we breathe,' said Omer. 'Y'all like mashed potatoes?'

'We do. Definitely.'

'Drop a turnip in there. Cook it and mash it in with your potatoes. Adds a really nice flavor.'

Shirlene stared at Omer.

'I've heard of doin' that,' she said. 'But I never met anybody that does it. Do you use real butter?'

'Yes, ma'am. Life is short.'

Patsy was straining at the leash and headed for the door. 'Gotta go, Father. See you at th' Feel Good. Patsy's after a squirrel.'

And there went Omer.

'Ohmigosh,' said Shirlene. 'Who was that?'

'That? Ah . . .'

'He was adorable.' She went to the window and looked out. Omer was dashing across to the post office, Patsy in the lead. 'Free as th' air we breathe. That was darlin'.'

'So, Shirlene, thanks for letting me transfer my certificate.

I've decided what I'd like to do with it, and thank you very much, it was very generous of you.'

'I wish you'd use it for yourself.'

'I know, and I probably should, but I'm putting the certificate in the spring auction for the Children's Hospital.'

'Oh, that is so *good*. That is absolutely *brilliant*.'

'Well, thanks,' he said. 'Are you spending Thanksgiving with your sister?'

'I'm goin' home to Bristol to see Mama and do her highlights. Who did you say that was?'

'I apologize for not introducing you.' Rude, indeed, but so be it. 'That was the fellow you see in the little yellow airplane, headed south.'

'I've never seen anybody headed south in a little yellow airplane.'

'You're probably working when he flies over.'

Shirlene gathered up her book. 'So, when are we goin' to have lunch with Homer?'

'One of these days, for sure.'

Winnie waited for Shirlene's departure before emerging from the poet's gallery. 'Holy smoke!' she said, grinning. 'You should fix them up.'

'Not me,' he said.

HE FOUND COOT in the storage room under the stairs, tears streaming.

'What is it, buddy?' He put his arm around the one who was their 'fixture.'

'I cain't say.'

'You can say it to me. I'm your friend. You're our friend.'

'Friend,' said Coot. 'F-R- . . .' Coot looked at him, at a loss. 'F-R- . . .'

'I-E-,' he said.

'N-D.'

'That's it!'

'I miss Mama.'

'Of course.'

'I always said she was mean as a rattler, an' she was, but I miss 'er. She was my mama.'

They stayed under the stairs awhile. It was a good place to have a cry.

Chapter
Twenty-seven

Saturday, December 1

Dear Henry,

A blessed Advent to you and Peggy and Sister!

Am writing from the bookstore to say what a wonderful Thanksgiving we had and I trust your own summoned a plenitude of grace. You sounded the best yet when we spoke.

And while we covered most of the bases, I feel the urge now to send something to greet you at the mailbox. I'm one for the cards and letters, myself, and am grateful for your faithfulness to us in that regard.

Dooley left here early on the 29th and Lace is on her way to Virginia as I write. D and L appear genuinely in love—it is a sight to see.

Actually, he had seen more than was intended.

On walking past the door to the deck, he had glanced out. They stood by the railing, wrapped in each other's arms. He saw plainly the look on Dooley's face, a look he had certainly never seen before. In something like slow motion, they kissed.

He had moved quickly into the kitchen, struck to the marrow by the power of that moment, a gift unwittingly captured for all time.

UP AND DOWN MAIN, an angel formed of tiny lights had been installed on every lamppost; alleluias and glorias poured forth from the sound system at the Town Hall, and ready or not, it was December first, and Christmas in Mitford was official.

HÉLÈNE PRINGLE WAS NOT ONE to let go of her notions.

Tomorrow was the first Sunday of Advent and, like the rest of the common horde, she was heading into full Christmas mode. She dropped by the bookstore on her way to the Local, toting her fold-up shopping cart.

'Hélène, you are Catholic. You know very well that Christmas cannot be had before Advent, any more than Easter can occur in advance of Lent! Further, I must be selling, don't you see, not lounging about in a hot suit trimmed in fake fur. We are shorthanded as it is, we cannot put an employee in the window.'

She didn't get it. He pressed on.

'Further still, there will be gift-wrapping to do.' Gift-wrapping! Right up there with locusts and plagues. He was stressed about this.

'I feel certain I can teach Coot to gift-wrap,' she said. 'He is surprisingly handy. And in any case, Saint Nicholas did not wear a suit, he was a bishop. He would have worn a cassock, a surplice, a stole, a cope, and a pectoral cross.'

'With mitre and crozier, I suppose,' he said, dry as crust.

'That, too.'

The torment of it.

'The mother of one of my old pupils is a marvelous seamstress. I tutored her daughter without charge for an entire year. She is willing to make you a most glorious costume—*if* she is provided the fabric, which can be purchased for a song in Wesley.'

She appeared to be running out of steam, but no.

'You can count on me,' she announced, 'to provide the sack.'

'Ah-h,' he said.

Hélène said something in French.

ESTHER CUNNINGHAM, now fully recovered from her stroke, was on the phone and none too happy.

'I've been meanin' to ask—do you have any idea why th' dadblame Christmas parade happened th' day before Thanksgivin'?'

'Not a clue.'

'Christmas does not come before Thanksgivin'.'

'Maybe they're working toward slipping it in around Halloween.'

'I need to talk to th' council. Just wait'll I get over this hackin' cough,' she said, proceeding to hack. 'How was th' candy?' she said. 'I'm not gettin' a good report on th' candy.'

Lord knows, he had stepped up to the corner of Main and Wisteria just to check on this item of concern. Santa had cruised in at the end on the back of a pink Thunderbird convertible, and as far as he could tell, it was all ho-ho and no candy.

'Um,' he said.

'My great-grans did not get a single piece. Fourteen great-grans scattered through th' crowd and not one piece of candy.'

'Lower dentist bills,' he said.

SALES HAD BEEN BRISK, albeit with no help from a couple of people who dropped by to read the Sunday *Times*, now entering the ravaged state. He was totting up the numbers when Hélène jangled in with a full cart.

No rest for the wicked, and the righteous don't need none.

'Think of it this way, Father. Saint Nicholas carried forth God's love by giving all his inheritance to the poor and needy. He dedicated his life to others, and was especially loving to children. We know the infant laid in the manger is almighty and supreme, now and forevermore. Saint Nicholas was but God's hands and feet, just as you are in your time in history.'

Cease! Desist! *Arrête!*

'Happy Endings could distribute sweets to the children who come to the store, and everyone who wishes could bring a small gift for the patients at Children's Hospital! Think how many of them come from the desperate parts of our mountains, Father. And so you see—your favorite charity would even today be served by a good man born long ago in the third century. How wonderfully it all ties together.'

She was breathless with conviction.

'How long would this . . . go on?' he said.

'We could start as soon as Polly gets the fabric and runs up the costume. *Tout de suite! Le temps c'est de l'argent!* We have no time to lose!'

'And who is to pay for the fabric?'

She gave him an expectant look. A French look, he thought, though he had no standard for what that might be.

'Not I,' he said, meaning it.

He agreed to nothing in her proposal. On the other hand, her pitch had succeeded, if only in making him feel the pressure of a fast-approaching Christmas. Something must be done.

He called Hope.

She directed him to a stack of author posters under the stairs.

He turned one over and uncapped a Magic Marker.

Christmas Help Wanted
Apply Within

'Take down the sign,' said his wife. 'I'll do it. My eyes will appreciate the break. And fun—it will be fun! A mom-and-pop operation!'

'I'd like you to gift-wrap,' he said, wanting to nail this issue immediately.

'I'm not terribly good at it.'

'I am not gift-wrapping,' he said in his pulpit voice. 'Not with help running around.'

'Okay, okay. I'll gift-wrap and you'll pack our lunches.'

'Deal.'

'No chicken for me, I am off chicken. And no salt on anything and no white bread, and by the way, I can't work but one day a week. I'm painting the other days and Christmas is coming and I have lists to make.'

Lists to make! Into the backpack went a notepad; he would knock his list out tomorrow.

'Saturday would be best for me,' she said. 'And no avocado, either. Too fattening.'

He mustn't forget chocolates for Hope House and Children's Hospital nurses. Lipstick for Louella, she was depending on him, and there was Walter, of course, who was difficult, not to mention costly, to shop for, and Katherine . . . why didn't he keep his lists from former years and just make minor revisions annually? This had never occurred to him before.

And what would he give Dooley? And Sammy, for that matter, and Kenny, who would be leaving straightaway and could use a warm jacket, and the grans, four of them, and Coot—there must be something under the store tree for Coot—and Marcie and Hélène, of course. Store tree! When did that go up? Not anytime soon—he would put his foot down on that nonsense.

'And no cheese or peanut butter,' she said.

Did Hope have gift-wrapping supplies stuck somewhere, or did he need to run to Wesley? And music. He hadn't seen any Christmas music in Hope's stash of CDs.

How had this happened? He had planned to keep his head about him this year, and on the day prior to Advent, he had already lost it.

THE PHONE WAS RINGING as he came through the side door at five-thirty. He had put the word out to clergy in Charlotte, and bingo!—Hope was being offered the use of a carriage house, by a member at St. John's. An early Christmas gift for certain.

Before he could drop the backpack into his desk chair, the phone bleated again.

'On the way home from the post office,' said Hélène, 'I saw your sign on the door. I'll give you Saturdays through Christmas, Father. I can certainly do that much.'

He had forgotten to take the sign down, and was getting what he asked for—help. Very likely, he'd also be getting a dose of Grieg that would last well into the afterlife.

'I HAVE A GREAT IDEA,' she said, climbing into bed.

'Do we have to do great ideas?' He had barely managed to assemble their Advent wreath on the coffee table in the study; he was beat.

'It can wait,' she said, turning out the lamp on her side. She gave him a kiss. He took her hand and prayed their old evening prayer, as worn as the velveteen of the fabled rabbit. '. . . the busy world is hushed and the fever of life is over, and our work is done. In thy mercy, grant us a safe lodging and a holy rest and peace at the last . . .'

'I love you,' she said.

'Love you back.'

The light from the streetlamp shimmered through the leaves of the maple and diffused itself in their draperies. They would be going out to Meadowgate in the morning and joining Hal and Marge at their small church in the country . . .

'I'm wide awake,' he said.

'Me, too.'

'What is your great idea?'

'The Nativity scene you restored for me. Why don't we share it this year? It's so beautiful; it would give joy to everyone who sees it.'

'But how?'

'It would be perfect in the window at Happy Endings.'

'We've been talking about using the window.' He had by no means consented to Hélène's elaborate scheme, and yet . . . 'There may be dibs on that window.'

'Yes, but there are two windows.'

He'd never thought about the other window, which was filled with freestanding bookcases. Fiction authors K through P, to be exact.

'We could move the bookcases out,' she said, 'and put them in the Poetry section. There's room back there if you move the wing chairs and the table and the rubber plant to the front.'

His peaceful days at the bookstore were over. *C'est la vie.*

ON TUESDAY, Coot learned to gift-wrap. Dealing with the Scotch tape, Hélène said, had given pause, but it all came around in the end. There were many rolls of green paper under the stairs; as for bows, they wouldn't do anything fancy—a strand of raffia tied simply, with a red and green sticker which she had found at the drugstore. Would he be so kind as to help her write the store name on the blank stickers? She had bought several packages out of her own funds and it all made a very smart presentation. Coot had taken a sample over to Hope, who called Hélène to pronounce it *très charmant*, and insisted Hélène reimburse herself.

He seemed to remember Hélène as studious, shy, possibly even timid.

What had happened?

What was the matter with people?

. . .

Word was on the street that Father Brad had wrapped up a two-bedroom rental house on the ridge, with a view 'to die for' and a heated garage, always handy in bad weather and, one hoped, a fairly decent place to winter over the gardenias.

Though he had not agreed to anything, Hélène and Marcie conducted a meeting early on Thursday. Saturdays would be the store's busiest days, they concluded, so that's when the Saint Nicholas business should happen.

There were but two Saturdays to go, since they couldn't make the one upcoming. What would the fabric cost? Hélène had roughly calculated the yardage in three different fabrics and was horrified by the reality of this scheme. Two hundred and fifty dollars at the discount store, plus tax.

'Be sure to make it one size fits all,' he said.

There was a further challenge. What to do about the beard?

'You can probably get a beard from Mitford School,' Winnie said, 'if it's not in use. They do plays all th' time.'

'Th' Santy in th' Christmas parade had a beard,' said Coot.

'Gone back to th' rental company in Atlanta,' said Marcie.

Who would seek and find the beard?

They looked at him. He adjusted his glasses and looked back, mute.

And who would be Saint Nick? Hélène declared she would do it herself. '*Si les choses se gâtent!*' she said, loosely meaning, 'If push came to shove.'

'People are nutty as fruitcakes,' he told his wife.

'Very seasonal,' she said.

. . .

ON FRIDAY AFTERNOON, he learned, Hélène had gotten in
her car, manufactured in a remote year, and careened down
the mountain to a community theater said to own an assort-
ment of beards.

He had once careened down the mountain with Hélène
Pringle and lived to tell it. He had learned all too late that her
brakes had gone bad and there were no funds to get them
replaced. It was a thrill ride that money couldn't buy, second
only to flying with Omer in a taildragger and eyeing the scen-
ery through a hole in the floorboard.

'Here's what somebody needs to do,' he said to Winnie
when he stopped by Sweet Stuff after the bank. 'Find a person
who has an actual beard. The woods are full of them back in
the coves and hollers. I guarantee it.'

'I'm not goin' back in there,' said Winnie. 'No way. That's
where all my cousins live.'

'In any case, there's the answer.'

'I cannot abide facial hair,' said Winnie. 'I'm makin' donut
holes for th' big day, an' that's it for me.'

The word blew along Main like a paper napkin from a fast-
food takeout. On Saturdays, starting next week, Abe would be
offering hot cider. The Woolen Shop would set out ginger
snaps. Winnie and Thomas were giving away donut holes, two
to a customer. And the bookstore would be putting on some
kind of a show.

COOT HAD GONE to their house and cleaned up the Nativity
scene.

The figures would be placed in the window right away, in an order suggesting the coming birth of the Bright and Morning Star.

First, the Virgin Mary and Joseph at the empty manger, seven sheep, a donkey, a cow, two members of the heavenly host, and a stable which someone had given anonymously the year he restored the figures.

After a few days, the wise men would be introduced into the fringes of the scene, looking none the worse for having tossed around for a couple of years on the humps of camels.

What a lot of rubble it had all been when he'd found the twentysomething pieces at Andrew's antique shop. Orange had been the operative color—skin, robes, even the camel. Andrew wondered why he'd bought the conglomeration, which took up costly container space on its way across the Pond from England. 'A reckless purchase!' said Andrew.

In buying it from Andrew, he had been uncharacteristically reckless, himself. Did he know how to restore plaster fingers and noses? No. Or how to paint realistic skin tones? No. Or what color anything should be, especially the wings of angels? Not a clue. He had solved this by consulting old Christmas cards and books showing crèche figures. As for the wings of angels, obviously they could be any color the artist chose to make them.

He had been intoxicated by the act of bringing each figure to life, thanks to help from Andrew and Fred. Dooley had painted the camel and its saddle blankets, and was also caught up in the thrill. It had been a huge challenge, but joy had overwhelmed fear, and the miracle had been accomplished.

On Friday night, he and Harley transported the whole caboodle in the truck bed, and Cynthia came along to give a hand.

They rolled the bookcases into the Poetry section, brought up the chairs, restationed the rubber plant.

Fiercely cold tonight. Not a soul on the street. They worked quickly. Harley toted in a bale of straw and let it loose in the window. The lighting, seldom used in this area and acting as the star, was pretty good.

They moved the figures around. That some of them were nearly two feet tall was useful in the large space.

The Virgin Mother to the left of the empty manger, Joseph to the right. Three sheep standing, four lying in the straw, along with the old shepherd he had learned to love as he'd painted the solemn face.

They stepped outside and looked in.

'Goose bumps,' said Cynthia.

'Where's th' baby Jesus at?' said Harley.

'He arrives on Christmas morning. Advent is a time of waiting.'

'People'll be lookin' f'r th' baby Jesus.'

'And there,' he said, happy, 'is the whole point.'

ON SATURDAY, there were more than a few noses pressed to the Nativity window, and more than a few of the curious came in to buy a book or two or three.

Marcie and Hélène convened at eleven, Winnie included.

'How's your mother?' he asked Marcie.

'Drivin' me crazy.'

Shirlene stopped by for a quick coffee. Maybe there was a Caftan-of-the-Month Club . . .

'How's business?' he asked Shirlene.

'On a scale of one to ten, a six. You would not believe who just walked out with a Boca.'

'Who?'

'I'll let it be a surprise!' said Shirlene. 'When do I get to meet Homer?'

'I'm not sure.'

'I don't know how I'm ever goin' to meet somebody. I guess he'll just have to fall out of th' sky.'

He had noted over the years that a good many single women counted on this very phenomenon, possibly influenced by what the Lord himself allowed through his servant James, 'All good and perfect gifts come down from the Father above.'

'The way you find a husband,' said Winnie, 'is you've got to get out there.'

'Winnie met Thomas on a cruise,' he said.

'I've always heard you can't meet men on a cruise,' said Shirlene. 'Single men do not go on cruises.'

Winnie beamed. 'Thomas wasn't a passenger, he was in th' kitchen, bakin'. Which I would consider totally out of th' sky.'

'Hey, people, I don't know about you, but I've got work to do.' Marcie, like her mother, did not like to fool around.

'The department store in Wesley!' said Hélène. 'They would have a beard, *pensez-vous pas?*'

'Hélène,' he said. 'If you were a department store at this time of year, would you lend your beard?'

'I heard y'all are lookin' for a beard,' said Shirlene. 'I have a great idea. Forget rentin' a beard and rent a Santa Claus! Gosh, I'd do it myself if I had time.'

'We don't want a Santa Claus,' said Hélène.

'We don't?' said Winnie. 'I thought that's what we'd been talkin' about all along!'

Hélène appeared fraught. 'We are talking about Saint *Nicholas*, the third-century precursor of the Victorian Santa, who had no basis whatever in real life, though their beards were similar.'

'Really,' said Winnie.

'I hear you went down the mountain,' he said.

'It was a gruesome business. Pirate beards, Viking beards, and a Gandalf beard, which was very stringy.'

Shirlene was busy with her cell phone. 'Ta-da! Santa beard! Just twenty-four ninety-five an' two-day shipping! "So real,"' she read aloud, '"you can convince even your own kids that you are Santa." Oops, wait. Out of stock.'

He retired to the back of the store, popped in a little Bach, turned it up pretty loud, ate a few raisins.

Five million. The thought came to mind, uninvited. A car dealership in Holding would donate a new van. The pizza parlor in Wesley would donate a pizza, fully loaded, each month for a year. And so on. The auction committee was out there at every opportunity, hoping to bring something to the table when the campaign launched next spring. Abe was keeping a low profile—he heard they were coming after him for a pair of Michael Jordan high-tops.

As for himself, he remembered what Nanny Howard said when she wasn't up to the job at hand: 'I feel like I was sent for and couldn't go.'

He slogged to the front. Hélène was on the phone, the meeting was winding down.

'The important thing,' said Marcie, 'is to find th' guy who'll be Saint Nick. I mean, we're puttin' th' cart before th' horse here.'

'How about J. C. Hogan?' said Shirlene. 'He's portly.'

'Too sour,' said Winnie.

'How about your daddy?' Winnie asked Marcie. 'He would be perfect.'

'Too wrung out takin' care of Mama.'

'Hamp Floyd,' said Abe, who had popped over for a coffee. 'I notice he's gettin' a little paunch.'

'Too short,' said Winnie. 'How about Mr. Abe Edelman here?'

'Too Jewish,' said Abe.

Heads turned as one; they were looking at him.

'Too busy,' he said. 'Go find a Saint Nick and let's get on with it.'

Running a bookstore or dealing with a vestry? Which was worse?

'I'm out of here,' said Winnie. 'But first—I just had a great idea. Put a sign on the door.'

'For what?' he said.

'Santa beard wanted. Gotta go.'

After lunch, he rounded up another author poster. He was scribing the suggested proclamation on the back when the phone rang.

'Father, *l'école est finis!* We are not a cooked goose! Polly just called, she will run up the costume out of remnants and I will contribute Mother's old fur for the trim! You will look wonderful in it, I assure you. You will not be disappointed in the least!'

Had Hélène Pringle gone deaf? How many times could he refuse to be part of this scheme?

It had spiraled out of control. It was a loose cannon.

'OH, MY GOSH,' said Vanita, 'your window is gorgeous. I love th' way th' afternoon light shines on th' straw an' that old man kneelin' down, he is so sweet. But where's th' baby Jesus?'

'He comes on Christmas Eve, around midnight.'

'Really? In my family, we pop him in his little basket right after Thanksgivin'.'

'Some do that,' he said.

'I brought you somethin'.' She dug in her enormous shoulder bag, pulled out a scrap of paper. 'A book quote.'

'You're a reader!' he said.

'Not really. I am way too busy to read a whole book, sometimes I just read th' first page an' scoot over to th' end. My cousin is th' reader, she said give you this.'

All good books are alike in that they are truer than if they had really happened [Ernest Hemingway]

'A gem. I'll post it right away.'

'You're not wearin' your ribbon.'

'Not today, but I've worn it a lot. Ask anybody.'

'You should wear it,' she said. 'So where's your tree? Everybody on th' street has a tree.'

'A little early for a tree.'

'We always pop ours in right after Thanksgivin'.'

'Some do that,' he said.

'So what's goin' on in the other window, with th' sign that says "Watch This Chair"?'

'Someone will be sitting in it the next two Saturdays.'

'Really! Who?'

'It's a surprise.' The gospel truth if he ever told it.

'I love surprises!' She wrangled a notebook from her shoulder bag, pulled out her point-and-shoot. 'I'm doin' a story on this, okay?'

'Okay,' he said.

'But I don't know about a front page, I can't guarantee a front page. It's Christmas, you know.'

DRIVING DOWN MAIN AFTER CHURCH, they noticed a plastic bag hanging on the knob of the front door at Happy Endings. He parked at the post office and went across to check it out.

'Good Lord!' he said. It was frightening.

A bag full of white beards.

He unloaded the bag in the garage. Three of the blasted things, one with eyebrows. Dusty. He had a sneezing fit.

A note read: Oh thank you forevermore for taking these off my hands. I would sign my name but you might try to give them back. Merry Christmas!

He stuffed them in the bag and trotted through the hedge to Hélène's. No answer to his knock on the rear door. He hung the bag on her doorknob, anonymous note included, and fled down the steps.

'Father Tim!'

Kenny was putting a bag of garbage in the can by Miss Pringle's driveway.

'How are you, Kenny?'

'Tryin' to get my head around leavin' in a couple of weeks. I've decided to take off the day after Christmas.'

'We'll miss you. You've been a fine influence on Sammy.'

'My grandparents are to thank for that. I was goin' wild like Sam, but they didn't give up on me, they kept prayin'. And my girl back in Eugene, she's been a huge help, she really understands why I had to come out here and find my brothers and little sister and stay awhile—not just find everybody and run back to Eugene. It's been hard to be away this long.'

'You've made your brothers and sister into a family again.'

'I'm tryin' to forgive my mother, but I don't know . . .'

He nodded, took Kenny's hand. 'If you need anything—anything at all, anytime at all—will you call?'

'I will.'

'I'm glad we'll be together for Christmas. Thanks for making that happen. We wish you a lot of success in school. You've saved some money, Dooley says . . .'

'Five thousand. Not easy in my pay range, but the rent was low.' Kenny smiled—he voted Kenny the best smiler in the family. 'Harley's a great guy, a really good influence. Sammy's pretty connected to Harley, but Harley needs to do a little butt-kickin'.'

He laughed. 'Somehow, I don't think that's going to happen.'

'Thanks for puttin' up with Sammy and helpin' him. He really likes you, he's probably never trusted an older guy before, especially somebody who lays down the law to him.'

'We all need the law laid down to us now and again, it was sure laid down to me.'

Nanny Howard had taken no prisoners when it came to making him toe the line. His mother and Peggy hadn't slacked in that department, either.

'We'll talk more before you leave,' he said. 'But I'd like to make sure you know you can call anytime. We all need to keep in touch, we can't afford to lose one of you—one of us—again.'

Kenny gave him a determined look.

'We're done bein' lost.'

ON SUNDAY EVENING, he took the Eucharist and a baked pasta dish to the Murphys'. They offered a prayer of thanks for the donor of the carriage house, and for Hope's sister, Louise, who was coming on board after Christmas.

'Louise once said that to be an aunt, she would give anything,' Hope told him. 'By not going to Denver and moving here, she's actually giving everything.'

'Starting a new life again in Mitford,' he said. 'A very good place to start a new life.' That's what he had done, and Cynthia, and Scott, and Hope, and Winnie's Thomas, and Abe, and Shirlene . . .

Hope looked at him, happy. 'Scott has something to tell you, Father.'

The chaplain sat on the side of the bed and took Hope's hand. There was a kind of radiance in Scott that he'd never seen before.

'Pretty soon, someone else will be starting a new life in Mitford. Her name is Grace.'

Chapter
Twenty-eight

People were watching the chair.

They were watching the manger.

They were watching the upstairs window for the appearance of 'the bookstore tree.'

And he, converted to the rigors of retail, was watching Hope's bottom line. According to Marcie, annual sales were 'up a little.' In these last ticking hours of the year, he was going for 'up a lot.'

He dug out the tree stand and several boxes of ornaments from under the stairs. Sammy and Harley were off to a tree farm to cut the finest specimen of Norway spruce they could find. 'Ten feet!' he said.

Marcie and Hélène would drop by after closing time to start the bedecking. Shirlene asked if she could pitch in.

He called home. 'Why don't you come up and join us? Sammy and Harley, Marcie, Hélène, Coot, Shirlene . . .'

'Shirlene!' said his wife. 'Why don't you invite Omer?'

'Should I?'

'Tell him there'll be food. Bachelors like that. I just made pimiento cheese for lunches at Irene's, but I'll do sandwiches for the tree-trimming instead. And I'll take a tray of lemon squares out of the freezer.'

'Bring a yogurt,' he said. 'Banana.'

'What time?'

'Anytime.'

THE NATIVITY WINDOW WAS PLEASING, but it lacked something.

Something tall.

Ha! He muscled the rubber plant to the window and positioned it left-rear of the camel coming from afar.

The painted pot just happened to be sympatico with the red in a saddle blanket.

Nice.

SAMMY AND HARLEY WERE WRANGLING the tree up the stairs with the help of Coot and Scott. Marcie was out buying drinks and chips; Hélène was on her way.

As he and Cynthia shelved new books close by, Shirlene and Omer tried out the chairs so long secluded in the Poetry section.

'How's Miss Patsy?' Shirlene asked Omer.

'She'd like to be here, but I didn't want her gettin' tangled up in th' tree lights.'

'She is adorable, you are both totally lucky. I would love to find a little dog just like her.'

'She's one of a kind, for sure. Don't know about findin' another one.'

'Th' breed books are so confusin', plus a lot of those breeds are a house payment.' Shirlene sighed. 'I guess I don't know how to find a dog.'

'SPCA,' said Omer. 'Somethin' for everyone.'

'But people say when you go over there, they're all barkin' at one time and they all want to go home with you. That is really sad, plus how do you know which one?'

'You just have to follow your heart. I hear you play Scrabble.'

'Scrabble is practically my life.'

'I pulled a bingo last night. My online partner played th' word SQUARE; I hooked on to her word with a *D*, used all seven tiles.'

A gasp from Shirlene; a jangle of bracelets.

'Got a triple word score both ways,' said Omer. 'Nailed a hundred and sixty points.'

'What . . . was your word?'

Omer looked ten feet tall, sitting down. 'J-A-P-Y-G-I-D.'

'Oh, my gosh.' Shirlene put her hand over her mouth. 'Oh, my gosh.'

'What?' said Omer. 'Are you okay?'

'Are you . . . could you possibly be . . . WingDipper?'

'Whoa. Are you . . . ?'

'BocaGirl! Yes! You're th' one who killed me with that crazy word I never heard of in my entire life! I cannot believe this . . .'

'Japygid!' said Omer. 'Any eyeless, wingless, primitive insect havin' a pair of pincers at the rear of its abdomen.'

There went the toothsome grin. It was Scott Joplin's 'Maple Leaf Rag,' it was Chopin's Scherzo No. 2, Opus 31.

'You're a great Scrabble player,' said Omer.

'Oh!' said Shirlene, fanning herself with a section of the *Times.*

'Around town, I'm Flyboy, down th' mountain, they call me Ragwing, but online, I'm WingDipper.'

'So many aliases,' she said, a mite breathless.

He and Cynthia stared at each other.

'Truth,' said his astonished wife, 'is very *much* stranger than fiction.'

'I HAVE A GREAT IDEA,' he announced to all who were decorating the tree.

'It's about time,' said Marcie. 'Ha, ha, just kidding.'

'Let's stay open Friday and Saturday nights until Christmas.'

You could hear a spruce needle drop. Hardly anyone in Mitford stayed open at night, except for the Feel Good. Shop-Mitford-during-the-day-and-stay-home-at-night-where-you-belong-or-be-a-traitor-and-unload-your-money-on-the-college-liberals-in-Wesley was thought to be the unspoken philosophy.

'I cannot work at night,' said Marcie. 'No way. I have a family last time I checked.'

'Oh, *vraiment*! At night?'

'I would help,' said Shirlene, 'but Fancy would kill me.'

'I can do it,' said Coot, who gave them all a rousing display of his dental condition.

His wife raised her hand. 'Only for you.'

'I'll d-do it,' said Sammy.

'Done, then.'

A shock wave. How little it took in a small town. This was revolutionary.

And then, another revolution. After all the work on the tree, they decided not to plug in the lights until Saturday at dusk. All but one of them would stand across the street at the PO and watch as it lit the dark window.

In a culture of instant gratification, it felt good to wait.

. . .

THE CROWD ON FRIDAY NIGHT was 'amazing' and 'huge,' not to mention 'unprecedented,' according to customer reviews.

Even with the tree window still dark, people were driving by, parking, coming in, nosing around in the display windows, delivering the occasional gift for Children's Hospital, asking about the empty chair, wondering about the baby Jesus—and actually buying books. At one point, the crèche included three small children on hands and knees, petting the sheep.

They had forgotten cookies—not a good thing. He sent Sammy to buy up 'the day's regrets,' as Winnie called them, for fifty percent off.

Free gift-wrapping was a hit; it kept Coot and Cynthia busy. He wished for the old-fashioned cash register that rang the sales, it would have made a cheering sound. Instead, they had Bach's Advent Cantatas going, a couple of which inclined toward the dark side and gave him new respect for the more upbeat 'Twelve Days of Christmas.'

The toilet was a big draw—big enough to require a plumber the next morning—but alas alack, such was doing business with the public.

ON SATURDAY MORNING, the coffee was ready at a quarter 'til ten. Abe said he could smell it through the wall and came over for a quick pour.

'You're spoiling it for the natives, Father. Open at night? When does a man get his deserved rest?'

'Abe, Abe, you're talking like a gentile.'

'True.' Abe took a sip of coffee. 'When is Saint Nick dropping in?'

'Around noon, according to the sign on the door.'

'So, okay, I'll stay open tonight and next Saturday. But if you're drumming up any such plans for Easter, I pass.'

'AT FIVE-THIRTY SHARP,' he announced, 'we're all going across to the post office and see the tree-lighting, and, of course, Saint Nicholas waving, and our wonderful Nativity scene.'

'The whole megillah,' said Abe.

Hélène raised her hand. 'Who will light the tree?'

'Somebody's got to light th' tree,' said Sammy. 'I'll d-do it.'

Coot raised his hand. 'I can do it!'

'Nope. Change of plan. We're all going across to the post office. The tree will be taken care of.'

'It's gon' plug itself in!' said Coot.

SCOTT CALLED TO SAY that he and Hope and Louise were planning a drive-by at six. Esther Cunningham called to announce a drive-by at seven, right after her meds.

'Tell your grans to turn out a little before five-thirty to get a good spot on the sidewalk,' he said. 'Cookies after.'

'What kind?'

'Chocolate chip.' He needed the word to get around.

Hélène arrived with the costume before noon. Flushed, rattling French like a house afire.

'Who's b-bein' Saint Nick?' said Sammy.

'Father Tim, of course!' said Hélène. 'He *is* Saint Nick!'

Hélène took the costume from the box, shook out the alb, the cassock, the stole, the cord, even a mitre concocted of an unknown material . . . Any bishop of any century would be dazzled.

'It's gorgeous!' said his wife. 'Every piece. Look at this! Real fur! Amazing! And these are scraps?'

'*Oui!* Forty years of sewing for the public!'

'Okay, got to get moving,' he said. 'Where are the beards?'

'The beards!' said Hélène. 'Oh, *non!*'

'And the sack, we must have the sack.'

'With all the excitement . . . *je suis désolée!* It is all on my kitchen table!'

'Is Harley home?'

'*Oui*, he is fixing the front burner on my stove!'

'Tell him to get everything to us right away, please. Could you bring it all up?' he asked his wife.

'Consider it done, honey.'

Honey. In front of everybody! He could scarcely bear so much excitement.

He hefted the costume box. 'A little privacy, please,' he said, proceeding up the stairs.

'There!' Hélène exclaimed to all present. 'I knew he would do it, I just knew it!'

MORE THAN A FEW CUSTOMERS dropped in before noon, one with a carry-out lunch from the Feel Good, which she ate sitting at the coffee station.

'I didn't know you had a café,' said a student from Wesley.

'We don't. Just c-coffee. Free.'

'Great. Cream and sugar, please.'

'It's s-self-help,' said Sammy.

And there went the bell jangling, and in came Miss Mooney's tribe with more than a few shouts and murmurs, not to mention gifts for Children's Hospital.

'Is Saint Nick on time?' said Miss Mooney. 'They've just had donut holes at Sweet Stuff and are absolutely wild; I can hold them down only so long.'

'He'll be here any minute,' said Hélène, thrilled to be instrumental in such splendid commotion.

'I shouldn't be here,' Vanita told Hélène. 'I won't get close to anybody, I don't know what it is. Maybe an allergy!' Vanita aimed her point-and-shoot at the door. 'I'm about to bust to see Saint Nick, I'll shoot 'im comin' in.'

'No, no,' said Hélène, 'he will be coming down from above.'

And down he came.

Every head turning. The intake of breath. Those sitting, stood. All cheered and applauded. Miss Mooney was agape, her tribe astonished. Hélène felt faint. 'Yay-y-y-y!' said Vanita.

The velvet robe, the fur trim, the solemn procession down the creaking stairs; the crozier, the mitre, the bulging sack, and behind the beard and frosty eyebrows, the twinkling eyes so often ascribed to yet another bearer of gifts . . .

'THAT AIN'T SANTY CLAUS,' said a disappointed five-year-old.

Hastings McCurdy put in his two cents' worth. 'Saint Nicholas fasted on Wednesdays and Fridays and gave all his money to the poor.'

'Bless you,' Saint Nicholas said to Hastings McCurdy, and gave him a sweet.

'Bless you,' Saint Nicholas said to Sissy and Sassy and Timmy and Tommy and Jessie and Pooh, and all the tribe of Miss Mooney.

'Do you live at th' North Pole?'

'Do you know Santy Claus? Why couldn't he come?'

'Do you go down chimneys?'

'Are they any reindeers on this roof?'

Saint Nicholas was silent before these and other bewildered inquiries, saying only, 'Bless you,' to one and all, and giving each a wrapped sweet from his sack. Then, trailed by fourteen third-graders, he stepped into the window and began his next command: waving to all who passed.

'That Santy,' a boy told his mother, 'ain't got no teeth.'

'It's all the Christmas candy,' she said.

In the ensuing hubbub, he and Cynthia slipped downstairs, where he was spied helping a customer.

'Oh, my goodness!' Hélène cried, as if seeing a ghost. 'It's you!'

Doing his best to keep up, he was praising the merits of biography, the raw vigor of Knut Hamsun, the earnest authenticity of the nearly forgotten Conrad Richter, the persistent charms of Mary Oliver and John O'Donahue, and the generous grace of Seamus Heaney . . .

Which fiction bestseller could he recommend? Did he have anything by Cynthia Rylant? How about John Grisham's latest, or James Patterson before he went co-op, or the book that came out ages ago about Julia Child that really wasn't Julia but someone who cooked in a tiny kitchen in New York City?

He was in over his head. Way in.

'I don't know what I'm doing,' he confessed to an English prof from Wesley.

'Join the club,' she said.

When he was priesting, people sat quietly, organized by rows, and listened—or pretended to. Now they scattered throughout the room like untended sheep, and when they had a question, as they often did, they rushed at him from every side. And of course there was no greeting them in an orderly fashion as they left the sanctuary of books. No, they simply went out into the world, packages under arm, and disappeared. Hardly any time to say, Have you read George Herbert or Patrick Kavanagh, and, Will I ever see you again, much less, Enjoy your book and peace be with you. They were customers, after all, not parishioners. Didn't he know that?

'How's it going?' he asked his wife.

'Holy smoke,' she said.

Miss Mooney was busy pinning a scrap to the corkboard.

IN A GOOD BOOK, THE BEST IS BETWEEN THE LINES. —*Swedish proverb*

She gave him a knowing smile. 'So, Father, who's your Saint Nicholas? He's quite wonderful!'

'Oh,' he said, 'just someone who's having a little fun that is funny.'

AT FIVE O'CLOCK, he met with his lighting techs. Last night, he had thought the thing through more clearly—why light only the tree in the upstairs window? He had a better plan. But how would they coordinate it?

'*Très simple*, Father.'

Hélène presented Pooh and Jessie, who seemed pretty wired,

and explained that he, Father Tim, would stand in front of the PO, under the streetlight, and when he raised his right arm, that would be their cue.

'Got it,' said Pooh.

'Awesome,' said Jessie, who would afterward post the results on Facebook.

'Depend upon us!' said Hélène, who refused to become a mere bystander at the PO.

At five-twenty, he wrangled the crowd across Main, whipped by a gusting wind—coattails flapping, one hat sailing.

In the light from streetlamps and angels, people thronged the sidewalk across from Happy Endings, hooting and coughing and waving to one another and generally being up for whatever might transpire.

There were Hoppy and Olivia, looking a handsome pair, and the mayor and his wife, and their new police chief with Puny and both sets of twins. There were Abe and his genial spouse, Sylvia, and Lew and Earlene, and, scattered among the legions, a major portion of the Cunningham troupe.

'Look,' said Cynthia. In the shadow beyond the light from an angel, Pauline and Buck.

He and Cynthia made their way to the lamppost where Bill Swanson and his grans—nine boys, to be exact—were congregated, and squeezed in among a contingent from Wesley, not to mention a few who wandered up from Holding, and a couple of Floridians looking dismayed in the wind . . .

Esther Bolick held fast to the arm of Adeline Douglas. 'There is no tellin',' said Esther, 'how many germs are bein' exchanged out here.'

Adeline patted Esther's hand. 'Too cold for germs, honey.'

'Okay,' said Bill Swanson. 'Tell us when.'

Only a soft lamplight shone forth from the bookstore's darkened windows. He looked at his watch.

'Go,' he whispered.

'Ten!' chorused the Swanson brotherhood.

'Nine!'

'Eight!'

The crowd chimed in, he and Cynthia chimed in.

'Seven!'

'Six!'

'Five!'

The wind had no mercy.

'Four!'

'Three!'

The goose bumps up his right leg, Cynthia's breath vaporizing on the air.

'Two!'

He raised his right arm as high as he could stretch it.

'One!'

Good Lord! The crowd stepped back, incredulous.

It was a launch at Cape Canaveral, it was the Eiffel Tower lit by eight million kilowatts; it was their night, in their town, with every possibility lying open before them.

'Ah!' they said, and 'Oh!' and all the things that might be uttered in wonderment and surprise, and then they cheered and applauded and hugged their neighbors on either side.

The high window cast its colored light onto the awning and splashed into the street below—blue, yellow, green, the colors of the tree lights many had known as children. Angels danced at the tips of branches, ornaments shimmered and gleamed, and above all, at the very top—the single, shining star.

He drew out his handkerchief and passed it to his wife.

In the north window, Mary and Joseph waited with the wizened shepherd and his sheep . . .

In the south window, Saint Nicholas, just in from the third century and arrayed in the splendor of remnants, stood in the sudden halo of light. The crowd cheered and waved for dear life. The pectoral cross glittered as the old bishop leaned his crozier against the wing chair, then raised both arms and waved back.

'Merry Christmas!' someone shouted.

He wiped his eyes with the back of his glove.

'Merry Christmas!'

'Merry Christmas!'

'C-cookies for ever'body!' Sammy hollered. And looking both ways, they all fled across to the light, and the warmth, and the books, and the mystery.

Chapter
Twenty-nine

Thank heaven for a chimney that, even in a strong wind, was drawing smoke sweetly up the flue.

On this gusty Sunday evening, their music was the sound of Sammy's and Kenny's laughter, punctuated by the sharp crack of cue tip against resin.

They turned their chairs to face the fire, rested their sock feet on the fender.

'She'll approve whatever we decide,' said Cynthia.

'There's Vanita, of course.' He was quite fond of Vanita, aka the Little Owl, as he sometimes called her privately. 'But . . .'

'But,' said his wife.

Here was real news, and they couldn't mess up. For the first time in history, the *Muse* might actually be a feed to the mighty *Observer*.

'I'll have to make a few calls,' he said. 'I'll talk to the right people, out of courtesy, but we can't let Wesley scoop us on this. The story absolutely belongs to Mitford. Would you write it?' Here was someone who made her living not only with pictures, but with words. Perfect.

'No,' she said.

'Just . . . *no?*'

'Yes. No.'

So. He could spill the beans to J.C., but the editor's literary skills were on par with Vanita's, minus the ardor for all-caps.

'Would you gather the facts and write them down? It would eliminate the nuisance of an interview by the *Muse* and perhaps help deliver the truth in recognizable form.'

'Consider it done,' she said, smug as anything when thinking of the information she'd been given by phone a half hour ago.

Hessie. It would have to be Hessie. She would do an earnest and workmanlike job. On the other hand, Vanita would be devastated if passed over.

Before getting in a swivet, they prayed the prayer that never fails.

ACROSS THE DATES of December 24 through 31, he had scrawled: *Dooley Home*. Across December 24 through 28: *Lace Home*.

Dooley and Lace would be staying at Meadowgate with Marge and Hal Owen, Dooley subbing for Hal's assistant, who was away for the holidays.

On Christmas Eve, he and Cynthia would finish decorating their tree and attend midnight mass in Wesley, and, on Christmas Day, drive out to Meadowgate with Dooley's siblings. Hoppy and Olivia would join them, making a baker's dozen around the farm table. It would be like going home, given the year he and Cynthia lived at the farm during the Owenses' stint in France.

Harley, so often included as family, would have Christmas dinner with his landlady, who was roasting a goose.

'First he buys dentures,' he said. 'Then there's the cologne business. And now roast goose. Do you think . . . ?'

'Wouldn't that be grand?' said his wife.

'I can't imagine it. She's an educated woman.'

'He's an educated man, remember? He majored in American history under Lace Harper, who also taught him to conjugate a verb.'

He shook his head. 'No way.' Harley at one of Miss Pringle's piano recitals at Mitford School? 'Just no way.'

'I have never conjugated a verb,' she said, gazing into the middle distance, 'and never will.'

ON THE WAY HOME from a frigid run on Monday, he stopped by Sweet Stuff.

He was eyeing the jelly donuts when she came through the curtains that divided customers from the kitchen.

'Merry Christmas, Father!'

'Winnie?'

'I look that different?'

'Well, yes. But . . .'

'You should see Thomas, he's a bronze god. He would step out an' prove it, but he's icin' cakes for th' Rotary tonight, an' believe me, he does not like to be bothered when he's icin' cakes. He looks exactly like he did when we met in th' ship's galley—I was admirin' his napoleons.' She gave him the once-over. 'You should use your gift certificate. They told me they gave you a gift certificate.'

'Don't start,' he said.

'Be careful whose hand you shake. Th' Mitford Crud is goin'

around. People come in here sneezin', coughin', eyes waterin' . . . Why don't people stay home when they're sick? People used to stay home out of respect for others. But that's th' trouble with people today, nobody has any respect for others. Lord knows, I'd like to get sick just so I could stay home for five minutes, but no way can I get sick 'til January. Have you heard about Vanita?'

'What?'

'Ended up in ER last night. Dehydrated. Mitford Crud, for sure. I think it's that little microphone she carries around, all those people breathin' in it.'

'Is she all right?'

'She's fine, just down for a week or two, her husband said. He came in for three brownies. I said she probably shouldn't have brownies right now; he said they were all for him, he was stressed.'

'I'll have two baguettes,' he said.

'What will you do with *two*?'

'Winnie, Winnie, what would anybody do with two baguettes? We'll have one this evening and use the other for crostini.'

'They say people in France used to eat two baguettes every single day. Fourteen a week! Can you believe it? Now everybody's down to half a baguette a day an' th' government's worried.'

'What are they worried about?'

'Well, because not eatin' baguettes is terrible for their cultural image.'

That would be his international news for the day.

'HESSIE, COULD YOU POSSIBLY meet me at Happy Endings? I'm subbing for Hélène Pringle. Noon to one, if that would work. You won't be disappointed.'

Noon to one could be busy with customers shopping on their lunch hour. Or the store could be empty as a gourd. The deepest truth he had learned about retail was that it's all about surprise. Right up there with farming.

'You want an apple?' Hessie said. 'I'll bring you an apple.'

He sat with her in the Poetry section and told her everything he was approved to tell. If she closed her mouth during the entire scenario, he didn't see it. 'And we'll have all the facts for you this afternoon. In black-and-white.'

'Lord help. And Vanita down with th' flu. I hate to admit this is th' chance I've waited for—an' now I'm scared to death. Th' turnaround . . .'

'You can do it,' he said.

'I guess you're wonderin' if I've forgiven her.'

'I haven't actually wondered that, but since you mention it . . .'

'She's a terrier, that one, but let her have her bone. Let her ruin her back in those spike heels if that's what she wants to do. I'll take my Social Security check an' fifteen bucks an hour, an' same time next year I'll be sittin' on a bench in St. Augustine. But yes, I forgive her, bless 'er heart.'

'Are you running this by J.C. before you write it?'

'No way. I'm just goin' to write it and hand it to him in person. It will never have contact with the Desk Dumpster.'

'How soon can we see it?'

'If I get your info by three and work half th' night, I can have it to him in th' mornin'. He'll have to tear up his whole front page, but he'll do it for this story. Definitely. He'll still be able to get the paper out on Thursday, just later than usual. What about pictures?'

'We'll give them to you with the facts.' His adrenaline was pumping like an oil derrick, and there came three customers through the door. 'Hessie, Hessie, thanks a million. Isn't life wonderful?'

'Stressful,' she snapped.

After selling four books and ordering two, he called Cynthia. 'Did you get what we need?'

'I think so. Maybe. I hope.'

'Hessie would like to have it by three at the latest.'

'I used your computer and will never do it again. Everything printed out triple-spaced, in red.'

'Seasonal!'

She was not amused.

'How old is your computer?' she said.

'Maybe ten years?'

'Ugh. Is Hessie home?'

'She was headed that way ten minutes ago.'

'I'll take it over after I mail the packages to New Jersey and Mississippi. We're out of wrapping paper, and Truman threw up on the pool room carpet.'

'So how's everything else at your end?'

'Stressful!' she said.

THE FEEL GOOD WAS DECKED OUT.

A life-sized bobblehead Santa greeted him at the door. On the wall behind the cash register, action reindeer circled the globe, hauling a sleigh with Santa waving at incoming customers. Bing Crosby was cranked up pretty loud, or was it Elvis?

'Merry Christmas, Padre,' said Wanda, who was wearing a Santa hat and western boots. 'New menu today.'

'I liked the old one.' Right there in one whining remark was living proof that *he* was old.

'This menu is lite, Father. L-I-T-E. As in healthy. As in good for you.'

He slunk to their table, where Mule was in discussion with a server wearing a Santa hat.

'It's not calories I'm worried about,' said Mule. 'It's cholesterol. My wife is watchin' my cholesterol.'

'We only know about calories,' said the server. 'We don't have th' expertise to advise people about cholesterol.'

'Are you okay?' he asked Mule.

'Why?'

'You're pale.'

'Fancy's got me off about everything but air an' water. Plus my tan ran out and I don't have time to strip down and get a refresher, I've got to find Fancy a present. What are you givin' Cynthia?'

'A cat door.'

'Is that supposed to be romantic?'

'She thinks so.'

'Fancy said give her somethin' romantic.'

'Like?'

'She didn't say, that's th' problem. What would I find in this town that's romantic?'

'Go online.'

'I don't go online. A cell phone is my limit when it comes to modern livin'. Help me out here.'

'I'll think about it. How's the new menu?'

'They took th' barbecue off, if that tells you anything. Turkey this, turkey that. Turkey is eatin' th' lunch of th' beef industry. I'm not goin' for anything turkey.'

'Have the vegetable plate.'

'Too many choices with a vegetable plate. You order for me.'

'Where's J.C.?'

'Out shoppin' for Adele, last I heard. Did you know he got a tan?'

Shirlene had said he'd be surprised. 'Living proof that hell has frozen over, or possibly that pigs do fly.'

'Said it made him feel like when he got out of th' Army and used to drive all night to Orlando.'

'Aha.'

'With th' top down.'

'So,' he told Mule, 'you're having the collard greens, the baby limas, and the sweet potato soufflé with homemade corn-bread. *Bon appetit.*'

'Sweet potatoes give me gas.'

'Okay, I'm done ordering for you; you're on your own. Hey! Meat loaf.'

'Made with turkey. Feel Good is obviously in th' pocket of th' turkey industry.'

'Here's chicken,' he said, hopeful. 'Grilled breast of chicken!'

Mule gave him a dark look. 'Read th' fine print. Made with turkey.'

Omer pulled out a chair and sat down, beaming. 'So what's new in town, y'all?'

Whoa! Look at this.

Omer Cunningham had either been spending a lot of time in the sun or . . . well, there you go.

HE OCCASIONALLY MISSED Henry in a way he hadn't experi-enced with anyone else. It wasn't the business that happened

with twins, of course, yet there was some sense of—call it a con-
nective tissue—that couldn't be explained. His stem cells had
traveled through Henry's bloodstream and into the very bone
cavities. Perhaps out of something so visceral had come this
sense of connection. If nothing else, their father had given each
of them a brother—and in their old age, when they knew how to
appreciate the gesture, God had brought them together.

> *Dear Henry,*
>
> *Am writing from the bookstore while listening to
> Grieg. I had dismissed him years ago, but was
> mistaken. I read that Liszt said to him as a struggling
> and physically handicapped musician, "Keep steadily
> on; I tell you, you have the capability and don't let
> them intimidate you."*
>
> *I would say this to you, defining "them" in this
> case as the Enemy and his minions: Believe that you
> can be up and driving and living very much as you
> once did. It's true that some transplants aren't
> successful, but equally true that survival outcomes
> are improving by up to 80%. I realize that you know
> this, but realize, too, there are times when hope is
> dim. God is near, brother. I miss you and pray
> for you faithfully and also remind you of what Julian
> of Norwich said as she suffered a devastating illness
> of her own:*
>
> *"All shall be well and all shall be well and all
> manner of thing shall be well." You may know that
> during her suffering she had gazed into the face of
> God, and out of that mighty encounter this truth was
> rendered for you, for all of us, for all time . . .*

Over the years, he had found little occasion to sit with a lap full of Christmas cards and pay attention to what they were saying. Oh, he had scanned them, noting with gratitude those who had remembered him. But he had skipped the more attentive reading of the personal greeting, and the good humor or outright awkwardness of the photocopied Christmas letter. At the end of the season, he had taken the whole lot from the large Delft bowl on the console and, too busy again to do the promised read-through, tied the bundle with string and, yes, kept it in a box in the basement. An unthinkable habit purloined from Nanny Howard, who threw nothing away, nothing. He was rather pleased to have in his DNA this single, harmless hoarding affectation—it could be worse.

From Sligo came a report that for the first time in years, Liam and all his household, including William, would be dining with Evelyn and Paddy at Broughadoon for Christmas. From the study, he called this news to Cynthia, who was making her Everlasting Pimiento Cheese for forthcoming hordes.

From the Fieldwalkers in Whitecap, where he had supplied for a year, a fold-out card with a brief gazette.

'Allelulia!' he called in to Cynthia. 'Morris Love is now St. John's minister of music. Marjorie says, "Every pew is filled but for two seats on the gospel side which are reserved for all time for you and Cynthia. Come soon. Fish for breakfast!"'

'And one from Otis and Marlene Bragg, signed "Bragg Paving Company for All Your Stone, Gravel, Asphalt and Concrete Needs."' Period. He was fond of the Braggs.

A handmade card with a line penned first by Christina Rossetti: 'Love Came Down at Christmas.'

'Agnes and Clarence send loving wishes for a happy Christmas season and good health for the new year, and ask that we come up for a visit in the spring.'

From Father Brad, a handsome card to be set on the mantel:

> *Comin' atcha Jan. 1. He is born that we might have*
> *life. Pretty astounding. Looking forward to being with*
> *you and yours.*

On he plowed, dredging time and memory, until the pimiento cheese was put away and the fire burned to embers and his wife went upstairs, followed by Truman. Violet had recently elected to watch through the night with Barnabas, a display of character which he found admirable in a cat.

A card from . . . Henry Talbot. Of all things:

> *Father, have ended up in New Mexico. Will try to*
> *stay in touch. Could you send me the prayer you*
> *mentioned when I was there? The one you prayed*
> *after you were ordained. Use this address until*
> *further notice. Pray for me. Yours, Henry*

He put Henry's card on his desk and the other cards in the bowl on the console, then turned off the lights and made his way up to bed.

On Thursday afternoon, Esther Cunningham was reclining in the chair pirated by her grandson, the police chief, from the furnace room. 'I had to call in th' cops to get my chair back,' she told anyone who would listen.

'Ray!'

'What is it, Honey Bun?'

Why was her husband lookin' old? She had not previously noticed this. After all these years, she still saw him as the boy at the picnic who brought fried chicken and coleslaw which he made himself, though he was clearly no sissy. She had eaten three pieces of his chicken, crispier than she'd ever tasted, and married him two months later—they were both nineteen.

'Didn't th' *Muse* come today? Is this Thursday or am I in a coma and lost track of time?'

'It's here somewhere,' he said, 'I hadn't had a minute to pick it up.'

'How come you hadn't had a minute?' She endured an extended coughing fit. 'What were you doin' all day?'

'Lookin' after you, Sugar Babe.' He poured a spoonful of cough syrup, put it to her lips. 'Down th' hatch.'

'What was there to look after? I had toast and a boiled egg for breakfast, Marcie brought a salad for lunch and decorated th' tree, and we've got th' Crockpot goin' for supper.' She could not understand people who thought themselves overworked.

'Right,' he said, thumping into his own recliner. 'You needed stamps from th' post office, said it was life or death. You wanted your green dress dry-cleaned for Christmas, so I ran that over to Wesley. I was on th' phone about th' hospital bill, they charged you for a urinary diversion which was twenty-four thousand an' I called to say they had not touched anything urinary, and they checked and took it off th' bill, which Medicare should truly appreciate. Then th' laundry—all th' beds needed changin' you said, since th' girls have been sleepin' over, so I washed and folded stuff like you told me to, and filled your medicine box an' called your sister in Dallas an' gave her an update an' invited Omer an' his new girlfriend to dinner since we're havin' his favorite. Then I set th' table an' laid th' phone off th' hook so you could take a nap.' Ray gave forth a shudder-ing sigh.

'Who's his girlfriend?'

'Fancy Skinner's sister, Shirlene.'

'Lord help, I hope we won't be gettin' Fancy Skinner in this family.'

'Shirlene's a nice girl. When you get better, she'll give you a tan. Her treat, she said.'

'That tan where you strip down to your birthday suit? I'll get my own tan, thank you. Is th' phone still off th' hook?'

'It is. An' thank God in his mercy.'

'I was wonderin' why nobody called.' She had figured people didn't care whether she lived or died.

'Then because th' school bus was in th' shop an' Marcie had a meetin', she asked me to pick up her grans at school.'

'Lord help!' she said, aghast. '*All* her grans?' She could not believe the wrinkles in his forehead.

'All of 'em that was in school.' As they climbed in the van, he'd done a head count—twelve, or was it eleven?—to be dropped off at a total of four different houses. To be absolutely sure, he asked them to count their own heads. Yellow house, Bitsy, Donna, and Albert; white house, green shutters, Sissy and Sassy; green house, white shutters, Buster, Harry, Susan, Paula, and Robbie; brick house, Jerry and Rosalind. And that was just Mar-cie's crowd. There were a dozen more distributed among their other four daughters, and nobody in the family was Catholic.

'Only one got off at the wrong house,' he said. The whole lot of them were famous for getting off at each other's houses and drivin' their mothers crazy. 'It's been a handful, Doll Face.'

This was a shock. The girls had certainly had their say about *her* wearin' their daddy out, an' now *they* were wearin' him out, sendin' him on a pick-up-and-deliver as if he had nothin' else to do.

She watched as he laid his head against the back of the chair and closed his eyes. Before he could hit the recline mode, his mouth dropped open and he was snoring to beat the band, bless his heart. She would have to do somethin' nice for him when she got stronger. Maybe she would buy a new nightgown, Lord knows they weren't dead yet, or take him up to Lucera, which would cost out th' kazoo, and maybe they should even have wine— bein' Baptist, they never had wine except for a communion or two at Lord's Chapel, didn't Jesus have wine?

In the meantime, she would climb out of this chair and round up her own dadblame newspaper.

She hobbled to the kitchen, where she found it on the counter with the mail, then she hobbled back to her chair and coughed a good bit and read the headline that ran clean across the front page.

'Ray!' she said.

He sat up and blinked. 'What is it, Honey Pie?'

'Go put th' bloomin' phone on th' hook and come listen to this.'

'HAVE YOU SEEN IT?' Esther Bolick held up today's *Muse* so Winnie could see it over the bake case.

'I read every word. Everybody's talkin' about it.'

'Have you ever?'

'Never!' said Winnie. 'Three million dollars! I can't get my feeble mind around that kind of money. So nice that th' movie star twin bought her sister's paintings for one and a half million, can you believe it? An' every dime to go to th' Children's Hospital! Then our own Miz McGraw turns around an' gives a million an' a half to match it.'

'They'll be needin' a lot of cakes for that big auction next spring. It's black-tie, you know.'

'I know,' said Winnie. 'An' how about them not havin' a clue all those years that they were twins? That is so sad.'

'I would say if they get th' two hundred people they're lookin' for, they'll need five fourteen-inch OMCs, sliced event-style.'

What had happened to Esther's bad knees? Was it a miracle healing? Never again would she, Winnie Ivey Kendall, sign an agreement of any kind. Not in this life.

'I think their names are really pretty,' said Winnie. 'Irene Elizabeth and Kimberly Frances.'

'That auction will be big-time,' said Esther. 'You should do three-layers. An' believe me, you'll need help to get that job done.' Esther was standing on tiptoe, eyeing her across the case.

'I've never seen one of Kim's movies, but Thomas is goin' to get 'em on Netflix.' Her dentist had told her not to grind her teeth and here she was grinding her teeth. 'I don't have any idea they'll come to me, anyway. There are other bakers in this world, Esther. They might even get a caterer from Charlotte.'

'*Charlotte*? That'll be a million and a half out of th' budget right there!'

She could not do this another minute. 'Besides, *formal* affairs these days go for a chocolate dessert every time. *That* . . . is *statistical*.' So saying, she marched back to the kitchen.

Esther fumbled in her pocketbook for the car keys. 'Chocolate!'

she muttered. 'An' when th' party's over, there's everybody won-derin' why they can't sleep, an' blamin' it on too much wine!'

'IT WAS A REALLY GOOD STORY,' Minnie Lomax told Hessie. They sat in the front window of the Woolen Shop, drinking hot cider schlepped from Village Shoes.

Minnie was fond of encouraging Hessie, who had no hus-band, no money to speak of, and was forced to work for pea-nuts for J. C. Hogan, who had never once made a purchase in this shop.

'I liked your headline—"Twin Gifts Kick Off Children's Hospital Campaign."'

'Well, thanks,' said Hessie. 'There was so dern much to that story, I didn't know where to start. I'm still in recovery.'

'I thought it was great that the movie star twin will make an appearance at the auction. That is really, really nice of her to come such a long way for children she doesn't even know. An' then Miz McGraw givin' that matching gift in memory of her poor dead husband—he used to buy all his woolen items from us. He played golf in Scotland, but bought all his woolen items from us. Wasn't that wonderful?'

Minnie wished Hessie would listen more carefully when she talked, but Hessie's mind was usually elsewhere.

'Way too many details to that story,' said Hessie. 'It half killed me. That's th' last big news this town needs for a long time, I can tell you that.'

'I HAVE SOME GOOD NEWS and some bad news,' said Puny, hands behind her back.

'But first, congratulations on all that money for Children's Hospital, I know you must have prayed up a storm. An' I'm so happy for Ms. McGraw that she has a twin, she deserves it! Sissy an' Sassy drew straws on which one of them would end up rich an' famous an' Sissy won. I tried to tell 'em they could both be rich an' famous, but . . .'

'Bad news first,' he said, weary in every bone, 'and get it over with.'

He had dragged himself out of bed this morning. Retail was definitely worse than priesting. It was Christmas Eve, and because his work schedule of Thursday, Friday, and Saturday was now ended, he had pitched in with Hélène and Coot for Christmas Eve, aka the last fling of his second career.

'Th' water heater's leakin',' it's runnin' out on th' basement floor.'

Their second water heater in four years. Where had American quality and ingenuity gone? What was the matter with people?

'I'll call th' plumber,' she said.

'Thank you. Is that the good news, that you'll call the plumber and I don't have to?'

'Th' good news is behind my back. Three guesses.'

'Puny, Puny. You know I don't like guessing.'

She handed over an envelope, grinning.

His letter to Cynthia? Yes! The lost letter was found!

He whooped.

'Where?'

'You know th' place under your desk where th' drawers are at? It has those little feet that set it up off th' floor a inch or two—I found it under there. When I was dustin' your desk, I dropped one of your pens and that's where it rolled an' I reached in there an' . . . Merry Christmas!'

She was beaming.

'Don't tell Cynthia,' he said.

HE WALKED OUT TO THE STOOP, the phone to his ear, and looked up. A snow sky. Big time.

'Sam! Good morning. Walk up to the bookstore with me.'

'I ain't got no clothes on.'

'Get 'em on,' he said. 'Paying job.'

Sammy could work 'til noon—bring in lunch, take the truck to have Lew check the ignition, and help Coot sort the recycling. He was scratching around for something for Sammy to do, as the cat door was finished and, as much for Truman as for Cynthia, covered by a hand-lettered sign: DO NOT OPEN TIL CHRISTMAS.

Kenny had been working on his kid brother; Harley had done his part, and Miss Pringle's terms and conditions hadn't hurt. Hair combed. Hands clean. A good-looking boy. He was grateful for the simple happiness of walking up the street with Sammy.

'Buck's goin' to take me to work with 'im next week.'

'Great.'

'He said he might find a job for me.'

'That should be pretty easy to do. You're a good carpenter, you can paint, and if they need any help with landscaping . . .'

As they rounded the corner onto Main, he saw a familiar figure walking their way.

'Father Tim! Merry Christmas! Joe Jordan, remember me? I was on th' vestry back in the day. We moved down th' mountain and I'm up to see my cousin. This your boy?'

This isn't Dooley, he was about to say, but hesitated.

He put his hand on Sammy's shoulder. Sammy didn't flinch.

'Yes,' he said. 'This is my boy. His name is Sammy.'

BEFORE HE OPENED THE STORE, they took a turn into Village Shoes.

'Happy Hanukkah, my friend.'

'Merry Christmas, Father!'

They embraced, each giving the other a rousing back slap.

'Shoes for Sammy while I open up, and I'll be back for brown loafers and a pair of black dress shoes. Ten and a half B.'

'Will do, and mazel tov. Sweet deal for the Children's Hospital.'

He paused outside the shoe store and looked up. A flake touched his cheek; one landed on his glove. It was snowing.

'ONCE IN ROYAL DAVID'S CITY,' 'In the Deep Mid-Winter' . . . a CD of his most-loved Christmas music . . .

Sugar, fake cream, napkins, and the sign turned around to OPEN . . .

It was his favorite part of the day. He would miss it.

He was shelving new inventory near the front when he heard the bell and looked up.

Good Lord. Edith Mallory. Pushed in her wheelchair by Ed Coffey.

He paused briefly with his mouth agape and went to them at once.

'Edith!' He felt an overwhelming flood of affection; stooped and embraced her. 'Edith.'

'Fa . . . ther.'

Snow mingled in the fur of her coat collar . . .

He took her gloved hand, not speaking. They had been through a great deal together. She had wooed him, once locked him in a room with herself, and pursued him unashamedly. And then, the catastrophic blow to her head and the loss of ability to form words and speech.

Edith's longtime driver had aged noticeably, but who hadn't? He embraced Ed, a spontaneous act that could never have happened in years past.

And here was his chance.

It had come to him; he had not been forced to seek it. But he knew he couldn't do it. Not at all. All those years with everyone hounding her for money; a never-ending procession of people to her door, hands out. He would not, could not do it. How would he tell the Children's Hospital board that she had dropped by to see him but he *could not do it*?

'We wanted to get up here before th' snow sets in,' said Ed. 'Miz Mallory's been missin' th' place. She's taken a house on th' ridge for a few days.'

'We're glad to have you, Edith. Welcome home. Merry Christmas.' His heart was painfully full.

Edith handed him an envelope inscribed with his name, gave him something that resembled a smile.

He opened the envelope. A folding card, handwritten by Edith's assistant, with a check tucked inside:

> *Father,*
>   *You have given when no one asked. I have given only when pressed. This is a new avenue for me, one*

I hope to travel until the end. I hear your favorite
charity is in dire straits. May God bless you to a
happy old age. Pray for me. Edith

He was touched by this; thought it could appear crass or impatient to look at the check now.

Ed Coffey cleared his throat.

He got Ed's message, studied the amount, blinked. This time, he might actually faint.

To: Children's Hospital.

Five hundred thousand dollars.

Edith spoke slowly and with precision the words she was first able to articulate after the disastrous head injury.

'God . . . is . . . good.'

The three of them held hands and wept together, a kind of family once bitterly estranged, now united.

PEOPLE ROAMING THE STORE, several youngsters in the Children's section, the bell jangling.

'Hey, Dad!'

Dooley striding in—a surprise visit on his way to Meadow-gate.

'Wanted to stop by and say we'll see you out there tomor-row. From Lace and me.'

Dooley brushed snow from his hair, handed over a bag filled with wrapped gifts. A first, this bag of gifts—with the impri-matur of the girl Dooley loved. So many firsts, all the time . . .

'I have somethin' else for you. It's the most important.'

Dooley pulled a twenty from his jeans pocket, and folded it.

Then he folded it again. And again. And once more. And handed it over, solemn.

'Merry Christmas, Dad. Thanks for all you do for me.'

Dooley gave him a quick hug and was gone before he could speak.

'EXCUSE ME.'

A smartly dressed woman he had never seen approached the sales counter. 'That plant in your window. What is it, may I ask?'

'Ah,' he said. 'A rubber plant. After a fashion.'

'I'm opening my house for Christmas and need something tall and green in my foyer. Where did you get it?'

'It was a gift.'

'Does it require much water?'

'Not much.'

'Must it have light? My foyer is dark.'

'Actually,' he said, 'it is completely maintenance-free.'

He carried it across the street to her SUV, and came back and totted up the take to date.

> $3,000,000 Kim and Irene
> 500,000 Edith
> 100.00 rubber plant

Including the spray tan certificate, which might go for twenty bucks:

> $3,500,120.00
> Not bad for openers.

. . .

IT WAS HARD TO SETTLE DOWN; he was flying, and it wasn't caffeine. This was a Christmas unlike any he'd ever known. So many gifts, a shower of gifts.

God was near, and he was all fingers. Still, he would wrap this one himself. When he started in the bookstore, Scott had paid for a book to be given away. He had prayed about that.

He scribed a greeting on one of the few remaining gift labels.

> *Merry Christmas To*
> *Coot*
> *From Your Friends*
> *At Happy Endings*

TO GET THE TRAIL PROJECT MOVING, he would need help with the details. Who would make the signs? They would want three estimates. What did they have to do to get council approval? There would be a good bit of bureaucratic hemming and hawing about the project. Where would they source litter bins and benches? There would be work to do on the Internet . . .

He had talked to Cynthia about his idea.

'Be specific,' was her advice.

He called from the store. 'Emma! Merry Christmas!' He was certifiably crazy.

'Merry Christmas! Who's this?'

'How quickly you forget.'

'Father Tim! I'll be et f'r a tater,' she said, quoting Uncle Billy. 'I've been checkin' th' obits to see if you're in there. I can't believe th' story in th' paper, you must be over th' moon.'

'And then some. Can hardly believe it myself. How's your Tuesday going?'

'South,' she said. 'My employer is movin' to Florida.'

'I'm gearing up for a project. How about four hours, eight to twelve on Tuesdays, starting the second week of January, with a possible cutoff at the end of March?'

Did he deserve her numerous skills? Should she play hard to get and show him what's what? He could hear her wheels turning.

'I thought you'd never ask!' she said. 'Are you at th' store?'

'I am.'

'Are you wearin' boots?'

'I am.'

'Good. It's comin' down out there. Do you have a hat?'

'Of course.'

'When you walk home, wear th' hat, th' temperature's droppin'.'

'I HAD SOMETHING to pick up at the Local. I should be on my way home, but I couldn't go without thanking you. There's just no time to say what I need to say. Our driveway is terrible in bad weather.' Sharon McCurdy was mildly breathless, distraught.

'You prayed and Hastings is completely fine. Is that a coincidence? I need to know this.'

'I can't say that I have any confidence in coincidence. I have confidence that God is with us in all things, both tender and tough.'

She glanced out to the street. 'I must hurry. It drives me crazy that God, if there is one, doesn't allow himself to be seen. It seems all smoke and mirrors, a fabrication of the silliest sort. How are we supposed to believe?'

'"All that I have seen," Mr. Emerson said and I say with him, "teaches me to trust the Creator for all that I have not seen."'

'I don't know. All these years and I don't know. How does one pray? If I don't believe in God, why would I pray? And yet I feel a great need to pray. About . . . something. Many things. Would God hear me? Must I believe to be heard? What would I say?'

'You would say whatever is in your heart.'

'I can't imagine that. It's frightening to even think it. You're saying, just . . . whatever?'

'When Hastings cries out to you, the door of your heart opens, just as prayer opens God's heart to us. There's a sense in which the questions you're asking are themselves a kind of prayer.'

'I cannot speak to God, it seems a sham. Why would he respond to what is shallow and forced?'

'God answers all our heartfelt petitions. He may answer no, or yes, or wait, or maybe. Yet there's one prayer for which he has only one answer, and the answer is yes.'

'Tell me,' she said, sharp.

'Thy will be done.'

'That's it?'

'That's it. There is a caveat.'

'There is always a caveat,' she said, bitter.

'One must pray it with a surrendered heart.'

She turned away from him, covered her face with her hand. 'My God.'

He was concerned for her, for the snow coming hard on their mountain roads . . .

'I'll make you a cup of tea and see you on your way.'

'There's no time to think, to ask the right questions,' she said, shaking her head. 'There's never enough time for anything, ever.'

He went at once to the coffee station and she followed.

'I'll pray for you,' he said.

'Pray for me now,' she said. 'Now! No one has ever prayed for me. Pray for Hastings, pray for my husband, who has Parkinson's. My God, pray for this crazy world, for the mess we're making of it.'

He switched on the kettle, and they went to the Poetry section and stood by a bookcase and he held forth his hands and she let him clasp her own.

'Lord, for the longing of Sharon McCurdy's heart and for her safety on these roads, for Professor McCurdy and the longings of his own heart, for the well-being of the bright and gifted Hastings and his rich curiosity, and yes, Lord, for the mess we're making of your inexpressible beauty, we ask one thing: Thy will be done. Thank you for your boundless grace, for your unconditional love, for your mighty power to heal. And thank you for making yourself present to Sharon in a way she is fully able to receive with joy. Through Christ our Lord. Amen.'

She was weeping.

'When I speak of God's will, it helps to know that he wants the best for us. If you can't believe he's there, pray anyway. If you feel he's cheap and withholding, thank him anyway. There will come a time when you'll thank him even for the hard places.'

'Perhaps somewhere I have the smallest bit of faith,' she said, 'something left over from my childhood. But it's almost nothing, not enough . . .'

'If you yield it up, God will make it enough.'

He put the tea bag in a to-go cup and poured hot water from the kettle.

She wiped her eyes with a paper napkin and composed herself. 'Two sugars,' she said.

HE WALKED HOME, the snow falling thickly. Louise had stopped in for a quick tutorial and he had done a mite of housekeeping, thus the bank had closed before he could get there. He would make the deposit after Christmas.

'You're our miracle on Main Street,' Hope had said. 'We're up twenty-seven percent over last year.'

Twenty-seven percent. Above all they could ask or think, a dream more than fulfilled. Indeed, the whole experience seemed a dream.

Another chapter had already begun. He wanted to see this present moment as clearly as possible—the procession of lighted angels wearing crowns of snow, an old Jeep moving along the street, slow as a dirge, the gnashing sounds of machinery plowing along Main.

He was grateful for his fleece-lined jacket with the hood, and the warmth of his mortal flesh. He walked faster, head bowed into the flurry.

'Thank you, thank you, thank you, thank you . . .' he whispered into the gathered dark. His breath was vapor on the mountain air.

Chapter
Thirty

M ark my words,' said the weatherman on the six o'clock news. 'It'll be over around seven.'

Viewers marked his words but it wasn't over. By the end of the newscast, the precip had piled up to seven-plus inches, and was still coming down.

He and Cynthia would not attend midnight mass in Wesley. And very likely wouldn't make it out to Meadowgate tomorrow.

Because he had for years celebrated a mass, and often two, on Christmas Eve, he was never able to figure the best time to open gifts. Exhausted both on Christmas Eve and Christmas morning by the second-busiest season of the church calendar, he considered it a toss-up. Christmas Eve was certainly Nanny Howard's preferred time. 'While the house is still warm!' she always said.

This year, they decided to do a little of both—open one present each tonight, and in the morning, all the rest. He was plenty curious about Sammy's gift in its simple wrap of newspaper and recycled ribbon, and eager to open his first Christmas present from his brother, to whom he'd sent a rare edition of the work of Henry's first poet hero, Dunbar.

In the meantime, there was the big box from Cynthia with his name on it, and the gifts from Dooley and Lace . . .

He pulled on his snow boots. He would blaze a trail for his

dog to the bed where their tulip bulbs lay dreaming. 'Deep in their roots,' Roethke had said, 'all flowers keep the light.'

When he stepped out with Barnabas, he stuck in a yard-stick. A little over eight inches. Definitely above his ankles and still coming down.

He imagined Hamp Floyd, hunkered behind his house with his own yardstick. This was serious business for the Worm.

'It's plenty deep,' he said, stomping snow onto the mat inside the door.

'We're going,' she said.

'You're sure about this?'

'We're going. How could we not?'

How could they not?

Harley rang. 'Don't you worry, Rev'ren'. We gon' have you shoveled out to th' street in plenty of time. You sure you don't want to take y'r truck?'

'Nossir,' he said, 'we're traveling up by camel.'

SHE HAD SET a small table in the study, where they could have dinner and see the tree strung with colored lights and ornaments of mixed vintage.

They were leaving the sign, DO NOT OPEN TIL CHRISTMAS, on the cat door. If Truman went out in this, they might not find him 'til the spring thaw.

Before dinner, she took the box from under the tree and presented it to him.

'It was going to arrive in January, but here it is by some miracle I won't even attempt to understand. Please try it on, I'm dying to see you in it.'

'Is this what I was measured for?' He was mildly dubious.

'It is,' she said. 'Please, honey.'

He tried it on.

A perfect fit. Already hemmed and ready to roll. He was vainer than he imagined. He stood looking in the mirror in their bedroom with a kind of delicious astonishment. He wasn't so fat. He wasn't so abbreviated in height. He even appeared to have more hair.

He wore the tuxedo, cummerbund, bow tie, the works, as they sat by the fire having a glass of champagne. She was in what she called her New Darling, the rather grand replacement robe for the one left behind in Ireland for cleaning rags.

'You're gorgeous,' she said.

He believed her. He couldn't help himself.

Then he read aloud the letter Puny had found, and they agreed that the timing couldn't have been better:

I once dreamed, but never truly imagined, that I would one day salute someone as "wife." It is a designation of the greatest virtue, and though a simple word, has deep and complex meaning.

As for the complex, you are nearly an entire family to me. Wife, mother, sister, child, and that bewildering cousin, daughter of Aunt Lily, who astounded us with her brains and ingenuity. She was after doing more than climbing a tree, she wanted a watchtower built among its topmost branches. This task she assigned to Louis and me and we were gravely honored to do it, though at risk of life and limb. Like you, Nealey could whistle loud enough to pierce the eardrums and was actually the first female I ever perceived to be truly sexy. You are the second.

*It is surely a tough go being almost an entire
family to someone who has but one living cousin,
a son, and a brother six hundred miles distant. I
congratulate you. The astonishing thing is, you
make this superhuman feat appear effortless.*

*I have searched for a more profound way to speak
my admiration for your courage in spending the rest
of your life with me. I will continue the search and
get back to you.*

In the meantime, beloved, just this—
You are the very best—to say the very least.
Bookends forever.
A viro tuo adorante

Following her traditional Christmas dinner of oyster pie, they enjoyed two treats verboten at this hour: coffee and chocolate. Tonight, caffeine had a practical virtue—it would keep them awake for their journey to the manger.

They were in the bedroom, changing into snow clothes, when the phone rang.

'Hey, buddy! Merry Christmas!'

'Hey, Dad.'

Dooley's breathing seemed rapid, as if he were just in from a run.

'Sorry to call so late.'

'Not so late at all. We're headed up the street in a few minutes.'

'I have somethin' to tell you. We were going to tell you tomorrow, but the weather . . .'

'Right. We won't see you tomorrow, but we'll have Sammy and Kenny over for a good meal. I'm all ears.'

'It's not a friendship ring.'

There went the breath out of him.

'I mean, it is, but it's really . . . you know.'

'Don't make me say it, son. You say it.'

'It's an engagement ring. It's done. I swear to God, I love her, it's done. I couldn't take it anymore.' Dooley laughing. 'Man!'

'Let me put you on speakerphone.'

'No, no, please. Whoa. You tell Cynthia. I'll tell Sammy and Kenny and Harley tomorrow. Gotta go, Dad, see you later. We love y'all. Pray for us.'

He stood with the cordless in his hand.

She walked in from the bathroom. 'Who was that?'

'It's not a friendship ring,' he said.

They burst into laughter that went on for some time. They hugged, he whooped, she whistled like Nealey. Downstairs, Barnabas barked. His dog had just passed a hearing test with flying colors.

'An engagement party!' she said. 'Maybe spring break. Olivia and I could do it together, what do you think?'

'Make me a list. Will work for food.'

He wouldn't say anything now, but he was thinking of the rose garden for the wedding. June, of course. The low stone wall. And they would need an arch. Seven Sisters would be the perfect climber. In four or five years, a sight to behold . . .

While she finished dressing, he imagined telling everyone who would listen.

'Fill 'er up,' he would say to Lew. 'Dooley's engaged.'

'To that good-lookin' girl of Doc Harper's with th' long legs? Drives th' BMW?'

'That very one.'

'Ol' Dooley, he's th' man,' Lew would say.

And Mule. 'Th' Dooley that used to wear overalls an' had a way of expressin' himself?'

'That Dooley, yes.'

High five. Mule would pass the word to J.C.

'If Esther is still on this earth,' Winnie might say, 'she will definitely want to bake th' cake. I hate that, but such is life. Congratulations, and have a brownie—just one won't hurt.'

'Mazel tov!' Abe would say. 'May you live to finance the education of your grandchildren!' That would be a stretch, but he enjoyed the thought.

He imagined the look on Hope's face, Hope who loved romance both in truth and fiction. 'Life goes on in such a wonderful way!'

Esther B. would no doubt be thrilled.

'Don't even think of lettin' anybody else bake th' cake,' she would say.

'He has to get through vet school first, Esther. The wedding could be a few years out.'

'I could be dead as a doornail a few years out. Let Winnie bake it, then, but tell her not so much buttermilk as th' one she did for th' Bradshaws' fiftieth.'

He could hardly wait to get the news out there.

HE HAD THE KEY in his pocket and the box in a basket.

They were close to heading out to the sidewalk to meet Sammy when the phone rang.

Lace's cell. He handed the phone to Cynthia and went searching in the hall closet for his warmest scarf. He fumbled around without finding the scarf, but fished out a far better hat.

'They're so happy!' Cynthia came along the hall with a report. Killer blue eyes, his wife.

'She says they've worked long and hard to make this important decision and they're still a bit fragile. She says they need to get used to knowing instead of wondering. No engagement party—not anytime soon, anyway.'

'I understand that.' He put on the old black hat, pulled it down as far as it would ride.

'And we don't need to tell anyone yet.'

'Aha.'

She buttoned her coat. 'She said they're thinking about a wedding after his first four years of vet school. A long time to wait for a great hurrah.'

'I agree.'

'That's how long I might have waited,' she said, 'if I hadn't taken matters into my own hands.'

'Say on, Kav'na.'

She squashed a knit cap on her head. 'She said if we wanted to do something around the time of the wedding . . .'

'Absolutely. Of course. Marching bands, elephants . . .'

'And llamas! They hope to be raising their own flock,' she said, brightening at the thought. 'They have such lovely eyelashes, llamas!'

OVERSEEN BY THE HEAVENLY HOST, the three Magi proceeded up the plowed street and let themselves into the darkened store.

They moved the camel close to the stable, along with two angels and the wise men—one kneeling, two bowing—and at midnight, the crèche was complete.

Cynthia laid the babe on the straw in the manger. '"Love came down at Christmas . . ."'

'"Love all lovely, love divine,"' he said, quoting the lyrics of the hymn by Christina Rossetti.

"'Love was born at Christmas . . .'" she said.

Sammy looked at his scrap of paper. "'Star an' angels g-gave th' sign.'"

When they glanced up, they were astounded to see a young family looking in, noses to the glass, and the father giving a thumbs-up. Someone else had come, possibly from afar, to visit the manger.

They had been in the store a day or two ago, they said, and the children had begged to come back for the child to be born.

Not knowing whether to laugh or cry, he did a little of both. It wasn't every day that a parson got payback.

It WAS LATE, but not too late. The round-trip in the snow had energized him, not to mention the coffee and chocolate. He sat at his desk and wrote Henry Talbot.

> *Dear Henry,*
>
>   *A blessed Christmastide to you. Am grateful to know of your whereabouts—please keep in touch. Here are the few words I prayed with a searching and repentant heart:*
>
>   *Thank you, God, for loving me and for sending your Son to die for my sins. I sincerely repent of my sins and receive Christ as my personal savior. Now as your child, I turn my entire life over to you.*
>
>   *Everything to gain and nothing to lose, my brother. With love in Him Who loved us first,*
>   *Timothy*

. . .

THE SNOW CONTINUED INTO THE NIGHT.

It undid the work of the snowplows and, in the wind that kicked up, laid a sixteen-foot drift against the north side of Happy Endings. It piled itself on the benches along Main Street, and covered Baxter Park so completely that it appeared as a white lake ringed by snow-burdened trees.

Something went haywire with the loudspeaker system at Town Hall and throughout the night, music played over the meadows of snow that were streets and parking lots on other days. 'Above thy deep and dreamless sleep, the silent stars . . .'

During a number by Bing Crosby, two deer paused briefly in front of the Feel Good and moved on, plowing south. Though big cities never sleep, little towns do, and no one was out to see the brilliance of the snow blanket reflected in the eastern sky.

Four miles from town, at a spot where two major creeks converge, a light still shone in the window of a house with a fallen chicken coop at the rear and a neglected lot where a pony once grazed.

Coot Hendrick was starting to read his Christmas book all over again. It was a book he literally could not put down.

'Mama,' he said, 'listen to this.'

He knew his mama wadn't over in th' bed, not a'tall, but he liked to think she was, for it helped to have somebody to read to.

'"I . . . am . . . Sam.

'"I am Sam!

'"Sam . . . I . . . am . . ."'

In this book, he was gettin' to be Sam and see what somebody named Sam was up to. He'd been a crazy cat in a hat, and here lately he'd been ol' Saint Nick, hisself, with all manner of people trailin' after him and askin' questions, and now, just as he was ready to be Coot again, they give him this book for a present an' he was gettin' to be Sam. That was his favorite thing about books—they took you off to other people's lives an' places, but you could still set in your own chair by th' oil heater, warm as a mouse in a churn.

HAMP FLOYD GOT OUT of a warm bed at four a.m., trying not to disturb his wife. He could feel it in his bones: his prediction this year was off, way off. He pulled on his socks, which he kept rolled up under the covers in case of a fire alarm, and padded into the kitchen and took his yardstick from the corner by the door. He slipped his sock feet into his old galoshes, which were cold as two trays of ice, and switched on the porch light and stepped out.

He counted the back steps. Two were missing, buried beneath the snow—he didn't have to put the stick in to know he had predicted wrong. Plus he'd said tomorrow afternoon was the cutoff, and here the precip had already shut down, so he was off on th' whole deal. He gazed up to the sky, which was clearing to reveal a waxing moon. He looked out to the white field behind his house which reflected light into the untroubled heavens. He listened to the muffled silence that comes only with snow, and then a dog barking somewhere.

Bein' right was good, no two ways about it, but bein' alive was better.

'Thank you,' he said, and went in the house without knowing exactly how far off his prediction had been, and crawled back in bed and put his arm around his wife and woke her up, which he figured was as fine a consolation as any man could wish for.

At six a.m., the TV weatherman admitted that he was only human. Fifteen inches of powder lay solemnly over the town and in the valley, and upon the ancient ridges to the west.

WHILE BUILDING THE FIRE on Christmas morning, he came across an old copy of the *Muse*.

Does Mitford Still Take Care of Its Own?

He tore off the cover page and folded and twisted it and struck a match and the page caught fire and he warmed the flue with its slight heat. Then he touched the blaze to the paper beneath the kindling, and the whole question of whether people are sufficiently kind to one another went up in smoke and flame. He thought they had stumbled, but not fallen; the town had answered the query in the affirmative, and Vanita was to be thanked for asking.

Truman rubbed against his leg. Violet peered down at such nonsense from the throne of Cynthia's wing chair. Barnabas gave a small yelp in his sleep.

His wife would be late to rise, and he would be early to start the roast in the slow cooker. In the afternoon they would gather in the study for a family service with Sammy and Kenny, whose flight home was delayed, then they'd break bread together at the kitchen counter.

Their celebration would be simple but good, quiet but merry, and afterward, all the pool Sammy and Kenny and Harley could shoot.

He stood away from the fireplace and glanced up to the portrait. The wisdom of the T-shirt might well be scribed over the mantel of every household.

Love is an act of endless forgiveness

He looked into the eyes of the subject. The painter had captured something steady and resolved; something wise and believing.

Dooley was their hope—a door opening to all that could be healing and genuine.

'Take it from here, buddy,' he said. 'Take it from here.

'And God be with you.'

SAVE THE DATE

Lacey Harper Harper
&
Dooley Russell Kavanagh

THE BIG KNOT
Sunday, June 14
Meadowgate Farm
Farmer, North Carolina

'Hey, Dad. Need th' crimper.'

Crimper, snipper, stapler, strainer . . .

He was scrub nurse to the fence doctor, who was repairing a section of Meadowgate's high-tensile cattle fencing. Two of Dooley's five heifers had broken out last night and wandered into a neighbor's yard down the road. Not good.

'Glad it happened with the heifers, so now we know. With Choo-Choo coming in a few weeks . . .'

'Don't want that big boy getting out,' he said.

'If he gets out we're dead in the water. He'd head straight for Mink Hershell's cows.'

'Ah.' He didn't know much about those things.

'Mink's cows are small, he's got Dexters—around six, seven hundred pounds. Choo-Choo is two years old and clocks in at fourteen-hundred pounds. He makes big calves, which can be a serious problem with a small breed. Mink could lose cows if our guy gets in his pasture. Dystocia.'

Life was happening fast. Dooley's graduation from vet school was coming up in a few weeks, then the bull delivery, then the practice turning over from Hal Owen, and on June fourteenth, the wedding . . .

'So how's Choo-Choo's disposition?'

'He's got calves all over the county. He's famous for gettin' the job done.'

'And you bought him because . . . ?'

'Not good timing, for sure, but the owner needed to let him go. It was me or somebody else. I could never top the price. Pliers.'

Tales about Choo-Choo were circulating at the co-op, at least one of them embellished with a direct warning.

'It'll be good to get out with your cattle in the evenings.' He was repeating what the neighbors said about having 'a few head' on the place. 'Relaxing.'

'We'll treat small animals at th' clinic and I'll have my large animal practice right here on th' back forty. Maybe we'll raise llamas one day.'

He was fond of llamas, they were a staple in Mitford's annual Fourth of July parade.

'I really wanted mixed practice but there's a great vet just a few miles north. She does it all and does it well.' Dooley wiped the sweat from his eyes. 'Hal loved doing it all but he says he won't miss it; he was on call twenty-four/seven. I'd like to give it everything I've got during the day, and have time in the evenings to spend with Lace—with, you know . . .'

'Sure. With family. When you have children . . .'

He didn't mean to say that, not at all, it had popped out from overlong suppression.

The look on Dooley's face . . .

He had said the wrong thing. Craving grandkids was the vice of those wishing to assure mortality. A change of subject was needed.

'So, will you sing on the big day?' Dooley had been a member of the UGA choir in his college days.

'No way. Will I breathe is the question.'

'Scared?'

Dooley gave him an ironic look. 'Were you scared?'

'I was. Then the peace flowed in.'

'Need th' crimper again,' said Dooley.

It was cool to know what this stuff was. He hauled the thing out of the workbox.

'Thanks, but that's the tamper.'

So this is what people called the simple life. He wiped his face with a bandana and went diving for the crimper.

Ever since they moved to Meadowgate a month ago, the entire household had gone hammer and tong making the old place ready for the Big Knot.

They had repainted the interior of the vet clinic, refinished the clinic floors and installed new exam tables. He declined to help Cynthia and Lace make curtains for the farmhouse kitchen and drove with Harley to Holding for a pickup load of furniture for the reception room. There had been repair work in the barn, guttering to replace on the house, and before Dooley came home yesterday for the weekend, he and Harley and Willie had weed-whacked a mile of fence line and had a serious conversation with the county agent about liming.

'It's your broom straw,' said the agent.

'What about it?'

'It tells you your place needs lime. Nature's messenger.'

The agent had given him a wealth of material to read on the subject of lime.

For today's nut to crack, they were awarded the high-tensile-fence-fix-off. He had prayed for a more challenging retirement and here it was in living color. It was the most fun he'd had in a coon's age. Not everybody got to watch a young couple build a whole new life.

LACE HARPER STUDIED THE CANVAS on the easel.

Being stuck happened a lot these days. Maybe she shouldn't be painting to focus her mind or clear it or settle it or whatever she was hoping to do. Maybe she should be painting for passion's sake or not at all.

But there was no passion in her—she was painting by a kind of rote. Every energy had lately been spent on this vast and overwhelming life they were entering, a life they had dreamed of for years and wanted with all their hearts—and now what had taken so long seemed so very sudden.

Suddenly their own kitchen with its amiable fireplace and big windows. Suddenly the old porches and creaking floors, the immense views, the enormous sky, the hundred acres, the doleful heifers with their bran breath—all theirs, and right next door, their own animal clinic. It seemed so grown-up to have a place like this.

A few years ago, Dooley and the trust people bought more land from Hal and Marge. If cattle were to be in the picture, additional acreage would be needed and Hal made sure the price was right, as he'd done when Dooley bought out the practice. Everybody had walked away happy, with the Owens keeping the remaining thirty-five acres. So now Hal and Marge and Rebecca Jane lived in the house they built on the hill to the south, and Hal would work part-time during Dooley's first year in practice.

They were surrounded on every side by people older, wiser, and definitely more patient. This big, new life seemed truly perfect—and also truly scary. The money Dooley inherited from Miss Sadie had stretched through his college and vet school and bought most of the Meadowgate enterprise, with something left over. But there would be no tapping into the remainder of Miss Sadie's amazing trust, not for a long time.

All that lay ahead would be totally up to them. They had declined any further help from parents and would be living by their wits and on income from the clinic. It was important that the rest of the journey be theirs.

She had no idea how to proceed with this painting. Maybe it was the subject itself. She was concocting apples out of a cell phone photo and blurred imagination instead of working plein air beneath a tree heavy with winesaps.

But she wasn't trying to paint apples as God made them, she was painting at a slant—slathering on color with a palette knife, trying to chase the way the light was moving. All she really wanted was an impression of apples, an impression of a basket, an impression of mountains in the background. Anyway, it wasn't a real painting, it was an exercise.

She stepped away and squinted at the work. Clearly, she was faking it. She could not afford the time required to fake a painting, exercise or not.

Somehow, she would make it work. Then maybe she could sell it. They needed money now, not just for the wedding, which would be really, really simple, but also for the upkeep of the property and payroll for Willie and Harley and the clinic employees. Only days ago she had sold an oil to Cynthia's friend, Irene McGraw, who was a fabulous painter. She hoped Irene hadn't bought the small picture because she knew 'the kids' were just starting out. Irene had asked the price, but she asked Irene to price it instead.

'I can't do that,' Irene said in her quiet way.

She had blurted out the first thing that came to mind. 'Four hundred!' She didn't want to overestimate her work, not with Irene. At the same time, four hundred seemed overly modest. She felt awkward and gauche.

Irene smiled. 'You've forced me to set the price, after all. It's a wonderful piece. Twelve hundred.'

She had the sensation that she might fall backward, and held on to the chair where she was standing. She had sold a lot of work before, but this was especially thrilling because Irene McGraw's paintings were masterful.

The blood had beat in her again for the work she loved, the gorgeous work with its resinous smells and silken brushes and the restless play of light.

She should stop now. Time was precious. The Big Knot, as Harley called it, was only weeks away and Dooley's graduation at NC State was practically here, with the bull arriving the day after and the new sign for the vet clinic going up and . . .

She turned away from the canvas.

. . . and maybe, hopefully, please, God—Jack Tyler.

She felt her heart thump, something like a book dropped to the floor.

She and Dooley were taking on too much, everyone said that except Father Tim and Cynthia. Father Tim and Cynthia gave them all the liberty they needed, expecting them to do their best. Harley was the biggest objector. 'Th' way y'all are goin', you gon' be gray-headed.'

'Put your teeth in and have a Snickers,' she said. 'It's a *pot-luck*, Harley. Everybody brings food. It's the least stressful thing in the world, a pot-luck wedding.'

'Then there's ol' Choo-Choo comin' in,' said Harley. 'He's got ever'body on th' place rattled.'

True, but why was their bull everybody's business? People

should be concentrating on the wedding, on getting the post in the ground for the new sign to be hung. Every time she went to Farmer, people were telling stories about this really mean bull named Choo-Choo—at the post office, the co-op, Jake's.

The grand wedding and honeymoon that her parents, Hoppy and Olivia, had hoped to give them would have eclipsed everything, bull included. She and Dooley were truly grateful, but they had to say they didn't want that.

She hated, hated to disappoint Olivia and Hoppy, who had been so eager to adopt her, Lace Turner, a total rebellious stray from the Creek who should be eager to please them and wear a gorgeous gown and have a wedding with all the frills at Lord's Chapel.

Olivia had come from a wealthy family. The silver-framed wedding portraits in Olivia's living room were a testament to her paternal line of coal money. But the day she and Dooley went to tell them the plan, both Hoppy and Olivia had laughed with a kind of childlike delight. Olivia thought a country wedding would be 'the best thing in the whole world' and the idea of a potluck was hilarious, but in a good way. 'It's not our wedding,' Olivia had said, giving them the best of hugs. 'It's yours.'

'I'll be your wedding photographer,' said Hoppy, who had a Nikon and loved to use it.

'I'll make the pies,' said Olivia, who had learned pie-baking from a former housekeeper and was proud to call it her specialty.

'Cherry!' Dooley had said, about to throw up from stress.

That had gone so much better than expected; she felt really grateful and later wrote them a long letter.

But she and Dooley still had to tell Father Tim. Everyone knew he hoped to marry them in the Lord's Chapel rose garden that he and Harley and Dooley's brother, Sammy, recovered from ruin. Everyone knew he had trained the Seven Sisters vines to climb in a really special way on the arch, just for this day.

Lord's Chapel was where she and Dooley were confirmed and baptized, and where Father Tim and Cynthia and Hoppy and Olivia were married. It was the family church.

She and Dooley had gone one evening to the yellow house. 'Give me a sign,' Dooley said, 'like when you think it's a good time.'

There is no good time for this, she thought.

Cynthia had made spaghetti and later, they all sat by the fire in the study. Dooley jiggled his leg a lot and was finally able to say it. 'We just want to get married at home, Dad. At Meadowgate. With family and a few friends.'

Father Tim had blinked and there was a long pause as if he were trying to absorb what he heard.

She looked at Dooley, who was miserable. But hadn't they waited through vet school, which everyone thought was a great idea, and gone through the awful hunger and frustration of being apart, and the endless road trips that connected the dots between Atlanta and Athens and Mitford and Chapel Hill and Farmer, and NC State where Dooley transferred after college? They had gone through four speeding tickets in as many years, two each, not to mention a stack of CDs. And now they both wanted to just be at home, please, God—at Meadowgate with family.

Father Tim had smiled then, and nodded. 'Good,' he said like he really meant it. 'Getting married at home is good.'

She had also written them a long letter.

So no Vera or Oscar or hair bound up in a chignon. She knew all about those beautiful, seductive things; she had spent years looking at dresses and hair styles and being a bridesmaid at glamorous weddings. Then for some reason she never expected, none of that mattered anymore. She had done it in her head over and over—the shoes, the jewelry, the music; she had walked down the aisle a thousand times and seen heads turning and heard the little gasps of approval. She felt a new kind of joy in knowing that she and Dooley would have something more wonderful than the grand wedding, the awesome honeymoon, the lingerie as ephemeral as mist.

'We could even go barefoot,' she said to Dooley. 'A barefoot wedding.'

'Wait'll y'uns step on a bee,' said Harley. 'Or one of them black snakes. That'll cure y' of barefooted, I can tell y' that.'

She and Dooley had dug deep to wait through the last years of college and vet school. And what would she do, Harley wanted to know, with all that learnin' Hoppy paid for? Her art instructors had been crazy about her portfolio; they said she could go anywhere and do anything and so she pursued jobs in publishing, in advertising, and then in design, but wherever she applied, it was 'the economy.' Here, there, everywhere, 'the economy.'

While Dooley was on a totally defined path, she was constantly trying to figure things out in a wandering sort of way. She resisted, without really understanding why, Olivia's generous offer to underwrite a graduate program in Art and Design at Pratt, which anybody in their right mind would go for, if they could get accepted. She adored Hoppy and Olivia, who had given her everything including their name and their amazing love, but the answer was no and so there she went again, wandering like an Israelite.

What saved her in these final couple of years was teaching art to children at a nonprofit in Chapel Hill, where she moved to be near Dooley. She had learned more from them than she could ever teach. It had been, in some ways, the time of her life, and she had loved each of them fiercely.

The experience had been pure joy and somehow helped the waiting make sense. Perhaps she would teach again one day. But what she wanted now was to work with Dooley. Though it was an established vet practice of thirty-five years, the change-over would be big and how they handled it would be important. She would be there for Dooley completely.

DOOLEY STOPPED AND WIPED the perspiration pearling on his forehead. 'You've been working really hard. You and Cynthia both. Thanks for everything. I want you to know we appreciate it.'

'Thank you,' he said, 'for the chance to do it. We're having a good time.'

Herding Dooley's new cattle into the pasture a couple of weeks ago had been the hoot of the month. They were a start-up herd of five heifers with the self-determination of a vestry. It had taken a village to get them off the truck and through the open cattle gate. The hauler had left more room than needed between the trailer doors and the gate, and so there went Willie and Harley, racing to head one off from the barn, and there was Lily, brandishing her apron like a matador as another trotted toward the corn crib. He had stood by the trailer like a bump on a log, waiting for directions from Dooley.

'I was no help,' he said later of receiving no directions.

'I didn't want you running around like that.'

'Because I'm old?'

'Not *old*. But well, you know . . .'

He did know. He'd be into the double-sevens at the end of June. Knees stiff, harder to keep the weight down, the occasional diabetic flare-up . . .

They worked for a time, silent. The buzzing of flies, a vagrant bee, the scent of grasses they were trampling.

Nobody was talking about the honeymoon. All he and Cynthia knew was that Hoppy and Olivia had offered something exotic, Hawaii or the Caymans, he couldn't remember, and according to Cynthia, the offer had been 'gently declined.'

'So. Any honeymoon plans yet?'

'See that house in the grove? That window over the front porch? That's it.'

'Aha. If you change your mind, you know we'll do anything we can. We'll help sit the farm, give a hand to Willie and Harley.' He and Cynthia had 'sat' the farm for the Owens a few years back and managed pretty well.

'What would you do if Choo-Choo and th' girls got out?'

'I'd do whatever Willie and Harley were doing.'

Dooley laughed. Things were okay. The strained look on his son's face had vanished.

'Sammy's pumped about coming to the wedding,' said Dooley. 'He texted me last night.'

Sammy. Almost twenty-two, now, with a manager and a hot name on the pro pool circuit. He had hoped to adopt Dooley's brother a few years back, but Sammy Barlowe didn't want to be adopted. 'My daddy made Barlowe a bad name,' Sammy said. 'I'm goin' to make Barlowe a good name.'

He had loved Sammy as well as he knew how. But it was Father Brad, the then-new hire at Lord's Chapel, who had stepped up to the plate and worked wonders. Thank God for Father Brad's Boot Camp.

'Okay,' said Dooley. 'That's it. We can pack up and go in.' Dooley's gaze scanned the field and the small herd lying beneath the trees along the creek.

He was more than proud of his son's vet school credentials and his wedding coming up and his bull coming in. Youth wasn't entirely wasted on the young. But he was sobered, too—by the big responsibilities that lay ahead. It was no dream anymore, it was the real deal.

'I'm in over my head, Dad. I look at you—always so patient. I can never be patient like you.'

'I don't know that I'm so patient. Ambrose Bierce called patience a minor form of despair, disguised as a virtue.' He had always liked that.

'You goin' to cry at my wedding?'

'I'm not planning to cry. I'll leave that to the women.'

Dooley grinned. 'I cried at your wedding.'

'You did?' What a wonderful thing to know. 'So, okay. I'll cry at yours.'

They had a laugh. He put his arm around his boy; slapped him on the back.

'I love you,' he said.

SHE SAT ON THE SIDE OF HER BED and stared at the painting without seeing it.

It was easy now to forget the fights and the tears, but still hard to forget the devastating disappointment that came nearly a year ago and the grieving that followed. She had wondered if they could survive that, but they did, because there was love they didn't even know they had til then. A raw, new strength was born from that grief and for the first time they both understood that no matter what, they could do this.

So the waiting had been a good thing, like a huge investment sufficient to pay out over a lifetime. Most important, the waiting had been worth it because she had lost the fear of surrendering her heart. For years, she had believed her strong will could be enough to make their relationship work. At one point, she decided her courage could be enough. And during one of her crazier phases she tried to believe that just being pretty, as some said she was, could be enough.

But none of that was enough for the journey they would be taking. She came to know this during his second year at vet school, after a long week of prayer and loneliness and weeping. She had surrendered her heart once before, when she was a kid, when Preacher Greer brought revival to the Creek. She had jumped down from the tree limb and Preacher Greer had prayed for her and she was warm for the first time in her life. To think that she must again surrender the core of her being was . . . too much. Surely it was more than was needed to get by.

He had come home to Mitford that last weekend of October— documented in her Dooley book for three long pages—and with an ease unlike any she might imagine, she had at last opened her heart to him completely.

It was every prayer answered, every benediction composed into one.

She remembered his weekend smell of a burger on the highway and his shampoo and his favorite jacket with the top button missing, all that, and his hands cold from the October wind. She had held him, unguarded and certain, and he looked at her and she knew that he understood. Dooley really got stuff that didn't come with words.

Words! For days she had wanted to write a special word in the Dooley book, but things had been so crazy. She cleaned her brushes and went to the shelf and took down the once-blank book and let it fall open of its own accord. Some days, it fell open to the really good times. Now it fell open to one of the other times.

Oct 19~ *He called last night and said he was sorry. We are always sorry about something with each other then we have to go back to school before we finish working things out. This is incredibly hard. Sometimes I don't want to do this anymore and he says he doesn't either. But we can't stop. I can't stop loving him.*

Oct 22~ *I painted all day yesterday. Drove to the country and had no idea where I was going. Found a farm and climbed over the fence and set up my easel in the field. D doesn't understand how solitude is the only way to get my work done—he is always 'up and doing with a heart for any fate,' according to Fr Tim. But people say we are so much alike—both of us with scary childhoods, both adopted by people who gave us everything, both working hard in school to prove whatever. But we aren't alike at all. It was our experiences that were alike. I am quick flame~ he is slow-burning ember. Or maybe it's the other way around. Our counselor, who has a wood stove, says any good fire is both.*

Maybe the 28th~*D and I talk a lot about living at Meadowgate. It has felt like home to us for years. If we ever marry~it is scary to write that word!~I want to stay home. But I never tell anyone I would like to stay home. What's so wrong with that anyway? Beth dreams of a big job at Goldman-Sachs and Laurel wants to design cars. Cars! And she doesn't want children. She says no way. D and I agree that four would be perfect. He helped raise his* four sibs when he was little. He was ten years old and feeding them out of cans and then they all got scattered to the wind and all but Pooh were lost for years. We will never let scattering happen.

Nov 6~It was this date ten years ago when I was legally adopted by Olivia and Hoppy and since I never had a middle name the lawyers said if I wanted one this would be a good time so I took Harper. That will be your last name, they said, do you also want it for a middle name? And I said yes.

I could not imagine O and H would keep me forever and if anything happened I would always have this special name. I thought they pitied me~a poor Creek kid in a mashed-up hat with stringy hair and dirty clothes.

They kept loving me but I had a terrible fear of loving them back. I did everything I could to keep from loving them back.

It was totally exhausting for all of us. I could see it in Hoppy's face where I also saw patients dying and his heart condition that he wouldn't confront and the years of lost sleep and Olivia's drained look when we tried to talk. All of it probably caused by regret that they had taken me in. All I knew is that I did not deserve to be loved~ it was their own fault for trying to do the impossible. I wanted them to just leave me alone because they didn't deserve to suffer because I couldn't love them back.

And then the year I studied in France and painted and they came to see me and somehow—I honestly think it was the way the light moved over the lavender fields and my heart was very full for them and grateful and I was able to say to the concierge, These are my parents!

*I felt a stone lift off my heart~after that I said it to
everyone~my parents, my parents!*
    Thank you, God, for helping us through hard times.
    They are my mom and dad forever.

She let the journal lie open in her lap. She shouldn't be
reading the old, hurting entries when there were so many
happy ones. But the old stuff was good, too—it was a reminder.

She was aware, then, of another reminder—the pain which
was so familiar she sometimes forgot it. She reached for the
pills which she kept in a box on a shelf with the old Brittani-
cas, and swallowed one with a glass of water from their well.

It was her night to make supper happen and she'd hardly
given it a thought. Meadowgate was a total commune right
now. When the Owens moved out a month ago, she and
Father Tim and Cynthia and Harley piled their belongings
into three vehicles and moved into this rambling old house
where everybody immediately went to work making things
ready for June fourteenth, for the beginning of another life.

Father Tim and Cynthia would move home to Mitford the
night of the wedding, but Harley would stay on, helping with
farm chores and general improvements and living in Rebecca
Jane's old room with the princess canopy bed. Harley had been
her true family when she lived at the Creek; he had been the
best place to run when she needed to hide from her father. Not
only had Harley protected her when he could, he had encouraged her passion for books and learning. Harley was the best,
and now she would take care of him, which was great with
Dooley, since he also considered Harley 'blood'.

She loved having family around, including Willie, who had
his own little house on the place. He had been the main hand

at Meadowgate for years and was always in and out with his weather predictions. Sometimes Blake Eddistoe, Hal's vet tech who would stay on in the practice, stuck around for supper, and sometimes Rebecca Jane Owen, almost sixteen and still crazy about Dooley, would come over with her mom and dad, and there was Lily Flower, who cleaned two days a week and was such a fun nut case and worked harder than anybody and sometimes had supper with them and washed up after.

Okay. Boiled red potatoes with chives and butter. A salad. And roast chicken with rosemary from the garden. Not two chickens, but three. Enough to make great sandwiches for tomorrow's lunch and soup after.

She paged forward to a blank sheet in the Dooley book, took a deep breath, and wrote the word.

Cherish

She did not date the entry.

She returned the book to the shelf and hurried to the north-facing windows of the attic studio. In the far corner of the fence line, she saw them. Dooley and Father Tim were specks as they climbed into the truck.

'Dooley!' Her breath formed a small vapor on the glass.

She lifted her hand and waved, though she knew he couldn't see her.

'I've been meaning to ask,' he told Cynthia as he changed clothes for supper. 'What do you wear to a potluck wedding?' He couldn't just float around all day with his vestments flapping in the breeze.

'Very casual.'

'A knit shirt?'

'I don't know about a knit shirt,' she said. 'Maybe too much of a golfer look.'

'So, a white dress shirt maybe? Without the starch?'

'How about your blue stripe or your blue check? And khakis, I think.'

Khakis. This would be a first. Back in the day, seersucker suits had been *de rigueur* for Mississippi summer weddings.

'And socks with your loafers,' she said. 'Loafers without socks is sort of a good-old-boy look, someone said.'

He ran a comb through what was left of his hair. 'I'm a pretty good old boy.'

'The chickens will be done in twenty minutes,' said Lace. 'If you could please take them out?'

'Will do.' Cynthia was putting potatoes on to boil.

'I just need to run up to Heaven. Back in a flash.'

'I know the feeling. Take your time.'

She did run. All the way to the top of the house to the room Cynthia had called Heaven and claimed as her art studio while living at Meadowgate years ago.

Right there! On just this apple at just this spot, this one simple thing. She brushed in a rough semblance of the *Coccinella septempunctata* and stood back. *Yes.* Cecil Kennedy would be crazy about it if he weren't dead as anything. She wished she could work on it right now, but no way; maybe tomorrow. This painting would rock.

Dooley had come in; she could hear his voice all the way from the kitchen.

She cleaned her brush and inhaling the aromas rising from the oven, ran down the stairs. Yes, yes, yes, yes, yes, yes, yes . . .

She was starved and he would be, too.